AMERICAN
HEART

AMERICAN

HEART

LAURA MORIARTY

HARPER **TEEN**

An Imprint of HarperCollinsPublishers

HarperTeen is an imprint of HarperCollins Publishers.

American Heart
Copyright © 2018 by Laura Moriarty
All rights reserved. Printed in the United States of America. No part of this
book may be used or reproduced in any manner whatsoever without written
permission except in the case of brief quotations embodied in critical articles
and reviews. For information address HarperCollins Children's Books, a
division of HarperCollins Publishers, 195 Broadway, New York, NY 10007.
www.epicreads.com

Library of Congress Control Number: 2017934829
ISBN 978-0-06-269410-2

Typography by Michelle Cunningham
17 18 19 20 21   PC/LSCH   10 9 8 7 6 5 4 3 2 1
❖
First Edition

AMERICAN
HEART

1

ONE THING SOMEONE just meeting me might want to know is why I have two first names. That was a question I always got when I was growing up, and the answer is that I'm named after both of my grandmothers. The Sarah part is there because when my mom was pregnant with me, her mom, Sarah, was thinking of giving her a car. The Mary part is there for my dad's mom, who was really nice and already getting sick, so everyone was careful to call me Sarah-Mary each time, and they were in the habit by the time she died. My mom said that just before I was born, she'd thought about doing a combination name, like Sary or Marah, hoping that would make everybody happy. But then I showed up with dark hair and dark eyes, and she worried people would think I was foreign. She said for all she knew, I might have ended up on the registry, sent off to Nevada by mistake.

Of course, if someone was meeting me just now, and knew everything, probably the first question they would have is how a person like me ended up doing something so illegal that if I got caught, I'd be in serious trouble. Like, forget juvenile detention. I'd go to a real prison, or even solitary confinement, in part for my own protection. A lot of people would want to kill me, or at least throw rocks or spit as I went by.

I guess they'd have a case to make. But some of them might be surprised to learn that up until a few days ago, I'd never broken a law, not counting truancy. And getting a fake ID. And I guess using the fake ID to get into a club. But other than that, nothing.

Aunt Jenny says I'm still in need of moral guidance, so that's where she's coming from with all her rules that make me crazy: No swearing. No watching or listening to anything with swearing. No books with swearing. No books with smut or references to demons. No makeup, no nail polish, no bare shoulders. I can't watch anything rated PG, and I'm fifteen years old. And forget the internet. Aunt Jenny's got this thing on her computer that lets her always see what I'm doing on mine. Let me tell you, she stays on top of it.

She might be surprised to learn I've got my own rules for myself, just in the secrecy of my own head. I follow them because I'm the one who decided on them, so no spying or outside enforcement is necessary. One of my rules is that I keep my promises. In fact, keeping a promise is what got me into this whole situation of breaking the law.

I think for someone to really understand why I've done what I've done, and why I made the promise that started everything in the first place, I would probably need to go back and explain that eight months ago, on the first day of summer vacation, my mom drove me and my brother Caleb from Joplin, where we'd always lived and where we had all our friends, to Aunt Jenny's house in Hannibal, which is way over on the other side of Missouri. Hannibal doesn't even have half as many people as Joplin. When my mom drove us through the downtown on our way in, she kept saying it was "cute" and "quaint." Caleb said something agreeable, even though he was sad, because that's his way. I didn't. To me, Hannibal looked like a town with nothing to do, and no friends to do it with.

We were supposed to just stay with my aunt for the summer. Our mom had gotten a job at a resort in Colorado, and she said she was going to make a ton of money, but she could only do it if she worked all the time, and anyway, she couldn't afford a place out there big enough for all three of us. She said Aunt Jenny would take good care of us and make sure we had so much fun, and when she came back to get us in August, we'd all go down to St. Louis and spend some of the money she was going to make.

Even then, I knew enough about Aunt Jenny to highly doubt the fun part.

It turns out I shouldn't have believed the part about our mom coming back in August, either, because now it's January, a whole new year, and Caleb and I still live with Aunt Jenny in Hannibal. Our mom didn't even come back for Christmas. As soon as she got out to Colorado, she met this guy Dan, and the only thing I know about him is that he has two houses: one in Denver, and another one up in the mountains so he doesn't have a long drive when he wants to go skiing. When my mom met him, she made it sound like we'd all hit the jackpot, but really, it was just her. He might not even know Caleb and I exist. She's sent money from Colorado, and sometimes presents, but what do we care about that? She knows her own sister, what she's like: three hours of church every Sunday, and serious consequences if you slip up even once and say "Oh my God" instead of "Oh my goodness" or something weird like "oh by golly by gosh."

Caleb is only eleven, and he just misses our mom. He's not disgusted with her like I am. I do miss her sometimes. I'll admit that. But from the start, I missed my freedom more.

Everybody at church is always telling Aunt Jenny how wonderful she is for taking us in. They say it right in front of us, like we're homeless dogs who can't understand, who should just wag our little tails and be grateful for our kibble. I've picked up that Aunt Jenny probably talks down on our mom to anyone who will listen, because nobody she introduces us to ever asks one word about her, or if we're homesick for Joplin. They just

4

tell us how lucky we are to have such a loving aunt, and to be in Hannibal, where we're safe and loved. If Aunt Jenny's standing there to hear, which she usually is, she lowers her eyes and smiles like she's waiting for angel wings to pop out of the back of one of her cardigan sweater sets so she can fly on up to heaven with everyone watching, cue the applause.

Sometimes I feel ungrateful, thinking of Aunt Jenny like that. She does take care of us. She buys the groceries. She makes sure we have shoes that fit. She drives us to school and picks us up on time. I know she means well. She's come right out and said that she's trying to undo some of the damage my mom's done to us, and trying to set a better example. But the thing is, we were way happier living with my mom. It's true her ex-boyfriend in Joplin sold weed for a living, but they broke up like two years ago, after he got arrested. Aunt Jenny still makes a big deal out of this, calling him only "the drug dealer" and not his name, which was Tom, and ignoring that he was always pretty nice to us. I've got the address for the prison where he is, and Caleb and I sent him cards on his birthday and Christmas, trying to cheer him up.

Early on, I told Aunt Jenny maybe she would set a better example if she wasn't always saying bad stuff about our mom or Tom. I think bad stuff about my mom all the time, but it's different if someone else says it. And it's not like I say bad things about her in front of Caleb, the way Aunt Jenny does.

After I made that suggestion to Aunt Jenny, she didn't seem to like me so much. Now when she gets mad at me, which is all the time, she tells me if I don't watch it, and if I don't reach for the hand extended to me now, I'm going to end up like my mom. I'm going to be selfish and flaky, the kind of person who drops off her kids with somebody else so she can go do what she likes. Or I'll end up like my dad. She says I need to let Jesus into my heart, even more than most people do, because obviously, whether you're talking nature or nurture, the cards are stacked against me.

I guess they are. I can't argue with one thing: our mom really did leave us, and she keeps on doing it. She calls sometimes to say she misses us, which makes me so mad I can barely talk. Caleb still falls for it. Or pretends to. He's a little kid, but he isn't stupid. He must know that if she really missed us, she'd come back.

The only good thing about coming to Hannibal was meeting Tess Villalobos, though I barely get to see her anymore. When I was at Hannibal High, we hung out every day. Tess is a senior, and I'm a sophomore, but we had morning study hall together in the cafeteria. There were something like sixty kids in there and just one teacher, so it was easy to go up separately and say you had to go to the bathroom, and then just meet in the parking lot. Tess has a nice truck, with tinted windows and speakers that could blow your ears out. Usually we'd drive over to the river and eat wasabi almonds from the big bag she kept under her seat, and we'd listen to music and talk, looking down at the water and out at the riverbank on the Illinois side. We'd always get back to school in time for third period. I wish we would have kept doing that, and not done the thing that ruined my life. But there was this perfect day in October, the sky bright and all the mugginess gone. Some of the trees along the river had just started to turn, and I love it when leaves go orange against a blue sky.

That day, when it was time to drive back to school, Tess squinted through the windshield, nodded once, and decided we should drive to St. Louis. If we left now, she said, we could be there by noon.

"Right now?" I asked. I was still crunching on almonds.

"Right now," she said.

She couldn't believe I'd never been to the Arch. She said if you grew up in Hannibal, the Arch and Mark Twain's house were the two field trips you could bet on. Mark Twain's boyhood home is right in Hannibal, and people come from all over the world to see it. They stand around taking pictures of this little plaque by Tom Sawyer's fence, even though it wasn't really his fence, because Tom Sawyer didn't really exist. The people of Hannibal know how to cash in—they've got a Mark Twain Avenue and Huckleberry Heights Drive, a Mark Twain Dinette and a Mark Twain Brew Company. They've got a big sign downtown that says *America's Hometown*, as if Mark Twain was the same as America, which, if you break it down, doesn't make a whole lot of sense.

"I've been sick of Mark Twain since fourth grade," Tess said, triple-wrapping a ponytail holder around the top of the almond bag. "But I never get tired of the Arch. You get up to the top, and you're so high up, let me tell you, it's a view. It'd be zip on a day like this." She put the almonds under the driver's seat and poked my leg with her sparkly fingernail. "Come on. We leave now, we can go up to the Arch, come down to have lunch, and be back before your aunt gets home. I'll buy your admission ticket."

If you didn't know Tess and were just talking to her for the first time, you might think she was on drugs. She gets really excited about things that don't make other people excited, like Jack Kerouac books, or a new song by Sketchy, or even the way sunlight happens to be reflecting off a particular cloud. Her eyes are so big that there's usually just a little white showing above and below her irises, so even when she's just sitting there, being calm, she looks pretty revved up. When she gets excited, her eyes can look ready to pop out at you, like one of those rubber toys you squeeze.

So maybe I was a little hypnotized, looking at her pop-out eyes. Or maybe I just wanted to go. I'd only been to St. Louis once, at night, to get fake IDs with Tess. And she was right. It was a perfect day.

"I knew you'd say yes." She was already backing up her truck, turning up the music. "Sarah-Mary, you're worth three seniors any day."

On the way down, we bought energy drinks, slammed them down fast, and sang with Sketchy into the empty cans. Tess leaned her head out the window, her blond hair slicked back by the wind, and shouted, "Stop acting so small! You are the universe in ecstatic motion!" to the drivers of other cars and to uninterested cows. Maybe she read those lines somewhere. Maybe she made them up. I don't know. But I started saying them too, like I meant every word, which at the time, I did. "Stop acting so small! You are the universe in ecstatic motion!" I think some people have to do drugs to feel that good, but we just had the energy drinks in us, and the cool wind coming in through the windows, and the music so loud you could feel the bass pumping in your chest like it was your own heartbeat.

I was still feeling good when we parked and got out to look up at the Arch, which was bigger and more impressive than I'd thought it would be, the metal of it glinting in the sun. Before you go up into the Arch, you go through security and then underground to the history museum part. While we were down there, I took a picture of Tess in front of a covered wagon, and she took one of me beside a stuffed buffalo, holding my palm out to it like I was getting ready to feed it some oats and pat its big head. That whole time, I felt fine. It was only when we had to get in the elevators to go up to the top that I started feeling weird.

I don't know what I was expecting—of course the Arch wouldn't have normal elevators. But the thing the attendant told us to climb into was more like a pod, something you'd see in a spaceship or a ride at an amusement park, with five plastic seats in a tight circle and just one window that wasn't even as big as my head. We had to sit with our shoulders hunched, and they put an Asian family in with us, two parents and a kid, all of us trying hard not to touch knees or look at each other's faces. The mom said something to the kid in another language, then took a picture of him with her phone.

"Where are you all from?" Tess asked, because she's like that. They smiled like they had no idea what she was saying. Then the man got it and said "Japan," though with his accent, it took me a second to understand. I guess even Tess thought another question might be too much work, as that was as far as the conversation went, which was fine with me. I was already starting to feel uneasy, thinking that the pod should have seat belts, or at least something to hang on to.

"It's not a long ride," Tess whispered. I guess she could see how I was feeling. I never thought of myself as claustrophobic, but when the attendant shut and locked the door, the one little window got covered up, and there was a humming sound, and then a big clank, and it was hard not to worry about what would happen if there was a power outage and we got stuck. Then we started to move up pretty fast, and you could feel we were going up at a diagonal. My stomach squeezed upward, sort of in an opposite diagonal, and it started to seem likely I would have to throw up in front of the Japanese family, or maybe on them, as there wasn't any room to turn away.

I put my head against my knees and counted to ten, and then twenty. And then a hundred. Tess patted my shoulder, saying it would be okay, that it would be so worth it when we got to the top, and we could look down at the Mississippi River and the barges, and all the buildings, and the stadium where the Cardinals play.

"Stay with me, Sarah-Mary," she said, still patting. "You're going to tough it out. You're going to be fine."

Finally, we clanked to a stop. When I raised my head, the Japanese family was looking at me all worried, even the little kid. The mom offered me a plastic water bottle, sealed, out of her purse, which was really just so nice. They let me out first, and Tess said, "It's okay. I'm right behind you," but then there were stairs and it was kind of dark, and all the people were getting out of the other pods and moving past me up the stairs to where you could see daylight coming in. I felt like everything was swinging, and I thought it was just me, and then I heard somebody at the top say, "Whoa! Cool. You can feel the whole thing swaying in the breeze."

I guess that's when I fainted.

I understand that they had to call the paramedics. It's a small space up there, narrow, with a lot of people, and Tess said I looked kind of dead for a minute, lying on the hard steps with my eyes closed and mouth open. She said she was so scared she wasn't even thinking about getting in trouble. They asked her my name and age, and she told them. Even after I was fine again, sitting up and drinking water, they said they had to call my parents.

To say Aunt Jenny overreacted about the Arch Incident would be an understatement. As soon as we got back to Hannibal, she had me tested for drugs. I'm absolutely serious. I had to go to her doctor, that very day, and pee in a cup. You would think she'd feel dumb when I tested negative, but nope. She was still crazy mad. She said she wasn't so upset that I had missed school as the fact that I had *left Marion County*. She told me I wasn't allowed to see Tess anymore. Not under any circumstances. She said she was saving me from myself, whether I liked it or not. I was thinking, okay, fine, I'll see Tess at school, and after a while, Aunt Jenny will calm down.

But the next day, she pulled me right out of Hannibal High and enrolled me in Berean Baptist.

I don't know where to start about what's wrong with Berean Baptist. First of all, it's not a real building. It's a double-wide trailer that somebody brought in on the back of a truck. It's good there are only nineteen kids that go there—I mean total, like K through 12—because we're packed in pretty tight, with everyone's cube facing a wall. That's right, I said cube. I sit facing a wall all day, and there's a wooden divider on each side of me. The dividers go from the height of my desk to how tall I am when I stand up, so when I'm sitting between them, it's like being a horse wearing blinders. Which is exactly the point. Same concept. There's just one teacher for everyone, Mrs. Harrison, but she's more like a monitor than a teacher—she doesn't get up and talk to the class, as we all sit facing the walls. There's no chalkboard or video screen, nothing like that. Berean Baptist uses these workbooks called *Light and Learning*, ordered from the national headquarters, and everybody just sits in their cube and does their assigned workbooks, from the little kindergartners to the one guy who's eighteen and already looks like he could be the dad of one of the kindergartners. If you don't get through your scheduled workbook on time, or if you don't do it right, you lose recess, and if you really fall behind, you get spanked. With a wooden paddle. I'm not lying.

I haven't gotten spanked, but I heard it happen to Jeremiah, who sits on my right. He's got allergies or something, and I always hear him sniffing on the other side of the divider. When he got spanked, they took him into the office, but the walls are thin, pretty much plywood. They made him pray first. Pastor Rasmussen said, "Foolishness is bound up in the heart of a child; the rod of discipline will remove it far from him," and then Mrs.

Harrison said, "Amen," and then Pastor Rasmussen told Jeremiah he needed to say amen too. He said, "Amen," and then I could hear it, each whack of the paddle loud enough to make me flinch. Jeremiah cried out on the third one, and then there was another.

Jeremiah told me later that he was supposed to get just three, but if you cry out, you get extra. He said you have to lean over and put your hands around your ankles, which sounds really embarrassing—I mean, Jeremiah's older than I am. But really, Pastor Rasmussen and Mrs. Harrison are the ones who should be embarrassed, hitting kids with wooden paddles. I said that to Jeremiah, and he just looked at me.

We do get to turn around and talk to each other at lunchtime, and twice a day we go outside for recess. But there's no monkey bars for the little kids or anything. They've just got a cordoned-off section of the parking lot with a basketball hoop on one end and a bucket of sidewalk chalk on the other. But being out there is fun compared to the rest of the day, when you're back in your cube, and if you turn around for even a second, that's a demerit. You're not allowed to raise your hand—you have to use the flag system. So here's what that is: everybody gets two miniature flags—the American flag, and the Christian flag. At the top of each desk divider, they've drilled these little holes for the flagpoles, which are about the size of a drinking straw. If you need to go to the bathroom, you put the American flag up on your divider, and you wait for Mrs. Harrison to come by and touch your shoulder; that's how you have permission to go. If you need help with a workbook, you put up the Christian flag, which is white with a blue square and a little red cross in the corner.

But like I said, Mrs. Harrison isn't really a teacher. I once asked her if I should write "between you and me" or "between you and I," and all she did was tug on her braid with this panicky look on her face, staring hard at the sentence, and then at me, until she wrinkled her nose and said, "It don't matter none. Just keep going." Another time, I could hear Jeremiah on the other side of my divider asking her about how electricity works, and Mrs. Harrison got all excited and whispered to him that electricity was a mystery, and that our relationship to it was a little like our relationship with God: we can know what electricity *does*, but we can't comprehend what it *is*.

I knew that wasn't right. I'm not Ms. Science or anything, but I remembered Mr. Petch at Hannibal High showing us a Bohr model of an atom and talking about valence electrons, the ones on the outside hopping from one atom to another because similar charges don't like each other, and how all that hopping can turn into a current with a charge. So without taking the time to consider the pros and cons of my actions, I leaned around the divider and said to Jeremiah, "I thought it had something to do with valence electrons."

Mrs. Harrison told me to hush and gave me a demerit. Three

demerits in one week means a spanking, so I didn't say anything else.

Another crazy thing about Berean Baptist is the dress code. The boys, even the little ones, have to wear ties and belts and keep their hair short. Girls have to wear dresses that go below the knee, and when it's cold out, we have to wear knee socks, not tights. Berean Baptist shares Aunt Jenny's suspicion of bare shoulders, but they're also weird about the backs of girls' necks. True story. You're not allowed to wear your hair in a high pony-tail. If you wear a ponytail, you have to pull it low. I could not for the life of me figure this one out, so I asked Mrs. Harrison, who told me in a whisper, like it was just a secret between us girls, that the back of the female neck was a "known erogenous zone," and they didn't want the boys to get distracted. Well, that threw me. I mean, I'm okay-looking. Let's just say guys have shown interest, both at Hannibal High and back in Joplin. But if just the sight of the back of my neck has ever made one of them have an instant erection or fall out of his chair in a convulsion of lust, I guess I missed it.

But the worst part about Berean Baptist is that I don't have any friends there. There are only two other girls even close to my age, Michelle and Shawna, and—surprise, surprise—they're both pretty uptight. Once, we were outside waiting in line to play foursquare, and I pointed out that Mrs. Harrison's breath usually smelled like cigarettes when she came out of the bathroom, which is 100 percent true, and Shawna looked at Michelle as if she was completely grossed out, like I'd farted or something, and said, "You shall not bear a false report. Do not join your hand with a wicked man to be a malicious witness," and then turned back to me and said, "Exodus twenty-three," as if that settled the matter.

Which it didn't.

Even before Berean Baptist, I had a pretty dim view of religion. Aunt Jenny's church isn't as bad as Berean Baptist—you can show your knees and the back of your neck. Still, when we go to the marathon services every Sunday, it all just sounds like made-up stories to me, nothing you should take so seriously that you have to be rude to people. Just because the Bible was written a long time ago doesn't mean it's true or even particularly smart, and some of it makes zero sense and is even pretty creepy. That thing about Abraham being all ready to kill his own son because God tells him to? He only stops because God tells him to stop, and if not, he would have gone ahead with it? That's not a good story. That's messed up. See, that's why I'm glad I have my own rules. I wouldn't kill my own son, or even an innocent ram that happened to wander by, because I thought God told me to. I mean, what's the difference between that and a crazy person today hearing voices and then killing somebody? Not much.

So all those hours when we're at church, I mostly sit and

think my own thoughts, like how pretty the sunlight looks coming in through the stained glass, or how much time I have left before I can leave. Caleb, on the other hand, loves church. But he still goes to Sunday school, and he said his teacher, this big-hipped woman who wears a ton of blush, is a wonderful person, with the softest, sweetest voice he ever heard, and everything she says to him makes him feel better. He told me that for him, Sunday school at Aunt Jenny's church has been the best thing about coming to Hannibal. He says sometimes he feels like he can't breathe and his heart starts pounding too hard because he gets so worried about our mom not coming back, and then he thinks about Jesus looking after him, and looking after her, and me, and even Aunt Jenny, and then he feels okay. He told me once that it was nice to have somebody like Jesus to think about, somebody he could admire and try to be like.

As soon as he said this, I could see he felt bad, like he worried I would take it as he didn't want to be like me. But I knew what he meant. I know Caleb loves me. He likes me, too. He started listening to Sketchy as soon as I did, and he's always wanting to come in my room and hang out. But we both know he's a lot nicer than I am. He's pretty much the nicest person I know. So if he wants to look up to somebody in that area, I guess it better be Jesus.

Still, I don't think it's true, what Aunt Jenny said about me needing Jesus, or any religion for that matter, for me to turn out okay. A person can think for herself about what being good is, and then just try to do it because it's the right thing to do, whether there's a God watching or not. And I know that Aunt Jenny would heartily disagree that I'm on the right path, and now, given what I've been up to, so would a lot of other people. But I've been thinking for myself, more and more, and that's still pretty much my plan.

This is how pathetic my life in Hannibal is: the most freedom I have, the best parts of my week, are the hours I'm working at Dairy Queen. I got a job there last summer because it's the only place in town that will hire you before you're sixteen. They didn't give me a lot of hours at first, but I was fast and neat and friendly to all the customers, and I didn't whine when it was my turn to clean the bathrooms. By the end of the summer, I was almost full-time. I had to go back down to part-time when school started, but I'd already made enough to pay for my phone every month, with quite a bit left over.

Plus everybody at work is pretty nice, and there's an old laptop in the break room. When I'm down there by myself, I can watch anything I want. Tess comes by to see me sometimes, and she'll hang around and do her homework in one of the booths until I'm on break. When my break comes, we go sit out at one of the picnic tables, or if it's cold out, my manager is nice about letting her come down to the break room with me. It's not like it's a super fun place to hang out, though, and it's not like Tess doesn't have other friends who could actually go and do fun things with her. Sometimes I worry she just feels guilty about getting me to go to the Arch and in so much trouble, and that's why she still comes around.

Other people I knew from public school have come by when I'm working, allegedly to see me, but they were mostly just looking for free food, which, sorry, I cannot give. Tess never even asks. She gets out money for whatever she orders. That's not as big a deal for her, of course, as she gets more from her allowance than I do from my paychecks, and all she has to do is stay in school and keep her truck filled with gas.

But free ice cream, especially ice cream with toppings, is a pretty big deal for Caleb. Aunt Jenny is anti-sugar, unless you count the molasses cookies she makes, which no one should. My manager lets us take a dessert home after every shift, so I always make something elaborate and bring it home for Caleb. It was harder to sneak things to him in the summer and the fall, but now that it's cold out, and dark by the time I get home, my window ledge is my mini-fridge. When I come back from work, I set the DQ bag outside on my ledge. And then I come in through the back door, tell Aunt Jenny I'm going to do my homework, and head back to my room. Caleb knows he can knock anytime.

On the last night of winter break, I made him a sundae with extra whipped cream and brownies. When he came to my room,

I took it off my window ledge and gave it to him with a little curtsy, saying, "Here you go, *monsieur*," before I went to shut my window against the cold. He said thank you, but he didn't look as thrilled as I thought he would. Usually it's pretty easy to make him happy.

"What's the matter?" I asked. "You sad that school's starting up again?" I pulled my curtain closed too. Hannibal is tiny, and like my mom said, quaint—but there could still be some creeper out there looking in.

He sat on my carpet, his back against the wall. He had the plump cheeks he'd had since he was a baby, but he already looked so much older than he had in Joplin, at least two inches taller, and all his light curls cut short. He was wearing the Sketchy shirt I got him for Christmas, and it made his arms look pale and skinny.

"I watched the news with Aunt Jenny," he said, setting the sundae beside him on the carpet without eating any of it. He didn't even take off the lid.

I sighed and sat on my bed. We'd been over this. Caleb isn't the kind of person who can watch the news and go on with his day or his evening. He gets upset when he hears about anybody, I mean anybody, suffering. Doesn't matter to him if the person is right here in Hannibal or in Miami or in China or in Timbuktu. That's his natural personality. And it's worse now that he goes to Sunday school, as not only does he get upset about people being poor or hungry or beaten in jail, he thinks he needs to be like Jesus and do something about it. He seriously asks himself *WWJD?* about the problems of people he's never met.

I understand it really is terrible to hear about people, no matter where they live, starving to death, or getting blown up or shot. And don't even talk to me about what happens to animals in this world. But Aunt Jenny's got the cable news on in the living room all the time, and if I let myself get caught up in all the sadness being reported, I'd never get through the day.

"You can't worry about everybody, Caleb. It's not your fault bad things happen."

He looked up at me, confused, like one of us had missed part of the conversation. "I know," he said. "But it's still sad." He brought his knees up, pressing a palm on each. "They showed a bunch of Muslims getting taken away to Nevada. You know. They were getting on the buses."

I picked up his sundae and put it back out on the ledge. I knew this might take a while.

"What did Aunt Jenny say?" I asked. This was sort of a lame question. I already knew the answer. Aunt Jenny had told me more than once she thought the containment was long overdue. She said she'd known it needed to happen years ago, before I was even born. She'd known since September 11.

"That if I wanted to be sad it was a free country." Caleb drummed his fingers on his knees. "But that we couldn't have them shooting up grocery stores and trying to assassinate people. And that we shouldn't keep spending tax dollars to protect them so they can buy more bombs to blow us up."

Aunt Jenny and I didn't agree on much, but that sounded right to me. "Well. I know you don't want that to keep happening."

It was true. Every time something bad happened, Caleb acted as if he knew the people who died. He got that upset.

"And you know," I said. "A lot of people live in Nevada because they like it. It's not like it's a terrible place."

He shook his head. "I'm going to show you. Can I use your computer?"

I almost said no. I didn't feel like getting all bummed out, and it seemed like I already knew what I needed to know. But I wanted Caleb to know that somebody besides Jesus cared about him and would listen to him when he was upset. There's something about Caleb's face, even now that he looks older, that always makes me want to be gentle with him, even when I don't think he's making sense. He looks a lot like our dad, the pictures I've seen of him.

So the video was pretty much what I thought it would be: a bunch of Arabic-looking people, some of them dressed normal, but a lot of the women with scarves covering their hair, getting on buses with their roller suitcases and backpacks and car seats and crying babies. The police were there, wearing helmets, holding back the crowd that was trying to get at the Muslims. Somebody had a sign that said *MUSLIMS OUT NOW*, which was a little redundant, because yeah, that's what was happening. The camera zeroed in on this one Muslim guy with a cello case who was yelling at the reporter that he didn't want to go to Nevada, that he wanted to keep playing in the orchestra in Michigan, and that his mother was too sick to travel and had to leave the cat she'd had for years, not to mention the house that his father had worked his whole life to pay for. This man was still yelling when all at once he sounded like he was going to cry, his voice going high and shaky. Caleb's eyes, steady on the screen, turned shiny, like if this man he didn't even know was crying, well then, he better cry too.

"Aw, Caleb," I said, but in a nice way, because I actually love that my little brother is so sweet, always thinking everybody's good like he is. I sat back on my bed. "For all we know, there's a bomb or a machine gun in that cello case. It's sad about the cat, but they gotta go." I squinted. "And he might be lying. I don't even know that Muslims can have cats. I'm serious. Not indoor ones, at least."

I wasn't a hundred percent sure if that was true or not. I'd never known any Muslims myself. There was the one guy who worked at the Pick-A-Dilly on Market Street who looked and talked like he might have been from somewhere Middle Eastern, but I don't know for sure. Anyway, he's not there anymore.

Caleb sat in my desk chair, staring at the freeze-frame of the man. "I think he really just had a cello."

"It's for their own protection, Caleb." I got up and walked over to him, patting his shoulder. Even when he was sitting in a chair, his head reached my elbow now. "And ours."

But he just kept looking at the freeze-frame of the man.

That's when I heard the first tap against my window. And then two taps. Then two more. Now I've seen enough horror movies, and enough of my own imaginings, to know that when you hear something tapping against your window at night, you don't just get up and go peek out so whatever's out there can bust through the glass and grab you or at least make you scream.

But Caleb heard it too, and of course he just turned around all calm, like the first-killed in a zombie movie, and pulled back the curtain. And there's Tess, standing out there in the cold, her bug eyes staring back at us, her face lit up by her phone, wearing her hat with the cat ears, so she really didn't look fully human. Caleb gave a startled cry.

"Shh!" I said. "It's just Tess."

"What's happening back there?" Aunt Jenny was still watching the news in the living room.

I held up a finger to Tess and turned around to crack open my bedroom door. "Caleb stubbed his toe." I could see down the hall to where the back of Aunt Jenny's head just cleared the edge of her recliner. "He's okay now."

I closed my door. There wasn't a lock. Of course there wasn't. But Aunt Jenny's recliner was hard to get out of, even for me. It would take more than a stubbed toe to get her vertical.

Tess is tall, with long, skinny legs, so it was no problem for her to climb into my room without knocking Caleb's sundae off the ledge. She knew enough to be quiet, but I was still nervous, whispering for her to sit on the floor of my closet. I was thinking if I heard Aunt Jenny coming, I could just turn my head and act like I'd been to talking to Caleb, who was still sitting at my desk, smiling now. He likes Tess. Back when I was still allowed to go over to her house, I sometimes brought him with me, and Tess would make him a plate of cheese and crackers and let him play video games while we talked or did her nails. Or sometimes she'd play with him. She's really good at this one game where your guy or girl jumps out of an airplane, and you have to shoot all the people on the ground who are shooting up at you while remembering to open your parachute on time. At first, Caleb was a little freaked out by all the shooting and the blood coming out of people's heads, and the ways they'd go "Ugh" and "Ahh!" when they got shot. But Tess told him it was all just play, just imagination, and there was no harm in them playing because they were both the kind of people who would never shoot anybody in real life. He was okay after that. I could tell Tess was letting him win sometimes, because she's really good. She plays with her dad almost every day when he comes home from work.

Once Tess was settled on the floor of my closet, she took off her hat, and her hair had enough static in it to start floating up toward my clothes. "Sorry," she whispered. Her cheeks were still pink from the cold. "I couldn't get to the Queen before the end of your shift."

This is what it had come to. She had to come to my window to talk to me, like we were Romeo and Juliet. She couldn't even call or text. After the Arch Incident, Aunt Jenny checked my phone bill, the one I was paying, every month for Tess's number, and she said if she saw it again, she'd take it away. It was like taxation without representation. Completely unfair, but what else was new? The plan was expensive, and Tess was the only person I really talked to, so when the contract ran out, I canceled.

I lowered myself to the floor, facing her. Nervous as I was, I was so grateful. She'd come to visit me in prison.

She pushed a sweater sleeve away from her face. "I wanted to tell you I'm going to Puerto Rico tomorrow. My mom has to go there for work, and she's taking me. It was all kind of last minute. I won't be back till Friday."

I couldn't tell if she was joking. It seemed like a crazy thing to say for a Sunday night in early January. Or anytime, really. But Tess was always getting to go places. The summer before I met her, her parents had taken her to France. She'd been to Holland, too. There's a picture of her standing in a field of red tulips on the Villalobos refrigerator. I'd been to Kansas, Arkansas, and Oklahoma, but only because their borders are all within an hour's drive from Joplin. I'd never even been to Illinois, and it was just across the river from Hannibal.

"What about school?" I asked. "You're going to miss a whole week?"

"My mom said she'd make it educational. She's going to take me to an art museum in Ponce to see her favorite painting."

I had to fake a smile. It would be annoying of me to act all pouty and jealous, and I especially didn't want to act that way in front of Caleb, who was just sitting there and watching us like we were having the most exciting conversation in the history of the planet. But I did feel jealous. I'd never even heard of Ponce, and the city's name had rolled right off Tess's tongue. That was probably because of her mom, who'd been an art history major. She'd been a nude model when she was in school and said it was fine, not embarrassing, because it was about art. Now she did indexing for some journal and still packed Tess a lunch every morning before school.

It made me kind of crazy sometimes, to think how different Tess's life was from mine. She didn't have to go to Berean Baptist. She had her truck. She lived with her mom and dad. She drove up to see her aunt and uncle in Omaha sometimes, by herself, just because she felt like it. And all because she got born into a different family than I did. That was it. But when I got to feeling too screwed over, I knew to get ahold of myself. I know I'm lucky, relatively speaking. I mean, all kinds of Mexicans and Central Americans were always dying of heat and dehydration trying to cross the border into America through the desert, and that's when people weren't going down to shoot at them. And lucky me, I just got to live in this country because it happened to be where I was born. It's not like I did anything to deserve it. So, you know, everything's relative.

"I'm sorry," Tess said. "I didn't know if I should tell you." She looked up at Caleb. "Did you know as soon as your sister turns eighteen, we're going to travel all over the country together? We're just going to go, for the whole summer. It'll be like Jack Kerouac, part two."

Caleb doesn't know who Jack Kerouac is, but he just said "Really?" and looked excited for me. I was grateful she'd gotten his mind off the Muslims, but I didn't know what I thought about this Kerouac plan of hers. Tess had been talking about this future road trip for a while, how we were going to go out to California, then up to Washington State, then back across Montana and North Dakota, down to Chicago and then all the way up and east to New England and down again to New York City, because that's probably where she'd be in college. We'd save the South for a winter trip.

I'd told her I would do it if we could take her truck, or if I could save up enough by then to buy my own. But she had this crazy idea of wanting to hitchhike. She said Kerouac hitched, and so did Bob Dylan. I pointed out they were both men, and that a couple of girls hitchhiking were likely to end up raped and murdered.

"That's what they want you to think," Tess argued. By *they* she meant the media. "They like to keep us scared, making a big deal of the few girl hitchhikers who get killed, and ignoring all the ones who get around just fine."

I guess she had her own experience to consider. She'd hitched all over Holland no problem. She said lots of people did over there, men and women alike, and that even over here we would be fine, especially if there were two of us. She said the trick was to ask for rides at a gas station, so if somebody said yes, you'd have the chance to check them out and decide if they were drunk or high or a creeper. And you let them see you take a picture of their license plate and text it to somebody, just as a precaution, before you even got in. She said if it would make me feel better, we could just get rides with women, and that Gloria Steinem herself said she didn't drive because that way the adventures could begin as soon as she left her door.

I don't know. I knew I could definitely use an adventure. I'd even say I was in desperate need of one. But I'd rather do it in my own car. I was thinking it would take me more than a few minutes of talking at a gas station to know if somebody was dangerous. A person with bad intentions can fake it for a while.

Tess stretched her long legs out of the closet, and a nugget of melting snow slid off the toe of her boot. She looked up at Caleb, and then at me. "So what have you all been up to?"

I glanced at my computer. The screen had gone dark, thankfully. I wasn't going to bring up the video, or how Caleb had been upset. Tess told me once that she knew some Muslims. Her aunt by marriage in Omaha is black, and she was never Muslim, but she had a couple of black Muslim friends, and then those friends had Muslim friends who were from Syria, either recently or a few generations back. Tess said the Muslims she'd met at her aunt and uncle's were all fine, even the ones from other countries. But this is coming from someone who'd prefer to get into a stranger's car when she has her own, who never thinks anything bad will happen to her, probably because nothing ever has.

In any case, I didn't want her telling Caleb how nice these Muslims in Omaha had been, because he'd just get more upset. He was being quiet, resting his chin on the back of the chair.

"Same old, same old," I said.

I hated how boring I sounded, but what was I going to say? At school, I sat in my little cube all day, working on *Light and Learning*. After that, I fried onion rings and french fries for a few hours, unless I got lucky and my manager put me on drive-thru. That all sounded pretty pathetic compared to going to Puerto Rico to see some painting. Plus I was getting nervous. Aunt Jenny could move fast and quiet sometimes, wearing just her socks, and if she came back and found Tess in here, my life would get even worse. She'd probably put an alarm on my window or take my bedroom door off its hinges.

I stood up. Tess got the message and held out her hands for me to pull her up too.

"I'd send you a postcard." She pulled her cat hat back over her hair. "But I guess I better not."

31

"Just bring back some sun." Through the window, even in the dark, I could see a frozen layer of snow in the yard. "Lucky you. It's going to be all warm and lovely there, isn't it?"

She nodded, but she didn't smile. I shimmied the window open and got Caleb's sundae out of her way. But she just stood there, looking back at me with her big eyes, the icy air drifting in.

"I wish I could rescue you," she said. "You're a whole lot of fun when you're not stuck in here. But you won't be stuck in here forever."

It almost hurt, how good it felt to hear her say that. Sometimes, sitting in my cube, I started to feel like nobody cared about me at all, except for Caleb, who cared about everyone. And I was glad to know Tess remembered that I'd once been a lot of fun. I felt my eyes go hot, and I lowered my head. I didn't want Caleb to see me cry either.

"All right," I said, when I was okay again. "Just come by when you get back. You can send me a postcard in your head. And I'll send you one from hell."

After she'd gone, I held the sundae out to Caleb. "You want this or not?"

He nodded and got up to take the cup. I turned back and left the window open for a while, my hand resting on the sill. It was true. I wouldn't be stuck here, or at Berean Baptist, forever. But a part of me wanted to climb out the window too, right out into the cold night, and just start walking. I didn't need to go to Puerto Rico. I just wanted a little freedom, to be able to make my own decisions about how I lived. I knew Caleb would forgive me if I left him, because that's the way he is. I wouldn't forgive myself, though. And anyway, Aunt Jenny would call the police.

It was a free country, but not for everyone.

"She's gonna come back," Caleb said. He was still at my desk, and he paused to slide a spoonful of sundae between his lips. I could tell by the way he'd said the words, like some kind of prophecy, very serious, that he wasn't talking about Tess. "She is," he said. "I've been praying about it every night. She's going to come back and get us."

I didn't say anything. Even I had hope. If he had his own way of going about hoping, good for him.

And I still think it was just a coincidence. I mean, nothing happened the next day, except the sun came out and melted all the snow. But the day after that, Tuesday, Mrs. Harrison tapped me on my shoulder and said Aunt Jenny was on the phone, and that I could take the call in the office, which is the little room where Jeremiah had been spanked. I was scared, thinking maybe something happened to my mother, but when I got on the phone, it *was* my mother.

"Act like I'm Jenny," she said.

"Okay," I said. Pastor Rasmussen was at his desk. The paddle hung by a hook on the wall. *DO NOT SPARE* was stenciled in black across the spanking part.

"I'm leaving Denver now, driving." She sounded out of breath. "Dan turned out to be no good. I'm getting a late start, and I'll have to stop for the night. I don't want Jenny to even know I'm coming, so don't say anything. I know where that crazy school is. Get yourself out by the Kwik Shop on the corner by two o'clock tomorrow. I'll be there to pick you up, and then we'll get your brother."

2

I TOLD CALEB to pack light, to make it look like we were just going to school for the day. I was hoping that we'd have a chance to come back and get the rest of our things—I hated to leave behind my nice clothes that I had worked to pay for. But I was more than a little excited about the next day being my last at Berean Baptist. I'd walk out with nothing if that's what it took.

Fortunately, the things I really couldn't leave behind were small enough to get in my backpack. My money didn't take up much room, though I had over eight hundred dollars saved. I'd been keeping it in a fire-safe file box I'd bought at Walmart, which I'd padlocked to the underside of my bed, tucked up in the box springs so you couldn't see it unless you got right underneath. I would have kept it at a bank, but they said I needed a guardian to cosign, and then Aunt Jenny would have had access. It's not that I thought she would steal from me. I don't think she would. But I didn't want her watching over. I could cash my paychecks at the 7-Eleven for a dollar, and that seemed a small price to pay for a little privacy.

I packed two shirts, an extra pair of jeans, three pairs of underwear, my pepper spray, my toothbrush, my comb, my fake ID, and the lipstick, mascara, and eyeliner I kept hidden in my closet. I also brought my old phone. It couldn't make calls anymore, but it still had all my old pictures on it. I thought about taking the computer, as it was small, but Aunt Jenny had paid for it.

Before I went to bed, I wrote a note.

Please excuse Sarah-Mary at 1:50 today. She has a dentist appointment downtown at 2:00, and I told her she could walk, as I'm not feeling well enough to drive.
Sincerely,
Jenny Veer

I was ready to make several attempts with the signature, but it wasn't that hard to make the big loop on the *J* the way Aunt Jenny did, and all the *e*'s like *i*'s. On the first try, I got it exactly right.

On the ride to school, Aunt Jenny asked Caleb if he was sure he was feeling okay. She was used to me not talking in the morning, but she and Caleb would usually chat on the way. Caleb said he was just tired, and he sounded convincing, even throwing in a little yawn, but when I turned around to look at him over my left shoulder, he had his arms crossed tight in front of him like he was literally holding himself together. The night before, when I'd told him our mom was coming, he'd put his hands flat against his ears and started breathing hard, and I worried he would have some kind of attack. Before I turned forward again, I bulged my eyes at him. I always got dropped off first, so he'd have to keep himself together, and his mouth shut, a while longer.

When we got to Berean Baptist, it looked just like it always did, all the kids still outside in the parking lot, the girls on one side, playing foursquare or waiting a turn with their coats zipped up over their dresses, and the boys on the other playing basketball. But that was fine. After today, I would never have to play another game of foursquare again, or worry about being spanked. I'd never again have to sit in that little cube. I smiled, just thinking about it, and Aunt Jenny must have seen me and misunderstood, because she smiled back and told me she hoped I would have a good day. I could hear in her voice, how high it was, that she was making one of her efforts—Caleb told me she'd told him once that she prayed every night for patience with me, and for understanding. But right then, with the early sunlight coming in through the windshield, I had this weird moment of having understanding for her. She wasn't wearing any makeup, and her hair was still uncombed, the sides tucked behind her ears.

Looking at her just then, I had a flash of how she must have looked when she was a girl, growing up with my mom, and with their mom, my grandma Sarah, who my mom said used to slap them across the face when she got mad and who was always telling them they were stupid. And now Aunt Jenny, who'd lived through all that, was sitting in the front seat of her car and looking at me so kindly that I started to feel bad for her. She was probably wondering why I wasn't getting out, but she just kept smiling, blinking at me with her thin-lashed eyes, and I could see clearly then that she really did think she was helping me and Caleb, and that she thought of herself, with all her rules, as a force for good in our lives. And this afternoon she would come to Berean Baptist to pick me up only to find out I was gone, which would be embarrassing for her. Soon after that, she would learn that even sweet Caleb had looked right at her and lied.

Still, what had to be done had to be done. I thanked her for the ride, nodded at Caleb as I climbed out, and told Aunt Jenny that I hoped she had a good day too, even though I knew that by around three o'clock, her day wouldn't be good at all.

But I guess I got back what I gave, and then some. Because I didn't know it then, but I wasn't about to have a good day either, or even like any kind of day I'd known before.

At 1:15, I put my Christian flag up on top of my divider and waited for Mrs. Harrison to come over. When she did, I gave her the note.

She frowned. "I didn't hear anything about this, Sarah-Mary. And why're you just giving this to me now?"

I looked down at my hands, and then up at the Christian flag, still poked into my divider. "I'm embarrassed to say," I said.

She crossed her arms and leaned in closer. "What is it?" Today, her breath smelled like cigarettes and also the minty gum she was chewing fast.

"I was going to tell my aunt I forgot about my appointment. I'm scared of the dentist." I looked down again. "I don't want to go. But then I felt bad about lying."

I kept looking down, waiting out the silence. I'd thought I'd said it just right, but it was sometimes hard to know.

Mrs. Harrison clicked her tongue. "Well. I'm glad you changed your mind about lying. And I understand. I don't like the dentist either." Her nose wrinkled. "My teeth aren't so good."

She didn't show me her teeth or anything, but still it felt like opposite day: everybody who was always mean had suddenly decided to be nice and kind of sad seeming, the very day I had to lie to them.

"They always look fine to me," I said.

She frowned again, squinting at the note. "This is pretty unusual, just getting a note like this. Seems like your aunt should have called."

"You can call her if it'd make you feel better," I suggested. "You've got her number?"

I held her gaze, no problem. I'd anticipated this part of the

39

conversation, which is why that morning, when Aunt Jenny was in the bathroom, I'd put her phone in airplane mode.

"That's okay. I believe you." She gave me a closed-lipped smile.

By 1:50, I was out the door, heading down the metal steps. I made myself walk slow and steady across the parking lot, but I was wincing the whole time, waiting for Mrs. Harrison or Pastor Rasmussen to open the door and yell at me to come back, or even rush down the steps to apprehend me. But no one did. As soon as I cleared the corner, I started to run like I was in a prison-break movie, my backpack bouncing behind me.

I didn't like that I still had no plan as to what I would do if my mom wasn't at the Kwik Shop. Obviously, she wasn't the most reliable person. I knew that well by now, and I knew it even as I was running. I imagined me just a few minutes into the future, getting to the Kwik Shop and not seeing her there, and waiting, and waiting, and then realizing she wasn't coming. Caleb would be in his classroom at the middle school, looking up at the clock, his fingers tapping on his desk as he started to get worried that our mom was worst-case-scenario dead, or bad-case-scenario still not wanting to be our mom. If she wasn't at the Kwik Shop, if she didn't come, I would have to head back to Berean Baptist and lie some more about having survived the dentist, which would probably just dig me in deeper, as Aunt Jenny sometimes liked to stay and talk with Mrs. Harrison when she picked me up. And

I'd have to face Caleb, and how brokenhearted he'd be.

And on top of all that, I would know I'd been stupid about my mom again, counting on her to do what she'd said.

But when I turned the last corner, breathing hard, she was there, leaning against the wall of the Kwik Shop. Her hair was longer than it had been, and she was wearing a coat I'd never seen, a red ski jacket that curved in at her waist. She was looking at her phone, smiling a little. She didn't hear me come up.

"Hi there," I said. I kept my thumbs hooked in the straps of my backpack. I wasn't going to hug her. I'd already decided.

She looked up, gave a little yelp, and in less than a second her arms were tight around me, squeezing my backpack into my back. She smelled like sunscreen, like lime and coconuts, and her cheek was cold against mine. She kissed the top of my head twice, making a *mwah* sound each time, and said she couldn't believe how tall I'd gotten, how I was almost as tall as she was now. I kept my own arms pulled in close to me, like to keep her a little away. But the corners of my mouth tugged up at the sound of her voice. And I didn't push her off.

When she finally stepped back, she looked me up and down. "You look good." She took off her sunglasses and squinted. "But my God. What *are* you wearing? You're like Sarah-Mary of the Prairie. Are those knee socks?"

"It's the dress code." I crossed my arms over my coat. I didn't appreciate her laughing at me, especially when she was wearing

41

jeans tucked into stylish boots. "I've got normal clothes in my backpack. I want to change somewhere after we pick up Caleb. I want to change right away."

"Yes, ma'am," she said. She started walking toward her car, gesturing for me to follow. It was the same old white Subaru she'd had forever, the back door of the driver's side dented in.

"Where are we going?"

She waited until we were both in the car, buckled in, to answer. "I don't know," she said. Her mascara was clumped, and she picked at her lashes, squinting into the rearview mirror. "Where do you want to go?"

I turned to look at her. She'd said it lightly, as if we were taking a spur-of-the-moment day trip, as if it would be fun to decide as we went along. Styrofoam coffee cups and empty candy bar wrappers surrounded my feet, and despite the pine-tree air freshener hanging from the mirror, the car smelled like spoiled milk.

"You don't have a plan?"

"I meant to eat." She play-slapped my skirt with the back of her mitten. "And I've got a plan, all right."

We were halfway to Caleb's school before I realized she wasn't even getting ready to tell me anything about her plan. She was still just talking about Dan and what a jerk he'd turned out to be.

"He *humiliated* me," she said. She'd taken her sunglasses

off, and her eyes looked dull, as if she were looking through the windshield at a sad movie instead of the road ahead. She'd taken off her mittens, too. She had red gel paint on her nails, the same color as her coat. "He got me to the point where I didn't think I was *anything*." She glanced at me. "I mean, he was so nice at first, so nice. We'd been shopping for a *ring*, Sarah-Mary. And he was going to buy me a new car so I could help him show clients around . . . and then all of a sudden"—she threw up her hands but put them back on the wheel fast when the car in front of us slowed—"all of sudden he's picking at me all the time, and telling me, 'Oh, those jeans don't really do anything for you' and 'Oh, too bad you didn't wear more sunscreen when you were younger.' And then I start finding these texts on his phone from this *Lauren* person I've never heard of. . . ."

"What's the plan?" I asked. We passed the Dairy Queen, and I saw my manager's little hybrid in the parking lot. I felt bad about not telling him I'd miss my shift that night.

She glanced at me again. "What?"

"What's the plan? How does this fit in with where we're going?"

She took a little breath before answering.

"Sarah-Mary. I was in the middle of telling you about something really painful that happened to me." Her eyes went aquamarine. "And I just drove eleven hours, all by myself, feeling so lonely and sad, and then I try to share with you just a little, and you interrupt me like you don't even care. Like you're not even listening."

I looked back out the window. We were already turning into the lot of the middle school. For all I knew, Caleb had been watching out the window and had already seen her car. I didn't want her to get more upset before we went in to get him. And anyway, it wouldn't do any good to try to point out which one of us was more self-centered. I knew that by now. It wasn't even like she was trying to be mean. My mom has her good qualities. I'm aware of them. But trying to get her to not think about herself for more than a minute was like asking her to spell a long word backward. You could see it in her expression, how her brain would just sort of freeze up.

"Sorry," I said. I turned back to her, my face as sad and serious as I could make it. "I do care."

It's probably why I'm so good at lying. I had a lot of practice, growing up with her.

I let Caleb sit up front. As she drove, he leaned across the parking brake, resting his head on her shoulder. She'd nuzzle him at stoplights, saying how much she loved him, and how grown-up and handsome he looked with his haircut, even though she missed his curls. I could see some of her face in the rearview mirror, and for the first time I noticed how much she looked like Aunt Jenny, especially with her sunglasses on. They had

44

the same overbite smile, the same rounded cheeks that Caleb got. But aside from wanting to love on Caleb and fight with me, they didn't have much in common.

"I'm starving," she said. She eyed me in the rearview. "But I don't want to eat in town and risk seeing somebody. I know you've both had lunch, but we could get out on the highway and find someplace for a snack."

"That sounds good," Caleb said. You could hear in his voice, the happiness in it, that she could have said, "Let's go stand in the middle of the road together," and his reply probably would have been the same.

And then we were moving fast, out on the same highway Tess and I took to St. Louis. The sky had clouded over, and the leafless tops of spindly trees waved around in the wind. My mom said something to Caleb I couldn't hear. They both laughed, and even though I still didn't know what the plan was, I felt a lightness across my shoulders, as if I'd taken off another backpack. We were leaving Hannibal. I would miss Tess, and some of my coworkers. But nothing else.

We stopped at a McDonald's next to a truck stop. I took my backpack in with me and said I was going to the bathroom to change. There was a line for the stalls, so when it was finally my turn, I hurried, coming out with the skirt and the knee socks tucked under my arm. I'd been thinking it would be such a pleasure to throw my Berean Baptist clothes away, but then

I wondered if someone else would want them. Maybe. After I washed my hands, I folded the skirt and put it on top of the hand dryer, along with the balled-up knee socks. On my way out, one of the women in line said, "Honey, you forgot something," and I said, "Nope. It's free for the taking," and walked out of the bathroom feeling great.

They were already eating by the time I got to their table. I'd had lunch just a few hours earlier, but the cheeseburger my mom was eating looked and smelled pretty good. Caleb had chicken nuggets, which he'd almost completely covered in ketchup.

"I guess I am hungry," I said.

My mom nodded and covered her mouth. "You should get something."

I waited, but she just sat there and took another bite. It seemed to me she might offer me some money, but I wasn't going to ask for it. I unzipped my backpack and got my purse out.

"Will you watch this?" I asked, passing my backpack over to Caleb.

He nodded. He looked dazed with joy, sitting with my mom and eating chicken nuggets in the middle of a school day. But I knew he'd heard me.

When I was standing in line, I could see one of the big TVs. The sound was turned off, or maybe turned low, so it was just annoying to see a newscaster with shiny lip gloss talking. But then there was a picture of a Muslim woman with a rose-colored headscarf, just dark bangs showing. She had high, wide cheekbones, and the hollows underneath looked real, not just contouring, though she did have on lipstick that was the same color as the scarf. She looked like a normal person except for the scarf, but below her picture was *REWARD $10,000.* I glanced around at the other people, in line and at tables, who were watching the screen too. Some of them were probably getting excited, thinking they were going to go out and catch themselves a Muslim and pay off their Visa bill. But looking up at the woman's face just made me anxious. If they were willing to pay that much to find her, they must have been worried about the fact that she was out running around. I was thinking that anybody who found her should just do the right thing and turn her in for free. Have some honor, for God's sake. As much as I liked money, that's what I would have done.

When I got back to the table with my burger, both my mom and Caleb were hunched over, looking at something in her hand.

"So you buy this ticket, and it attaches to the zipper of your coat like this," she was saying. "And then you can ride the chair-lifts as many times as you want for the whole day."

"Wow," Caleb said. "Is it scary?"

"Oh, no, it's fun." She had a smear of ketchup on her chin. "I mean, I started out on the bunny slope, and that's what you'll do too. I'll teach you."

"Really?"

She nodded, but by then I'd shrugged off my coat, and she'd looked up and noticed my watch. "Oooh," she said, reaching over to rub her fingertip along the metal band. "I guess you've been making good money at your job, Sarah-Mary. I know those aren't cheap."

"My friend gave it to me," I said, turning my wrist so she could see the face better. Tess had given it to me when she got a new model. She'd switched her contract over to her new watch, so this one didn't work as a phone anymore. But it still had all Tess's music on it, over five hundred songs, and little wireless earbuds that snapped right out of the band. Her trash was definitely my treasure.

"No friend like a rich friend," my mother said, nudging Caleb.

I didn't like that so much. I didn't like it when she acted like I thought the same way she did about people, or about anything. But it was fine. Wherever we were going, I'd probably be able to talk to Tess more than I did living right in Hannibal. Maybe she could come visit.

I put my purse in my lap and unwrapped my burger. "So you're taking us back to Colorado?" I was up for it. I'd only seen mountains in pictures, but I thought I'd like living around them. I could learn to ski. Tess knew how to ski already. Her family had gone out to Breckenridge over Christmas.

My mom looked at me like I was crazy. "Why would I take

you to Colorado? There's nothing for me there."

I had to wait to chew and swallow. "Okay. Then where are we going?"

She only hesitated for a moment. But I felt the heat in my arms, the anger bright in me right away. I knew it then. Wherever she was headed, we weren't going with her. I looked out the window, where a woman in a white coat was jogging to her car.

"Where are we going?" I asked again, because stupid me, I was still hoping. I couldn't go back to Berean Baptist. I couldn't.

She wiped the ketchup off her chin with her napkin. "Sarah-Mary. I don't have any money. I can't take you anywhere just yet." She said it with a little laugh, like I'd had the nerve to ask when our limo was arriving.

I put down my burger and stared at her. If she noticed my distress, you couldn't tell.

"Are we going to stay in Hannibal?" Caleb asked. He was still munching on the last of his nuggets, not even looking upset yet. But I already knew that wasn't happening either. Only two of us would be staying in Hannibal. Our mom already had a sad look on her face, or rather, a look she hoped made her seem sad. She wasn't good at faking.

"I don't have a job in Hannibal." She sighed with puffed cheeks. "I don't have anywhere for us to stay."

"I've got money," I said, patting my purse like a gun in a holster. "I've got enough to rent a place for a month, in Hannibal or

49

about anywhere. That should give you time to find a job."

She leaned forward on the table. "You've got it with you?"

"Yeah," I said, a little surprised. I didn't think she'd take me up on it. Not just like that. All those hours at Dairy Queen. But it would be worth it to keep her from doing what I worried she was getting ready to do to Caleb. And to me.

She squinted. "You have a checking account?"

"No. I've been saving cash. But we could just open an account and deposit it. I'm sure we could find something."

"That's a good idea," she said, like she was really impressed. "But you know, if you hear me out, I've got a better plan."

"You can stay with Aunt Jenny," Caleb said. He was already frantic, talking too fast. His hands were flexed on the table. "We can all stay there together."

She reached over and smoothed his short hair. "I said I've got a better plan, honey. You'll just have to hold on a little longer."

I could see he'd started breathing hard, his narrow shoulders moving up and down under his gray coat. My own heart started to pound. She was doing this. She was really doing this to us again. I wanted to reach across the table and shake her. I wanted to pick up the plastic fork on the table and stab it into her cheek.

"The thing is," she said in a low voice, "I've been chatting with this man in Virginia. He's a little older than I am, and he's not in the best shape physically." She held up her palms as if calming a crowd. "But he's extremely nice. Extremely nice. And he's already crazy about me." Clearly, she didn't understand that she was in imminent danger, the plastic fork lying close to my hand. She smiled, leaning back in her chair. "And he's got so much money that if I can pull this off, we'll all be vacationing in the Bahamas next Christmas."

"You're leaving again?" Caleb shook his head, like he was trying to answer the question the way he wanted. "Virginia? We're not going with you?"

"Just for a little while." When she saw his face, she clicked her tongue. "Come on. This is an exploratory visit. I can't exactly show up with the kids in the back of the car. You know what I'm saying? I don't want to scare him. I'm trying to keep things casual for now. I told him I was going to be out there anyway. On a business trip."

"Well, you kind of are," I said. I meant it mean. But she only tilted her head for a moment, as if I'd helped her see the situation in a new light. She nodded thoughtfully.

"I've got to go to the bathroom," Caleb mumbled. He kept his head down as he got up, and I knew he was trying not to cry. My mom frowned as he walked away, then popped another fry into her mouth.

"Why'd you even come here?" I whispered, surprised by how calm I sounded. "Why'd you even call?" I knew this was the most I might get out of her. You couldn't ask her questions like *How can you do this?* or *What's wrong with you?* She didn't know.

51

"I mean, we're not even on the interstate. This is out of your way."

"I wanted to see you." She tucked her chin in like she was hurt. "I wanted to see my kids. Is that so strange?"

"Mm-hmm." I glanced back up at one of the big TVs, which now showed an overturned semi under a bridge. "Well. It probably would have been better if you hadn't called at all."

Caleb would have been better off for sure. And me too, though my concerns for myself were more practical. I was going to get spanked with that damn paddle over this. I was going to have to hold on to my ankles and pray.

"I'm sorry," she said, and right then, she sounded like she meant it. I don't know. Maybe some part of her was truly sorry. It was confusing. She'd taken care of us when we were little. She'd changed our diapers, I guess, and gotten us both through fevers and colds, and at least four incidences of head lice. I had a memory of her singing "Dream a Little Dream" to me, when I was little enough to sit in her lap.

"To tell you the truth"—she half smiled—"I was hoping you could help me out a bit."

I shook my head. Whatever she wanted, no way.

"I'll pay you back. Every penny."

I shook my head again, laughing a little, though I could feel the pressure of tears. But it was funny. Really. That's all it was. This didn't have anything to do with me. She was just a woman who'd happened to give birth to me, and she was even more out of her mind than I'd thought. I held tight to my purse. I wanted to put it away, to zip it back in my backpack, but my backpack was still over by Caleb's chair. I put my purse on the floor and leaned my chair to one side so I could loop the strap under one of the legs. Out of sight probably wasn't out of mind. Not for her. But I'd made my point.

"Please," she said. "I'll pay you back with interest. How much do you have? Let me make you a deal. A good one."

"No." I looked past her. The big clock on the wall read 3:25. Aunt Jenny would be at Caleb's school to pick him up in five minutes. I was trying to think of what I could say to her, and to Mrs. Harrison, if there was any way to still fix this. But there was nothing but consequence in my future.

"Sarah-Mary. Don't you see? It would be so much better if I could fly into Richmond and stay in a halfway-decent hotel. Think about it. Think about how much better that would look."

"He's only eleven." I shoved my tray toward her. "I mean, I understand leaving me. I don't really need you. But he does. His dad is dead, and you're his mom."

I was being foolish, doing the very thing I knew better than to do. I was trying to make her feel bad. It'd never worked before, and I don't know why I was thinking it would work now. But to my surprise, she winced. She rubbed the back of her neck.

"He's got you," she said. "I would never leave him if he didn't have you."

I wasn't enough. Of course I wasn't.

She sighed. "And you've both got Jenny. Don't act like you're in some prison camp. I know she's a little rigid, but you've got a roof over your head and enough to eat." She held up her hands. "You may think you have it rough, Sarah-Mary. But you've got everything you need."

I shook my head. "You can't make yourself feel better because we're not going *hungry*!" A man at another table turned around, but I didn't care. Let him look. "You have no idea what Berean Baptist is like! I don't have any freedom! You understand? None!"

She didn't have anything to say to that. And I'd said all I could. We sat in silence for a few minutes, not even looking at each other. A woman started to sit at the table connected to ours, but when she saw my face, how mad I looked, she backed right up to go find a different table. Just then, it occurred to me that Caleb had been in the bathroom for a long time. I turned around, craning my neck, but the bathrooms were down a hallway. I couldn't see the door to the men's room.

"You think he's okay?" I asked. I didn't wait for her to answer. I was thinking of highway pedophiles, and how little he was, and the idea of him all alone in a bathroom while his mother and his sister weren't paying attention. I got up and hurried across the lobby, dodging people coming through with trays. The hallway was empty, the doors to both bathrooms closed.

I knocked on the door of the men's room. "Hello?"

A toilet flushed, but no answer. I knocked again, louder.

"Hello?"

A man in a baseball cap opened the door.

"Hello," he said, and laughed a little. I got the joke. I was standing there with my fist raised, ready to knock again, and it was like he'd opened the front door to his house. But when he saw my face, he stopped laughing. "What?"

"Did you see a boy in there? Around eleven?" I used the flat of my hand to show how tall Caleb was. "He's wearing a gray coat?"

"Uh . . ." The man turned around and looked. I ducked under his arm and moved past him. Another man coming out of a stall, still buckling his belt, looked at me like my head was on fire. I moved to the side to let him through.

"Caleb? Are you in here?"

"Yes." It was his voice. He sounded mad, and a little choked from crying, but it was him. "Sarah-Mary, get out of here. I'll be out in a minute."

"Okay," I said. "Sorry. I was worried." I nodded at the belt-buckle man, who was at the sink, washing his hands. "Sorry," I said again.

I felt pretty stupid, coming out of the men's bathroom. I'd embarrassed Caleb, made him feel like a little kid, when that was the last thing he needed. Also, those poor men had just been using the bathroom, and I'd pretty much accused them of being creepers. I kept my head down as I moved across the lobby, so

I was almost back at the table before I saw my mother's empty chair.

Her tray was still there, and ours too.

"Miss?" A McDonald's worker in a polo shirt pointed at the table. "Are you done here? May I clear the table?"

"Hold on." I turned back to the counter. There was a line, but she wasn't in it. She'd gone to the bathroom? I glanced back to the hallway, and just as I did this, out of the corner of my eye, I saw the dented Subaru backing out of the parking lot. I stood there like a fool, openmouthed, with the girl in the polo shirt still standing beside me.

"Oh my God," I said. The Subaru was already rolling forward. I could see the red sleeve of her jacket. She was really doing it. She was leaving us here. I'd never catch her, even if I ran. And if I did catch her, and said everything I could say, it would make no difference.

"Are you all right?" the girl asked. "Is everything okay?"

I nodded, sinking into my chair. "We're still sitting here," I said.

I'd been stupid. I'd been so stupid to believe. But to my credit, even before I looked down, I knew my purse was gone.

3

WHEN CALEB CAME out of the bathroom, I was standing by the exit, my coat zipped, my mittens on, my backpack strapped to my shoulders. I told him we had to go out to the parking lot.

He looked over at our table, where the man in the baseball hat was now sitting. "Where's Mom?"

"We need to go around back," I said, already moving to the exit. I knew I was making it sound like she'd be out there waiting for us, but that was for his own good. On the other side of the parking lot was a little grassy area with two picnic tables set back from the road. I figured we'd go out and sit at one, away from everybody else. If he started to cry when I told him, he at least wouldn't have to be embarrassed.

But he didn't cry when I told him. He sat at the picnic table and cradled his belly, his eyes shut tight like he had a stomachache, and really, that was worse than seeing him cry. I reached across the table and patted his shoulder. I didn't know what to say. The sky was gray and heavy looking, and I could smell car exhaust from the drive-thru. Still, I just wanted to sit out there with him for a while. I didn't want to have to go inside and call Aunt Jenny. Life was feeling hard enough without bringing her in just yet.

And we were actually in kind of a pretty spot, if I looked in the right direction. Behind Caleb, there was the McDonald's, with the dumpster mostly hidden by a fence, and then a parking lot that stretched out to the truck stop. But if I turned my head to the right, away from the highway, there was just a big, winter-dead field, with nothing but wooded hills on the other side of it. The trees didn't have any leaves, but they looked so peaceful, their branches black against the gray sky. I've always liked the way trees look in winter, like arms and hands reaching up for something, or like they're trying to get bigger than they are. I guess that's what's really happening, even if they don't know it.

"When did she say she'd come back?" Caleb asked.

"Does it matter?" I laughed a little, picking at a loose thread on my mitten. A drop of rain fell on my forehead, and then another. I pulled up my hood and checked Tess's watch. It was after four, too late to try to fix things. Aunt Jenny was already losing her mind.

And Tess was in Puerto Rico. I couldn't even go borrow

someone's phone to call her for a ride. Or advice.

A white car rolled into the parking lot, and Caleb sat up straight, though it wasn't even a Subaru. When he saw it wasn't her, he folded his arms on the picnic table and rested his head on the sleeves of his coat. I blew into my mittens, looking back at the trees. Aunt Jenny would have a lot to say to me tonight. There would be the scolding, especially because I'd taken Caleb along, but worse than that, there would be her barely disguised smugness that she'd been right about our mom. I wouldn't tell her about the money. She would love that too much.

"She didn't even say good-bye," Caleb said. He still had his head down against his arms. I couldn't see his face, just the gold whorl of hair at his crown.

"I'm sure she wanted to," I said. "She just wanted my purse a little more."

That was a bad enough thing to say to him. I don't know why I had to say what I said next. I was just so mad, thinking about what an idiot I'd been. And before I could get ahold of it, the mad turned into mean.

"And if your plan is to sit around and wait for her to love us like a normal mom?" I leaned across the table. "And come back? I'm sorry, but you're just being stupid."

When he lifted his head, I could see it in his eyes, how much that hurt him. Before I could say I was sorry, he jumped up and ran out of the picnic area, straight out into the field. I called out

59

his name, but he didn't stop, and he was moving fast. I could see the soles of his shoes as he ran. By the time I gave up shouting at him to come back, he was about a quarter of the way across the field. Still, I sat there for a few more stupid seconds. I was thinking he'd get tired and stop, or at least slow down.

But when he was about halfway to the trees, not slowing at all, I realized I might have a situation. The trees didn't have their leaves, but there were so many of them, so close together, their bare branches entwined.

"Caleb!"

I'm a fast runner usually, but I was still wearing my backpack. Also, the boots I'd changed into had low heels, and the field was uneven and muddy. After stumbling and almost falling, I looked up just in time to see him slip in through the trees.

"Goddamn it, Caleb!" I tried to sound scary, but now I was scared. I didn't know what was in those woods. Somebody's property? I didn't know. My hood had fallen back, and cold rain seeped through my hair to my scalp. "You come back here right now!"

He scurried up a little rise in the land, and then over it, and I couldn't see him anymore. I shook my head, like I could refuse what was happening. I was so used to him being good.

"Caleb, I'm sorry! Come back!"

I reached the trees and hurried up the rise. It was steeper than it looked, and I had to turn and dig the sides of my boots into the slick grass so I wouldn't slide back down. When I made it to the top, no Caleb. I could hear the hum of the highway behind me, but in front of me there was nothing but wilderness, so many shades of brown and gray. Faded leaves carpeted the ground between trees, and more trees, as far as I could see.

"Okay," I yelled, "you win. I'm scared now, Caleb. I'm going back, and if you're not with me by the time I get to the McDonald's, I'm gonna have them call the police."

I waited. Branches creaked overhead. It seemed the best thing to do was just wait where I was, perched up like a resting hawk. He couldn't get back across the field without me seeing him. And it wasn't like he was going to try to spend the night in the woods. His coat didn't even have a hood.

I waited, and waited. I didn't see or hear him.

"Caleb?"

The sky started to change, turning a deeper shade of gray, and the darkness of the tree trunks was getting harder to pick out against the darkness of the earth in between. If I ran back to the McDonald's to call the police, they might come out with dogs and searchlights. I didn't want to think about that. I didn't want that story to start.

And for all I knew, he was just hiding behind a tree, watching me. I stood with one foot in front of the other, my hands tight on my backpack's straps.

"Caleb, I'm sorry!" My teeth were chattering. "But if you

don't come back to me right now, I have to go call the police. I mean it. You've got five minutes."

I moved farther into the trees, listening. There was the tapping of raindrops against the ground and the trees, and a squirrel skittering across my path. But other than that, quiet.

I kept walking. Rain started to fall in earnest, cold against my cheeks and forehead. I didn't pull up my hood. I wanted to be able to see all around, and to hear him if he called out. The air seemed to grow dark before my eyes, but the farther I walked, the faster I walked, the harder it was to give up and turn around, to admit that he had really vanished. My backpack thumped against my back like it was pushing me forward with every step, and then I started to run, calling his name, my voice getting louder, again and again, until I was out of breath.

I almost stumbled when I came to a dirt road cutting through the trees. Nobody was on it, and my armpits pricked with sweat. Someone could have been driving through. Someone could have picked him up.

"Caleb?"

I heard the tremble in my voice. I'd called him stupid. I hadn't meant to.

"Please," I whispered. "Please let him be okay."

I don't know who I thought I was begging. Anyone who thinks they can yell up to God for sympathy or help in times of need doesn't pay much attention to the news. Little kids die in the hospital, whether people are praying for them or not. People die horrible deaths in coal mines and earthquakes and tornadoes and wars and airplane crashes and convenience store robberies, and you know some of them had time to guess they were dying, and to pray as hard as they could.

But knowing all that didn't stop me, now that I was really scared. I kept saying please, over and over, as if I were begging someone who might change their mind. "I promise, if he's okay, I'll be so nice to him," I whispered. "I'll never be mean to him again." I looked at Tess's watch. I'd been looking for him for almost forty minutes. It felt like hours.

"CALEB!"

The trees on either side of the road stayed silent. All I could hear was soft rainfall. I called his name again, shouting so loud my throat hurt, my mittens cupped to my mouth.

And then he was up in front of me, just before a turn in the road. He held a big umbrella, lime green, but it was him, his gray coat zippered up to his chin. I started toward him, and he held up his hand like STOP.

"I'll run again!" he yelled. "I'll run again, and you won't catch me. You stop right there, Sarah-Mary!"

I stopped. He wasn't that far away—maybe two hundred feet—but it was uphill. If he ran again, I might lose him. Even in my relief, I felt unease creeping back. I didn't recognize the umbrella.

"Caleb. I'm sorry. Okay? I'm sorry. I was just mad. Mad at her. Not you. Come on back. It'll be okay. I'm sorry for what I said."

He didn't move, and he kept his palm raised in front of him.

"I need you to promise me something."

"Okay, sure." I stepped forward, just one step. But he stepped back, ready to run. I went still.

"Anything," I said. "You name it." I was just so happy to see him. He wasn't dead, chopped up somewhere, or stuffed inside somebody's trunk. He was fine. I would never be unhappy about anything again.

He glanced back over his shoulder. "There's someone over here who needs help. I need you to promise to help her. And to not get her in trouble."

It took me a moment to get what he was saying, but once I did, I had to work not to smile. I could guess what he meant. Even when he'd been so upset, realizing his mom had left him again and his sister had called him stupid, he'd found someone to help. I figured it was a homeless woman, living in the woods. Of course he would want to help her. That was just him all over.

But it also seemed dangerous, talking to a stranger out here.

"I'll see what I can do," I said.

He shook his head. "No. You promise me, Sarah-Mary. You promise you'll help her. You make a promise to me right now." He had his jaw set; the hand that wasn't holding the umbrella was clenched in a tight fist. "Promise." He moved the umbrella to his other hand.

I nodded. Whoever she was, she couldn't be that bad. She hadn't murdered him yet, and she'd apparently given him an umbrella. And in this particular circumstance, Aunt Jenny might actually be of use. She sometimes volunteered at a soup kitchen with other people in her church. She would know how to help.

"Say it," he said. "Say you promise to help her. Say you promise not to get her in trouble."

"I promise," I said, not even thinking about it.

And that's what sealed my fate.

I was expecting him to lead me to a little tent, or some kind of lean-to made out of branches and a tarp. But when I saw a dark red car parked a few hundred feet from the turn in the road, I wasn't that surprised. People lived in their cars sometimes, when they didn't have anywhere else to go. She had the engine running, probably for the heat, so right now she was better off, or at least warmer and drier, than I was.

But as we got closer, coming up on the passenger side, I saw the car was pretty nice and new looking. The windows on the side were tinted dark, and there weren't any dents or chips in the paint. I didn't know what kind of car it was, just some kind of sedan, but it looked newer than my mom's, and newer than Aunt Jenny's. If this woman was living in it, and it was hers, she should have sold it. She would have had rent for at least a year. She could have put a down payment on a mobile home.

I slowed my steps. "Caleb. What's going on with this person?"

"She's nice," he said. He'd been walking next to me, letting me hold the umbrella over both of us, but now he jogged ahead. "Come on and get in."

He opened the door to the backseat of the car. I threw down the umbrella and shouted his name, reaching the car just as he closed the door.

"Get out of there!" I grabbed for the door handle, slick with rain, just as I heard the click of the lock. I stood there, looking at my freaked-out reflection in the dark window, my hair wet, and some of it stuck dark against my pale face. Nothing in me could believe he'd just done what he did, but I was looking down at the proof.

"Caleb!" I stomped my foot. I could see from my reflection that I looked like a cartoon villain who'd just been had—I only needed steam coming out of my ears. But I really wanted to throttle him. I pounded on the glass.

"Damn it, Caleb!"

Finally, the back window moved down a little. But even if I could get my hand through, he'd scooted just out of my reach. "Get in the other side," he said. "Up front."

I shook my head. I couldn't believe how he was acting, giving me orders like that. It was like he'd turned into a different person, just because he'd decided, in his eleven-year-old brain, that this woman needed his help. Through the half-open window, I could see the back of her head clearing the top of the driver's seat. She was wearing a knit blue hat over dark hair that almost reached her shoulders. But that's all I could see—she was facing straight ahead, and she didn't turn around. Which was weird.

I walked to the back of the car. It had an Arkansas plate—red, white, and blue, *The Natural State* etched along the bottom. I coughed on the exhaust and moved back around to the side of the car.

"Caleb." My teeth were chattering again. I put my mouth against the crack of the window. "Tell her to roll down her window, and I'll talk to her right here. Meanwhile I want you to get out. Right now. Right this instant. Or I'm walking away. I mean it."

"No," he said. "You get in, Sarah-Mary. She's not dangerous. I promise."

"You don't sit in a stranger's car."

"She's nice. She gave me dry socks. I'm wearing them. She gave me peanuts, too." He held up a bulk bag of shelled peanuts for me to see.

I shook my head. I knew Caleb well enough to know it wasn't the promise of peanuts that had lured him into the backseat of this woman's car. He could be naïve, but he wasn't a complete idiot, and anyway, he wasn't starving—he'd just eaten at McDonald's. He was just dead set on helping her.

I moved to the front of the car, wiping rain from my forehead. The windshield wasn't dark like the other windows, and now I could see her clearly, staring back at me through eyeglasses with thin frames and square lenses. She didn't look young, but she didn't look old. She might have been thirty-five, or forty-five, or anywhere in between. She had both hands on the steering wheel, but whatever she tried next, I was ready: I had my backpack slung on just one shoulder, and I'd already unzipped the little compartment where I'd packed my pepper spray.

"Tell my brother to get out of the car," I yelled, loud enough, plenty loud enough, for her to hear me through the glass. But she kept staring at me. She wore a white puffy coat, and just like the car, it looked too nice, and too clean, for someone who didn't have a place to live. It seemed like she must be hiding, probably from the police.

"I'll help you," I said. "Okay? Whatever it is, I'll help you. But I need you to make my brother get out of the car. I'm not comfortable with him being in there with someone we don't know. I'm sure you understand."

Caleb opened the back window again, sticking his head out just a little. "I'm not getting out, Sarah-Mary! I'm not getting out until I know you'll help. Just get in. Get in the front."

He said it as if I were the one being unreasonable, standing

68

out there in the rain. Before I could make it back to his side of the car, he'd put his window back up. I glared down at my reflection. Aside from the part about getting in a stranger's car, he really was being smart. He knew better than to even let me in the backseat with him—he knew I'd drag or push him out.

"I'm going to leave," I said. "I'm going to leave you here, and I'm going back to the McDonald's. I'm going to have someone call the police. And she'll be in a whole lot more trouble than she is now. She'll be ARRESTED. For KIDNAPPING." I pounded on the glass of her window, hard enough that I hurt my hand. I turned away. "Seriously, Caleb. Here I go."

I only walked a few steps back up the road. We both knew I couldn't go anywhere. What if she drove away with him inside? What if I came back with the police and the car was gone, and he was gone with it? Right now, I was at least here, and if the car so much as rolled forward one inch, I'd jump up on the hood. I'd get my fingers into the edges by the windshield, and she couldn't make me let go. I didn't know how hard it would be to kick in the glass of a windshield. But I was ready to try.

The car didn't roll forward, though. It stayed where it was, the engine still running, so there was nothing for me to do but stay there as well. I pulled my hood back up over my head and crossed my arms, staring at the passenger side's front window. Finally, it rolled down.

I crouched down enough to see in, staying a few feet away.

She leaned across the parking brake and looked up at me, her eyebrows raised as if she'd asked me a question. She waved me in with her hand, smiling a little. She didn't say anything.

Caleb moved his head up into my view. "She's not a killer, Sarah-Mary. Geez. If she was a killer she would have killed me by now."

I ignored him, my eyes on her. I was shivering, and my teeth were still clacking together. I knew I wasn't thinking straight. I had to be careful. I couldn't use the pepper spray. Not with Caleb inside.

I bent my knees to get a better look at her. She'd ducked her head to get a better look up at me. Her eyes were sort of greenish behind her glasses, but she looked like she might be Mexican. I guessed that was it, the reason she was hiding. She maybe didn't have papers.

"What's your name?" I asked.

She didn't answer. Caleb was still pressed up behind her headrest, giving me a scolding look, like I was being rude.

I tried again. *"Cómo se llama?"* I'd been taking Spanish since ninth grade, and I could write it okay, though both teachers had told me my pronunciation was terrible.

Still she didn't answer. She held up a little plastic orange packet. When I squinted, I could make out *HOT* and *6 HOURS* on the side, and I realized it was those little toe warmers they sold in bins at Appliance Depot. People put them in their boots when they had to be out in the cold. She was offering them to me, but only as a condition. I had to get in the car.

Caleb was still pressed up against the back of her seat. I glared at him as he brought a peanut up to his mouth. He slipped it through his lips, still looking at me. I heard the crunch of it in his teeth.

I shook my head at him, my fury plain for him to see. I didn't give a damn about the toe warmers. I wasn't stupid. At least not usually. I would have stood out there all night, getting frostbite or whatever, if it had been just me.

4

THE INSIDE OF the car smelled musty, like wool that had gotten wet, with an undersmell of Caleb's peanut breath wafting up from the back. But it was clean enough—there wasn't any junk I could see on the floor or around the gearshift—just her keys, with a little silver *S* attached to the ring.

"She's nice," Caleb said. I whipped my head around to tell him that if he told me the woman we didn't know was nice one more time, I was going to lose my mind. But then I saw he wasn't talking to me. He was talking to the woman. About me.

"She doesn't always seem nice." He cupped more peanuts beneath his chin, ready for delivery. "Especially at first. But she is. She'll help you out."

The woman nodded, though she'd scooted close to her door. I gave her a look to let her know that was probably a good idea. I'd taken off my mittens, and I had my backpack in my lap, my right hand inside the pocket with the pepper spray. She glanced down at my hidden hand, looking anxious. That was fine. Let her be anxious.

"You understood what he said?" I asked. "You understand English?"

She nodded again, pushing up her glasses. She'd put the Toasty Toes packet away, back in her coat pocket. I'd already refused it. I curled my toes inside my damp socks.

"Then you better start talking," I said. I was acting tough, like I had a card to play. Which, of course, I did not. Caleb started to say something, but I held up my hand. "I want to hear it from her."

She shifted in her seat. The nylon of her white coat made a *sh-sh* sound, but she didn't say anything. She kept staring at me through her glasses. Even with her coat, I could see the rise and fall of her shoulders, and I knew she was breathing hard.

"*Rápido,*" I said. I couldn't roll the *r*, but I snapped my fingers. She knew what I meant. "Come on. Start talking."

"I just want to leave," she whispered.

Or maybe she said, "I just want to live." I couldn't tell. What was clear was that she had some kind of accent, and it didn't sound Mexican at all. *Want* had come out like *vant*, like the way a German in a movie would say it. But I didn't think she was German. I looked at the bones of her face, the hollows of her cheeks, her scared eyes. My heart started to pound. I knew where

I'd seen her. She looked different with the knit hat and more of her hair showing, and no lipstick now. But I knew.

I leaned away from her, a siren going off in my head. Caleb was right behind her seat. I pulled the pepper spray out and aimed it at her. She held up her gloved hands in surrender. I didn't care.

"Caleb!" I kept my eyes on her hands. "Get out of the car! Get out now! She's a criminal. They're looking for her. I just saw her on TV."

My whole arm was shaking. I grabbed my elbow with my left hand to try to keep it steady. But I was going to do it. I'd already popped the release. As soon as he got out, I would jump out too, and I'd give her a good spray, right in the face, before I slammed my door.

"Caleb?"

He didn't answer. When I let myself glance into the back-seat, he was just sitting there with his arms crossed.

The woman turned away and covered her face with her hands, leaning down against the steering wheel.

"Caleb. You listen to me." I tried to keep my voice calm, but my finger stayed on the trigger. "This is serious. Even if you think she's nice, understand she's done something wrong. They were showing her on TV. I don't know just what she did, but they're telling people to watch for her. She's maybe hurt people. And even if you don't believe that, it's for sure true that we would be in trouble with the police for sitting here with her like this." I clenched my teeth. "Now get yourself out of this car right now."

He shook his head. The sun had started to set, and the silvery light coming in through his window cast half his face in shadow. It was still him. Still Caleb, my little brother. But all at once—maybe it was the serious way he was looking at me—I could picture how he would look when he was grown, older than I was now.

"No way," he said. "She didn't do anything wrong. She didn't hurt anyone. She just didn't want to go to Nevada. That's the only reason they're looking for her."

"You don't know that," I snapped. "You think that's true because that's what she told you?" I didn't want to call him stupid again, but my God. I was trying not to breathe so hard. I didn't want her to know I was scared.

"It is true," the woman said. She sat up straight again, resting both hands on the wheel.

"You stay quiet," I said. But I lowered the pepper spray to my lap. I couldn't spray it with us both in the car with her. "Caleb. You don't know if she's telling the truth. But she probably isn't. It's only the bad ones that didn't go when they were supposed to." I eyed her from the side. "The ones who are still killing people."

"I have killed no one." She acted all offended, rolling her eyes, which, it seemed to me, is what any good actress would do. "And I won't ever kill anyone. I just didn't want to go to a"—she

75

paused to make quote marks with her fingers—"detention center. I'm not going to participate in my own persecution."

Now I rolled my eyes. That was a little much. First of all, they weren't called detention centers. They were security zones. It was true that a lot of Muslims were living in those little trailers, and that they had to use public bathrooms that they all shared, but that's only because the government was still trying to build housing, and hello, they were in the middle of a desert, so everything needed to be brought in by truck or train. But the trailers seemed fine for now. I mean, I'd been going to school in a glorified trailer every day.

And second of all, the government was sending them off to Nevada for their own good. We'd talked about it in social studies when I was at Hannibal High. Mr. Gordon said the security zones had fences and barbed wire and tower guards holding machine guns, but that was just as much to keep out people who wanted to kill Muslims as it was to keep the Muslims in. That's how mad everybody was. It was all costing taxpayers a whole lot of money, and Mr. Gordon didn't see how it could go on forever.

"Well. You should have gone," I said. "Cause now you're probably going to end up in a real detention center, and it won't be the kind with quote marks around it."

"No, she isn't!" Caleb slapped the back of my seat hard enough so I felt it on the other side. "We're going to help her, Sarah-Mary. You promised!"

I swallowed. It was true. I'd promised him. He knew what

that meant for me, and that I wasn't like our mom. But this was crazy, too much. He didn't understand how serious this was. He was trying to be like Jesus, and judge not. He was going to welcome the stranger and love everyone the same. That was all very nice, usually, but not for this. Sometimes you had to judge, or you were going to get killed. Or arrested.

She looked at Caleb in the rearview. "Your sister is right. You should go with her. You would get in trouble, and it's very serious." She glanced at me. "I am sorry. I should not have told him to get in the car. But he looked cold and wet. I thought he was lost." She pressed her hand to her ear and lowered her voice. "He was crying. I thought he was hurt."

"She gave me dry socks," Caleb said. "And now we're going to help her back."

The woman gestured at her face. "And he guessed right away. He knew."

I nodded. I'd already figured out what to do. There was only one way I could think to keep my promise to him without doing something illegal.

"We'll help her, Caleb." I looked back at the woman. "We'll help you turn yourself in. They won't be as hard on you if you turn yourself in." I didn't know if that was true, but it seemed likely. It seemed fair. "And however bad you think it's going to be in Nevada, it can't be half as bad as sitting out here in your car." I shook my head. "And they're going to get you eventually."

She looked at me, tilting her head. "How old are you?"

I raised my chin so I was looking down at her. I didn't want her to think I was some kid she could talk down to. And I knew for a fact that when I put my mind to it, and with a certain fake driver's license, I could pass for twenty-one, though I was more convincing when I had the chance to pile on the mascara. I would have lied and said I was older, but Caleb probably would tell her I was lying.

"I'll be sixteen in March."

She sighed, closing her eyes. "He told me you were nineteen."

I turned around and gave Caleb a look. He stared back at me and shrugged.

"Where are your parents?" she asked. The look on her face made it seem like we were the ones with the weird situation.

"Don't worry about that," I said.

She still looked confused. "You live close to here? It is dark now. They must be expecting you home for dinner soon."

Caleb started to say something, and I turned around to shush him. We didn't need to start telling some Muslim woman anything about our parents. Or even Aunt Jenny. I looked back at her to let her know we weren't giving out more information.

"Well," she said. "Even at fifteen, you have studied history. You know why any group of people that is first registered, and then rounded up, should be very nervous."

She was talking about the Holocaust. But that was totally different. The Nazis registered people and then killed them, even the little kids. America was just making Muslims go to the safety zones for their own protection, and for ours.

She sighed. "Not to mention the internment of Japanese Americans and German Americans during the same time period."

She talked funny. It wasn't just her accent, whatever it was. It was the words she chose, most of them bigger than they needed to be, and also the way she said them, like you were maybe a little bit stupid if you didn't automatically agree with every single one.

"Where you from?" I asked.

"Originally?"

I nodded. Duh.

"Iran."

I shrank back. That just pretty much sounded scary, especially the weird way she said it, like *EE-dan*, not *Eye-ran*. I knew the capital of Iran was Tehran, which sounded even worse, like *terror*. It's from a different language, okay, but if they ever wanted to make a better impression, they should probably change it.

"It's just a country. A place." She looked annoyed. "And for the last seven years, I've lived in Jonesboro, Arkansas. I taught at the university."

That made sense, that she was a teacher. She totally had that way about her, like she knew everything you didn't.

"What did you teach?" Caleb asked. He'd moved to the middle of the backseat, one hand resting on each headrest. Still, I guessed if I tried to grab him and pull him out, he'd go all rigid. He'd hook his feet under one of the seats.

She rubbed her eyes. "Electrical engineering."

"Wow," Caleb said. "You must be smart."

Or she was lying, I thought. But it was a pretty smart lie. I didn't know anything about electrical engineering. It wasn't like I could quiz her and trip her up. And even if it was the truth, it seemed kind of suspect. Somebody who knew about electrical engineering probably knew how to make a bomb.

"She's got to get to Canada," Caleb said. "You promised you'd help her, Sarah-Mary."

I turned around and gave him a look to let him know how crazy he sounded. "Uh, how am I going to do that?"

"I don't know. But you'll think of something." He turned to the woman. "She's really sneaky," he said. "She makes up the best lies."

The woman did not look especially relieved. But I have to say, I knew Caleb had meant it as a compliment, and I took it as one. If I were a foreigner trying to sneak out of the country, I'd for sure come up with a better plan than sitting out here in my car.

"You should turn yourself in," I said. I knew I'd already made that clear, but I wanted to say it again, and hear myself saying it, just for my conscience. My brain was already starting to think of what else she could do, what I would do if I were her. Even that, just thinking about it, seemed morally wrong.

"That's not an option." She looked at me like I'd said something stupid. "Do you think your parents would help me?"

I rolled my eyes. She was really stuck on this parent thing. She was acting like I was nine or something. I'd be a whole lot more help to her than any adult I knew. Unless they had a car.

"We live with our aunt," Caleb said. "And she'd turn you in."

He was right. Any adult we knew would turn her in.

She nodded, looking through the windshield up at the sky. "Then there is nothing you can do." She turned back to him. "I'm sorry. I don't want to get you into trouble. Please go with your sister. She is right. And I'm glad you found her."

"No," Caleb said. "Sarah-Mary promised. She's going to help. She'll think of something. You've just got to give her time."

I shook my head. It would be better if I could just tell him, in all honesty, that there was nothing I could possibly think up. But my wheels were already turning. I couldn't help it. It was like somebody put jigsaw pieces in front of me and said, *Okay now, don't try to put this together.*

"Why don't you just keep driving?" I asked. "Why you parked out here?"

She waved in the direction of the highway. "They are showing my face and my car on television. I saw it when I was getting gas just now—my picture up on the screen. That wasn't happening when I was still in Arkansas, when my car was parked in my friend's garage. One of the toll cameras must have scanned my plates when I drove through yesterday. That's how they know I'm driving. I ran out of the gas station and drove here to hide, and here's where I've been sitting. If the police have my license number, I'll never make it. This car is no good to me now."

She was right. If she was out on the highway, they'd get her in no time. Even I'd noticed her Arkansas plates.

"You could take a bus." I couldn't believe I was giving her ideas. But Greyhound stopped in Hannibal. Anyway, I didn't know how she would get from here to there. It wasn't like Aunt Jenny was going to come out here and give her a ride.

She shook her head. "You need identification to buy a ticket." She looked down. "Same with a train, or a flight, of course. I have a license, and an American passport. But given my name, I'm sure I would be pulled aside."

That was true. I didn't even want to know her name. The less I knew, the better.

"She'll think of something," Caleb assured her.

But I couldn't think of anything. We were a long, long way from Canada, and they were looking for her car. But I like to think that every problem has a solution, or at least most of them do. You just have to figure it out. I tried to think what Tess would do.

"Can you talk normal?" I asked. I tried to say it in a nice way.

She looked confused.

"Like without an accent?" I pointed at my mouth. "Can you talk like me?"

Now she looked like I'd said something funny. I didn't know what. It seemed to me she better listen up.

"Let me hear you try it," I said. "Say, 'Hi. I'm from Arkansas and my name is . . . Lindsey. I'm trying to get up to . . . Minnesota.'"

She tried it. She saw I was serious, so she was too. But no matter how many times I corrected her, she didn't sound normal. She sounded like she had a hook tugging hard on one side of her mouth.

"No," I said. "Try to sound like me."

"This does sound like you," she said, like she still had the hook.

I shook my head. It wouldn't work. As soon as she said anything, people would know. "How've you been getting around up till now?"

"I have been hiding at a friend's house." She touched her ear again. "In a basement. But the neighbor was getting suspicious. He'd seen my car in the garage."

"Your friend you stayed with's a Muslim?"

"Of course not." One of her thin brows moved high. "All of my Muslim friends are gone."

I knew she might be lying. But the story about the friend hiding her seemed true—I couldn't think of any other way that she wouldn't have been caught already with her accent, not if she had a Muslim-sounding name on her passport giving her away. The fact that somebody else, somebody in Arkansas, somebody who wasn't a Muslim, had already helped her made me helping her, if I really had to, not seem so bad. I was still holding the pepper spray, but I switched the safety cap back on.

"Are you thinking of something, Sarah-Mary?" Caleb asked. "You look like you're thinking of something."

I didn't answer him. But an idea had already come to me—it was exactly what Tess would do, if she were sitting in this car in the cold rain with a Muslim fugitive, and not in Puerto Rico, probably wearing a bathing suit and walking along a beach, or smiling pleasantly at a painting in a museum. It was exactly what she would try. And if I tried it, whatever happened, at least I wouldn't be headed back to Aunt Jenny's. Or Berean Baptist. Not right away. It would certainly be an adventure, maybe free of charge.

"She's coming up with something." Caleb slapped twice on the back of my seat. "I knew you would, Sarah-Mary! You're the best! You're the best person in the world!"

I shook my head. Now there was some irony for you. I looked over at the woman's face, at the faint wrinkles that branched out from her eyes, and the thin wire frames of her glasses. She didn't look particularly dangerous or crazy. Then again, she was dressed normal, wearing a blue knit hat and not the headscarf she'd been wearing in the picture. I tried to think of what I should ask her, something that might put me more at ease: *Are you sure you haven't hurt anyone? Are you sure you don't plan to? You absolutely promise you're not going to blow anyone up? Or help anyone who's planning to?*

It wouldn't matter if I asked or not. If she was lying, she'd just keep doing it.

"Do you have money?" I asked.

She nodded.

"How much?"

Now she looked all nervous about me. I could see it in the way she pulled her head back a little, her eyes going small behind her glasses. Good for her. I should have been that smart.

"I'm not going to steal it," I said. "But I know someone in St. Louis who makes fake IDs. He charges three hundred dollars, and he's really good. I can get you to him. Maybe tonight. And you'll need to buy me a bus ticket home."

She nodded. "I have that. But . . . he'll make one for me? A license?"

I didn't know for sure. "Yeah." I'd figure out how to get him to do it. "You have cash?"

She nodded again. But she still looked unsure. "I don't understand. Won't your aunt be upset if you are out so late? What are you going to tell her?"

I waved her off. "You got a phone?"

She shook her head. "No. They can use it for tracking."

"Then I'll need some cash now." I wriggled my toes in my boots. "Sorry. I just got robbed myself. Ten dollars should do it. Maybe fifteen."

"What's your plan?" Caleb asked. I waved him off as she turned away from me, fidgeting in one of her coat pockets. When she turned back, she held out a folded twenty-dollar bill.

"Okay," I said, taking the twenty. "Here's what we'll do. Up by the highway, there's a McDonald's. Right next to that is a truck stop. It's big. You can't miss it."

"Yes," she said. "I was just there."

"Okay. I'm going to walk Caleb back to the McDonald's." I zippered the pepper spray in my backpack. "I'll meet you at the truck stop in an hour. Just leave your car here and walk over. Take what you can carry. If you stay bundled up, I don't think anyone will recognize you."

"Why can't I go to the truck stop?" Caleb asked. He usually wasn't whiny. But he was whining now. "I want to go! Sarah-Mary! I want to help!"

I turned around, but before I said anything, I took a breath and made my voice soft. "It won't work, Caleb. If you want to help her, you need to listen to me. You've got to go back to Aunt Jenny's. Okay? That's the only way this is going to work."

He nodded, looking miserable. He zipped his coat and put his hand on the door release. Before he pulled it, he gave me a long look. "But you promise? You promise you'll help her?"

I nodded. I'd already promised. I was a little insulted that he'd made me promise again. But the woman just sat there looking at me, sort of peering at me through her glasses, like she was trying to see in through my eyes to my brain, to better guess how it was really working. That was fine. If she didn't trust me, there wasn't much I could do. If she thought she had a better option, she was free to take it. The best thing for me would be for her not to show up at the truck stop. I could tell Caleb I'd done my best, and it would be the truth.

I looked at Tess's watch. It was almost twenty till six.

"I'll wait until seven," I told her. "You got that?"

Caleb leaned up between the seats. "You've got to do it," he told her. "You can't just sit out here in your car. They'll get you if you do. And Sarah-Mary will help you. She will."

The woman nodded. I couldn't tell if she was nodding like she agreed or nodding like, *yeah, whatever,* but after I'd opened the door and started to pull my hood up, she touched the sleeve of my coat. "Take the umbrella." She gestured to where I'd thrown it down earlier, its green so bright I could see it in the dark. "Just take it," she said, like it was totally normal for her to tell me what to do. "Stay dry. Keep your brother dry."

The dark actually made it easier to find our way back to the McDonald's, as we could see the glow of the lights from the signs and the highway reflected off the clouds. Not long after we started walking, the rain eased up enough that I closed the umbrella and put it in my backpack. At one point, I stopped to ask Caleb why he was walking funny. He pulled up one leg of his jeans to show me one of the pink socks the woman had given him to wear.

"They're thick," he said. "They make my shoes tight."

But other than that, we didn't talk. It wasn't until we got out of the trees, walking side by side through the field, that I started to tell him the plan.

"Listen," I said. "If you want me to do this, you've got to do everything just like I say."

He nodded. I'd been thinking maybe he would chicken out and say I didn't have to go help her. But he just kept walking, waiting for me to say more.

"Okay." I nodded up at the McDonald's. "You're going to go in there, find a manager, or anybody who works there, and ask to use their phone. You call Aunt Jenny and tell her that Mom left you there. Only tell her I went with Mom."

When I got to that last part, he slowed his walking and shook his head. "She won't believe that, Sarah-Mary. She won't believe you left me."

I thought on that. He was probably right. And it was nice to hear that even Aunt Jenny knew me that well. There was no way I would have left him at a freaking McDonald's by himself. If I would have been in the car with my mom, I would have made her turn around, no matter what. I would have jumped out of the car. That was a difference between me and her. One of many.

"You've got to make her believe," I said. "That's your job, okay? Go ahead and tell her that you were so upset you ran out into the woods, but just say you sat out there by yourself for a while. Don't say anything about the woman in the car."

He made a face. "I know that. I'm not stupid."

"I know you're not." I stopped walking and looked down at him, so he could see that I meant it. I'd already said I was sorry, so it didn't seem like I should have to keep saying it. But I was still feeling it. So I said it again.

"Okay." He held up his palm like he got it, and he'd had enough of it too. But the hurt was still in there, lodged in his brain. I'd put it in, and I couldn't take it out.

"But you're going to have to have one story and stick to it, no matter what." I started walking again. "Even if you have to say it to the police."

Here was where I really thought he would get scared and have second thoughts. His eyes did widen for a second, like he was trying to imagine having to lie to a police officer with a notebook. But then he just nodded and waited for me to say more.

"Tell everybody the exact same story. Tell them you and I went out to the picnic table together, in case anybody saw us out there. Say we were waiting while she got gas, but we'd already told you we couldn't take you with us." I could hear how false it all sounded. "Say you tried to argue, whatever, but I just kept saying I'd call in a few days, and that it would be okay, and when Mom came back, we both gave you a hug and told you we loved you, but only I went with her. Say it over and over, the same way each time. Picture it in your head like it really happened, and then it'll seem like a real memory. Nobody'll be able to trip you up."

I felt like I was giving him a gift, telling him my best strategy. At Hannibal High, I'd told a couple of girls that my dad died when he pushed a little boy out of the way of a tow truck. I told them I saw it happen, and I remembered how his body had flown higher than the roof of the truck before landing on the curb, and how I knew he was dead as soon as my mom and I ran up because I could see his wide-open eyes staring up at the sky. I'd told them the tow truck had *HERE COMES HELP* painted on the door, and that the driver kept yelling that it wasn't his fault, like the only thing he cared about was not getting a ticket. I told them about how the little boy's mom had come to my dad's funeral, and how she'd been crying when she hugged me and my mom, and how my mom could barely hug her back because she was so pregnant with Caleb.

Only Tess knew the real story: when Caleb was just a baby, our dad had been walking home from a bar by himself in the middle of the night, maybe too drunk to be careful, and he'd been hit by a car.

We got to the edge of the field, just out of reach of the McDonald's security lights. It was cold enough that I could see my breath, but Caleb kept standing there, looking up at me, and I realized he was trying not to cry.

"Hey," I said, poking his shoulder. "This is your idea, remember? Do you want me to help her or not?"

He nodded, but he turned away from me, rubbing the back of his neck. "How long will you be gone?"

"I don't know." I looked up at the sky. There were no stars. There was no moon, even. "I'll probably get back tomorrow. But if I don't, you still can't tell anyone. Just sit tight and wait. You gotta promise me, Caleb. I could get in a lot of trouble for this. And not just with Aunt Jenny."

"I won't tell," he said. "I promise."

We nodded at each other, and I wasn't worried anymore. I leaned down to kiss him on the top of his head, and then I backed away, watching him walk out into the light.

The Muslim woman wasn't at the truck stop when I got there, but it was only six thirty. After I used the bathroom and did what I could to dry my hair with the hand dryer, I waited by the counter, looking at maps in a spinning rack until there wasn't a line. The clerk behind the counter had little dreamcatcher earrings and called every customer "honey"—male or female, young or old. *Okay, honey, thank you. Mm-hmm. You have a nice day now.* Her voice sounded friendly, even a little musical, but everything she said came out with the same tune, so it sounded more like the fake voice you can use when you have to get through a long shift of saying the same thing over and over, and you know very well somebody could be rude to you any second and you can't say anything back if you want to keep your job. I know. I've used that voice at Dairy Queen. When I came up to the counter, the clerk smiled and used the singsongy voice on me.

"Honey, you look like a drowned rat. Did you get stuck out in the rain?"

"I'm all right." I smiled back. "But is there a phone I could use?" I got out the twenty. "I could pay."

She turned her head and looked at me from the side, so I was looking at the wing of her eyeliner. It was like all of a sudden she didn't have to be so friendly just because I didn't have a phone.

"We got a booth." She nodded toward the back of the store. The music in her voice was gone.

"A booth?" I stood on my toes, but I couldn't see anything over the shelves. "Like a phone booth?"

"With a lock." She lowered her voice. "Some of our customers prefer not to use their own phones for certain numbers, and they still want the video component that the disposables don't have." She gave me a knowing look. "And they usually want privacy."

I wrinkled my nose. She was talking about sex calls.

"I'm just trying to make a regular call," I said. "I'm calling an arcade in St. Louis. I don't need any privacy."

She held up her hands. "Not my business. You buy the card up here and tell me how much you want to put on it. First minute is a dollar. After that, every minute is fifty cents."

"Can I get change back if I don't use it all up?"

"Nope."

I got a card with five dollars on it and headed back. The booth was at the end of a long hallway that went past the bathrooms and the changing rooms for the showers. I kept my head down as I moved past people, like I was so worried some truck driver I was never going to see again would think I was headed to make a sex call.

The door to the phone booth had a slide thing for the card I'd just bought and a dial that read *VACANT* over the knob. After I slid my card, I heard a timer start ticking, and I peeked my head in. The booth was a little bigger than my closet at Aunt Jenny's, and there was a touch screen and a plastic seat to sit on. Everything looked clean, and I smelled something lemony that I hoped was disinfectant. But after I closed and locked the door, I didn't sit.

It was easy enough to ask the screen for the number, though I typed in *Bobo's Good Times* instead of saying it, as I didn't want anyone to overhear and think I was making a sex call after all. Tess and I had laughed about the name of the

93

arcade when we'd called last September.

Before I touched the Call button, I turned off the video.

"Bobo's."

I kept my eyes on the speaker by the dark screen. "Hey. Is Matt P. working?"

"Hold on."

I took a breath. This was the part I was most worried about. I doubted Matt P. worked every night. I might be out of luck. But I got ready in my head, just in case. I'd been thinking about whether or not I wanted to try out an accent, to sort of get a read on how he would feel about making an ID for somebody foreign. But I wasn't sure I could do any kind of accent right. I didn't want him to think I was playing a joke.

The line rustled. "This is Matt."

"Matt P.?"

"'Sup."

"Uh, hi." I'd already started in my normal voice. It was too late to go back. "I remember you once helped me and a friend out with some identification issues?"

There was a long pause. I could hear beeps and whirls in the background, and then some kind of lion or dragon roar.

"I don't know what you're talking about."

He seemed to mean it. I bit my lip. It was possible that I had the wrong Matt P. But it sounded like him, as well as I could remember. He had the same low voice, and a lazy way of barely using consonants, like he had chew in his mouth when he didn't. Tess had done a great impersonation of him after we'd left with our new IDs.

"We went to your apartment? I remember it was across the street from a pancake house. And you had a dog. I forget its name."

"Well," he said. "I'm from the Show-Me State. How come I can't see you?"

"I'm calling from a booth at a truck stop, and their screen isn't working right."

He was quiet again.

"Boogie." It came to me, just like that. I jumped a little in the booth. "Your dog's name is Boogie!"

"Okay," he said. "What do you want?"

"Um, to get your services? I lost the first one. And I remember how much it cost last time. I can do that again. You going to be around tonight?"

He was quiet. The timer on the booth was still ticking.

"Hello?" I said. "Are you there?"

"Yeah," he said. "What do you look like? I need to know if I can find a good picture."

That was a lie. When Tess and I were at his apartment, he'd bragged that he had access to some database of something like two million ID photos, all of them electronically sorted by height and weight and hair and eye color. He was just a skeeve.

When we went to his apartment in September, he was looking us both up and down, even though he must have been at least twenty-five, and he knew for a fact we were minors. Tess took me aside and told me not to drink anything he offered, even just water. She said it wouldn't matter if there were two of us if we were both passed out.

Still, I needed to bait the hook.

"Um, let's see. I'm about five foot eight." I'd always wanted to be taller. "A hundred and twenty-five pounds. Dark hair, dark eyes." I waited. "And if it matters, they're unusually big."

He laughed. "Excuse me?"

"My eyes," I said, and laughed back at him, exactly the way my mom would have. "My God. You're terrible!"

That did it. He told me he got off work at eleven, and he'd be home by quarter past, and that he'd be available until midnight.

"I'll turn on the light over my door when I get home. Don't knock until you see it turn on. If I've turned it off again, then you'll know you're too late."

That didn't give us a lot of time. But he wasn't so suspicious anymore. I got him to remind me of the number for the highway exit he was by, and then, with just a little more pushing, he gave me the number of his apartment. But that's as close as he would come to giving me an address. He said if I'd really been there before, I should be able to remember the name of the complex, or at least how to find it.

"I'm sure I'll remember," I said. I kept my voice steady, but unseen to him, I pumped my fist in victory. It had all worked just how I thought it would. I was a freaking mastermind.

Then I caught sight of my reflected smile in the dark screen, and just like that, my conscience rose up and made me put my fist down, embarrassed. I didn't recognize the person who was looking back at me, the person who was breaking the law and not even stopping to feel bad. Just now I'd been caught up in the game of it, in seeing how much of a solution I could put together. I hadn't even been thinking about how what I was doing was wrong. But it was wrong. There was a reason she was on the run, a reason the government or whoever put up the money for the reward was looking for her. Maybe a better reason than I knew. Either way, I was betraying my country.

I wished more than anything I could talk with Tess. She would help me think this through.

"We're all set, then?" Matt asked.

"Yeah," I said, quieter now. "Thanks. I'll see you soon."

We weren't all set, of course. Just because he was okay with making fake IDs for girls to get into bars didn't mean he'd help a Muslim get out of the country, whatever she was willing to pay. I guess she'd find out when she got to his apartment. Even if she didn't say a word, he'd know as soon as he looked at her she wasn't under twenty-one. But it wasn't like I could go in and get it for her—she'd need the license to say she was older for it to be believable, and if I asked him to do that, he'd still guess what was really going on, only I'd be the one standing there if he felt patriotic and called the police. I didn't think Caleb meant for me to promise to be stupid and put myself at that much risk.

Still, after I hung up and walked out of the booth I started to feel worried for her, which was crazy. I was doing all I could. More than most people would. I'd get her to St. Louis, and right up to the door of Matt's apartment. The rest was out of my hands.

5

WITH THE CHANGE from the twenty, I bought an energy drink, a roll of clear tape, a spiral notebook, and a black hat with ear flaps on clearance because it was missing a button. I'd already spied a marker by the cash register, and when I asked the winged-eyeliner woman behind the counter if I could borrow it, she looked at me like I'd asked her to lend me a thousand dollars. But then she slid the marker across the counter and told me to be sure I brought it back. In the little eating area, I found an empty table tucked away from the front windows. But I still put on the black hat and pulled it low, on the off chance Aunt Jenny might stop for gas after coming out to pick up Caleb.

It didn't seem likely that she would. It seemed more likely that there would be no further complications, and that soon, I'd be heading to St. Louis with a fugitive to break the law. It was hard to believe, sitting there with the truck stop's stereo tuned to a basketball game, the sound of the referees' whistles and the time buzzer making me even more jumpy. I tried to focus on making the sign. But even as I worked, it occurred to me that if I got caught with her, I'd have to think fast to make it seem like I'd had no idea she was Muslim. I'd have to play super dumb, and do a good job of it. If I didn't, and I got caught in the lie, everyone would think I was really stupid anyway, helping a Muslim, when everyone knows they only pretend to be innocent until they do their damage.

Only Caleb wouldn't think I was stupid.

A family with two little kids, the parents wearing matching blue windbreakers, sat at the table across from mine. When the dad caught my eye, he smiled, not in a creeper way, just friendly, like maybe he felt sorry for me sitting all by myself in a truck stop. The energy drink went warm in my mouth, and I looked down without smiling back. He thought I was a nice girl, a good American. His face would change if he knew.

The door dinged. I looked up to see the Muslim woman in her white coat. She was just inside, standing by a display of beef jerky packets like she wasn't sure which way to go. She turned away from the lady at the counter, which was smart, and she had her hood pulled up over her blue knit hat. She carried a messenger bag like it was heavy, her right arm cradling it against her hip.

I gave a little wave. She put her head down and started walking toward me.

"Hello," she whispered, sliding in across from me. She looked at the sign I'd been working on, and the two lines between her eyebrows went deep above the frames of her glasses.

"What is this?" she asked.

I picked up my handiwork to give her a better a view. I was kind of proud about how well it had turned out.

NEEDING RIDE
TO ST. LOUIS FROM A WOMAN.
HELP A SISTER OUT! :)

I'd added the smiley face to keep it friendly, and then I'd gone over the whole thing with the clear tape to give it some structure. It wasn't exactly laminated, but it was the same idea.

She didn't look impressed.

"You said you could get me there!" She was whispering, but you could tell by her eyes she was mad. "You said you had a way!"

I put the sign in my lap. Geez, I thought. So much for beggars not being choosers. So much for gratitude. Maybe she'd like to go back out to the woods and sit in her car with her radioactive license plate.

"I do have a way. We're gonna hitch."

She touched her glove to her ear and winced. "Hitchhike? To St. Louis?"

"Sure. I do it all the time." It wouldn't do her any good if I showed a lack of confidence. I rolled my eyes. "Listen. You can't believe all that stuff you hear about how dangerous it is. That's just the media trying to scare you. It's perfectly safe if you do it right. And that's how we'll be doing it." I held up my hand to count on my fingers. "One, there'll be two of us. Two, we'll only get rides from women. And three, we're not going to be standing out on the highway. We'll get rides from places like this, where we have a chance to size somebody up. And I'll take a picture of the license plate before we get in, and say I'm texting it to someone as a precaution. That's about as safe as it gets."

She stared at me for a good long while. Then she squinted. "You have a phone? I thought you didn't have a phone."

Good for her. She was paying attention. I took my phone out of my backpack.

"Just the camera part works," I said, showing it to her. "It doesn't have service. Nobody would know that, though." I held up my hands. "That's just an extra precaution anyway. If we just get rides with women, we'll be fine."

She pursed her lips, then leaned back. With the fluorescent light over the table, I could see she had freckles, very faint, along her cheekbones.

"Oh," I said, remembering. "I got ahold of the guy in St. Louis, so he knows you're coming. He says he can do it. You sure you have the cash to give him?"

She nodded.

"And enough left over to give me bus fare back to Hannibal?"

She nodded again.

"Why don't you give it to me now, then?" I said. "Probably a hundred dollars should do it." I wasn't trying to rip her off. If a ticket home was less than that, I'd give her back the change at the station. What I was doing would be even worse if I made any profit doing it.

She got a leather wallet out of her messenger bag, and she looked around to make sure no one was watching before she slid five twenties across the table. I guess she wasn't in any position to hold back.

"But who will give us rides?" she asked. "It's dangerous for them. They don't know us."

She was right. That was the bigger problem. That was the part I didn't get about hitchhiking. I mean, why take the risk if you were the one with the car?

"Well," I said. "I've never had any trouble. But we've got to make up a story about you. Do you speak anything else besides English and, you know"—the basketball fans were cheering too loud for the family across from us to hear, but I lowered my voice anyway—"Arabic?"

"I don't speak Arabic." Her voice was even quieter than mine. I had to lean across the table to hear her. "I speak Farsi. Farsi and English."

"Nothing else?"

She shook her head.

"Okay," I said. "I was thinking I could say you're Italian, and that you don't speak any English. I'll say you're my mother's cousin, visiting from Verona. That way you won't have to talk." I sat back and waited for her to be impressed. I thought it was a pretty good story. I'd gotten Verona from *Romeo and Juliet.* Most people wouldn't have thought of it.

She frowned, looking at my empty energy drink can, then back up at my eyes. I don't know what she was trying to imply. I'd only had one.

"What if someone knows Italian?" she asked. "And they try to speak to me?"

"You're in Northeast Missouri. No one's gonna know Italian." I tried to say it just reassuring, not like she was being dumb.

She looked past me, out through the windows. It was full-on night now, but the lights over the pumps were bright, making rainbows out of puddles of oil. There were cars lined up, waiting, and that seemed like a good sign. We were already south of Hannibal, so maybe an hour and a half from St. Louis. We would only need one person to say yes.

"Portuguese. It's even less likely." She said it like she was in charge all of a sudden. "Say I'm visiting from Lisbon." She waited. "It's the capital."

"I know that, thanks." I probably did know it. I'd just forgotten. It's not like I'd recently had a reason to walk around thinking about the capital of Portugal. "Fine. Now we've got to come up with a name for you, something that sounds Portuguese."

She shrugged. "Maria."

I shook my head. That sounded kind of Mexican. That was the last thing we needed. Actually, I wasn't sure even her saying she was Portuguese would go over so well with everybody. But it would probably be fine. "Let's go with . . . Chloe," I said.

She tilted her head. "Chloe? From Portugal?"

"Yeah. Say your mom heard it in a movie and thought it was pretty. It'll be fine. And we need a last name. What's a Portuguese last name?"

I rolled my lips in like I was thinking. I didn't know if a Portuguese last name would sound like a Mexican last name. But I didn't want her to know I didn't know.

Her gaze moved up to the fluorescent light. "Da Gama." She half smiled. "Like the explorer."

I thought about saying, "Oh yeah, good ol' Vasco," just to prove I knew something. But I didn't really care what she thought. "All right," I said. "You're Chloe da Gama, my mother's cousin visiting from Lisbon. But you don't say any of that, okay? Don't talk at all. Act like you don't know any English."

She nodded. She put her glove to her ear again.

"Why you keep doing that? Why you keep rubbing your ear like that?"

"It's clogged," she said. "I got some water in it a few days ago, and I couldn't shake it out. Now it feels as if a soaked cotton ball is stuck inside."

"Did you try putting hydrogen peroxide in it?" My mom used to do that for me and Caleb when we got water in our ears.

She nodded. "I did try this. It still feels clogged." She waved her hand. "It's not so bad, though. I'll get drops for it when I can."

"Okay." I unzipped my backpack and started squishing stuff down to make room for the tape and the notebook. "Hey. I got your umbrella in here. You want it back?"

She shook her head.

"Okay. I'm going to use the bathroom and then we'll head out with the sign."

She stared down at the table like she was either thinking hard or getting ready to throw up.

"You'll be all right, Chloe," I said, part for a joke, and part for practice. And also because I didn't feel so bad about what I was doing when I thought of her as Chloe, a nice Portuguese woman. I still didn't want to know her real name.

On the way to the bathroom, I stopped at the register to give the clerk her marker back. I asked if they had any ear drops, just to see. They didn't have any, though.

We stood outside the truck stop's door, staying under the roof because of the rain. I held the sign, and Chloe kept her head down and her hood pulled up. I understood she was worried about being recognized, but to make up for her looking kind of depressed and weird, I smiled at everyone walking by and tried to look as normal and as American as I could.

It didn't work. An hour went by and nobody stopped. It was mostly men getting gas or coming into the store, or sometimes a man and a woman together, or a man and a woman with kids, and when anyone in these categories looked at the sign, they seemed relieved we were only looking for a ride with a woman, as then they didn't have to feel bad about not wanting to help a sister out. One man on his way in even smiled and said, "Sorry. I'm a dude," and held up his palms like, *What are you going to do?*

Sometimes just women walked by, by themselves or with kids, but they all lowered their eyes and hurried past us. I didn't want to call out to any of them because it would be embarrassing, and also because I was nervous someone would complain at the counter. I was pretty sure it was legal to hitchhike in Missouri—Tess had acted like it was, and I remembered I'd seen people with their thumbs out on the side of the highway. Still, the clerk could probably throw us off the property if she wanted to. So there was nothing to do but keep standing there, looking pathetic. Chloe and I didn't say one word to each other, as she was already in character.

After a while, my cheeks started to hurt from forcing a smile for so long. It was getting colder out, and I wished I'd taken the toe warmers from her when we were back in her car.

It was almost nine when a black woman wearing a pink pea coat and a matching beret gave us and our sign a dirty look as she was walking into the store. That about did me in. It was hard enough standing out there and shivering and feeling more and more worried that we might not make it to St. Louis before Matt turned out his light and closed up shop—I didn't need someone walking by and giving me a look that made me feel even worse. I didn't even want to look at Chloe. I felt dumb, like I'd been caught in a lie. I'd made it sound like I knew what I was doing.

A few minutes later, the black woman came out with two sodas with straws in the lids. She'd only got a few steps past us when she stopped and turned around.

"I have one question," she said, emphasizing the *one*. "Are you two out of your minds?"

I shook my head, in case she was really asking. "No ma'am," I said. "We're just trying to get to St. Louis."

"Hmm." She looked me up and down like she didn't quite like what she saw. Right then I knew why I'd called her ma'am. She reminded me, so much, of a teacher I'd had back in Joplin who used to hand out lunch detentions like they were nothing, and I'd quickly found it was a good idea to be as polite to her as possible. This woman standing before us now was even wearing slacks with low heels, just like that teacher wore—I remember they used to click on the linoleum, and it was always scary. You could hear her coming.

She took a sip from the one of the sodas and shook her head. "Well, that's a good way to get yourself killed," she said. "I see your sign says women only, but it's still not smart, what you're doing. Not in this day and age."

I shrugged. There wasn't a lot I could say in response. Apparently it wasn't that smart, but not because someone would murder us—we would just freeze to death waiting for a ride. But I wished she would go away, and take her stupid beret and her sodas with her, and not keep calling me out in front of Chloe.

"Why do you have to get to St. Louis?" She took another sip from the straw. "What's in St. Louis?"

"My sister works at a pancake house there. She's got the night shift. We're supposed to meet her."

"Hmm-hmm. What pancake house? What's it called?"

I couldn't remember the name of it, but I gave her the exit number, and I told her it was just to the right of the exit. She said she knew the exit I meant. Still, I saw the look she was giving me. She was one of those people who could spot a lie, even a good one. Her gaze moved to Chloe.

"She's Portuguese," I said. "She doesn't speak English."

She narrowed her eyes, still looking at Chloe, so I went right into the whole deal, how this was my aunt Chloe, who was really my mom's cousin, visiting us from Portugal. I said she wanted to meet my sister before she went home to Lisbon, so my mom asked me to take her down to St. Louis, since my sister couldn't get off work. I was ready with more details if she required them. I knew my sister's name, and how long she'd worked at the pancake house, and I knew that she'd promised us a free meal when we arrived. If needed, I could tell her what I was going to order.

But I didn't have to go into all that. Judging by the look on the woman's face, she no longer seemed suspicious, just horrified, or maybe disgusted.

"Your *mother*? You're telling me your *mother* told you to hitchhike to St. Louis with this poor woman who doesn't speak any English? At night?"

"Yes ma'am," I said. "We don't have a car. And the bus is expensive."

She looked over at Chloe again, and I could guess what she was thinking. I looked like someone who maybe couldn't afford a bus ticket, but Chloe's white coat was pretty nice, and so were her boots.

The woman looked back at me. "How old are you?"

"I'm eighteen."

She frowned, but didn't say anything. And then she just turned around and walked away. She got into the driver's side of a dark blue van parked at one of the pumps. I gave it a hateful stare, thinking about her sitting inside it, all warm and self-righteous, leaving us here with just her opinions and her rudeness.

I was still staring at the van when she got out again, and started walking fast toward us. She didn't have the sodas anymore, and she looked like she had something on her mind, like maybe she'd heard my thoughts. Her shoes clicked on the pavement. Right before she reached us, I took a few steps back.

"Okay," she said. "We can give you a ride. Now, my husband and my son are with me. If you don't feel comfortable with that, we can't help you. But if you want to come meet them, come on over and have a look in."

I had to make a decision fast. She didn't seem like the kind of person who would take well to ingratitude, and even worse, she might think my hesitation was a race thing, which it wasn't. The problem was I'd told Chloe we would only get a ride with a woman, and technically, that's not what this was anymore. Then again, it seemed pretty unlikely that we were going to get robbed, raped, or murdered by an entire family, and I was freezing, so I said, "Oh, thank you so much!" and touched Chloe's arm. I pointed at the van and the woman, nodding my head, and if Chloe was mad about me breaking the rules, she didn't show it. She pressed her gloved hand over the strap of the messenger bag, and gave the woman a grateful smile.

When we were about halfway to the van, the woman turned back to me. "And I just want to let you know my husband spent seven years in the service. He's a trained soldier."

That gave me a jolt. I had no idea what she meant by that, and I worried she meant something having to do with Chloe. But then I realized she was saying that we shouldn't plan to try anything funny once we got on the road. She was thinking we were thieves.

"I'm Gayle, by the way. And just to save us all trouble, I want you to know we don't have any cash. I'm not exaggerating. I had to dig around in the console to get enough change for those sodas. We've got credit cards, but they're all about maxed out. You don't want them." When we got to the far side of the van, she took off her glove and showed me one of her hands. "And this is my wedding ring, okay? No stone. Just a band. It means a lot to me, but you could not get ten dollars for it."

"Oh," I said. "Don't worry, ma'am. We're not . . ." But then I stopped, because what was the point? That's exactly what someone who wanted to rob them would say. And anyway, Gayle wasn't listening. She opened the van's sliding door, and instead of a long seat, there was a boy in a big wheelchair who might have been anywhere between six and ten years old, with a plaid blanket over his legs. His head was sort of leaned back and tilted to one side in a headrest, but you could see by his eyes he was looking at us. On the other side of him was the man I guessed was the dad, the trained soldier, who looked friendly enough. He wore a Cardinals jacket, and he held a soda in one hand; in the other, he held a water bottle with a long straw that had an unusual bend in the middle, which I guessed was for his son.

"This is my husband, Reggie, and this is our son, Aaron. They have terrible taste in music, but they're generally good people."

The boy made a groaning sound that might have just been a hello. The man waved. I waved back at both of them.

"Reggie and Aaron, this is Chloe. She's visiting our country from Portugal, and with her is . . ."

"Amy," I said.

Gayle gave me a look. I don't know how she would know I was lying about that. But she gave me a look.

The man smiled, leaning around his son to see Chloe better. "I never made it to Portugal," he said. "Wanted to. I was stationed in Italy for a few years. Vicenza. But I didn't get to travel much."

Chloe stayed quiet.

"She doesn't speak English," I said, very aware that Chloe had heard and understood every word he just said, and was probably feeling pretty good that we'd gone with her Portuguese plan and not my Italian one. Two points for her. Fine.

Gayle leaned into the van to fix the blanket so it covered her son's feet. Then she straightened back up and looked at me.

"Amy, I want you to know we don't normally pick up strangers at truck stops."

I swallowed. She was looking right at me, and she'd said "Amy" like we both knew it was fake.

"We're doing this because we try to walk with Jesus through this life, and back there I felt very strongly, very clearly, that Jesus was telling me to help you."

I nodded. That was about all I could do. I wasn't going to lie to her and be all *Oh yeah, Jesus told me I could trust you too, so it all works out!* I was feeling bad enough. These people had their own problems, with their maxed-out credit cards and their boy who was watching us, taking us in, but who couldn't walk or talk. I didn't know how they would feel if they knew that Jesus was telling them to help an atheist and a Muslim who were breaking the law.

"Thank you," I said. My teeth were chattering again. I worried that maybe she was going to spend the drive trying to save our souls, or at least mine. Lucky Chloe would just get to sit there and act like she couldn't understand.

"Okay," Gayle said. "I was thinking your aunt could sit in the very back. There's a little seat next to the lift. And you could ride up in the passenger seat next to me."

I was about to nudge Chloe and point to the back of the van when I remembered I was supposed to get a picture of the license plate. But the words wouldn't come out of my mouth. It'd seemed like such an easy rule when I was making it, but now, in front of actual people who were giving us a ride, I felt bad. I mean, they were trusting us. And now I was going to act like we had to worry about them. Still, I'd told Chloe we were going to take a picture of the plate, and I'd already gone back on one rule. It didn't seem fair to keep switching rules around on her when she wasn't allowed to talk.

"I'm really so appreciative," I said. "But before we get in, I need to take a picture of your license plate and send it to my dad. He made me promise."

Gayle tilted her head so that her pink beret, which sat on her head at an angle, looked level with the ground. Her eyebrows went up, but the rest of her face didn't move. It seemed like she might be offended, or maybe thinking that I obviously didn't hear Jesus the way she did and maybe didn't deserve her help after all. But then she smiled.

"That," she said, "is the first sensible thing that's come out of your mouth." She held one arm out to the back of the van, as if she were a waiter showing me to my table. "Please. Be my guest."

I ended up being wrong about Gayle wanting to save my soul. The whole way to St. Louis, she barely talked. She played gospel music on the stereo, and she sang along with the chorus to one of the songs, "everything's gonna be all right," over and over, but that was kind of nice, actually. She had a good voice—it was deeper than her talking voice, and she could still go up high without sounding like she was straining. When her husband told her Aaron was asleep, she turned off the music, and we were all quiet the rest of the way. I put on my headphones and clicked through Tess's music until I got to a slow, pretty song by Gallatin Sky. I was in the mood for something soft like that, now that I was warm and cozy, and looking at the red taillights in front of us.

Tess told me once that she loved the feeling of being driven on the highway at night. She said when she was little, her parents would wrap her up in blankets in the backseat so she would sleep, and she'd open her eyes sometimes and see just a strip of white from the roadside lights reflected on their faces, the rest of the car still dark, and it didn't matter if it was raining out, or even snowing. She felt safe, she said, like they were all together in a little egg. I'd nodded like I knew what she meant, but I didn't. I've probably been in the backseat at night while my mom was driving, maybe even back when she was still with Tom. I suppose I might have had a blanket over me at some point. But I'd never felt like I was in an egg, nestled in and safe. So it was pretty weird that just now, sitting in a van that belonged to people I didn't even know, with Chloe quiet in the far back, I kind of understood what she meant. I could hear the tires *shush*ing over the wet road, and the hum of the engine, and Aaron snoring softly behind me. His mom was wide awake and driving steady, so all I had to do was sit back and be whisked along. I had this feeling, true or not, that for now, at least, we were one of them. Part of their egg.

I thought of Caleb, and hoped he was safe and tucked in his bed, though I knew he probably wouldn't be asleep. He'd be too worried about me, and about Chloe. He couldn't know we were both safe in this van, on our way to St. Louis. I even had warm air blowing on my feet.

We were just outside the city, coming up on the suburbs,

when I looked up and saw a digital billboard maybe a quarter of a mile ahead. I'd been keeping watch for them the whole trip, hoping we wouldn't pass any. Highway digitals usually just showed the forecast, or traffic warnings, or a picture of some smiling real estate agent going back and forth with the featured Home of the Month. But sometimes they showed photos of fugitives, and I could see that's what this one was doing, showing a picture of a bearded man. But as we got closer, it switched to the picture of Chloe in her headscarf, her face bigger than any moon, her eyes gazing out over the highway. My whole body tensed, and I waited for Gayle to slow the car and look at me like, *What the heck?*, or for her to just make big eyes at her husband in the rearview. But she didn't do any of that. She just kept on driving, humming some Jesus song to herself.

I thought, thank you Jesus for the distraction. Ha ha.

When we got to the pancake house, I was nervous someone from the family would need to use the bathroom, and that they'd all come in, maybe expecting to be introduced to my waitress sister. But the son was still sleeping, and after Gayle pulled the van in front of the door, she didn't even cut off the engine.

"It's open?" she asked, squinting at the entrance. The parking lot was empty, and though the windows were lit, all the tables I could see were empty. But I pointed to the *Open 24/7* neon sign, and she nodded and pushed a button that made the side door roll open. She must have forgotten that Chloe didn't know any

English, because she told her in a quiet voice to be careful not to trip on the brace for the wheelchair on her way up.

I got out with my backpack, but before I shut my door, I said thank you again, looking back at the man to show I meant to thank him, too. They both nodded and smiled, but that was it. They didn't want anything else.

"Good luck," I said, which was sort of weird, because it wasn't like they were getting ready to do something. I meant good luck in general, like with their lives, and their son. I meant they'd been nice when they didn't have to be, and I felt it.

"Good luck to you," the man said. He nodded at me, and then at Chloe.

I shut the door, and the side door hummed and clicked back into place. Dry and delivered, and holding our bags, we watched the van roll away.

6

WE HAD OVER half an hour to wait at the pancake house before Matt P. got home from work. Chloe said she'd buy me something to eat.

"You must be hungry," she added, saying *hungry* like it was spelled *hung-a-dy*. But she was right—I was hung-a-dy. I hadn't eaten anything since the cheeseburger I'd gotten with my mom and Caleb at the McDonald's how many hours ago.

"But I can't buy sausage or bacon," she whispered. "No pork. I'm sorry."

I frowned. "Why not?"

"It's haram." She shrugged. "It's not allowed for us."

"I'd be the one eating it."

"But I would be paying. I'm very sorry." She did look like she felt bad. "I'm grateful you're helping me. Anything else, I will get you."

I rolled my eyes, which I guess was a little rude. But seriously? Leave it to a religion to rule out something as amazing as bacon. And I didn't like her telling me what I could and couldn't eat. Then again, I had a friend back in Joplin whose mom was a vegetarian, and she had a rule that she didn't want meat in her house. I went over there once for a sleepover, and the mom said she'd order us two big pizzas, which was really nice, but she made it clear we could order veggies or cheese or nothing. My friend said we couldn't even order meat and go outside and eat it on the steps—her mom wouldn't spend her money on it. I wasn't the only one who thought that was a little nutty, but all I said to the mom was, "Cheese would be great, and thank you for the pizza."

"Okay," I said. "I'll just get pancakes. Thanks."

Once we were inside, Chloe went back to not talking, looking at one of her gloves like it was fascinating when the hostess walked up. I asked if we could get a booth by the window, which we got, as the place was pretty much empty. After we were seated, I was pleased to look over at the apartment building across the street and see the Budweiser sign still hung in a window on the bottom floor.

I pointed the sign out to Chloe. "His is the one right next to it," I whispered. "On the right. Our right. That's the one. See the door light is still dark?"

"You are not coming?" She leaned across her side of the table.

She didn't seem scared so much as just making sure. Even in the warm restaurant, she was still wearing the blue hat, the ends of her hair a little tangled above her shoulders. But she'd taken off her coat, and with just the black of the turtleneck against her skin, her face looked older, or at least tired. The hollows under her cheekbones were too deep, and her eyes were squinty behind her glasses.

"I'll wait for you here," I said. I'd for sure decided on that. If Matt P. didn't like illegals, if he was a more ethical person than I hoped, me being with her wouldn't do her any good, and it might do me real harm.

"You'll be fine," I said. I didn't mean it like a lie. It was more like wishing her well.

She nodded, looking hopeful. "You know him? He is your friend?"

"He's not my friend," I said. I'd never said he was, and it was important that she understand this. I wasn't going to make her think she was more safe than she was. If she didn't want to go over there, she shouldn't. "I can only tell you that the last time I saw him, I paid him for a fake ID, and he gave me one. He's a legitimate businessman."

One of her brows went high. "But if he's seen me on the reward sites, he knows he could make much more money if he turns me in."

I frowned. I hadn't thought of that.

"Well," I said, "he didn't strike me as the kind of person who pays much attention to the news." It was the only thing I could think to say that was true but that also might make her feel better. I could have also mentioned that really, she was taking the same chance of being found out right now. There were only maybe six other people in the restaurant, including the waiter and the hostess, but any one of them might have seen her picture, and maybe recognize her from five booths away. That might have just made her more nervous, though, so I kept the point to myself.

And when our waiter finally came over, he just seemed friendly, not suspicious at all. Chloe ordered by pointing to what she wanted on the menu. I explained she was Portuguese and didn't speak any English.

"Not even a little?" he asked. He was old, with bad teeth, but he gave her a wide smile and kept looking at her as if he were expecting an answer. Chloe was good, though. She only smiled back, looking confused.

"Not even a lick," I said. I ordered a tall stack of pancakes and a Diet Coke. When the waiter walked away, Chloe shook her head.

"This is not healthy for you, this soda." She made a *tsk-tsk* sound. "And the energy drink you had earlier. It was big. It is too much for you."

I gave her a look to let her know that I didn't appreciate the advice. Maybe it was some kind of Muslim thing. Some kind of

122

Muslim anti-soda thing. Or she just personally felt like she could tell everybody else what to do. It seemed to me she might lay off after the whole bacon denial.

"You ordered coffee," I said.

She shook her head. "It's not as bad for the body as these soda drinks, with the sugar, or the fake sugars, even worse. And you are still growing." She paused to click her tongue. "You need to be careful with your body."

"I've had a long day," I reminded her, though it was pretty crazy that I should need to. "And I imagine I'll be up all night. I don't know when the next bus leaves for Hannibal." I smiled in a bitchy way. I was American, and I liked my freedom and my soda, thank you very much.

She didn't say anything. She looked like she was studying me, the lines between her brows gone deep again. "Where are your parents? Why do you live with your aunt?"

"They died," I said. "Car accident." That was a half-truth, sort of. That was all she needed to know.

"Oh." She put a palm against her chest. She sucked in her breath, like someone *she* knew had died. "Oh, I am so sorry."

I shrugged. Her greenish eyes had gone all soft, and I felt a little bad about lying. Her hand was still pressed to her chest, and I noticed her diamond ring. She'd been wearing gloves before.

"You married?" I asked.

She put her hand in her lap, but didn't say anything else. I guess only she got to ask the personal questions.

"So that's a no? You're not married? No kids?"

She held up her hand to show me she didn't want to talk about it.

It occurred to me that maybe her husband was mean to her. Or maybe he was already in Nevada, and that was really why she was trying to escape. My mom told me that when she was a teenager, she was in the mall in Springfield and she saw an Arabic man walking around with this woman who was always a few steps behind him, wearing a black burqa with just her eyes peeking out. The woman even stood behind the man on the escalators, like she was his servant, but my mom said the woman was wearing those designer shoes with the red on the bottom that cost about a million dollars, so she was most likely his wife. "I wouldn't make a dog walk behind me like that," she told me, and I'd agreed it sounded messed up.

I leaned across the table, my voice quiet. "Are you on the run from your husband? You can tell me if that's what's going on."

She tilted her head. "Why do you ask me this? Why do you think this?"

It felt kind of awkward, coming out and saying that I knew Muslim women didn't have rights. So I told her what my mom had seen at the mall in Springfield. That was awkward even, but I felt like I needed to be honest and get across what I meant. And I wanted her to know how crazy it was that a woman should have to walk behind her husband like that. I was thinking I knew it was messed up because I'd grown up in America.

She listened to the story, the two frown lines between her brows showing again. When I was done, the frown lines stayed there, but she said, "It is not perhaps anyone else's business, how this married couple walks through a mall."

I stared at her. I couldn't believe she thought that was okay.

She waved her hand. "But this story has nothing to do with Islam, or with me, or any Muslim I know." She leaned across the table and pressed the backs of her fingers into the palm of her other hand. "You understand. This is not Islam. I have literally never met a Muslim woman who walks behind her husband. Not once in my life. This is as strange to me as it was to your mother." She lifted her chin. "What, you think because your mother saw one woman in a burqa walking behind her husband that all Muslim women in the world do this? You take one story and generalize it to the lives of over a billion people? From all different countries? Who don't even all speak the same language?"

I chewed my bottom lip, thinking. When she put it like that, it did sound like kind of a jump.

One of her eyebrows went high. "Do you think that no Christian woman in the world has ever walked behind her husband? No Jewish woman? And yet you do not generalize this to all of them. Yes, I am very aware there are places in the world that use Islam as an excuse to oppress women, as is true with all religions. But this is not actual Islam."

I leaned back against the booth. I didn't know enough about it to argue with her. But I wasn't convinced. It wasn't just that one story. I was always hearing about terrible things happening to women in Muslim countries. One of Aunt Jenny's news shows did a report on how in this one Muslim country, if a girl had anything to do with sex before marriage, their fathers or brothers could kill them in front of everybody, and it wasn't illegal, cause even the government agreed she was better off dead. It didn't matter if you were rich or poor. And it wasn't made-up. They interviewed actual women who were almost killed, some of them crying, their words translated to English at the bottom of the screen. And I'd once done an oral report about how girls in Afghanistan couldn't even go to school without getting acid thrown in their faces by Muslim men.

Chloe must have gone to school, though, to speak a whole other language so well. And if she really did teach electrical engineering, she'd gone to school a lot. So obviously, if I brought that up, she could say I was generalizing again.

But I wasn't done asking questions. I was thinking this would be the last time I'd ever get to talk to a real live Muslim, face-to-face, and there were so many things about them, including Chloe, that I just didn't get.

"You usually wear a headscarf?" I gestured at my own head. "Like in your picture?"

"I used to. When it was safe."

"Your husband made you wear it?"

She shook her head. She looked annoyed, like she'd heard the question before. "It is my decision. In Iran it was compulsory. But here it is my choice. Or it was. Think of a habit for a nun. No one is making her. It is her decision."

I tried not to make a rude face, but nun, Muslim, whatever, it seemed like a pretty bad decision to make. I would hate covering up my hair all the time, not to mention my ears. And all for what? It was about as dumb of a rule as not being able to wear a high ponytail at Berean Baptist. Nobody was going to die or go to hell if they saw your hair or the back of your neck.

"Don't you like to feel the breeze in your hair?" I couldn't imagine otherwise. I loved that feeling. Even sitting here, inside at night in the middle of winter, I could imagine the sun warming the hair on my scalp, a cool breeze moving through it. If there was a God, he or she or whatever it was would probably want you to feel the pleasure of that. Plus earrings.

"You sound like my sister." She smiled, picking at the edge of her rolled-up napkin. "She hates hijab. She never wore it once she got here. She could not understand why I would come all the way from Iran and decide to wear the very thing so many women back home resent." She wagged her finger at me, which seemed a little rude. "But there is a difference between being free to wear it, and being made to wear it. It is a personal decision. When my grandmother was young, women in Iran weren't allowed to wear hijab. All of a sudden, the police could come up and tear it right off women's heads, so they would look modern, so they would look Western." She shook her head. "My grandmother didn't leave the house for years. She was too embarrassed. You understand? For her, it was strange to go out uncovered. It would be as if the police told you you could no longer wear a shirt."

"No," I said, still thinking it through. "It's not like wearing a shirt."

"How is the difference?"

"Because men have to wear shirts too."

"Not at swimming. Not at the beach. You see? If all at once there was a rule, here in the United States, that men and women could both swim topless, some women would choose to go topless, no doubt, but most, I think, would choose to keep their tops." She put her hand to her chest. "I choose to wear hijab because it is pleasing to God." She made a slicing motion with her hand. "But it should be my choice."

I nodded. That very last part made sense. But only that last part. I didn't want to get into the rest of it with her, the pleasing to God part. I'd been around enough religion to know you couldn't talk sense with people about it. They were going to think what they thought.

The waiter came back, and we went quiet. As soon as he set down my Diet Coke, I took a big long gulp and smiled at her. I could drink as much as I wanted. It wasn't her business.

She blew across the top of her coffee to cool it, but didn't say anything.

"Where's your sister now?" I asked.

"Nevada." She set down her coffee and her lips went tight. "She registered. She did everything she was supposed to do, and now her whole family, her husband, her children, they're all in Nevada, along with all my Muslim friends, including those who never wore hijab in this country, or who thought they belonged here through and through, or who came here because they wanted to be free. Free to decide for themselves how to please God." She said *free* both times like the word tasted bad in her mouth. "And including people who were born here, whose families have been here for generations. They are all detained in Nevada, it is told for their protection, because it is too dangerous for them to be free."

"It got pretty dangerous for everybody," I said, and I could see that she got my point. She didn't look mad, though. She stared down at the empty place between her knife and fork like she felt sorry for the whole world.

By the time our food came, I was thinking that I really wasn't doing anything so bad if I was just getting her out of the country so she could go back to wearing a scarf over her hair if it meant that much to her. Probably she was telling the truth when she'd said she hadn't hurt anyone, and that she didn't plan to. So really, I was helping everybody out, including the United States, by getting her up to Canada. That was where she wanted to be, and there'd be one less Muslim down here. No harm, no foul.

"See, that's why I don't like religion," I said, taking a bite of pancake. "It makes people act crazy."

That was the truth. I once saw a pastor on television saying that gay people should be killed because that's what the Bible said. And he meant it. You could hear it in his voice, like he really felt he needed to go out and murder innocent gay people because that's what Leviticus said he should do. It would have been bad enough if he was just some lunatic screaming on a street corner. But he wasn't. He was wearing a nice suit and tie, and he was a real pastor of a real church in Colorado. And a lot of people were listening to him, I guess thinking that would make them better Christians.

I reached for more syrup. "If you ask me, the world would be a better place if there weren't any religion at all. A whole lot of people would have one less reason to kill other people." Even as I said it, a part of me thought, but they'd just come up with another reason. Still, I thought I was being nice, showing Chloe that when I said I didn't like religion, I didn't just mean hers. But she crossed her arms and frowned.

"What about the people who just gave us the ride here?" She pointed vaguely out the window. "The woman said it was for Jesus."

Well, yeah, I thought. They were fine. I guess religion made some people nicer. Or maybe they were just nice to begin with. Caleb was Christian, after all, and he'd never want to kill anybody, or even hurt anyone's feelings. And the Sunday school teacher who was so nice to Caleb, she seemed like a good person. And Martin Luther King, Jr. He was way better than I'd ever be, to say the least. But so many religious people were messed up, wanting to force everybody to follow rules that didn't always make a lot of sense and frequently made people miserable.

"Well," I said, "I think it usually causes more problems than it helps. Personally, for myself, I don't believe in God."

She nodded. From the look on her face, I could have just told her I was left-handed. She didn't seem at all upset. But that was the kind of thing I could say if I wanted to make Aunt Jenny cry. And I thought Muslims were supposed to freak out even more.

"That makes me an infidel, right? You're supposed to want to rid the earth of me?" I tilted my head and smiled. "Make me a slave or something?" I knew that from Aunt Jenny's news shows.

She held up her hand. "Yes, yes," she said. "I am familiar with all of this. I am to strike off your head and the very tips of your fingers."

That sounded like a quote. I glanced at my fingers. "That the Koran?"

"It is a mistranslation of the Koran. It ignores the context of war." She waved her hand like she was refusing an offer. "When others incline toward peace, Muslims must incline toward peace. The Koran clearly forbids harming anyone unless in self-defense. It commands us to repel evil with what is better. To exercise patience and self-restraint. To encourage kindness and compassion. Not just with other Muslims, but with all."

We stared at each other. She rubbed her ear.

"Hmm," I said, pushing my plate away. I hoped she got it was a polite way of saying I was still thinking things over. All those last lines sounded nice, but apparently there was plenty in there that made at least a few Muslims kill innocent people in airplanes and grocery stores. Then again, I saw an interview once with a Ku Klux Klan guy who said his favorite book was the Bible, and so he was reading the same book that a lot of noncrazy people read, including Caleb, who was about as far as you could get from somebody who would be in the KKK.

"In any case"—she lifted her chin—"it does me no injury for my neighbor to say there are twenty gods or no God. It neither picks my pocket nor breaks my leg."

I squinted. That sounded like another quote. "That's the Koran too?" Geez, I thought. It really couldn't make up its mind.

"Thomas Jefferson." She raised her coffee mug like she was making a toast, glancing out the window. "That is the apartment you mean?" She put the mug down. "The light over the door is on now."

I followed her gaze across the street. "Yeah," I said. "He's home."

She swallowed, looking scared, but then she closed her eyes for a few seconds, and when she opened them, she seemed calm. She got her wallet out of her bag. "Here," she said, passing me a five and a twenty. "In case they want you to pay before I come back."

I didn't say anything, but I was thinking she sounded a little overconfident. We didn't know for sure if she would be coming back. She started to put on her coat, and all of a sudden I wanted to tell her not to go. I wanted to come up with another plan. But there wasn't any other plan. This was the only way.

"He's got a dog," I said. "You'll hear it when you knock."

She looked up from her zipper.

"And it's a pit. Just so you know."

She tilted her head. "A pit?"

"A pit bull. You know, the kind with the super strong jaw? It's a fighting dog. The breed is, I mean. Or it can be. They're not all bad. They get trained to be mean. Some of them are really sweet."

She looked like she couldn't move. Her hand stayed on her zipper.

"Matt's isn't a fighter. I don't think it is," I said. "And it's really well-trained. It just stands in between him and you and looks up at you like, you know, it would do something to you if he told it to. But I don't see why he would. He's expecting you. Or he's expecting someone. And you're gonna give him money."

She closed her eyes again, and this time she kept them closed.

I felt bad for making her so scared. I just didn't want her to be surprised.

"It'll be fine," I said. "I was fine when I went. The dog didn't do anything to me." I waited a moment, remembering. "But just get in and out as fast as you can. And don't drink anything he offers you. Even water."

She opened her eyes, and she looked so scared right then I knew I should just shut up. I was being paranoid, probably. But Tess had meant that warning when she gave it.

"Here," I said. I unzipped the pocket of my backpack and pulled out my pepper spray. "Take this with you. This is how you unlock it, and make sure this arrow part is facing away from you. And you hold it real far from your own face, like this." I glanced around quick to make sure no one was looking, and held the sprayer out like a gun. "And then after you press this part down, you turn around and run, and try not to breathe in for a while."

She whispered something under her breath, something with a *szhhh* sound in it. But she took the pepper spray and put it in her coat pocket.

"You won't need it," I said. "Don't even get it out unless something crazy happens." I wasn't sure if I should add that I meant if something crazy happened with just Matt P. or his dog—that's when she should get out the pepper spray. If the police or Homeland Security was the crazy thing that happened, she shouldn't get out the pepper spray, unless she wanted to be dead.

The waiter came over, smiling again. We smiled back at him, looking normal, I hoped. But inside, I was thinking about how I'd just given pepper spray to a Muslim fugitive, and how that might look to a judge.

"Everything all right?" the waiter asked.

I nodded, and he went away.

"You'll be fine," I said. "I'll be right here, and I can see his door." Like that would do her any good.

But she nodded, her eyes on mine, as if what I'd just said mattered. And then she pulled her hood up over her hat, stood up, and walked out.

I watched her white coat as she made her way across the parking lot. After she waited for a pause in traffic, she jogged across the street. And then cars rolled by from both directions, and I couldn't see her anymore.

After a while, the waiter came by with another Diet Coke, and I drank down half of it in just a few gulps, the Patchouli Kings blasting in my earbuds. I kept looking at Tess's watch and tapping my foot. I told myself I shouldn't feel guilty or worried, and that it was crazy that I felt both. I'd done what I'd promised. Anyway, she'd been over there for ten minutes already, and I didn't see any police lights. I didn't hear any sirens.

She was fine. She was for sure probably fine.

But I was also thinking that maybe I should have gone

over there with her. If I put myself in her shoes, I wouldn't have wanted to knock on that door all by myself. And it was pretty clear she was scared of dogs. It seemed like maybe, as part of the promise, I should have stayed right with her until she was at a bus station, ID and ticket in hand. That's what Caleb would have done, if he could have. That's what I would want somebody to do for me, or for him, if everything was changed up.

She'd been gone for sixteen minutes when I saw her running back across the street, her white coat bright under the streetlights. She was moving fast, her boots keeping time with the drums of my music. I popped out the earbuds and sat up straight. She was still alive. And not in handcuffs. All of this was good. But then she got close enough to see my face in the window, she shook her head, and I saw she was crying.

I put the money on the table, grabbed my coat and both bags, and hurried out. But by the time I got out into the parking lot, she wasn't there. I turned in a circle, a bag hanging off each shoulder, until I saw her. She'd moved back to the brick side of the restaurant, where she couldn't be seen from the road. She was still crying, but as I got closer, I saw she didn't look sad or scared so much as crazy mad.

"He stole it!" She pointed across the street. "He took my money, and then he said his computer wasn't working, and he would not give the money back."

"No," I said, like I was arguing with her, like I didn't believe what she was saying was true. But even then, I knew how stupid that was. Of course it was true. Of course that was what he did. That way he could get paid without having to take any risk himself, or even do any work. She was lucky he didn't turn her in. And I saw now that I should have known he would take her money, just because he could.

"There was nothing I could do." She wiped her face with the sleeve of her coat. "He said if I didn't leave, he would call the police. He said he could put his equipment away in five minutes, and no one would believe what I said."

I still had a bag hanging off each shoulder, and my coat was rolled under one arm. The vapor of my breath floated out into the night. "Goddamn him," I said. "Goddamn." I probably shouldn't have said that in front of a religious person, but I was so mad I couldn't help it. And at least at the moment, she didn't seem to care.

"He made the dog growl and bark at me. There was nothing I could do. Nothing." She put her hand to her mouth. "And now I don't have much money left. I have just enough for the tickets now." She put her arms up around her head, like she was blocking a punch. "I'm finished because of this. I'm over."

"Did you pepper-spray him?"

She looked confused, peeking out at me from between her elbows.

"You should have pepper-sprayed him," I said. It was sort of a jerk thing to say to her then, because obviously it was too late. But it made me feel better to say what she should've done, to make it seem like she'd messed up. I wanted this to not be my fault.

She shook her head. "He did not attack me."

"Well, he robbed you," I said. "Same thing. You should have pepper-sprayed him."

She gave me a hard look. "You are a frightening people."

I blinked. "What?" But I knew what she'd said. And I knew what she'd meant. She meant Americans. She was upset, okay. I understood. But Americans weren't bad or frightening or whatever. She was lumping me, and all of us, in with Matt P. That wasn't fair.

"I wanted to come to this country since I was a girl," she said, laughing, though her eyes were still shiny. "Everyone I knew did. I worked so hard, so hard to get here." She shook her head, looking back across the street. "But this is the reality. This man can steal from me, and there is nothing I can do. There is no Bill of Rights for me. It means nothing. It's a lie. You live in a lie. I worked for a lie." She thumped her hand against her chest. "I was in love with this country. But it has broken my heart. And no. No, I did not use the pepper spray, because this is not the person I am."

I shook my head. I understood she was having a hard time, but it wasn't fair, what she was saying. I mean, okay, maybe she didn't want to use the pepper spray, but the whole country wasn't a thief. The whole country wasn't a skeevy guy who made fake IDs and scared foreign women with a pit bull. He was just one person. But I guess she'd been having a pretty bad experience with us in general by now.

I looked back across the street, to the light still shining over his door. I damned him in my mind once again. You shouldn't take somebody's money, even a runaway Muslim's, and not give them what they were owed. That just seemed un-American to me. However you felt about foreigners, if you had a deal, you had a deal.

And really, it was my fault she'd gone over there. I'd kind of screwed her over.

"Gimme the pepper spray." I set the bags down and held out my hand.

She waited a second, like she wasn't sure. She started to shake her head, but I snapped my fingers. "It's mine," I said. "And I'd like it back."

She reached into her pocket and pulled out the pepper spray, setting it carefully in my palm. I pushed an arm through each sleeve of my coat.

"You got money to go back in?" I asked, nodding back at the restaurant.

She frowned. "Yes, but—"

"Can you take my backpack in with you?" I was already

walking away, my eyes trained on the Budweiser sign. She was saying something else to me now, but I didn't hear what. I was too busy listening to my own head.

We were not a frightening people. We were not all disappointing cheats. I knew it wasn't true, but I didn't even like that she thought it. And that she maybe had good reason.

I was going to get that money back. I would do what I had to do.

7

MATT P. ANSWERED the door all mad-looking and frantic, like he was expecting a fight. He had on a red hooded sweatshirt and jeans, and his belt was undone, the ends of it hanging out from under the sweatshirt. The dog stood beside him, staring up at me with wide-set, serious eyes.

"What?" Matt waved his hands at me like he was trying to break a spell. He was only a head taller than I was, short for a grown man, but he was twice as wide across the shoulders. I wouldn't do well in hand-to-hand combat.

"Sorry," I said. My right hand clutched the pepper spray in my coat pocket, my finger on the trigger. "I'm looking for some help with some . . . laminated documents?"

He leaned out onto the covered walkway a little, and glanced from side to side. When he saw the coast was clear, he gave me a long look. "You been here before?"

I nodded. "Last September. I came by with my friend."

He bobbed his eyebrows. "I always remember the cute ones."

I forced a smile. I have to say, Matt P. might have been considered good-looking if you just saw him in a photograph—he had a full head of sandy hair, and pale blue eyes with dark lashes. But in real life he just wasn't that appealing, maybe because of the lazy way he talked paired with this twitchy thing his eyes did sometimes. Like there was a glitch, and every now and then, it showed.

He reached down to buckle his belt. "Why you need another one?"

"My purse was stolen."

His gaze was free of sympathy.

"You got cash?"

I nodded, blowing on my hands. I'd left my mittens in my backpack.

"Just you? You by yourself?"

I nodded again, and he stepped aside to let me in. The dog backed up, his eyes moving back and forth between us. He was almost all white, with just a few brown spots on his muscled back, and another around one of his eyes.

"Hey Boogie," I said, looking down. "How you doing?"

I didn't get so much as a wiggle of a tail stub. Matt shut the door behind me.

"He's not doing so well. Excuse me, but he just puked on

the carpet. I got to finish cleaning it, or it'll stain. Take off your shoes and come on in."

I didn't like the idea of that. My plan had been to keep by the door for easy escape—I remembered that his apartment was laid out like a snake den, with a long hall you had to go down before you got to any rooms. But Matt was already walking down the hall. Boogie stayed behind, staring up at me. I held out my hand for him to sniff, but he wasn't interested.

"You coming?" Matt called out. "You're perfectly safe. He only attacks on command."

"Hold on." I pulled off my boots and followed his voice down the hall and into the living room, Boogie's collar jingling beside me. I remembered the living room's track lighting and cream-colored carpet, which looked as freshly vacuumed now as it had in September. That had surprised me and Tess both. If I'd met somebody like Matt P. on the street, or when he was working at the arcade, I would have probably guessed right away he was a skeeve, but I wouldn't have guessed in a million years he was a big neat freak. That's what he was, though. His living room looked like something you'd see in a catalog—the furniture was all modern and black, and there was no clutter anywhere, no dust. The remotes and game controllers were all lined up parallel on the glass coffee table, and the black throw pillows were set on the white couch just so.

So it made sense that he was freaking out about the stain on the carpet. The stain was mossy green, about the size of an out-stretched hand, and not too far from the couch. Matt was down on his hands and knees, and he'd pulled on yellow rubber gloves, going after the stain hard with a sponge and frequent sprays from a bottle of pink liquid. Boogie went over and sat beside him, looking up at me like maybe I shouldn't move too fast.

"Take a seat," Matt said.

I walked slowly to the other side of the couch and sat on the very edge.

"I'm sorry he's feeling sick," I said.

"Yeah. He just does this sometimes. He'll be all right." He looked up from his scrubbing and leaned over to nuzzle the dog's forehead. Boogie looked up to lick his face, and Matt turned away, gagging.

"He's got breath that'll burn your eyes." He laughed, his eyes twitching a little. I had to smile back to be polite, but nothing in me was happy. The whole way over here, I'd been so mad I hadn't considered that I didn't have a real plan. I was just going to come over here with the pepper spray and get Chloe's money back. But I hadn't really thought things through. If you threaten somebody with something like pepper spray, you've got to be prepared to actually use it. You've got to be ready to pull the trig-ger. And I wasn't sure that I could do it anymore—not looking at Matt the way he was now, cleaning up dog puke and rubbing the neck of the dog who did it. He'd stolen Chloe's money. I hadn't forgotten that. Still, there was a big difference between thinking you should pepper-spray someone in the face, and actually doing it when he was a real person sitting four feet away from you.

Also, if I pepper-sprayed Matt, or even threatened to do it, Boogie would probably come after me. So I'd have to spray him, too. I didn't like to think of myself as the kind of person who would hurt a dog.

"Boy," I said, looking down at the stain, or what was left of it. "That stuff's zip. It's really working."

I said this to get him friendly with me. I knew from experience, mostly with my manager at Dairy Queen, that people who really like things clean love to talk about their methods. You start conversing with them about what kind of cloth or spray or special concoction to use to make something especially germ-free and shiny, or what kind of tool you need to get down into that little crack where the gunk hides, and they get this look in their eye like finally they met someone who gets it, and they don't have to be alone anymore.

Matt was exactly the same. He held up the spray bottle and showed me the label, which had some kind of Asian writing on it.

"I had to order it special from Japan," he said. "Let me tell you, it gets out anything. But it doesn't have bleach in it, so it doesn't affect the color of the carpet. I don't get it. But it's a game-changer, for sure."

"For sure," I agreed, leaning down to look at the carpet, which was just damp now, no stain. It really was impressive. So I wasn't completely acting, and when I looked up, he smiled at me like he was having a moment with an old cleaning friend.

"Where'd you come in from?" He stood, pulling off the gloves. The dog stood too, stretching.

"Joplin."

He nodded and carried the cleaning supplies through an open doorway to the kitchen. Boogie followed him as far as the doorway then stopped, turning back to keep an eye on me. He was like the Secret Service with a jingling collar, who sometimes puked on the carpet.

"You drove here all the way from Joplin?" I heard water running, shutting off. "All by yourself?"

"That's right." As soon as I said it, I wasn't sure that had been the smartest thing to say. I should have said I had a friend, or friends, waiting for me. Too late. I'd already committed.

"Last time you came with a friend." He was back in the doorway now, drying his hands on a checkered dishcloth. "Your blond friend." His eyes did the twitchy thing.

I nodded, but I had to pretend to sneeze so he wouldn't see how skeeved out I was.

"Bless you," he said. "And I'll need the money now."

"Okay. But I got something to tell you." I lowered my chin and tried to sound as sweet and pitiful as I could. "I only have a hundred dollars."

"Forget it. Get out."

I pressed my palms together, like a child saying her prayers. "Please? For a loyal customer?" I was as desperate as I sounded. If he said no, I was going to have to do something drastic immediately. "Look," I said. "I could have gone to somebody right in Joplin, but I drove all the way here because you do such a good job. My friend Tess said you were the best in the state."

"Yeah." He blew through his teeth. "Which is why I don't work for cheap." But then he checked his watch, and he was quiet for a few seconds. I guessed he was thinking that it didn't look like the tall girl with the huge eyes, who'd called earlier from a truck stop, was going to show after all. He twisted his mouth to the side and looked back at me like he was making a calculation.

"Whatever. It's a slow night. Give me the hundred now, and I'll do it if you have a drink with me."

It was like my body got scared before I did. My stomach clenched, and my forehead went damp.

"That's great!" I laughed. "But first let's make the ID, okay?"

"Nope. Drink first. I want to unwind. And you gotta pay me now, too."

I took a deep breath. I'd be fine. I could be careful. I just had to think. I took out the five twenties that Chloe had given me. He took his wallet out of the back pocket of his jeans and slipped the money in.

"Pick your poison," he called out, heading back to the kitchen. "I got wine, stout beer, some hard stuff . . ."

I could see the outline of his wallet in one of the back pockets of his jeans. "I'll have what you're having," I said.

I didn't know what to do. It wasn't like I could run in after him. Boogie stood just outside the arched doorway to the kitchen, watching me.

Matt leaned back out, bending down to rub the dog's head. "Gin and tonic okay? I got limes."

"Whatever you're having." I wiped my palms on my jeans. "Hold up. I'll come talk to you while you make them."

"Nope. Don't come in." He was back in the kitchen. "I've got to feed the dog in here, and he gets anxious about his food." He made a sound like a clucking squirrel. "Come here, Boogie. You ready to eat? Come here, boy."

He poured Boogie's food into a silver bowl that was right off the doorway to the kitchen, so Boogie's body, once he started to gobble up his food, made a little fence that I wasn't about to try to jump. I craned my neck, trying to see where Matt was making the drinks. But the wall hid him. I looked down, rubbing the back of my neck. I supposed it was possible that he really did need to feed the dog just then, and that he wasn't just trying to keep me out while he made the drinks. It seemed pretty late at night to feed a dog. Then again, that was when he usually got off work.

Anyway, it didn't matter now. If he was putting something in my drink, he'd already had time to do it.

"Can I use your bathroom?"

"Yup. Down the hall. You'll find it."

The bathroom smelled faintly of bleach, and everything in it was too-bright white: the towels, the walls, the little rug in front of the toilet, the shower curtain, and even the shower curtain rings. I sat on the toilet with my face in my hands, my breath warm on my palms. I could get out of this now. I could come out and say that I'd changed my mind about the drink, and that I'd called my friend when I was in the bathroom, and he was coming by to pick me up right now, and oh, by the way, this friend's dad was a cop. Maybe Matt wouldn't give back the hundred dollars. I'd still be fine. I'd be a whole lot better off than I might be if I stayed here and had a drink.

But then Chloe would just be waiting at the pancake house, let down twice, by two Americans in a row.

I washed my hands, and looked in the mirror, smoothing down my hair. I kept my gaze steady on my own eyes, like I was trying to ask myself for advice and give it at the same time. I rubbed my lips together. I had to get that wallet. I'd figure out a way.

When I came back to the living room, the doorway to the kitchen was clear.

"Hey, we're gonna drink in here," Matt called out. He was in the kitchen, and I still couldn't see him. "It's a carpet and white couch thing. House rules. And you can come in now. Boogie's done eating."

"Okay," I said. I could smell the cut limes as I moved through the doorway. The kitchen had a low ceiling and ugly brass fixtures on the cabinets, but it was even cleaner than the living room. There were no magnets on the refrigerator and no crumbs on the floor. Aside from the red-and-white checkered dish towel folded over the oven handle, the silver dog bowl and water dish, and a plastic tub of dog treats on top of the fridge, there was no evidence of life—not until I turned and looked in the corner, where Matt P. sat at a table by the kitchen's only window, which was covered by black Venetian blinds. He was already sipping his drink, and he gestured to the other chair, where my drink sat waiting for me, a slice of lime floating between the ice cubes. I looked back at his glass and felt my lungs go tight. He'd given me a glass that was tall and thin, and his was short and fat.

"What's the matter?" he asked. Boogie jingled over and sat on the linoleum by his feet.

"We got different glasses." It was all I could come up with.

"So?"

I waited, trying to think. "So that's bad luck."

"What?" He shook his head. "No, it isn't."

I shrugged, but I didn't sit down. I rested my hand on the back of the empty chair. "You can think what you want," I said. "But don't you have matching glasses? You seem like the kind of person who would. I mean, most of your stuff is really nice."

He looked at me like he couldn't believe I was serious, like he was waiting for me to start laughing. When I didn't, he laughed some more.

"I got matching glasses," he said. "But what are you talking about mismatched glasses being bad luck? I've never heard that in my life."

"It's for real," I said, and all of a sudden it was like I believed it, not at all like I'd just made it up. I looked him right in the eye, no problem. "My friend Tess and her mom were drinking out of mismatched glasses one time when I came over, and I told them what they were risking. They laughed at me, just like you're doing now. And let me tell you something." I leaned away from the table, giving my glass a dirty look. "Ten minutes later, the phone rang. It was the police. Tess's dad had been hit by a car. And he was dead."

I hoped Mr. Villalobos wouldn't mind me killing him off in a story. Probably not. He was in good health, and generally pretty relaxed.

Matt crossed his arms over the front of his sweatshirt, still chuckling. "That's what you call a coincidence, sweetheart. He didn't die cause they were drinking out of mismatched glasses."

I shook my head. "No. There are a lot of stories like that. My grandma could tell you three other stories just like that. And that's just people she knew."

"I'm sure she could," he said.

I held my ground. "I don't mean to be rude to your hospitality.

But I'm not giving in on this. Sorry. I'll sit and talk with you, though." I sat, but I kept my hands in my lap.

"You are one nutty girl." He took another sip from his short glass. "But okay. I'll get you a matching glass."

He got up, opened a cabinet, and got out a tall glass like mine. He poured his drink in, the ice clinking against the new glass, and I could see he'd already sipped enough that it wasn't going to fill up as high as mine. When his back was still turned, I picked an ice cube out of my glass and slipped it into my coat pocket.

He came back to the table. "There," he said. "We got matching glasses now." He tilted his head. "You want to take off your coat? It's not exactly cold in here."

The apartment was warm, actually. But I needed easy access to the pepper spray. "I'm a little chilled, actually. Would you mind turning up the heat?"

I thought that was pretty clever. I didn't see the thermostat in the kitchen. I would only need a few seconds alone with the drinks.

"I think it's at seventy. But I'll go check it."

Out he went, but his drink stayed in his hand. And Boogie remained in the kitchen, watching me like he wasn't fooled by my nice-girl routine at all. It occurred to me that the ice cube in my pocket would be better off melting on the window sill, behind the Venetian blinds. I took it out of my pocket and put it there just before he came back.

"I bumped it up to seventy-two," he said. "You'll probably warm up soon." When he sat back down, he frowned at my glass. "You're still not drinking? Even with the matching glasses?"

I realized he hadn't asked my name. I guess he didn't need to know it.

"You got any milk?" I asked.

He made a face. "Milk? In a gin and tonic?"

"No. To drink first. To settle my stomach. Sorry. I always do better if I drink milk first."

He just sat there looking at me, no response at all. I worried he guessed I was up to something. I was having to come up with lies so fast, I couldn't tell how crazy they sounded. I stared back at him, waiting.

"Girl, you get stranger and stranger." He got up and headed to the fridge, his back to me again. But it did me no good. He never set down his drink. I stared down at the half-submerged lime in my own drink, my options moving fast through my head: I could leave. I could say I left my phone in the car, and then just not come back. Or I could get up and aim the pepper spray at him, and tell him to give me back Chloe's money, taking my chances with the dog. Or I could go ahead and take a sip of my drink, and hope that it was fine.

He set a glass of milk in front of me. A new option appeared in my mind.

"Thank you," I said. He turned to put away the milk carton, and before I could overthink it or get too nervous, I knocked the glass of milk off the table. The crash of it made Matt jump. Boogie stood up fast.

"Oh crap!" I said. "I'm so sorry!"

He put his hands to his head and looked down at the mess like it was the first sign of the apocalypse. Boogie started to whimper, looking up at his face, and for a second, it seemed I'd very much made the wrong decision.

"Let me clean it up," I said. "Oh my God, I'm so sorry." I put my foot out like I was trying to figure out where to step. There was glass and milk all over the floor, and I was only wearing socks.

"Just stay put," he said, and not nicely. "Boogie." He snapped his fingers. "Get in the corner."

The dog jingled over to the corner and cocked its head, waiting for further instruction. Matt looked back at me. "Don't touch anything. I'll be right back." He set his drink on the table and took one careful step, and then another, until he was out of the room.

I grabbed my glass and poured a third of my drink over the mess on the floor, letting it mix with the milk and using my free hand to hold back the ice and the lime. Boogie watched me do it. He was still watching when I switched the glasses.

Matt came back in wearing slippers over his socks. He headed straight for the pantry, getting out a dustpan and a little broom.

"I'm so sorry," I said again. I tucked my feet up on my chair, taking a sip of the drink. I could taste the lime, and the pine of the gin. There was a good chance Tess had been paranoid, and that I was being ridiculous.

After Matt had the glass cleaned up, and the milk wiped away with a wet dish towel, then the floor dried with a clean one, he asked if I wanted a new glass of milk.

"Thanks, but I'm okay," I said. "This is actually going down easy." I shook the glass, and the ice rattled. "I have to say, you make a good gin and tonic."

As if I knew what I was talking about. As if I sat around drinking gin and tonics all the time. He sat down and took a swallow of his drink, pausing to crunch some ice between his molars.

"How long have you had Boogie?" I asked. People always want to talk about their dogs. But Matt seemed particularly pleased by the question. He told me he'd gotten him at the pound, on what would have been Boogie's last day.

"No lie," he said, setting down his glass. "It was July first, and the sign on his cage said, 'This dog may be destroyed on July second.'"

"Destroyed? It actually said 'destroyed'?" I shook my head and pretended to take a longer sip than I actually did. Even if it was just a gin and tonic, no drugs. I needed to keep my head. "That's terrible."

"I know it," he said, looking down at Boogie, who was lying

by his feet again. "A good dog like that, wasted. Not right." He blew through his teeth again. "Not right at all. Makes me sick to think about it. I never had a better friend in my life."

He went on about Boogie for a while, telling me how quickly he'd learned to mind, and how the vet said he had such terrible breath because of gingivitis. He talked for a long time about Boogie's trials at the dog park, where everybody had been afraid of him just because he was a pit bull, and how he'd slowly won everybody over because he was such a good dog. I was watching Matt closely as he talked, waiting for him to crash on the floor or go paralyzed or something, but the whole time he was talking, he was just fine, talking in the lazy way he always talked. He got up and made himself another drink, and after he drank half of that one, he still seemed fine.

He nodded at my half-empty glass. "You're not drinking much."

"I like to pace myself," I said. He shrugged like that was okay with him, no big deal. By then, I was starting to feel pretty dumb—he definitely wasn't a rapist, or at least he wasn't being one tonight. He was just a guy, a little skeevy, who loved his dog. He was also a thief, I remembered.

"So no other customers tonight?" I asked, taking another pretend sip. "Nobody else needing a license?"

He looked at the clock on the stove. It was 12:09. "Guess not."

"Even before me? Nobody?"

He laughed into his glass. "It's not like there's always a stampede every night. Some nights I get two people, even three. Sometimes nobody at all."

"But I was the first one tonight?"

He smiled and fluttered his eyelashes. "Yes," he said, his voice going up like a girl's. "You're my first. Honey, nobody's been here but you."

I smiled back, the chill of the drink moving through me. I couldn't figure out why he would lie and act like Chloe hadn't just come by. It came to me then, the gin buzzing my brain a little, that maybe he wasn't lying. Maybe Chloe was. I hadn't actually seen her knock on his door. When she'd come back to the pancake house so upset, saying he'd taken her money, I'd just gone ahead and believed her. I didn't know what was wrong with me. Based on the word of a foreign-born Muslim I barely knew, I'd gotten myself so worked up that I'd been ready to pepper-spray an innocent man and maybe his dog. I didn't know why she would have lied. But that didn't mean she didn't have a reason.

"I'm gonna have another," Matt said, scooting back his chair. "You want more milk or something?"

I shook my head. I didn't even know if she was still at the pancake house. For all I knew, she was long gone. What had she been up to? Why had she lied to me? I put my hand to my mouth, watching Matt as he took a lime slice out of a little container from the refrigerator. All I knew was that I'd been foolish.

I'd been played. Twice in one damn day, the first time by my own mother. It was like I just couldn't learn. I'd be too embarrassed to tell anyone but Tess.

Matt turned around and looked at me, still holding the lime slice. "You feeling all right? You look like you're not feeling well."

"I'm okay," I said. I really was, physically speaking, at least. He actually sounded a little drunk, like the wad of chew in his mouth was bigger than usual. For all I knew, he'd been drinking before I even arrived. Maybe that's what he did every night—came home and drank with Boogie, his best friend. I was at least glad I hadn't pepper-sprayed him, and made his life even worse.

He nodded, making a face like something was stuck in his throat. "Cause you look kinda . . . kinda . . . kinda . . . kinda . . ."

He was looking down at me like he meant to finish what he was saying, but couldn't get the word out. He grabbed the edge of the counter. The lime slice fell to the floor.

"You okay?" I asked. But by the time I got the words out, I knew. I jumped out of my chair and got behind it.

Ho-ly hell, I thought. He was roofied.

He lowered himself to the floor, still holding the counter with one hand, like he didn't quite trust his legs. When his rear finally made contact with the linoleum, Boogie walked over, nails clicking. He sniffed Matt's open mouth; his tail stub wagged a little. He was thinking this was a good thing, his master sitting on the floor, maybe wanting to cuddle. Matt turned his face away, but Boogie jingled over his legs to breathe in his face again. Matt stared hard into the dog's eyes, like he was trying to communicate something without any words. I put my hand on the pepper spray. I didn't know how Matt usually told the dog to attack, but the longer I waited, the more it seemed like it was a word he needed to say.

And now he couldn't say anything.

I felt frozen myself. I mean, I knew I could move if I really had to. But I felt like I couldn't stop staring down at him, at the way his head seemed to be slowly sliding down the cabinets toward the floor, or the way he kept trying to lift one of his arms. That would have been me, if Tess hadn't warned me. That would have been me sitting on the floor, my arms and legs limp as a doll's, and he would have been the one sitting up in his chair, feeling just fine, looking down at me. He would have raped me, whether my eyes were open or not. That had been his plan, from the time he said I had to have a drink with him. Even after we'd had that nice talk about the cleaning stuff from Japan. Even when he was laughing with me about the matching glasses, and when he was telling me about how he got Boogie from the pound. He'd just been waiting.

But now he couldn't even talk. His mouth started to open and close, over and over, like he was a fish dying on a dock. And something about seeing that made hot tears press against my eyes.

I was tired of people who didn't have any standards for themselves. I was tired of people moving through the world like they were playing a game on a screen, like everybody they hurt wasn't real, and all that mattered was that they won.

"Tables have turned, haven't they?" I dried my eyes with the sleeve of my coat. His eyes went wide, but he still didn't say anything.

I made my way to the pantry, bringing my chair with me like I was a lion tamer in a circus. I kept my distance from Matt, and though Boogie kept his gaze on me, he didn't seem alarmed.

I found a jar of peanut butter in the pantry. There was probably something better in the refrigerator, but Matt's legs were blocking its door. I unscrewed the lid, reached in for a big dollop, and flicked it, aiming for the floor by Boogie. But the dollop landed on Matt's hand. Boogie's tail-stub wagged. When Matt just stared back at him, openmouthed, the dog helped himself, licking the peanut butter off his hand. Matt lifted the hand and turned his head away, blinking. I rinsed off my fingers in the sink, singing a little. I wanted the dog to stay calm, to not think anything worrisome was happening. So I started to hum, and then sing.

". . . everything's gonna be all right, everything's gonna be all right."

I slid open drawers until I found a spoon.

"You want more?" I asked, holding out a big spoonful of peanut butter. Boogie turned to check with Matt again, and hearing no disagreement, he jingled over to me. I nearly fell back when he opened his mouth. Matt hadn't been lying about his breath—it smelled like rotten eggs, even with the peanut butter. I turned my face away to inhale fast, like a swimmer, and I held the breath in as I started to walk backward toward the doorway. Boogie had a big tongue, and he licked up the entire spoonful by the time we got out of the kitchen. I got a little more stingy when we were back in the living room, and then even more stingy as I lured him down the hall. But when we got in the bathroom, I dug as much peanut butter out as I could. I was still singing, and I pretended like I was icing a cake, using the spoon to smear peanut butter across one of the white towels.

"Bye, Boogie," I said, shutting the door.

When I got back to the kitchen, Matt was lying under the open silverware drawer, a metal cheese grater and a butter knife lying on his outstretched legs. I pieced it together. He'd made a last-ditch effort. Bold and brave. But it just hadn't worked out.

"Were you gonna try to stab me?" I asked, crouching down beside him. I picked up the butter knife. He stared at me with his pale blue eyes, helpless as a baby.

"But your original plan was to rape me." I twirled the knife like a small baton. It was just a butter knife, too dull to do any real damage. Unless it got shoved up somewhere he wouldn't like. I wouldn't be a complete animal. I'd keep the blade side in my hand, and the handle wasn't that big. An eye for eye. Or an eye for the plan of taking an eye. Matt P. could learn how it felt, to have something shoved up where you didn't want it. He could wake up on his kitchen floor with his own butter knife sticking out of his rectum, and maybe not remember how it got there. Or maybe he would remember. That would be fine, too.

I set the knife down and reached around him into his back pocket, pulling out his wallet. And there they were. Three folded hundred-dollar bills that belonged to Chloe, plus the five twenties I'd given him. There was also a coupon for a free car wash, and a folded piece of yellow notepaper that read *I LOVE DADDY* in purple crayon.

His blue eyes watched, heavy lidded, as I re-folded the note. He made a sound like a kitten mewling. I picked up the butter knife, looking at my reflection in the blade. I could only see a sliver of myself, some of my nose, and half of one dark eye. No one would know. No one was watching, not even Boogie, and not anyone from above. Only Matt himself might remember.

But this was not the person I was, either. Not when it came down to really doing it. I still didn't believe anyone was watching, watching out, or watching over. But I could repel evil with what was better. I could turn the other cheek.

I stood up and put the butter knife back in the drawer. I put the cheese grater away too. The spoon I'd used to lure Boogie to the bathroom was still on the counter, but Boogie had licked it clean. I could only smell the faint whiff of Boogie breath if I brought it right up to my nose, but just doing that made me gag.

I put the spoon back in the drawer with the clean ones—it's not like I was applying for sainthood. I shut the drawer and crouched low again, looking down at his sleeping face. His mouth was open. He breathed softly, in and out. I could see a flake of yellow wax in his ear.

"I'm Sarah-Mary, by the way," I said.

I slipped the bills in my coat pocket and left him there, just with himself.

8

I WAS JUST getting ready to jog back across the street to the pancake house when Chloe stepped out from behind a parked car and scared me so much I said a bad word. When I saw it was just her, I said another one. She was holding both our bags, and even in just the dim glow of the streetlight, I could see she looked mad, like I was the one who'd scared her.

"I told you to wait in the restaurant!" I whispered. "How long you been out here?"

She reached forward and slapped my shoulder. It didn't hurt because of the thickness of my coat, and because she didn't do it hard. But she definitely slapped me. I stepped away from her. "Watch it," I said.

"You were gone so long. I was scared for you!" Her blue hat was on crooked. "Why were you there for so much time?"

I nodded. I guess I had been in Matt's apartment for a while. So it wasn't exactly crazy for her to start to worry that I was getting killed or raped or chopped up into little pieces. I don't know how she was planning to help me out, but I have to say, it was sort of sweet that she was worried enough to come across the street and wait in the cold.

"I'm fine," I said. I looked over each of my shoulders. Cars were still rolling by in the street, but no one seemed to notice us. I took my backpack from her and reached in my coat pocket. "And here you go. That's all you gave him, right there."

She looked at the bills, then back up at me. "How . . . ? How did you . . . ?"

"I got my methods." I might have had a little swagger in my step, hearing myself say that. I liked that she was looking at me all impressed, and anyway, I didn't want to tell her about the roofie in the drink, or why my hand still smelled like peanut butter. She already seemed stressed out enough. She was breathing deep, one glove pressed against the cross strap of her bag.

"So you'll pay for a hotel?" I asked. "That's a Super 8 up the road. See it?" I pointed at the lit-up sign, maybe a quarter of a mile away. "We can share a room if you want to save money." I moved over to the sidewalk and started walking, waving her over. It was too cold to just stand and talk.

"Yes, okay." She hurried over and fell in beside me. "But you don't . . . you don't want to go to the bus station now? Maybe it would be better to call from the hotel room and see when the next bus leaves for your town?"

I waited before I answered. She was going to argue with

me, as soon as I told her. But I'd already thought my decision through. I had two reasons for changing the plan. One, I felt bad for falsely accusing her of lying to me, even in my own head. And two, she still didn't have ID. The new plan was the only one that would work. I could hear our footsteps on the pavement, and the cars purring by on the street.

"I'm not going home tomorrow," I said. "I'm going to hitch with you all the way. Up to Canada."

She stopped walking. "You can't do this," she said. "What about your aunt? What will she think?"

I didn't even slow my step. She hurried to catch up.

"Sarah-Mary!" she said. She said my name like it rhymed with *secretary*. I looked back at her, but I didn't stop walking.

"Sarah-Mary! Answer me, please. What about your aunt? She'll be alarmed if you don't come home."

"Don't worry about that," I said, my tone hard, like I meant it. Which I did. It was really none of her business. I'd deal with Aunt Jenny when the time came. I was already in so much trouble that it made no sense to get more worried about it now. Also, it seemed to me Aunt Jenny was the last thing Chloe should be concerned about. If I left her now, she was done. She might as well go turn herself in. She couldn't buy any kind of ticket, not without ID. And she couldn't hitchhike on her own. She couldn't even get a hotel room with her accent. Really, if I went home now, I'd either have to lie to Caleb and tell him I got her an ID and a bus ticket to Canada no problem, or I'd have to tell him the truth and explain that I'd left her in St. Louis in as bad a shape as he'd found her, or actually a little worse off, as now she didn't have a car to sleep in, and she was about a hundred miles farther south of Canada than she had been.

When I pictured Caleb looking back at me, neither of those options sounded very appealing.

"Look," I told Chloe. "It's no problem if you can buy me a bus ticket home from Canada. I don't know how much that'll be."

She nodded, still looking worried. But what else was she going to do? She didn't even point out that she'd already given me a hundred dollars for a bus ticket. But I planned to use that on food. I wanted to be able to buy whatever I wanted, without her going all nutritionally obsessed every time, or not letting me order bacon.

"What's your plan for the border?" I asked.

She didn't say anything. This time, I was the one who stopped walking.

"You don't have a plan?"

She took off one of her gloves and rubbed her eyes. "I don't know," she said. And just the way she said it, I could tell she was tired.

"I was just headed north," she said. "That is all I could think to do."

I didn't say anything. That made zero sense, for her to have just started driving north from Arkansas, with no plan about how to cross into Canada. Canada might let her in, but it didn't seem like the US would just let her out, like *Oh, what the hey, you made it this far!* And it wasn't like she could just sneak across, and not go through a checkpoint. They would for sure have drones cruising around, even out in the countryside. And it would be a lot colder up there. What did she think she was going to do? Burrow through in the snow? In her nice boots with the little heels?

"We'll figure something out," I said, starting to walk again. That's how it worked sometimes. When you really had to find a way, that's when you found it.

I sounded like Tess. That's what she would have said. But I knew it wasn't exactly true. Obviously, sometimes there isn't a way, no matter how hard you look.

Even though I was paying in cash, the clerk at the Super 8 wanted to see my ID. That was no problem—my fake ID was still tucked in with my makeup in my backpack. I have to say, Matt P. really had done good work back in September: Rachel Robbins of Bend, Oregon, who'd turned twenty-one just the previous August, really did look like me, and the weight and height were exactly right. The clerk squinted at the photo for a long time, and then she quizzed me on my address and my date of birth like she was a grouchy bouncer in a club. But please. I could have rattled off the answers in my sleep.

"Sorry," she said, sliding the license back across the counter. "You just look so young."

"Oh, thanks." I gave her a nice smile. "Lucky genes. My mom's half Portuguese."

That was just a safety lie, in case for some reason she had to meet Chloe. For now, Chloe was outside, waiting while I paid and got a key. We didn't know how often they were showing her picture on television, and even though she looked different now, wearing her eyeglasses and the knit hat, there was no point taking extra risks. When I came out and told Chloe our room was on the third floor, she knew, without me saying anything, that we should walk right past the elevator and take the back stairs up instead.

The room was just a normal hotel room, freshly vacuumed, with two double beds and a heater humming under the closed blinds of the big window. But it felt strange, the two of us standing there in the doorway together, looking at the yellow bedspreads with their matching green pillows. For all I knew, Muslims had some special rule about how and where they were supposed to sleep. But I guess she decided it was okay. After she walked in, the first thing she did was unzip her boots and wriggle out of them. She left them right by the door.

"You are going to shower?" She pointed toward the bathroom. Its flickering fluorescent light had been left on. "Before bed? Or in the morning?"

"I think tonight," I said. Now that we were inside where it

was warm, I felt how tired I was. But I hated to go to bed with cold toes. "If you want to go first, you can."

"Yes, thank you." She rubbed her ear. "I will be fast. You need to use the toilet?"

I shook my head. She took off her white coat and hung it in the little closet. But then, still wearing the knit hat, she went right into the bathroom, with her whole bag, and closed the door.

Weirdo city, I thought. I couldn't figure out why she'd take her whole bag in with her. Even if she'd wanted to change in there, even if she was just modest, she could have taken what she needed out.

I could hear heavy footsteps overhead, somebody walking around in the room above. Without even taking off my backpack, I went over to the bed by the window and fell down at a diagonal across it, holding my hands over the heating vents. I heard the toilet flush in our bathroom, the sink running, and then the first spatter of shower water. I pulled both my arms in close to my body, trying to think.

Maybe she took her bag in the bathroom because she was worried I would go through her things. I don't know if I would have thought of it, but now that she was being all cagey, looking through her bag seemed like it would have been the responsible thing for me to do. I wouldn't have been super nosy. I would have done just a quick search for suspicious materials, like they did at malls, and some of the grocery stores too now. Really, it would be my right to tell her I needed to look through it, and now I was thinking that maybe I'd do just that when she came out of the bathroom. I mean, I was going pretty far out on a limb here, believing that she hadn't hurt anyone, and that she didn't plan to. I'd feel awful if she turned out to be lying.

But she might not be lying. And she might be offended if I said I wanted to look through her bag. She probably would be offended—she seemed the type. She might even say no, even if it was just a bunch of clothes in there, just as a point of pride. I might say no, if it were me. And if she said no, what exactly would I do in response? Leave her here? Turn her in? It wouldn't do any good to give her ultimatums I didn't plan to carry out.

I was still lying there and worrying about it when she came out wearing black wide-legged pants, a white sweatshirt, and a pair of fluffy pink socks just like the ones she'd given Caleb. But the big difference was she'd taken off the knit hat, so I could see her hair. She hadn't gotten it wet, and it looked thick and wavy, maybe from the humidity of the shower. When she came over closer to the lamp, you could see a little red in it, glossy in the light.

"You got pretty hair," I said, because it was true, and because it surprised me. I mean, you would think if your religion made you keep your head covered all the time, you wouldn't put too much work or even thought into how your hair looked. But she'd definitely dyed it.

She made a groaning sound, touching the top of her scalp. "It's henna," she said. "But I haven't been able to get it done since

171

summer. My roots are atrocious."

She set her bag, all zipped up, between the other bed and the nightstand. I looked down at it, but I didn't say anything. She'd left her glasses off, and her face was shiny from some kind of moisturizer.

"The water pressure is good," she said, sitting on her bed with one leg tucked in, her other foot resting on the floor. She had a dry washcloth pressed up against the ear that she'd been rubbing. "But it gets very hot. Be careful."

I rolled my eyes. I was pretty sure I knew how to take a shower. I picked up my backpack and headed to the closet. Before I hung up my coat, I took off Tess's watch and zipped it in the pocket, as I wanted to protect it from the steam of the shower. But I'd already decided I was going to take everything else, my whole backpack, in the bathroom with me. If I couldn't look through her stuff, she couldn't look through mine.

"Do you take long showers?" she asked.

I already had one foot in the bathroom, but I leaned back out so I could see her. She was sitting there on the bed, her hands resting on the knees of her black pants, looking at me like she'd asked something that wasn't strange at all.

"Excuse me?" I asked.

"You'll be in there how many minutes? Do you think?" She was smiling at me, but I'm sorry—it was an odd question. I didn't know what she was planning on doing while I was in there. I looked at the old telephone on the nightstand. She was going to call someone, maybe.

"I take a normal time in the shower," I said. "Why?"

She nodded, still smiling. "I'm going to pray. It will take longer than usual, because I could not pray during the day. I do not want to startle you when you come out."

I kind of made a face. I know it sounds rude, and I didn't mean to be, but I couldn't help it. I was thinking, yeah, I would have been startled if I'd come out and seen that. I knew the way Muslims prayed from television and movies. They weren't like Christians, who could pretty much do it on the sly if they felt like it, just bowing their heads with their fingers clasped. For Muslims, it was this whole-body workout, with all the standing up and kneeling down and bowing and then standing up again, over and over. I'd seen videos of thousands of them doing it all at once, the women separated from the men, and something about it, so many people doing the exact same thing at once, seemed a little sci-fi to me.

I felt bad about making the face, though, so I tried to say something nice.

"Don't you have to, like, face a special direction or something?"

"That's right!" she said, real enthusiastic, like I was a third grader who'd gotten two times two correct. "We face the direction of Mecca. I have a compass. I keep it with me, just for that."

She unzipped her bag like she was getting ready to show me.

"Okay, well . . ." I'd already ducked into the bathroom. "Have fun."

Probably not the best thing to say. But it was safe to say, by anyone's measure, that I'd had a long day. And I didn't want to see her compass. I didn't want to know which way Mecca was. I was getting scared again. I just wanted to shut the door.

It felt strange, taking a shower right after she'd been in it. It probably shouldn't have. At Hannibal High, all the girls in my gym class had to jump in and out of little shower stalls one after the other, soaping down and rinsing off fast, with Mrs. Reisig waiting there with her whistle if anyone took too long. But this was different, because it was just one bathroom, with a proper tub and a door. It was like all of a sudden Chloe and I were roommates, or even family, like we knew each other way better than we did. Her damp towel was hanging on the hook behind the door, and she'd left her pink-handled toothbrush out. As quick as she'd been, there was still steam along the edges of the mirror, and I could smell her mint-smelling soap, or maybe her lotion. She'd already packed it away, whatever it was, so I just used the shampoo and soap and lotion that the hotel set out for free. The shower did get plenty hot, but I didn't mind. I stood under the faucet with my eyes closed for as long as I could stand it, trying to let the heat of the water seep into my bones.

Almost eight hours had passed since I'd said good-bye to Caleb and watched him walk back to the McDonald's alone. I doubted Aunt Jenny had called the police. She might have called my mom to yell at her, but my mom probably wouldn't pick up. I just hoped Caleb wasn't in trouble. Probably not. Aunt Jenny was probably being good to him, consoling him for getting left behind. And secretly pleased that I was gone.

After I turned off the water, even when I turned off the fan, I couldn't hear anything through the door. I had no idea how long it would take a Muslim to pray, but she'd made it sound like something extended, even by regular Muslim standards. I dried off slowly and got into my pajamas, and I took my time combing through my hair. I started to wrap my hair in a towel to keep it from dripping, but then, just to see, I stretched the towel out long, pulled one edge of it over my hair, and criss-crossed it at the neck so just my face was showing. It didn't look exactly right. The towel was thicker than a scarf, and probably not as long. But it gave me the general idea. I turned my head from side to side, my gaze on my reflection.

I still didn't look foreign, even with my dark hair and eyes. I'm pretty much almost 100 percent Scotch-Irish, with just a little French, so it would take more than a headscarf to do it. But it was interesting to think about what I'd be like if I'd been born someplace else. I'd still be me. I guess I would. But I might think it was perfectly normal to go around with a scarf on my head, and so going around without something on my head might really feel as crazy as walking around without a shirt. Even if I moved to a country where nobody wore one, I'd be like, *Uh, no thanks, I'll leave mine on.* And I'd probably have some weird name that wouldn't even seem weird to me. I might be out there praying with her right now. Maybe not. If I was still me, I might have stopped praying, and believing in the rules, just like I did here. I mean, underneath, scarf or not, it would still be my head.

It turned out I stayed in the bathroom way longer than I had to. When I came out, just the little lamp on the nightstand was on, and Chloe was in bed, either sleeping or pretending to sleep, the shiny back of her hair facing my bed. She had a hand cupped over her ear, and I guessed it must still be bothering her.

I pulled down the covers of the other bed and eased myself between the sheets. They were scratchier than the sheets at Aunt Jenny's, but I would have been happy to go to sleep on the ground at that point. Seriously, it felt so good to finally lie down, all clean and warm, with a soft pillow under my head, and the heater humming beside me. It was all I could do not to sigh. But I stayed quiet, wanting to be considerate, in case Chloe was really asleep.

9

I WOKE TO the clatter of the blinds going up, and the sting of sunlight on my eyes. When I stopped blinking enough to focus, I saw Chloe standing by the window, already dressed in different pants and a red sweater. The coffee maker gurgled in its corner.

"Jesus," I said, pulling the blanket over my eyes. "What's wrong with you? Pull that back down."

"Sarah-Mary." She said my name the weird way again. "It's after nine o'clock. We should go. The daylight is burning away. Do you want coffee? I had some. It is not so bad."

My mouth was dry, and I could tell, even before I lifted my head, that I was going to have a headache. I'd only had half of a gin and tonic, but it wasn't like I was used to them. Or maybe it was just that the room's heat was on too high, with no humidifier like at Aunt Jenny's. I peeked out from under the blanket. Chloe had already made her bed, which was a weird thing to do, as the maid was going to have to strip the sheets. Her messenger bag was zipped up and set on the table by the television. A hardback book sat next to it with some kind of Arabic, or I guess Farsi, writing on the spine.

"I hope I did not disturb you when I did my prayers this morning? I'm sorry."

Here we were with the prayers again. I shook my head. Tess once said that every time she was in a hotel room, she cracked herself up thinking of all the people who'd been in it before, and all the strange situations they could have been in, and how some of them had probably woken up in the very bed she was lying in, smiled uncomfortably at another person, and wondered what the heck they'd been thinking the night before. I know she meant that in a sex way, but whatever the history of this room was, as far as waking up and feeling awkward with someone, it seemed like Chloe and I should get first prize.

"Okay," I said, sitting up and rubbing my eyes. "I'll have some coffee."

By the time she brought me a cup, I was sitting over at the little built-in desk, and I'd taken the yellow notepad out of my bag. She was right that we needed to get going, but I wanted to make a new sign before we left. I didn't have a marker, just the pen that the hotel left out on the desk. I had to keep going over the words to make them big and dark enough to be legible from a few feet away.

Going North?
We'd Like a Ride!

I looked up. Chloe sat at the foot of her bed, frowning at the sign.

"What?" I asked. "You think you could do a better job, go ahead." I held out the pen.

She waved it away, crossing one leg over the other. "You have better handwriting. But 'north' is not good. It is too general. People will think of Canada, and they'll know why."

"Well," I said. "We don't want to get too specific. At this point, we just got to go *up*."

She looked out the window, two fingers to her lips. The lines between her eyebrows went especially deep, or they just looked that way in the sunlight. She pushed up her glasses. "Iowa," she said.

"Just Iowa?" I made a face. "That seems pretty general." It also didn't seem that ambitious.

"When someone asks you, you can say we are trying to get to Minneapolis. But just getting to Iowa would help."

I looked down at what I'd written. She was maybe right. I got out two new pieces of paper, taped them side by side, and tried again.

Headed to Iowa?
We'd Love a Ride!

I added a smiley face, and looked up at Chloe. "And we're still just getting rides with women?"

It's not like I wanted her to be the boss all of a sudden. But after last night, I wasn't sure about the women-only rule. We'd had to wait a long time for a ride, and by just saying no to all men, we were cutting out half our possibilities.

"Right," she said, no question in her voice. "It is much more safe."

I drummed my fingers on the table, thinking. That was probably right, too. Most men weren't rapists and killers. But most rapists and killers were men. Even Tess had made that rule.

"And no more black people," Chloe said. "Unless we are very, very desperate."

I about spit out my coffee. Before I could swallow, I was already shaking my head, revving myself up to tell her right off. Who the hell did she think she was, of all people, saying racist stuff, when it was those nice black people, black *Americans*, thank you very much, who'd been the ones to help us out last night when we were out there freezing our butts off? Talk about being an ingrate.

"That's *racist*," I said. "Shame on you. You got a lot of nerve, considering everything, and—"

"Not racist. Just practical." She shrugged and rubbed her ear. "Black people are more likely to be pulled over, much more likely in some places. We should avoid riding with them, at least in the

180

daytime. Last night was fine. But in the daytime, we shouldn't take the risk if we can avoid it."

I stared at her. She didn't know what she was talking about. I was the one who'd grown up here.

"That's crazy," I said. "They do not get pulled over more. Not if they're just driving a regular car down the highway and not doing anything."

"They do," she said. "There have been studies."

She said that last part like that was the end of it, like if there'd been studies, well, oh my God, or oh my Allah, everybody better just bow down and accept it as truth. I took another sip of coffee. I supposed it might be true. There didn't seem any reason for her to make something like that up. I looked down at my hand holding my coffee cup, my skin pale and dry in the sunlight.

Somebody started up a vacuum cleaner in the hallway. Chloe rubbed her ear again. Her glasses went crooked, but she fixed them.

"I did not say that is the way it should be," she said. "I'm saying that is the way it is."

The sign for a gas station, just in front of the highway overpass, didn't seem so far away from the window of our hotel room. But it seemed a lot farther when we were actually out walking, as even with the sun, it was way colder out than it had been the night before. I wore the black hat pulled down over my ears, and

Chloe and I both kept our heads lowered against the wind. Some guy leaned out the window of a growling truck and wolf-whistled as he went by, laughing when we both jumped. "Sexy!" he yelled, which was just so dumb. Even by Berean Baptist standards, we were both pretty bundled up. Somebody who whistles out the window like that just wants to scare you because you're female and out walking without a male, like a dog without an owner. Nine times out of ten, in my experience, it's got nothing to do with showing skin.

We'd already decided we would get something to eat at the gas station, so we would be, at least officially, paying customers, and then the cashier might not be so put out about us using the bathroom or standing out by the door with our sign. Chloe got a bag of unsalted peanuts and a banana. Judging from the look on her face, she didn't think much of my breakfast choice, which was a pack of glazed mini-doughnuts and an energy drink. But she couldn't say anything about it, as she was a Portuguese-only speaker again. Which was nice.

We ate fast and quiet at a table by the window. And then there was nothing to do but throw away our trash, take out the sign, and go back out in the cold.

It was same as last time. Most people didn't even read the sign, and the ones who did were men. Women acted like they couldn't see us, or if they did look at the sign, they didn't stop to ask questions. I kept smiling, real friendly, like, *Oop! I see you're walking away, ma'am. No hard feelings. I get it. I really do. But if you change your mind, you know where we'll be.* That didn't help, though. If anybody looked at our sign on their way into the gas station, they didn't look at it when they were coming out.

So we kept standing there, breathing in car exhaust and gas fumes from the pumps, the bell on the entrance going *ding!* every few seconds. My toes felt snug and warm, as Chloe had given me a packet of toe-warmers. But even after the energy drink, my head still ached a little, and after what seemed like an hour, I started to wonder if my dumb smile could actually freeze to my face.

But it hadn't been an hour. I made the mistake of checking Tess's watch and saw we'd only been out for thirty-five minutes.

"You need a break?" Chloe murmured. "You need to go inside?" She hardly moved her lips at all. She was like a trained ventriloquist. Pretty good for a second language.

I shook my head. "You?" That was all I could manage. She shook her head too, though I could see her eyes were watery, maybe from the cold, maybe from the car exhaust. I turned away from her, smiling again.

And then a short white woman was standing in front of us, squinting down at the sign. She looked about ten years older than Chloe, though her hair was dark blond, no gray. She wore a black leather coat that had fringes all over it and little rhinestones along the collar, with glittery swirls running down the front by the zipper. It wasn't nice of me, but just in the privacy of my head, I was thinking no matter how cold I was, I would never wear a coat that ugly. Seriously. I'd rather freeze.

"What part of Iowa?" she asked. Her eyebrows were really high up on her forehead, maybe naturally, maybe not.

"Oh!" I said, all excited. "Well, we're actually trying to get home to Minneapolis, but we thought Iowa would be a good start. So anywhere in Iowa is good."

"I'm headed to Hamilton," she said.

Chloe looked at me, and I looked back at the woman. "Hamilton," I said. "I'm afraid I don't know even know where that is."

She shook her head like she felt sorry for me. "Hamilton, Missouri?"

I was right. The dumb smile really had frozen to my face. I waited for her to go on.

"Have you heard of J. C. Penney?"

I nodded. The woman looked at Chloe like she couldn't believe she wasn't nodding too.

"She's my mother's cousin visiting from Portugal," I said. "She only knows Portuguese."

"Hmm," the woman said. "Even Portuguese people have probably heard of J. C. Penney. And he's right from Hamilton. That's where he was born."

"Oh," I said. "That's nice." It wasn't especially helpful information, but this was the closest thing to a nibble we'd had all

184

morning. "Where is Hamilton?"

"It's also the quilting capital of the world. It has more quilting stores than about any place. That's where all the bees are."

"Bees?"

She laughed, not in an especially nice way. Her teeth were as white as Chloe's coat.

"The quilting bees," she said, like I was pretty much the stupidest person in the world. "Anyway, I'm taking the long way to Hamilton so I can stop by the Walmart in Cameron. I could drop you there. You'd be a lot closer to Iowa than you are now, and Cameron is right on thirty-five. From there it's a straight shot up to Minneapolis."

"Oh yeah," I said, like I already knew, like I was just agreeing with her.

She raised her chin. "I could use some gas money."

"Yeah." I was still nodding, still smiling, still trying to look friendly. "Of course. How much were you thinking?"

"Well it's over four hours to Cameron. Maybe twenty dollars?"

I kept nodding. "That sounds fair."

"Or thirty," she said. "Thirty."

"Thirty," I said, but I said it like it pained me. I didn't want her to keep going up, but more than that, I didn't want her to think we had a lot of cash on us in case she was a thief. I turned to Chloe and held up three fingers, and then made a zero with my

185

forefinger and thumb, and then rubbed my fingers and thumb together, like we had a special sign language. Chloe watched my hands then nodded as if she just now understood.

"Do . . . we . . . have . . . that . . . much?" I asked. I had thirteen dollars and change left over from the twenty I'd spent on the doughnuts and energy drink. I pulled that out, all crumpled, keeping my remaining twenties out of sight. For a second, I was worried Chloe wouldn't know not to whip out one of her hundreds and say she had to go get change for it. But she was smart. She unzipped a little side pocket of her bag and took out a five and a ten, and then, after pushing her hand deep in the pocket for a while and looking unsure, she pulled out three more ones and two quarters.

"Okay," I said. "That's twenty-nine fifty." I fished out a dime and a nickel from my coat pocket. "Twenty-nine sixty-five."

"That's fine," said the woman. "I can let the rest go." She said it like she had a magic wand, and was touching each of our heads with it. She took the money and pointed behind her. "I'm over there, at pump four."

I thought she was kidding. A silver Striker was parked at pump four, its long hood low to the ground. It's not like I know a lot about luxury cars, but I recognized the little cobra hood ornament, and I knew a new Striker cost more than most people's houses. But she wasn't kidding. She pointed her clicker at it, and the headlights came on with their reddish glow, which made the shiny grill below it look even more like a set of bared teeth. My first thought was: Whoa—I get to ride in that car? My second thought was maybe it wasn't such a hardship for her to spot us the thirty-five cents.

But I acted like it was no big deal. I just walked over to the passenger side like I didn't even notice the little cobra on the hood, like I rode in cars like this all the time. Chloe followed me over. Neither of us got in. I liked that Chloe was thinking the same way I was—nice car or not, we had a system.

"Oh, hey," I said to the woman. "I promised my dad I'd text him a picture of the license plate every time somebody was nice enough to give us a ride. That okay?"

The woman frowned, though her high eyebrows stayed high. I waited too, still smiling, but not moving at all. If she didn't let me take a picture, we weren't getting in, even if we lost our money. It seemed unlikely she was out to rob us, but then again, it was super weird she'd asked us for gas money when she had a car like this.

"It's just for my dad," I said. "He deletes them when I come home."

The woman blew through her teeth. "We're already on video." She pointed up at the little roof over the pumps. Her black gloves were trimmed with gray fur. "Everything we do these days is watched and recorded."

I nodded. I hadn't thought about that, how we were being

filmed right now. I didn't look up, and neither did Chloe.

"It's just for my dad," I said. "He's a worrier."

She clicked her tongue, opening the door to the driver's seat. "Yeah. My husband is the same way with me and our daughters. You know what we each got for Christmas? A new gun. Go ahead and take your picture."

I thought for a second she was trying to give me some kind of double message about her having a gun. But she shrugged and got into the car, so I think she was really just telling me her husband worried about her as much as my made-up dad worried about me. I took out my phone and went around to the back of the car. The bumper stickers were hard to miss.

QUILTERS LOVE YOU TO PIECES

IF LIFE GIVES YOU SCRAPS, MAKE A QUILT!

GET 'EM OUTTA HERE!
No Refuge for Illegals and Islamic Terrorists!

It's not Islamophobia when they're really trying to kill you!

My chest went hot under my coat. Chloe had already gotten in the backseat—I could see the back of her blue hat through the rear window. The woman started the engine, probably watching me in the rearview. There was nothing to do but hold up my phone and act like I was taking a picture. And then I had to come around to the passenger side, smiling again, pretending hard to both of them that everything was fine.

The woman took off her gloves to drive. Her nails were short and unpainted, but I couldn't believe the size of the diamond on her ring. I was thinking maybe it was just a big rhinestone, to match the ones on her jacket, but if it was real, I guess it made sense she'd gotten a gun for Christmas, especially if she was going to go around picking up hitchhikers in her Striker.

"Did you see my bumper stickers?" she asked.

Exactly no part of me wanted to have this conversation. Or really, any conversation at all. We were already cruising up the entrance ramp to the highway, the ride smooth even as we picked up speed. It seemed like we could all just get through this, and maybe quite comfortably, if we kept the talking to a minimum. My seat had a control for heat, and another for a back massage, and I was thinking that after a while, if it didn't seem awkward, I might ask if I could turn them both on. Already the seat was so comfortable, the headrest made of soft leather, and tilted up just right. It was like being in a dentist chair, but without the dentist.

The Quilter glanced at me, waiting for an answer.

"I did," I said. Simple question, simple answer. Yes, I'd seen the bumper stickers. But I guessed that wouldn't be the end of it.

"Do you like them?" she asked. "I'd say you better like them today."

"Oh yeah," I said. "Get 'em outta here. For sure." I waved my hand like I was shooing smoke. Even on the highway, the car was silent, and Chloe could of course hear us from the backseat. She must have known what that particular phrase meant, as it was on a lot of bumper stickers and T-shirts. The topic of conversation was likely making her nervous.

"I liked your other bumper stickers too," I said. "You know what's funny, or I guess lucky?"

I waited for her to glance at me like, *No I don't. What is it?*

"Well," I said. "I've always been curious about how quilts are made, how somebody gets started doing something like that. And I suppose you know all about it."

I thought that was pretty smart of me, changing the subject like that. And I kept feeling smart for a while. Just as I'd hoped, once I got her on the subject of quilts, forget it, she wasn't thinking about Muslims, or terrorists, or illegals, or even the other cars flashing their lights behind us because even though that Striker could probably go two hundred miles an hour, she never took it above sixty. She just wanted to talk quilts. She told me about how she'd started making quilts with her sisters when she was young, and how she'd made one all by herself when she was just nine years old, and though the stitching wasn't exactly right, most people couldn't believe it was as good as it had been. And then when she was fourteen, she'd won a big contest, and some-body named Sharon had been so jealous, but too bad for Sharon, as everyone knew which one was the best—even though it was just a strip quilt. The stitching had been perfect on that one.

"Uh-huh," I said. It was getting harder to keep showing interest. To be clear, I don't have anything against quilts. But after about an hour, when we were out in the country, and she was still talking about quilting and all her quilting accomplish-ments, not so much. I hoped Chloe appreciated I'd taken one for the team.

"You're not going to believe this," the woman said. "But my eldest daughter won the same contest when she was fourteen. Now she lives out in California, but she's got that same quilt on her and her husband's bed, even now."

"That's great," I said. "Hey, I see this seat has controls for heat and massage? Okay if I turn them on?"

She shook her head. "Sorry. That one's not working right. I've got to take it in. Anyway, her win was really surprising for a lot of people, as she chose a very modern pattern. I'll try and describe it. It was like . . ."

And so on. And so on. I was stuck in listening hell. And it's not like the scenery was that interesting, either—just win-ter-dead fields and every now and then a billboard advertising homemade fudge or an adult video store at the next exit. I could see in through the windows of cars in the passing lane. Most people were just driving by themselves, probably listening to music as loud as they wanted, or just quiet if they preferred that. I glanced in the back and saw Chloe was asleep, her mouth open, her head lolling on one shoulder.

"And a gun-boat quilt," the woman said, "that's what they called quilts made by Southern women during the Civil War to raise funds for gun boats."

"Thanks," I said, real firm, hoping she'd take the hint. "Now I feel like I know what I was curious about. Like everything. I know everything I wanted to know. Thank you."

That didn't do any good. Neither did me asking if she had any pets, or if she'd seen any good movies lately. She stayed focused on quilts. She told me how she got the best loft. She told me how she'd learned the feather stitch, the satin stitch, the running stitch, and the French knot.

"How long do you think the average quilt lasts?"

"I don't know," I said, leaning against my window. I just wanted to watch the cobra hood ornament coast over the road.

"Just guess," she said.

"I don't know."

"Guess!"

I held up my hands and turned back to her. "A hundred years!"

She looked at me, her mouth open. "Wow," she said. "That's exactly right."

Around the time we got to her telling me what a wedding

ring pattern was, my eyelids got way heavy. I yawned twice, but she didn't take the hint. So I got more obvious. I stopped saying "uh-huh" or even "hmm." And then I bent my arm up so it was like a pillow against my window and leaned my head on the soft part of my forearm. I don't know how long I got to close my eyes.

"Hey!" she said, elbowing my arm. "If I gotta be awake, I should have company, don't you think?"

I opened my eyes and saw a digital billboard flickering up ahead. Even from a distance, I could see it was showing pictures of faces, two at a time, with *CASH REWARD* in bright red at the bottom. It wasn't Chloe's picture. But it could change to hers any second.

"So, hey"—I turned to the Quilter, trying to sound and look calm—"what's the hardest quilt you ever made? Like what's the one that gave you the most trouble?" I leaned forward, thinking maybe I could block her view.

She didn't answer. She held up her finger like telling me to wait, and her gray eyes moved back and forth between the road ahead and the billboard.

"They wouldn't have to give me a penny," she said.

I nodded, holding my breath.

We were just outside of Kansas City when the Quilter said she needed to stop at a gas station—"to use the facilities," was how she put it. I had to pee myself, and so did Chloe, but we were both fast, and out waiting by the Striker while the Quilter was still inside. I didn't know if Chloe had seen the Striker's bumper stickers on her way to the restroom or coming back. If she had, she was probably thinking, *Yeah, lady, I'd like nothing more than to get outta here, thank you very much. In fact, why don't you drive me to the border?* I didn't think I should bring them up.

"You're lucky you're in the backseat," I whispered, bringing my knee up by my waist to give my hips a stretch. "You're not trapped in a four-hour talk-u-mentary about quilting. My God. I'm about to throw myself out the window."

Chloe gave me a scolding look, like the kind I got from the other girls at Berean Baptist if I said something about Mrs. Harrison or Pastor Rasmussen. So I guess it was the same thing for Muslims as it was for Christians—you weren't allowed to talk about someone behind their backs, which to me seemed like a good way to take the joy out of life. It was true that I was biting the hand that fed me, or I guess the hand that gave us a ride. But still. It seemed to me that if somebody was going to drive around with bumper stickers telling you to get outta the country, you could at least let somebody make fun of them a little, Muslim or not.

Chloe wasn't having it, though.

"Sorry," I said, not meaning it. I turned away from the door to the gas station and changed my voice so I sounded like a robot. "I will not com-plain a-ny-more a-bout her talk-ing. I will be hap-py to hear about quilt-ing for as long as ne-cess-ar-y."

I knew I was being immature. But I was tired, and not happy at all about having to get back in the car. To my surprise, Chloe's mouth did a funny thing, like she was trying to frown at me, but couldn't quite manage it, and then—whoa, hold on, sound the alarm—it was pretty clear she was trying not to laugh.

So of course as soon as we're back on the highway, the Quilter told me something that made me feel bad for making fun of her. Basically, the whole reason she'd gone down to St. Louis was that in her free time, when she wasn't helping out with filing the insurance at her husband's practice, she made grief quilts, which were quilts made out of pieces of clothing of people who'd died. She figured that over the years, she'd made about fifty or sixty of them. That was what she was doing now, driving a box of clothes back from St. Louis for some poor woman who'd lost her son and didn't know what to do with his baby clothes and blankets. When she got back to her house, she said, she'd figure out the best pattern for what she had to work with, and then start cutting up the material.

"How long does it take you to make one of those?" I couldn't believe I was asking her a quilt question, getting her started again. But I really wanted to know.

"Hmmm." She tilted her head. "About twenty hours for a smaller one. I have to space it out, of course."

"How much do you charge?" Not like I was in the market

for one. But I wouldn't have minded having a quilt like that of my dad's clothes, and I didn't even remember him. Anyway, his clothes were long gone by now.

"I don't charge anything." She glanced at me, her mouth wrinkled up like she was looking at a dead animal. "It's just something nice I do."

"For strangers? These aren't people you know?"

"They're my fellow human beings. In pain," she said, and I could tell from the look on her face that she didn't think it was so great she had to explain this to me, even though I was one of the two people she'd just charged for gas money even though she was already making the trip. I turned around and saw Chloe staring out the window. I didn't know if she'd been listening or not.

We passed a car lot with a big video screen that, to my relief, only flashed on the different models of cars they had. An American flag snapped in the wind at half-mast above the lot.

"Why's it at half-mast?" I asked. "Did somebody die?"

Now the Quilter looked at me like I was crazy.

"I imagine it's for the bombing," she said, with the same smirk she'd used to ask me if I'd heard of J. C. Penney.

"What bombing?"

She glanced at me again. "In Detroit? You didn't hear? Seven people were killed by a bomb last night. Seven Americans. Innocent people. Not doing anything but riding a bus home from work. Those crazies blew it up."

My stomach seized as if we'd lurched to a stop, but the car

was still gliding along. I didn't risk looking back at Chloe. She better be listening now.

"They know who did it, then?" I asked, trying to keep my voice even. But I already knew who she meant, who the crazies were. When we'd first gotten in her car, back in St. Louis, she'd asked me if I liked her bumper stickers, and she'd said I'd better like them, especially today. She'd meant what happened in Detroit. That was why the video billboards were all showing pictures of Muslims, and not showing weather or traffic reports at all.

But maybe they didn't know for sure it was Muslims. Muslims weren't the only ones who blew things up or shot people. Sometimes it was just a crazy white guy, born right here, and mad about something not going his way. Last year when the Statue of Liberty got bombed, everybody assumed it was Muslims, but it turned out to be a group from here that did it because they didn't like the poem at the bottom.

"You're asking me who did it?" The Quilter blew through her paper-white teeth.

She looked at me from the side, and I could see that she didn't like that I'd asked the question. "They haven't said who, officially. Not yet." Her small eyes got smaller. "But pretend your life depended on it. And take a wild guess."

10

YOU MIGHT THINK that the Walmart Supercenter in Cameron, Missouri, wouldn't be that crowded on a Thursday afternoon in January, the sky threatening cold rain. But you would be wrong. The Quilter had to circle the entire lot twice before she found a spot she liked, and when she was pulling into it, she almost hit a man carrying a box of firewood in one hand and a bag of groceries in the other. He gave her a mean look, and she gave him one right back.

"People need to be careful," she said, pushing the gear into park.

I nodded, already feeling queasy. Walking into a crowded Walmart with a well-advertised fugitive didn't seem like the smartest move. But the Quilter was already getting out of her car, so there was nothing to do but pick up my backpack and get out, too. As soon as I did, the wind pushed the car door against me, and I pulled my hood up. Chloe got out of the backseat with her head down, her blue hat already pulled low.

"That wind, huh?" the Quilter yelled. Her blond hair was flying all around, and so was the fringe on her coat.

We'd only been walking for about ten seconds when I noticed a big man in a flannel jacket watching us. He'd just finished loading his groceries into his truck, and the door to the backseat was still open. I smiled fast and then looked away.

"Excuse me," he said. And then he said it again, like he wasn't going to be ignored.

All three of us turned. He took a step toward Chloe. Even in the cold, a layer of sweat pushed out of my hairline. I didn't know what we would do if he recognized her. We didn't have a plan.

"She's my aunt from Portugal!" I started. I had to shout because of the wind. "She doesn't speak English!"

"Okay." The man stepped back, one pale palm raised. "I was just going to ask if she wanted my cart. They're hard to come by once you get in."

"I'll take it." The Quilter stepped in front of me and took the cart. "Thank you so much! You have a nice day. God bless!"

When we got to the front curb of the store, Chloe started rummaging through her messenger bag, and she kept doing that as we passed through the first set of automatic doors. Just above the second set of doors was a black-and-white screen showing what the security cameras saw, and I could see me in it, no problem, looking up with an open mouth. I could see the Quilter, too, pushing the empty cart. But all that showed of Chloe was the top of her hat and her white coat. I thought she was smart to hide her face, but inside the store, when the greeter said "Welcome to Walmart," Chloe looked up to give a quick smile, and all the greeter did was smile back.

Nobody was putting it together. It was like without the headscarf, and with the knit hat and the glasses, and maybe because she was walking next to me and now the Quilter, she just blended in. All she had to do was not talk.

"I guess this is good-bye," the Quilter said. She nodded at Chloe, then at me. "I hope you remember everything you learned today." She leaned on the handle of the cart and put one hand on her lean hip. "I hope I wasn't just talking my voice out for nothing."

"Thank you," I managed. And then I added, more sincerely, "Thank you for the ride, too."

Over her shoulder, I could see a man wearing a *GET 'EM OUTTA HERE* T-shirt under his coat, a rifle slung over his shoulder. He was over by the greeting cards, trying to pick one out.

"You're welcome," the Quilter said, already rolling the cart away. "You two be safe now."

I frowned at the fringe on the back of her coat. She'd said

it like she was making a strong suggestion. Like being safe was something we could choose.

There weren't any available shopping carts, but that was fine. All we needed was a basket. Chloe was going over the handle of one with an antibacterial wipe when she nudged my arm, and touched her ear.

"I know," I whispered. "We'll get that first, then just what we need to make a new sign."

That must have felt bad for her, being a grown woman but having to ask me for what she needed, like she was a little kid with her mom. We didn't look at each other as we walked, but she stayed close to me, her gaze moving along the bottom shelf of every aisle. Some people glanced at us, and some didn't. The stereo was playing that old doo-wop song, "One Fine Day," and I tried to focus on its happy rhythm so I wouldn't feel so tense. But I couldn't forget it would only take one person to recognize her face.

"One more thing," I whispered, standing on my toes to look for the electronics section. Chloe nodded and followed me to the other side of the store. It was only when I stopped in front of the disposable phones that she gave me a nervous look. Too bad, I thought. She couldn't say anything, not with so many people around. If I wanted a phone, I'd get one. I wanted to talk to Tess.

At the register, the cashier asked if I wanted to buy a flag pin.

"All the proceeds for today's sales go to the victims' families in Detroit." He touched the glinting pin on his own blue smock. "I mean for just the pins," he added quickly. "Not for everything."

I nodded. Even if I was by myself, I would have bought one, because of the families. I wasn't just being smart.

"Thanks," I said. "I'll take two."

We got lunch at the little Subway right inside the Walmart. At Chloe's request, I ordered her a salad with ranch dressing, and I got chips and a ham sandwich for myself. I only took enough money from her to pay for her salad, so I was the one paying for the ham.

As busy as the store was, it was late enough in the afternoon that the lunch crowd was long gone from the seating area. I found a table that didn't have anyone close by except a short-haired mom with a baby and a toddler, and they were three tables away. Two men in overalls and work jackets were laughing about something in the far corner, and there were still oldies playing on the sound system, with the same lady's voice breaking in every now and then to give coded messages to the employees. The toddler started to fuss at the mom about something, his voice high-pitched and whiny. So you couldn't exactly hear a pin drop. I could have leaned across the table and said to Chloe in a normal voice, "Hello there, Muslim!" and probably nobody would have heard.

Chloe didn't seem to want to talk, though. Before she even took the lid off her salad, she opened the box of ear drops, took out the bottle, and tore off the plastic wrap around the cap with her teeth. She pulled up one side of her hat, laid her head on the table, bad ear up, and squeezed in a few drops. She stayed like that for a while, not even folding her arms under her head.

I unwrapped my sandwich, looking up at the television on the wall behind Chloe. The volume was turned down, or I was too far away to hear, but I could see they were showing video of the blown-up bus in Detroit—flames shooting high out the windows, bright against the night sky. You could tell it was colder up there. Snowflakes fell in front of the camera, and even the newscasters wore hats or earmuffs. They interviewed people who were crying and shaking their heads, their gloved hands cupped over their mouths and noses. Sometimes the newscasters hugged people, or looked down like they were crying too. They showed video of the bus as it looked today, charred and still smoking, surrounded by armed guards and tape that said *DO NOT CROSS*, and lots of flowers and a few stuffed animals, too.

I'd only had two bites of my sandwich when I put it down. My throat had closed up, and my tongue felt cold. I rested my elbows on the table, my hands folded over my mouth.

When Chloe sat up, her hand on her ear, she saw that I was looking past her. She turned around and looked up at the television. When she turned back to me, her eyes were lowered. She'd pinned her flag to the right side of her hat.

"It was probably your people who did that," I whispered, wrapping up my sandwich. Her greenish eyes opened, steady on mine. I shrugged. It was a harsh thing to say, but I was feeling harsh. They were showing the victims now, their smiling faces, one at a time. An old black woman playing a piano. A handsome white man with an earring wearing a red graduation cap. An Asian boy about the same age as Caleb, sitting by his cat. I shook my head. They were all alive yesterday. The Quilter said it happened at night, so they were alive when I was in the woods with Caleb. We used to take the bus in Joplin sometimes—the city had tried to dress it up and call it a trolley, but it was just a bus. I knew what it was like to ride one, tired with your head against the window, but not thinking for a second it would be the last place you got to sit.

"They are not my people," Chloe said. She said it quietly, just through her teeth. "Whatever they call themselves, whatever they think they are, they are not. They are not Muslims."

She started to say something else, but she took a deep breath like she was trying to stay calm.

"Well"—I wiped my mouth with a napkin and nodded up to the screen—"a lot of them seem to be confused on that point. Maybe the rest of you should straighten them out."

And maybe I shouldn't be helping her, I thought. Because they didn't mean us well. That's what I was really thinking.

204

"And how are we supposed to do that?" She said it like she was really asking, but then she held up her finger. With her other hand, she mimed holding a phone to her ear. "Oh hello," she said into her hand. "ISIS? Yes. *As-salam alaykum*. This is Sadaf."

I didn't want to know her name. Also she needed to be quieter. I bulged my eyes at her and looked around to make sure no one was listening. The mom was cooing to the baby, and the toddler was sitting beside her now, playing with an empty cup.

"Yes, hello." Chloe still had the pretend phone pressed to her ear. "Listen. I have something to say to you. Please either stop murdering innocent people or stop saying you follow Mohammed, peace be upon him." She cocked her head. "What's that? Oh. You want to kill me, too? Oh. Because I am a woman with an education?" She stared just over my shoulder, like she was really talking to someone on the phone. "Because I believe in democracy? Ohhhh. I see. I am an infidel as well because I don't live my life the exact way you say I should, either?"

"Keep your voice down," I hissed. She was whispering, but there was no need for her to say words like *infidel*. My God. We were in a Subway in a Walmart.

"Oh," she said into her hand. "I deserve to die as well? Ahhhh, I see. And all my family and friends, you want to kill them too? Most of the people you've killed have been Muslim? Oh. Well. This is not a very productive conversation, then. Bye-bye."

She threw up her hands and glared at me.

"Okay," I whispered. "Sorry." I said it to get her to stop talking, and also because I was sorry. I guessed me acting like she had anything to do with a blown-up bus was pretty mean. I'd be mad, if it were me.

She started to pry off the lid of her salad, but she had trouble because her hands were shaking. I reached over to help, but she jerked the salad away from me. Once she got the lid off, she stabbed her plastic fork in a cherry tomato, but when she got it up close to her mouth, she made a face and set it back in the bowl like she'd lost her appetite too. She turned away, staring out the window. The sky was still low with steel-colored clouds, and a skinny boy without a jacket was pushing a train of carts up to the doors.

"Why did you get a disposable phone?" she asked. "I deserve to know who you will call."

I looked down at the plastic bag beside me, where I could see the outline of the phone. I'd call Tess as soon as I could have some privacy. "I'm just going to let my friend know where I am. She won't tell anyone. She won't."

Chloe took off her glasses, closed her eyes, and pinched the bridge of her nose.

"I need someone to know where I am," I said. "The only person who knows is Caleb, and he's eleven."

I don't know why I was explaining myself. Maybe it was in my head that I had to, as she was an adult. Still, she wasn't exactly in a position to tell me what I could and couldn't do.

She shook her head. "You want to tell your friend, but not your aunt? I do not understand." She held out one hand, dangling her glasses. "Your aunt must be afraid for you. You are young to be out by yourself. Where does she think you are? She has probably called the police."

I rolled my eyes. She needed to drop this whole *your aunt must be worried* business. Like she knew one thing about Aunt Jenny.

She put her glasses back on. "I hate to think she is so worried, your aunt, she must—"

"Stop," I said. "She thinks I'm with my mom."

She blinked. "But . . . your mother is . . . dead? The car accident?"

"She's sort of dead," I said, and then I felt bad for saying it, like in a superstitious way. I didn't want my mom dead, sort of or otherwise. What I meant was that she was only sort of my mother. More than anything, I was getting annoyed with all the questions. I especially didn't like Chloe looking at me the way she was doing now, like she felt sorry for me, her eyes all sad behind her glasses.

"Look," I said. "You got bigger problems than worrying about my mom. Okay?" I met her gaze and nodded. Over her head, the television was showing the burning bus again. "And you know what I think? I think people like you need to just stay in their own country. Then we wouldn't have these problems. You wouldn't be in this mess. Couldn't you have just stayed"— I didn't want to say *Iran*—"where you were?"

She forked the cherry tomato again, and this time she managed to slip it into her mouth. She chewed fast with closed lips, like a rabbit.

"You wouldn't be here," she said. "You are not Native American."

I shook my head. I wasn't going for that. People who wanted to let immigrants in were always bringing up the Native Americans, which, if you ask me, wasn't the best argument for their case. I mean, the Native Americans tried being nice to foreigners. And look what happened there.

"I mean recently," I said.

"That is convenient." She took a big bite of lettuce, and then we both had to just sit there and wait until she chewed. She took her time, too, dabbing at her mouth with a napkin before she started talking again. "I came here for the same reasons I imagine your ancestors did. As I told you, I had admiration for this country. Or the idea of it. What it is supposed to have. Freedom of religion. Separation of church and state."

"You wouldn't need it if you just stayed where everybody was Muslim," I whispered.

"To the contrary." She took another bite of salad, and this time, she held her hand over her mouth as she chewed. "My husband is Sunni. Most of Iran's population is Shia, and the government is Shia." She put her hand to her chest. "I am Shia. To some people, that is a strange marriage. Sunnis in Iran are mostly tolerated. Mostly. But not always. And they are often at a disadvantage with government positions, and positions in universities."

"Well," I said. "It couldn't have been any better for him here."

"It was. For a while. There was a mosque in Chapel Hill when I was there, and there was one in Jonesboro. We had Shia friends, Sunni friends. And at work, I made Jewish friends. I loved it. It is why I became a citizen." She tilted her head to the right, like she was trying to drain out her ear. "And also, there was much more chance for education, for work." She paused, squinting. "Why aren't you in school? Are you missing school right now?"

I shrugged.

"What does this mean?" She mimicked my shrug. "You don't care? You don't care that you are missing school?"

"The school I go to is pretty wacko," I said. "I'm not learning much there."

She didn't look like she believed me. "It's up to you how much you learn. Don't you want to go to college? Don't you want to study history and literature and science? And how will you make yourself useful?"

I made a face to let her know I didn't appreciate her turning all guidance counselor on me.

"I'm probably not going to college," I said.

She frowned. "Why not?"

"I've had it with school. When I'm finally free, the last thing I'll want to do is sign up for more imprisonment. Especially if I have to pay for it."

She wadded up her napkin. "That sounds spoiled to me, if I am honest with you. I'm sorry to say, because you are helping me. I appreciate that. But you are also spoiled."

I let my mouth fall open. I've been called a few insulting things in my life, but never once had anybody called me spoiled, not even Aunt Jenny. Excuse me that I wasn't already making plans for the rest of my life that somebody else needed to approve of. Tess was going to college, but that was because her parents would probably die if she didn't, as they'd been saving since she was a baby so she could go anywhere she wanted, as long as she got in. She'd gotten her applications in over winter break, and now she was waiting to hear. Columbia. Northwestern. Grinnell. She'd gone on campus tours with her parents in late summer, when I was full-time at Dairy Queen. I still had a couple of years to think things through, but I didn't exactly have the setup that Tess did.

"I'm sorry." Chloe gave me a look like she wasn't sorry at all. "But yes, to me, you sound spoiled, talking about an opportunity as if it is something you can throw away, like it is candy you do not want. You are talking to someone who had much greater obstacles, who still got herself to a university, into a graduate program, into a doctoral program, in a field that, even here, is not overrun with women. A university in another country, mind you. And my family was not wealthy." She pointed a forkful of salad in my direction. "You are smart, Sarah-Mary. Quick." With her free hand, she snapped her fingers three times. "You should care more about school, about your future. You should have a goal to do your part."

I fiddled with my sandwich wrapper. I guess it was impressive that she'd gotten through all that school. And now she was a professor. Or at least she had been. But I didn't see how that gave her the moral high ground over someone like me.

"So I guess teaching electrical engineering makes you Mother Teresa? You're just doing it to help everybody out? That's so good of you." I smiled. "It's like you've opened a shelter for the homeless. Or given your hair to Locks of Love."

She squinted. "You do not see how engineering helps people? You are joking?" She looked like she was going to say something else, but then she set her fork down and touched her ear, wincing.

"They're not working?" I asked. I glanced at the bottle of ear drops.

"No. Not yet."

I leaned back, looking over her head at the television screen. They were showing Muslim fugitives again, two at a time.

211

I waited as the screen changed to two more faces that weren't Chloe's, two more faces I didn't know. But then Chloe appeared on the left side of the screen, with no glasses and the rose-colored headscarf. *SADAF BEHZADI* was written below. And beneath that, *REWARD*. But that didn't tell me what I really wanted to know, which was why they were looking for her, what it was, according to them, that she'd done. If all she'd done was not show up for her bus to Nevada, then what I was doing wasn't so bad.

The screen changed again to two new faces, another man, and another woman. With them, too, it didn't say what they'd done. Like with all of them, you could only guess.

We'd only been standing out in front of the Walmart with our sign maybe ten, fifteen minutes when a white van pulled up at the curb, and three Amish people, two women and a man, came out and started loading groceries into the back of it. The driver got out to help, and he wasn't Amish, obviously. He wore a hooded sweatshirt and jeans, and a John Deere snapback with the visor pushed low. The Amish were of course dressed old-fashioned— the women wore long dark dresses and white bonnets over their hair, and the man had a gray beard that almost reached down to the black vest underneath his black coat. When the wind tried to snatch his wide-brimmed hat, he tucked it under his arm and kept loading groceries.

Chloe stared and stared.

I wasn't sure what was fascinating her about them. Maybe they didn't have too many Amish down in Arkansas. But in Missouri, in some parts, you saw Amish all the time, and yes, they did go to Walmart. I did a report on the Amish in eighth grade, and I included a section about a Walmart in Ohio that had so many Amish going to it that the managers set up a little covered stable area for buggies in the parking lot. They even put out water for the horses. That system works for some Amish, but in Missouri, most of the Amish towns are too far away from cities and stores for them to get there by buggy. But the Amish have a way around the no-car rule: they can hire a non-Amish person to drive them. In my opinion, that's a pretty crazy rule, with an even crazier loophole. I mean, saying you can't drive because of religion, and then hiring someone else to do it, all just seems like rigmarole that doesn't help anybody out.

I got a B-minus on my report. My teacher said my research was good, and that the paragraphs were well organized, but it seemed obvious to her that the no-car rule was about maintaining community, and I should try not to be so judgmental.

That's how it is. People like the Amish because they're religious but they don't bother anybody, and they definitely don't blow anybody up. They just make bread and pies with real butter and also high-quality furniture that you can buy at their markets or just by the side of the road. I agree it's kind of neat, eating something or sitting on something that somebody made without the help of any machine. And I know the Amish are healthier than we are because they eat food without chemicals and they don't spend all their time sitting around playing video games or watching television. My teacher said they were probably happier, too, because they were so deeply spiritual. But I once read this book by a girl who'd run away from being Amish, and she didn't have much good to say about it. It turns out some of the Amish have the same problems our world does, with girls getting raped and wives and kids getting beaten, and it's not like they have any social workers to go in and make an assessment. That girl who wrote the book said if you're Amish and you get raped or beaten, you're just supposed to forgive.

So I can see how being Amish might be a good life if you were lucky and born into a nice family and you were okay with lots of physical labor in every kind of weather, and not having any air conditioning or central heat, or zippers, or bras, or phones, or energy drinks, or earbuds to listen to music, or any music at all except your neighbor's fiddle. But if you were born into a family with mental problems, or if you were the kind of person who liked to sit and read or just do your own thing, you were going to be pretty unhappy. Or you were going to leave and be shunned.

I was thinking about all this when I noticed that the Amish man, who had eyebrows as crazy bushy as his beard, was standing still at the back of the van, and looking right at me and

Chloe. I smiled, but he didn't smile back. He said something to the two Amish women, and then they all turned around and looked at us. One of the women said something to the guy in the John Deere hat, and then he looked at us too.

I told myself to just stay calm. But my heart was already pounding. Wouldn't that be something, I thought, if it was the Amish that turned us in. I was being paranoid, probably. They didn't even have televisions. Or internet. But they might have driven past a billboard on the highway. That old man might have looked at a screen in Walmart even if he wasn't supposed to.

The driver jogged up to us, keys jangling. He had to hold on to his John Deere hat because of the wind.

"We're headed up to the Amish Country Store in Lamoni," he said, looking at Chloe, and then at me. "You know it? It's just over the state line. About an hour away. They're only dropping off a few items, and we'll turn right around and come back. But they said I could give you a ride if you wanted it."

"Oh, thank you!" I maybe said it with too much enthusiasm. John Deere hat took a step back.

"I'm only the driver," he said. "You can thank them. But just so you know, they don't speak much English. It's usually a quiet ride."

"That's great," I said, meaning it. A quiet ride sounded fine to me. I might not even have to go into the Portuguese business, or explain anything about Chloe. I was already feeling guilty enough. While the Amish had been loading up their van, I'd been thinking about how their rules and loopholes didn't make sense, and how miserable it might be to be one of them. And then I'd been scared they were going to turn us in. And the whole time, that old man who maybe only spoke Pennsylvania Dutch had been thinking about how they could help us out.

When we got over to the van, all three of them, the man and the two women, were in the very back seat. The man, who was tall, was hunched up between the women. They'd left the middle seat open for us. As I climbed in, the two women looked down at their laps, so all I saw was the tops of their bonnets, and a little of their sniffling noses and pink cheeks. But the man nodded at me, and then at Chloe.

"Thank you," I said. "Thanks."

He nodded again, just once, to show he understood.

11

THE AMISH COUNTRY Store in Lamoni had an old-fashioned wagon on its front lawn, and also a covered porch with a swing, and it was connected to a little barn-looking building that was really a Maid-Rite restaurant. Nobody working in the store was Amish, which made sense, as it would be against their religion to run the credit card machine or turn on the overhead lights. But the store had the feel of a museum gift shop, with a wooden floor that creaked under your feet, and a high tin roof, and copper cooking kettles hanging on the walls. The place was bigger than any gift shop I'd ever seen, though. There was a section for rocking chairs, and another one for tables, and an entire alcove devoted to Christmas decorations, now part of the *JANUARY SALE*. Up by the registers, they had dolls made out of cornhusks, and butter churns and wooden bird houses, and a wheelbarrow full of needlepoint pillows that said things like *Bless*

This House. You would think with all that stuff, it would start to feel sort of garage-sale cluttered, but the whole place smelled like cinnamon, and all the shelves and little alcoves looked tidy, everything polished and neatly arranged. A tabby cat with a red collar slinked around a corner, and Chloe crouched by a bin of wooden napkin holders to rub its little orange chin until it purred loud enough for me to hear. She couldn't talk to it and call it a good kitty because people were around, but she held its cool gaze for a long moment.

I was most interested in the food. Chloe and I had just come in to use the bathroom, and I knew we didn't have time to actually sit and eat at the Maid-Rite. But when we were supposedly on our way back out, I stopped at the little counter, pointing at the pastries and banana bread slices to show Chloe I'd get her something if she wanted. She shook her head, so I just got myself a cinnamon roll, still warm in its foil pouch. It tasted so soft and buttery on my tongue I pushed half of it in my mouth all at once.

Chloe stared at me. By then, we'd walked over to the woven baskets, away from everybody, but my cheeks were still too full to talk. So I just looked at her like, *What?*

"It's getting late," she whispered. "We should go out."

I wiped my nose, but I took another bite, acting like she hadn't said it. It was so cold out, the wind still blowing hard, and it was embarrassing to go out with the sign.

But I felt optimistic, looking around at the other customers.

It turns out that if you ever need a ride with a safe-looking woman, an Amish store on a weekday is a good place to look. At least the day we were there, it was pretty much older-lady central. I mean, nobody was scooting around with a walker or anything, but it seemed like Iowa women who hadn't yet reached retirement age maybe had to wait until the weekend to buy their Amish goods. And these were older ladies in a good mood, loading up on half-priced hand-carved nativity scenes and jars of jam with ribbons around the lids. There was one man following his wife around, holding her coat and squinting at his phone, and another man was on his hands and knees, looking up to study the joints of a table. But other than that, all older women. One of them, wearing little snowflake earrings, raised her paper cup of sample hazelnut coffee to us, like a toast, as she passed.

"I like your pins," she said, nodding at where I'd pinned my flag on the collar of my coat, and then at the flag on Chloe's hat. She didn't smile when she said it, but it was nothing against us. She just meant she was sad about Detroit.

Still, I wasn't prepared for all the attention we got when we went outside with our sign. It was the exact opposite of how it had been at the gas stations: nobody just walked by. We weren't out in front of the store's covered porch for even ten minutes before we had not just one, and not just two, but three different old women and one old man standing around worrying about us needing a ride to Minnesota. And then every time I heard the front door jangle, the new old person coming out would see that there was a huddle of other old people, and the new one would stop to ask what was going on, and then join right in on the conversation about how it didn't really seem safe for two women to hitchhike, even in Iowa.

But for a while, none of them actually offered us a ride.

"I'm afraid I'm headed south," said the man, ignoring the fact that our sign specifically said we were looking for a woman, and also that he was holding a newly purchased ladder-back rocking chair, which looked heavy, and which he probably should have set down. "But I've got a granddaughter about your age." He nodded at me. "I'd like to get you two to a bus station."

I didn't like the way he said it, kind of bossy, like I actually *was* his granddaughter and so he had some kind of right to tell me what to do. But I had a feeling that if I said we didn't have enough money for a bus, he might have opened his wallet.

So I said we were hitching on purpose, as I was writing about the experience of hitching through America with my Portuguese relative for a school project, to show her America. Taking a bus would be cheating.

One of the women narrowed her eyes behind bifocal glasses. Former teacher, I'd bet on it. "A high school project?"

"I go to MU," I said, acting offended, and already thinking about whether I meant Minnesota or Missouri, in case one of them asked.

But they didn't ask. I don't know if it was an Iowa thing, or an old-person thing, or maybe just that particular group of people, but for them, it was like hearing something had to do with school was the same as hearing it had been ordained from above. Just like that, they laid off about the bus, and one of the women, with a fuchsia streak in her gray hair, said she was going to Sherburn, right on the interstate, an hour north of Ames.

"And I've been to Portugal," she added with a little laugh, looking at Chloe, and then at me. "Though that was years ago."

I wasn't happy about that, of course. She didn't say if she'd picked up any of the language when she was over there. Either way, I hoped she didn't plan on going down a Portuguese memory lane with Chloe. At that point, though, there was no getting out of it. The rest of them agreed, like they were a committee, that Sherburn was our best bet.

The woman with the pink streak had a big sedan that looked like nobody had ever been allowed to eat in it, or even drink a soda. It wasn't a new model, but it had gold, sort of velvet-looking upholstery with no stains, and there was nothing in the little cave in front of the gearshift except for a packet of tissues and a coin purse. My seat didn't have any options for heating or massage, but it was comfortable enough, and the woman told me I could scoot it back if I wanted more legroom. Chloe was sitting behind the driver's seat, and by the time we were on the interstate, she'd leaned her head against the back window, her hat pulled over her eyes.

"I'm Val, by the way," the woman said. She didn't ask for Chloe's name, so I just said my name was Amy.

"I like your hair," I added. I was mostly just wanting to stay off the topic of Portugal. But I really did like how the pink of the streak was the exact shade of the frames of her eyeglasses. That was the way to get old, I thought. No need to get drab and boring.

"Oh, thank you." She glanced in the rearview with a smile. "My granddaughter talked me into it."

Boom, I thought. I knew now I could definitely keep her off of Portugal, however long it was to Sherburn. My grandparents were all dead by the time I was old enough to know them, but in my experience, asking a grandparent if they want to talk about their grandkids—how many they have, how old they are, or all about the clever thing one of them did the other day—is like asking a kid if they'd like some ice cream. You may get a few who aren't interested, but not many. At Dairy Queen, I worked with two grandmothers, Lily and Dana, and if either one of them happened to come down to the break room while I was in it, it didn't matter if I was spending time on the laptop or probably if my finger had just been cut off, it was guaranteed I'd be spending my break looking at pictures of little Skyler or little Tayra or not-so-little Evan, and saying, "yes, uh-huh, he sure is cute" and "oh, yeah, she's getting tall," until it was time to go back to work.

It was probably something that just happened to you, like getting wrinkles or arthritis. You could swear that if you got old and had grandkids, you weren't going to obsess on them and bore everybody to death talking about every little thing they ever did, but then you had them, and it was like getting zombied—you couldn't help yourself.

This lady with the pink streak, Val, was no different. She told me she had five grandchildren, two living on the same street as her in Sherburn, two more in Iowa City, and the other one in San Diego, because their dad was in the military. She was more than happy to answer my questions about which sports they played, what instruments, what they were good at. And I kept going for details.

"Aren't you the curious one?" she asked, but you could tell she was happy about it.

I got her to keep it up for quite a while, her big car rolling along under the darkening sky. I'd never been this far out of Missouri before, and at least so far, I thought Iowa was pretty, as much as it could be without any snow in the middle of winter. There were more hills than I was used to, and even in the clouded dusk, each rise and fall of the land seemed a different shade of brown, purple, or dark green, depending on how the fading light fell on it. We passed a caved-in barn, the paint long gone, with a huge oak growing right out the top. I got out my phone and took a picture.

Best of all, we were far enough away from any city that there weren't any billboards to worry about, digital or otherwise.

But then Val looked in the rearview, touched her own ear, and asked, "Is something wrong with your ear?"

I turned around. Chloe had her hand cupped over her bad ear. She blinked in the direction of the mirror.

"She doesn't speak English," I said, though I'd said that back in Lamoni. "She just got some water in her ear. It'll be okay. She's got medicine for it."

"It seems like it's really hurting her." Val frowned into the rearview. "*¿Te duele el oído? ¿Necesita un médico?*"

For a second, I thought she was speaking Portuguese. I felt like my heart stopped.

Val looked at me and shrugged. "I thought she might understand Spanish," she said. "Some words are similar. You probably speak a little Portuguese, right? You want to ask her if she needs a doctor?"

"She just told me she was okay back at the store." I turned around to nod at Chloe, like she needed convincing. She'd stopped tugging on her ear, and she was smiling out her window like she wanted to prove my point. But I knew it must still be hurting her. I hated to think she had to keep smiling when she was in pain. "She saw a doctor in St. Louis yesterday. He said the medicine would need a couple days to kick in."

I didn't want her to think about that too long. I opened my mouth to say something else before I had any plan what to say.

"Your Spanish is really good," I said. "I've been taking it at school, and I'm okay. But you could be a native speaker."

I meant it in a friendly way—really, I was just trying to get her off the subject of Chloe's ear. But whoa, she didn't take it friendly. She moved her hand through the pink streak and gave me a hard look before turning back to the road.

"I'm a US citizen. A legal citizen. I have all the documentation, right with me."

I shook my head. I hadn't meant anything like that. I wasn't thinking she was a foreigner. She didn't even have an accent.

"I didn't mean . . . ," I started. But she wasn't listening. She took her right hand off the wheel and opened the console between the seats. The console of my mom's car has always been a swamp of melted candy bars and gum wrappers and old lipsticks and pens that were out of ink, and Tess's and even Aunt Jenny's consoles were pretty bad, too. But not this woman's. Her console just had a neat stack of little tissue packets like the one by the gearshift, a roll of breath mints, a folded twenty, and a laminated card that she took out and handed to me.

It was a birth certificate for Valentina Maria Martinez, born in McAllen, Texas, on December 24, 1955, at 3:14 a.m.

"Okay," I said. "But listen. I wasn't saying anything like that."

She tugged the certificate out of my hands and slipped it back into the console. "Well," she said. "Some people start to make assumptions."

I'm not proud of this, but if I'm being honest, I'll say that it did occur to me how helpful it would be to Chloe, and therefore to me, if I could get hold of that birth certificate. Chloe was quite a bit younger than Val, or Valentina, but we could figure out a way to make it work. It would be stealing, but it would be for a good reason, and it wouldn't hurt Val any. She probably had another copy in her purse, or maybe even in the glove compartment, the way she was so touchy about it.

I stretched my neck a little, checking the gas gauge. She had over half a tank left, which was probably enough to get wherever Sherburn was. And even if she did stop for anything, that didn't mean she'd leave me alone in the car for even a second. She knew I'd seen the twenty in there, and she didn't seem particularly dumb.

"That's neat you were born on Christmas Eve," I said. "Or maybe you don't like it."

She tilted her head from side to side. "It has its pros and cons." She smiled like maybe we were friends again. "My mother was born on Christmas Eve, too."

"You're kidding me," I said. "What are the chances?"

"I know," she said. "Even now we think it's funny. She calls me on my birthday and says 'Happy birthday, my daughter!' and I say, 'Happy birthday, my mother!'"

She smiled, and I smiled too. I was thinking her mom must be pretty old, if Val herself was a grandmother. "Does she live close to you?"

"She's in Mexico. In Reynosa." She gave me another glance. "She and my father were both sent back, with two of my sisters. The two who weren't born here."

"Oh," I said. I wasn't sure what else to say. Unless she hated her parents, and also her sisters, that was a pretty sad story. It wasn't like the old days, when you could go back and forth for a visit. There was just that one little spot in San Diego where people could reach through a fence and hold each other's fingers and try to press cheeks through the wire. Right then I knew I wasn't going to take her certificate, even if I had the chance.

"I'm sorry you got separated," I said.

"No reason for you to be sorry." She lifted her chin enough so she was looking down her nose at the road. "We have video calls. It's almost the same. And my parents shouldn't have broken the rules." Her voice was calm, like she was reading something she'd memorized, but her knuckles were white on the steering wheel.

I nodded. I thought about Caleb, how I would feel if I only got to see him through a fence. Video calls might only make me feel farther away, and more lonely. Especially if I was old.

Val glanced in the rearview.

"Either her ear really is bothering her, or your aunt understands more English than you know. I think she's crying."

I turned around. Chloe was turned to the window, her hand shielding her face. I swallowed, trying to guess what had set her off. It seemed unlikely her ear would have gotten that much worse that quickly. If it was the story about Val's parents, well, okay, that was sad. Chloe had to be more careful, though. She wasn't supposed to let on that she understood.

But maybe she had people she was missing too. Maybe she had people she worried she would never see again. If that were true, I couldn't blame her for getting upset, for crying even. It seemed like it probably would be true, and thinking about that, how she probably had at least one person that she missed and worried about the way I would miss and worry about Caleb, I felt my own eyes get hot.

"She understands a little," I said, turning back around. "And she's okay. She just gets sad for other people."

Val nodded like this didn't surprise her. "I love the Portuguese people, the ones I've met. They're so caring." She glanced at me. "Are you all with the church?"

"What church?" I asked. Normally I'd be worried that I was walking right into a let-me-tell-you-about-my-personal-savior trap, but at the moment, I was happy to talk about anything but Portugal.

"Sorry. Catholic." Val squinted, somebody's undimmed headlights bright against her face. "I figured she is, at least, coming from Portugal." She looked up at the mirror. "Catholic?" she said, real slow and loud. I turned around and saw Chloe was facing forward again, but she'd lowered her gaze to her knees.

"Yeah, she is," I said. "And my mom, too. But we're sort of laxed on this side of the ocean."

Val smiled a little, and as soon as she did, I knew it was *lapsed* I meant. But I'd never been Catholic, even a little bit. I was doing my best.

"Well," she said, "I'm Catholic, and you can tell her that gives me great comfort. The Holy Virgin, especially. She helped me when my dad died and I couldn't be there. I do miss my mother. And I worry about her. But I have Mary everywhere, you know? It's like that song." She started to sing, her voice low. "'When I find myself in times of trouble, Mother Mary comes to me.'"

I was so glad I hadn't tried to pretend I was really Catholic, or at least not the serious kind. Because I could hear from the shakiness in Val's voice how much the song meant to her, how much Mother Mary did, and I didn't want to lie to her about it, or pretend I understood what I didn't.

She sniffed, glancing in the mirror. "You know that song. I can tell. You understand Mother Mary."

I turned around to see Chloe nodding. There wasn't a lot else she could have done. But the skin around her eyes was still pink, and just looking at her, how sad she seemed, Muslim or not, you would have thought she truly agreed with Val that that Mother Mary song was the most beautiful song in the world.

We rode in friendly silence for just a few minutes before I

saw a digital billboard up ahead. Even from a distance I could tell it was showing faces, a lot of them all at once. I strained my eyes, searching for Chloe. But as we got closer, I saw there were exactly seven faces, and there were no headscarves, and just one man with a beard. There was the handsome man with the graduation cap. There was the close-up of the boy who'd been sitting with his cat. And five more smiling faces I had to take in without looking away because even though I'd never been to Detroit, I owed them at least that much.

"Those poor souls," Val said. She touched her forehead, her chest, and then each of her shoulders. "Eternal rest grant unto them."

I lowered my head, as that seemed the right thing to do. So I don't know if Val was looking in the mirror or not. But out of the corner of my eye, I saw Chloe's right hand move in a quick cross, forehead to chest, shoulder to shoulder, as if she'd been making crosses her whole Portuguese life, and with enough clear sorrow in her face that you could tell she meant it too.

12

WHEN WE GOT to our hotel room in Sherburn, I shook off my backpack, left my coat on, and told Chloe I was going for a walk.

Right away, the two lines between her eyebrows showed up. "So late?" she asked. "By yourself?"

"Nope." I turned around and looked at the wall behind me. I could hear the television in the next room. "I'm going with one of my many good friends here in Sherburn."

I hoped she got that I was being sarcastic. We'd only been in town for an hour. Val had dropped us off at a diner that was just over a bridge from the interstate exit and cheap hotels, and when our waitress came over to take our order, I told her I liked her Sketchy shirt. After that she was super friendly, coming over to our table when she wasn't busy to tell me she'd seen Sketchy play in Iowa City, and how they sounded better live. She even brought over two free cookies when she was leaving the bill, though Chloe hadn't wanted hers. But other than that, and my brief interaction with the desk clerk downstairs, I hadn't talked to anyone.

Chloe sat on one of the beds and tugged off her hat. Some of her hair stuck straight up from static electricity. "You are sure it is safe?"

I lowered my voice. "Uh. Probably a lot safer than walking around with you."

I wasn't trying to be mean, but that was the truth. Maybe in Iran a girl couldn't go for a walk in the dark by herself, but I walked around after dark by myself all the time, hair showing and everything. I had the pepper spray. I had the disposable phone, too, already free from its plastic packaging and tucked in my pocket, ready to go. But I didn't want to bring up the phone to Chloe, and stress her out even more. I just wanted to go call Tess.

"Just be careful." Chloe yawned, rubbing her neck. The skin beneath her eyes was thin and shadowy, and just then, even with her mostly hennaed hair curling to her shoulders, she looked older than she did in the picture on the billboards, where she didn't have her glasses, and she'd been wearing the headscarf. I didn't know how long ago that picture was taken, but maybe it wasn't that long ago. She might just look older because she'd been hiding in her friends' house in Arkansas, not able to go for any walks or even stand outside, day or night.

She made a groaning sound and tugged on her ear.

"Hey," I said. "There was a CVS over by that diner. You want me to get you more drops? Maybe try a different brand?"

"No," she said. "Thank you. I'll be fine." She closed her eyes and nodded like she was trying to convince herself.

I'd planned to call Tess from the hotel's parking lot. But when I stepped outside, a couple of bundled-up smokers were over in their designated area by a bench and a little sign, and even with the low rumble of the interstate behind the hotel, I worried they'd overhear. I bowed my head to the cold and started walking toward the bridge we'd crossed to get home from the diner. It had a walled-off lane for pedestrians, and as no one else was walking on it, it seemed a good place to make the call.

"She'll answer," I told myself, talking out loud like a crazy person. "She will."

The moon had come out, shining on the river below, which was wide and moving so slowly that the water looked still, like the water of a lake. Cars rolled by behind me, and I pressed the phone tight against my ear.

The first ring. I crossed my fingers and closed my eyes.

She might tell me to leave Chloe right where she was and come home. She might say I'd been doing something crazy. She might say I'd done enough, getting Chloe as far north as I had, and that Caleb would just have to get over the half-fulfilled promise, as he was eleven years old and maybe not clear on what would happen to me if we got caught.

Another ring.

She might even say that what I was doing was wrong. Tess had always been one to defend Muslims, the ones she'd known, at least. But she might remind me that I didn't really know Chloe, or if she was an innocent one or not.

Another ring. I didn't know what time it was in Puerto Rico, if they had Daylight Savings or what.

I heard a click, an intake of breath, and I was so grateful I actually whimpered. But the joke was on me. It was just her outgoing message.

"Don't be difficult." Her recorded voice sounded tinny. *"If you didn't catch me, send a text."*

The beep was so loud it made me flinch, and I hit the wrong button before I ended the call. I didn't want to leave a voice message, but it seemed even riskier to send a text, something her mom might see. I pulled up my coat sleeve and checked Tess's watch. It was only eight thirty.

I tapped in her number again. While I waited for the beep, I kept my gaze on the water, the strip of wavy moonlight shimmering in its center. The disposable phone didn't have a camera, and I'd left my phone that wasn't really a phone back at the hotel. So I did my trick from when I was little, pretending I could take a picture of something by just staring at it then blinking slowly.

"Hey there. It's me." My voice came out wobbly, and I could feel ambush tears pressing up. "Uhhhh . . . sorry to be difficult with the voice mail. I'm in sort of an emergency. I'm out of town." I bounced on my toes to stay warm. "Out of state, actually. I know you don't get home until tomorrow, but don't say anything to Aunt Jenny or anybody. Even your parents. Don't tell anybody I called. I'm okay, but call back at this number as soon as you can. Okay. Hope Puerto Rico's been fun."

I didn't go back to the hotel. I wanted to answer and talk in private as soon as Tess called back, so I slipped in my earbuds and walked the rest of the way across the bridge, trying to look like I knew where I was headed.

Sherburn didn't seem much bigger than Hannibal. The downtown storefronts had striped awnings and names like Fabrics and More! and Shiffenburger's Used Books and Novelties, and also a dessert shop with a hand-painted sign that said their ice cream was MADE FRESH WITH MILK FROM IOWA DAIRIES and DELICIOUS ANYTIME, but apparently not after eight thirty, as it was closed for the night, like almost everything else. The sidewalks were empty, and only the diner and the CVS were still open.

Just as I was walking up to the door of the diner, the waitress who'd given me the free cookies pushed it open and almost bumped into me. She had a letter jacket on over the Sketchy shirt now—but her red hair, pulled back in a ponytail, made her easy to recognize.

"Oh, hey there." She jingled her keys. "Back again?"

"I was just out for a walk, and I got cold," I said. She didn't look much older than I was. I would say seventeen at the most. When she was waiting on us, she'd asked if we were visiting from out of town, and I'd told her that Chloe and I were just passing through. I'd been careful not to lie to her about my age. She wouldn't have believed for a second I was older than she was, fake ID or not.

"Where's your Portuguese aunt?" She tapped her glove to her head. It was yellow and black, like her jacket. "Or your cousin?"

"My mom's cousin. She's back at the hotel." Nosy Nelly, I thought. "She was tired."

"Yeah?" She half-smiled and shimmied her shoulders. "Well. If you're out free for a while . . . you want to go on a Sherburn adventure?"

I didn't know what to say to that. We'd had a good discussion about Sketchy in the diner. But this girl didn't know who I was. Maybe Sherburn, Iowa, was just a really friendly town. The whole time I'd been out walking, no one had honked or whistled or yelled anything gross at me. Still, this girl and I were pretty much strangers.

"What kind of adventure?" I didn't want to be rude.

"There's gonna be a raid." As she passed by me, she tossed her keys up in the air, at least a foot, then caught them with the same glove. "Somebody's been hiding Muslims, right here in town. There's going to be some big action."

I clenched my teeth, working to make my face calm before I turned around. She'd said Muslims. Plural. Not just one. Chloe was fine. She was back at the hotel.

"Where? Where're they hiding them?"

"Not even two miles away. I can't believe it." She was walking backward toward the parked cars. "But my boyfriend follows somebody who knows a hacker, and he says it looks for real. I got my manager to let me off early. My parents are headed down there, too."

Behind me, the engine of a car moved fast and loud down the otherwise quiet street. By the time I turned, I only saw taillights. They were probably racing to the raid as well, trying to get there before the police. That's how it worked—one of Aunt Jenny's news shows did an episode about it. People kept hacking in on the police and then blabbing about it so much that by the time the police got anywhere, they had an audience waiting. The police didn't like it one bit. They kept switching their software and their codes and their passwords, everything, but the hackers kept getting through. Tess said her mom thought it was actually the news stations, and that they were lying whenever they said they'd gotten an anonymous tip. She thought the news stations had spies on the police force, and that the law should come down on this anonymous-tip business hard.

But Aunt Jenny said regular people showing up for arrests was just democracy in action, and if the people weren't listening in and personally showing up to make sure justice was getting served, the police might not do their jobs as well as they should. Aunt Jenny had been disappointed that there'd never been a Muslim raid in Hannibal, but there'd been one for a couple of Mexican families on one side of a duplex. With just a half hour of lead time, something like two hundred people showed up to watch. I guess Aunt Jenny knew about it, but she didn't go. She didn't really have it in for illegal Mexicans as much as the Muslims because she'd once gone to Mexico on a church thing. But her friend Tracy went, and she told Aunt Jenny that somebody had brought a tuba, of all things, to serenade the illegals as they were being led out.

"Want to come? Last chance." The red-haired girl was already getting into the driver's seat of a little black car. "I promise I'll bring you right back. I'm Sophie, by the way."

Like she knew me. Because we were about the same age and because we both liked Sketchy, and because I more or less looked and sounded like her. She didn't wonder for a second if I was someone she should trust.

Sherburn didn't seem to have a lot of stop signs or stoplights, which was good, as whenever we came to one, the girl, Sophie, just slowed and looked to see if anyone was coming—if not, she rolled on through. She drove over a set of railroad tracks without braking, and the car went airborne for a second. She laughed when we hit the ground.

"Sorry," she said, like she didn't mean it. "I do that every morning when I'm late for school. I have to be there at seven when there's track practice."

I held tight to the handle above my door. "So how many Muslims are these people hiding?"

"My boyfriend heard this guy's got like seven of them, right in his house." She turned to me, her blue eyes wide. "Sounds crazy, I know, but they just caught a woman in Ames with ten in her basement, though I think some of them were Guatemalans." She let go of the steering wheel long enough to tug up her ponytail with both hands. "It's like my nutty aunt Kate with her cats. We're looking for Quaker Road, by the way. Oh! There it is." She slowed the car, barely, and cranked the wheel to the right. "That was all just the other night. There were two more raids in Iowa City today, and something like four in Minneapolis. Cause of Detroit, you know. Everybody's motivated."

"Uh-huh." I kept my face turned toward the window so she wouldn't see that I had my hand pressed tight over my mouth. She was talking about these raids like there was nothing sad about them, like they weren't the end of the road for some people. It would be the end for someone tonight. Someone like Chloe. I hoped the hackers were wrong about the raid that was coming, and really, it seemed like they might be. Quaker Road was lined by flat-roofed, one-story houses. None of them looked big enough to hide seven people, at least not comfortably, for very long.

"Did they say who was hiding them?"

"Some weird old guy. One of his neighbors noticed he was all of a sudden carrying in way more groceries than usual, bags and bags every few days. She asked him what he was up to, since he'd lived alone after his wife died. He said he'd been having company, relatives visiting. But she lived across the street from him, and she never saw anybody coming or going except for him. That's what tipped her off."

I rolled my lips in. He should have brought in the bags at night, maybe. That's what I would have done. But that might have been even more suspicious. Really, there was no way to convince myself that I'd been too careful to be in his shoes. Whatever he'd done, it wasn't as risky as hitching through two different states with Chloe and telling everyone she was Portuguese. We'd just been lucky. So far.

We crested a hill, and Sophie squinted. "Okay. Here we go. This is it."

Up ahead, a floodlight was mounted to the top of a lime-green van with *NEWS YOU CAN USE* and *CHANNEL 4* in black on the side door. The van was parked in the middle of the street, and the curb on either side was lined with cars and trucks.

Sophie pulled in behind a powder-blue SUV with a bumper sticker that read *PROUD PARENT OF AN SMS HONOR STUDENT* and a license plate that read *#BLESSED*.

I took out the phone and checked the screen. No calls. Tess would call back, though. Any minute. Of course she would.

"You okay?" Sophie asked. Her door was already open, and she looked at me over her shoulder. "Sorry I was driving so fast. I don't want to miss it."

I took that as a cue that I should put away the phone and hustle out. It would look pretty strange, even suspicious, if I said now that I just wanted to stay in the car. But I wasn't sure why I'd come along, what it was I wanted to see. It felt like the time my mom woke me and Caleb up in the middle of the night because the house down the street was on fire. All the people had already gotten out, and even their dog was safe, but everything they owned was burning up or getting soaked by the hoses, and it was awful to stand out there in humid dark, breathing in the smoke, the flames popping and cracking while the family stayed over by the fire trucks breathing through oxygen masks and probably hating all of us for standing around and watching like their misery was a movie. Nothing in me had wanted to stop watching, though. Even Caleb had just stood there, openmouthed in his pajamas. It was like our eyes and ears and noses needed to take it in, maybe to prove to our brains that something like that could happen to a house, any house, including ours.

I hurried over to the sidewalk, falling in next to Sophie. We jogged past parked cars, and also a woman on her front porch across the street, talking on her phone. When she saw us, she gave us a dirty look, so I guessed she wasn't the neighbor who turned the man in. *I don't like this either,* I wanted to say, and I wished there was some way she could know it, like I could shine some secret light at her so she would know I was on her side. If she was on my side. All she did was go back in her house.

As we got closer, I could see that the news van's floodlight was focused on a red-brick house's front door, so bright it made a circle of daylight. Whoever was inside had turned out all the lights except for a line of red and green Christmas lights blinking along the front gutter. An upright wagon wheel, surrounded by white rocks, had been put in the middle of the front yard for decoration, and maybe thirty people stood between it and the van—not as many as I thought there would be—though I could hear the slamming of more car doors behind me. The people already on the lawn were mostly silhouettes, some of them shining flashlights into the house's dark windows.

I slowed my steps, holding my breath. I knew the people inside, whoever they were, must be scared out of their minds, watching the flashlights shine through the curtains. If Caleb were here, he'd run up and tell everyone to stop. He'd tell them all to get away, and to take their flashlights with them.

And I'd have to drag him away, with maybe my hand over

his mouth. Because we would be very much outnumbered.

One flashlight started moving toward us, bouncing along, and then I could see it was held by a tall, lean boy in a denim jacket. When he got to Sophie, he put his arm around her and kissed the top of her red hair.

"We didn't miss it?" she asked. "They're not here?"

"No. But what took you so long?" He gave me a friendly nod. "Who's this?"

"A stray I picked up." She winked, half-nuzzled into the armpit of his jean jacket. "Amy, this is Jayden. Jayden, this is Amy. She's just tagging along."

I couldn't quite pull off a smile. I didn't belong here. I tried to think of myself as some kind of spy. But a spy for who? Who would I report to? Caleb? Chloe? The lady who'd been on the phone?

"Cool," Jayden said, like he really meant it, though he turned back to Sophie fast. "Listen. Your parents are over there, sort of close to the driveway. They got interviewed, so they'll probably be on TV." He turned and waved behind him. "I'll just wait to let you see their set-up."

"Oh God." Sophie winced, her hand over her eyes. "I don't even want to know."

"No, you don't. But you will soon." He took hold of the sleeve of her letter jacket and tugged her toward the cluster of people in front of the house. She turned around and grabbed the sleeve of my coat, so we were a little chain as we moved through. I kept my head down and said "excuse me" a lot, and everybody was polite about stepping back so we could pass. A woman holding a little boy on her hip told me she liked my flag pin.

"And you're wearing it for real, not as sacrilege," she added, hitching the child higher on her hip. "The neighbor said this son-of-a-b puts the American flag out by his front door every morning. Takes it down at sunset."

"The nerve," somebody else said. "Using that as a cover."

I kept my eyes on the back of Sophie's head.

"Do they think he's in there now?" It was Sophie, asking Jayden.

"They're all in there. People were already watching the back of the house and all around the sides when I got here. And the lights went out about ten minutes ago."

"Except for the Christmas lights," somebody said. "On a timer in January. Tacky."

Someone tapped on my shoulder. I turned around to see a tall, bird-necked woman wearing a lot of makeup and holding a microphone. She smiled, but her eyes stayed big.

"Hello," she said, her voice friendly and sort of musical, like my kindergarten teacher that I'd loved. "I'm Ava Montgomery with Channel 4 News. Would you mind if I asked you a few questions about how you're feeling right now?"

I shook my head and turned away so my hair covered my cheek. I didn't want Aunt Jenny seeing me on television. I didn't want anyone seeing me here.

"Honey? Honey? We're over here." A woman in a puffy green coat, her moussed-up hair the same red as Sophie's, was sitting in a straight-backed lawn chair in the yellowed grass at the far edge of the driveway. A man wearing earmuffs sat next to her, also in a lawn chair, a pair of binoculars resting on his belly. They both had flashlights held between their knees, and even though they were both smiling, their underlit faces looked kind of horror movie.

"Oh God, Mom. Lawn chairs? Are you kidding me?"

"Well, excuse me if I want to be comfortable." The mom glanced at her phone. "We've been out here for almost forty-five minutes." She looked at her husband and rolled her eyes. "To protect and to serve, my foot."

"It doesn't look like a safe place to sit," Sophie said. "What if the police drive right over you when they come?"

"Then I'll sue."

The dad laughed, blowing on his hands. "They aren't gonna drive up on the grass, Soph. They'll probably just walk up so they don't get blocked in." He smiled at me. "Who's your friend?"

"This is Amy."

Her mom gave me a worried look. "You want to sit, honey? We've got an extra chair in the car. You look like you're not feeling well."

"I'm okay," I said. "Thanks."

She didn't seem convinced, and I couldn't blame her. Even

I can't make every lie smooth. I was thinking I didn't want her smiling at me and asking if I needed a chair when she was the kind of person who'd bring a lawn chair to something like this, like she was watching fireworks in a city park. Maybe she was being nice to me, even though she didn't know me, because I looked and talked the way she did. But what she was doing right now was no good. And the standing people weren't any better. I could understand being scared and mad about Detroit. But nobody I'd just walked past looked especially scared, and they didn't seem mad so much as pumped up, like fans at a football game. Fans of the team about to win.

"At least you're dressed appropriately." The mom clicked her tongue. "Jayden, I'm getting cold just looking at you. You need an actual coat on a night like this. Not just that jacket."

Jayden smiled, though he had his arms crossed tight in front of his chest. "I didn't think we'd be out here this long."

"No joke," somebody said. "Where the hell are they?"

"I don't know if they're even coming." It was another voice behind me, a man's, and he sounded a little madder than everyone else. I didn't turn around.

"They better. And they better get here soon. I'll go in there myself. I've got a sister in Detroit. Or more the suburbs. But I'll go in there myself."

I lowered my head in the darkness. These people around me must have known what they were saying didn't make any sense.

If whoever was inside had anything to do with what happened in Detroit, there wouldn't be just a bunch of random people standing around, or sitting in lawn chairs, and waiting on the local police. There'd be a freaking SWAT team here. Helicopters. Serious military. And I didn't think Sophie would have beaten them here from the diner, even if her manager let her off early.

"I'm tired of waiting," the man behind me said. "Are you tired of waiting, people? Who's with me? Who's with me?"

Plenty of them were, it turned out, judging from all the clapping and hooting. So I don't know if he was the one who threw the rock. I don't even know if it was a rock. I just heard the shatter of glass, and the louder whooping and clapping that came after. Jayden aimed his flashlight at the shards of glass in the front window. A white curtain fluttered behind it. "Somebody's got good aim," he said.

"Thank you," a woman's voice said, and people laughed and clapped some more.

The light behind the front door switched on, and everyone went quiet. It was one of those old-fashioned doors with the three little rectangles of glass for decoration. But the glass was glazed so you couldn't see in.

"Open the door, traitor! You coward!"

The door opened, as if the person behind it had just been waiting for the command. A big, wide-shouldered man with a white buzz cut stood in the doorway, squinting into the floodlight, and because of the way the light made a circle around the door, he looked like he was in a spotlight, up on an old-fashioned stage. He was clean shaven, with a bit of a wattle under his chin and a paunch under his sweatshirt. He definitely didn't look Muslim. He looked like one of those old guys who used to hang out in front of the doughnut shop in Joplin, always looking grouchy and chewing tobacco and yelling at the high school kids not to smoke. He held the door wide with his left arm, and he kept his right hand tucked in the front pocket of his sweatshirt like he couldn't be bothered to take it out.

"What's wrong with you people?" He leaned out of the doorway, the red and green Christmas lights reflecting off his forehead. "I'm a veteran! I fought for this country, which is more than I can say for you idiots. Get off my property! You're vultures! Cowards in a mob! You make me sick! You want a piece of me, you come get it!"

I don't know if there was any right thing he could have said just then, but that was definitely the wrong one, as more people started yelling back at him, and some of them moved closer, like they were all saying yes, they certainly did want a piece of him, and they'd be glad to come get it, thank you very much. I could hear sirens in the distance, still faint, and I wished they would come faster. I knew the police weren't exactly going to give the old man, or anybody inside, flowers when they showed up. But it would be better for everyone if they got here soon.

"Who you got in there with you?" somebody yelled. "Who you hiding?"

The old man shook his head and made a face like he was going to spit. "Innocent people," he said. "Including women and children. One of them has a condition, and needs to be where he can get medicine. Have some decency, people."

"That's a laugh," somebody said. "You talking about decency."

I heard another shatter of glass, but before I could see where it came from, the man started yelling again. "I said get off my property! You don't want to mess with me tonight." When he took his hand out from his pocket, he had a pistol in it. He held it out in front of him, pointed straight up.

I took a step back, my eyes on the gun, the shiny silver of it glinting in the floodlight. But almost everyone else moved forward, and all around me I heard *clack, clack, clack*, a chorus of clacks, some quiet, some loud. My eyeballs moved to the right. Just a few inches from my shoulder was the kind of gun that didn't look like it shot bullets so much as sprayed them, and it was held steady and aimed at the old man by hands wearing red fingernail polish. On my left, somebody else had just a regular gun. Sophie's mom had stood up from her chair, her face all business now. She had a green gun, the exact same color as her jacket, pointed at him as well. I could still hear more clacking behind me.

I dropped to my knees and crouched forward, my hands on the back of my head. The asphalt of the driveway was hard and cold, but I pressed my forehead against it, wishing I could burrow right into it. I thought of the little boy on his mother's hip, but I was too scared to turn around. My lips moved without me meaning them to. *I love you, Caleb. I love you, Tess. It's okay, Mom. I'm sorry, Chloe.*

"Freeze!" New voices. Running footsteps. "Drop your weapons! Drop your weapons!" More shouting. "Drop it! Drop it!"

I didn't think my body could tense up any more, but when the shot fired, it did. The boom of it shuddered through me. I tried to make myself take up negative space, to pull my head down into my neck and my feet up under my butt, so I was crouched up the way Caleb used to sleep when he was a baby in his crib. My hands went to my ears, then back to my head. I heard a thud, and then another.

"Suspect down. I repeat, suspect down. Weapons down, people. Weapons down."

A woman behind me yelled, "Way to go!" And then there was more clapping, more hooting.

"Bull's-eye." It was the guy from before, the one who said he hadn't been kidding.

I lifted my forehead, my chin scraping against the asphalt. I was eye level with the backs of someone's tennis shoes, but when I tilted my head just a little to the side, I could see the old man was lying in his doorway now, the thick sole of one of his shoes facing me. Bright blood was smeared on his white door in the shape of a sloppy number seven.

A police officer crouched over the man while four more officers, weapons raised, moved past him into the house. Six more officers stood in the yard, facing the crowd. They held long black shields in front of their bodies, though I could see the tips of their guns over the tops of the shields. They wore dark glasses, maybe because of the floodlight, so you couldn't see their faces. But some of them must have been scared, facing all those people with guns.

"Step back, people. We're your police force. Let us do our job. Please keep all weapons down."

The tennis shoes in front of me started to move backward, and I had to sit up fast so the person who owned them wouldn't trip over me and maybe accidentally shoot somebody's head off. But when I tried to stand, my knees didn't work. It was like they didn't have bones in them, nothing to hold them upright. I might as well have tried to stand on my hair.

"You okay, honey?" It was Sophie's mom. She was sitting in her lawn chair again, leaning forward, her flashlight shining on her own face. She'd put away her gun. "Scared you, didn't it? Jayden, help Sophie's friend up, would you?"

"Oh, no, I'm okay," I said. My knees would have to go solid again. They would have to. I didn't want Jayden touching me.

I didn't want any of them touching me. I imagined my knees solidifying, the jelly of them turning hard and strong. I raised one knee, put my weight on it, and willed myself up to my feet. I wouldn't look at the old man sprawled out in his doorway, the Christmas lights still blinking over him. I didn't need to. The man behind me had said "bull's-eye." That meant he was dead.

And I didn't want to see the Muslims come out. I didn't want to see their faces and think of Chloe, and I didn't want to hear what people would yell at them. If I did, my knees might give out again, and I needed them to stay strong, strong enough for me to move out of the crowd slowly and politely, saying "excuse me" without sounding particularly upset, so I could get away from the news van's light and slip into the darkness, away from all of them, as far as I could run.

I don't know if I've ever run that fast, that far. I ignored the cold air, sharp in my lungs, and the hardness of the pavement beneath my boots. Sweat cooled and itched under my coat, but I didn't stop. I could only hear my own breath, moving fast and strong in and out of me. I almost didn't hear the phone when it buzzed. At first, I thought it was a car or a motorcycle coming up from behind. But then I knew. I took the phone out of my pocket and looked at the screen, as if I needed to check the number, as if anyone else in the world would be calling this disposable phone. My heart was still pounding, and I felt sweaty and cold at the same time, but seeing the number, so familiar, made me smile while I gasped for breath.

I didn't answer it, though. I knew I couldn't. As Sophie had said, people were motivated, and now I understood what that meant. This wasn't a game. That man was dead, partly because he'd gotten out a gun, but mostly because he'd been hiding people. I couldn't bring Tess into this kind of mess. Once I told her where I was, and what I was doing, if she didn't turn me in, she'd be in trouble too.

She was a good friend, calling me back like I knew she would. So I'd be a good friend to her.

I touched the phone against my forehead, letting it buzz just one more time before I set it down on the pavement in front of me. I looked up at a streetlight as I brought the heel of my boot down hard on it once, and then again, and again, until the ringing went dead.

Chloe met me at the door, her hand in her hair.

"Where have you been?" She locked the door behind me. "Why is your face red? You've been running? You were gone so long. I was worried." She turned to the side, pointing at the television. "There was a raid on a house, right in this town. Sarah-Mary, they killed the man who was hiding them. They shot him in his doorway!"

"I heard," I said, shaking out of my coat, which had turned clammy against my skin. I didn't want to tell her I meant I'd actually heard the shot, and then the thud of his body against the door, and then another thud when he hit the ground. She was wearing the white sweatshirt and wide-legged pants again, dressed for bed. Her eyes were wide behind her glasses, and she crossed her arms like she was cold.

"They took everyone else away." She went over to the edge of one of the beds, nodding at the television. "He had two families in his house, three children. They were crying when they came out, the younger two holding their mother's coat. Someone threw something at her. At a mother, with crying children!"

She was sort of yelling and whispering at the same time, which was good, as the hotel walls were so thin. I had to pee, pretty badly in fact, but I could tell she wanted me to see what she meant, and she wanted me to see it now. I went over to the edge of the bed and sat next to her, wiping sweat from my forehead. The news van must have pulled back the floodlight, or switched to a different one, because the spotlight shining on just the doorway was gone, and now you could see the whole front of the house, and the man lying dead in his doorway, though now there was a blue sheet pulled over him. The Christmas lights were still blinking, and the garage door was open now, showing the back end of a pickup truck. A younger man with his head lowered was walking out on one side of the truck, his hands behind his back, an officer close behind him. The crowd, which you couldn't see, clapped and whistled. The bottom of the screen read *CHANNEL 4 EXCLUSIVE: ONE DEAD, SEVEN*

APPREHENDED IN SHERBURN RAID.

"They're just bringing them out now?"

She shook her head. "They keep replaying it." She held a palm in front of the screen and squinted like she was trying to block the sun.

"Maybe stop watching," I said. I said it in a nice way, but when she didn't move, I reached up to the bureau for the remote and turned off the power. She couldn't do those people any good, no matter how many times she watched. And I didn't want to see the kids coming out and holding their mother's coat.

Even with the TV off, she stayed still and quiet, staring at the black screen. I swallowed. The back of my throat felt raw from running.

"I'm going to Canada too," I said. "For good." I didn't know if she'd be surprised or not, or if she wouldn't believe me. I didn't care if she believed me or not. I believed me. I'd decided when I was running, and I hadn't changed my mind. Even the caption on the news was like a scoreboard. A win for the home team.

She turned to me and shook her head.

"No," she said, like I was a little kid. "No, you're not going to Canada."

That was irritating. I know some people say they're going to move to Canada every time they get mad at the government, like it's some big threat that's supposed to impress you. But nobody ever really does it. At least I've never known anyone who has.

255

People start saying it after every election, no matter which way it goes, and then four years later, what do you know, all those would-be emigrants are still down here complaining about everything. I knew that was irritating too.

But I meant what I'd said. I wanted to get out. I kept hearing the *clack, clack, clack* of those guns coming out all around me. And I kept picturing the old man, and the bottom of one of his shoes as he was lying there, and the bloody seven on the door. He was a veteran, he'd said. He'd said they didn't want to mess with him. But they did. And they'd won.

"Uh, yes I am," I said. I didn't know much about Canada. It was supposed to be cleaner. It was definitely colder. There weren't nearly as many guns. I was sure they had their problems. But if that's where people were trying to escape to, it must be a gentler place.

"You can't go to Canada," she said.

I didn't like her tone, like she knew something or even everything that I didn't.

"If they let you stay, they'll let me stay," I said, though I didn't know that was true. I wasn't Muslim, and that was a big plus on this side of the border. But the Canadians had a whole different way of thinking about it. They might be more okay with letting in a Muslim who could teach electrical engineers than somebody like me, who hadn't finished high school, who only knew how to fry onion rings and make change and clean bathrooms. "I can do whatever I want," I added, because that was really the point I wanted to make.

"You won't go, then." She looked back over her shoulder at me. "Because of your brother."

Shame moved over me, like a wave of heat. I'd forgotten about him. I really had. It was just for a little bit, and I was tired, and still sweaty and scared. But even forgetting about him for a little bit, no matter what, was too long. I sat up, rubbing my palms against the thin bedspread like I was trying to wipe something off. Now that we'd turned off our television, we could hear another television through the wall again. I heard applause and laughter, the nice kind. They weren't watching the news.

"You would never do it," she said. "I saw you with him. You love him." She ducked her chin and looked at me over the top of her glasses. "And you said your mother is only a sort-of mother. Your brother needs you, I think."

I crossed my legs, as I still had to pee. I didn't nod, or even say anything, but of course we both knew she was right. That was probably why a lot of people didn't actually move to Canada, even the ones who would be allowed. I mean, not because of Caleb. But because of whoever it was they loved. No matter how mad they got, or how scared, the people they loved were all down here.

"And that's why you need to go home," she said, in the same know-it-all voice. "You need to go be with your brother. And you need to be home, and safe. I'm so thankful for all you have done, Sarah-Mary. But in the morning, I will give you enough money for your bus ticket home. We will go separate ways."

I snapped my head up. She'd said it like it was a done deal, like the whole decision was hers. "I'm not going home tomorrow," I said. "How would you get by without me?"

"They shot that man," she said, like that answered my question. "They shot him dead. I am putting you at risk. And you are a child. I cannot do this."

That was pretty irritating, having her call me a child. I mean technically, I was a minor, okay. But I didn't feel like one. I didn't think I'd been acting like one, either. I would think she'd give me credit for that.

She frowned, shaking her head. "Do not take offense. What I mean is, if something happened to you, I wouldn't forgive myself." Her eyes went shiny, but she looked away. "I've hurt enough people already."

I stared at her, surprised.

Chloe winced. "No. Not like that. Please."

"What do you mean, then? Who'd you hurt?" I leaned away from her, watching her face.

"I meant my son. And my husband."

It took a second for her words to make sense. "You got a son?"

She sniffed, smiling a little, though she started crying at the same time. "Jahan. He turned six in November. Would you like to see a picture?"

I nodded. She got up and went over to one of the bureau

drawers, where she'd put her bag. I was expecting her to show me a little picture, but she came back with a frame the size of a magazine.

"This is at our house in Jonesboro," she said. "My friend Yasmin took it. Jahan is very happy because the oven was not working and so we ordered pizza."

It was a picture of Chloe and a man and a little boy, the three of them leaning in together. The boy was in the middle, smiling, his chin in his hands, his elbows on the table. Chloe and the man were sort of leaned in on either side of him, their heads almost touching. They weren't smiling as hard as the boy, but their eyes looked happy, like they'd both just gotten done laughing about something. Chloe wore a green headscarf with little white flowers on it. The man, her husband, had one of those little dimples in his chin, and he actually looked a whole lot like my old science teacher Mr. Borland, which was weird, because Mr. Borland wasn't Iranian. I didn't think so, at least.

"That's nice," I said. The frame was white wood, smooth against my fingers. "Your son's cute." He was. He had the same greenish eyes as Chloe, and he had a little bump on the bridge of his nose. "Where are they now?"

She put her hand flat against the front of her sweatshirt. "Toronto."

That was good. I was worried she'd say Nevada.

"How'd you hurt them?"

She opened her mouth, then closed it like she wanted to

think some more. She still had the frame against her chest.

"For years, even when Jahan was just a baby, my husband wanted to leave, to find jobs in Canada. He was scared for Jahan, scared for all of us. I told him he was overreacting, though when the registry came, I was nervous as well. But even then, I was not so afraid. We had friends, colleagues who I knew would protect us." She shrugged. "But in September, we heard rumors about the buses, the plans for them. I said we didn't know if it was true or not. I still wasn't ready to leave. I kept saying wait, it won't get worse. It will get better. We have to make it better. Baraz said it was my choice, but he'd go without me, right away, and he'd take Jahan." She started to raise her hand to her ear but then stopped and put it back in her lap. "My plan was to finish out the semester. I still believed I was in a position to help. I was writing, posting pictures of people I knew, friends who were suddenly gone." She shook her head. "I didn't want to just give up. I loved my job. I loved where we lived. I loved biking to campus. I loved our cats, two brothers. I loved our house." She laughed like she was embarrassed to say she'd loved a house. "I loved this country. I thought of it as mine. I wanted to fight for it, for what it is supposed to be." She shrugged. "And then they sealed the borders."

I wiped my forehead again. I could already feel the soreness in my legs settling in, my muscles tight and tired from running. I didn't think of myself as a weak person, but here was Chloe talking about how she loved this country too much to leave, and too much to just give up on it. And here I was, born and raised here, and after one bad night—a really bad night—I'd wanted to get up and go.

She winced again, tugging on her ear.

"It's not any better, is it? Those drops aren't helping?"

She shook her head. She got up and put the frame back in her bag. After she closed the drawer, she leaned against the wall, her arms crossed again.

"I'm glad they're safe. I'm so grateful for this. But I was foolish. And selfish. Not a good mother. And because of that, for the past four months, my son has been without me." Pink splotches shaped like jigsaw pieces moved up from the collar of her sweatshirt to her chin. "I can't imagine that he is not hurting, with me not being there to tuck him in, to kiss his forehead in the morning. And I don't know how I will get to him again. But if I don't find a way, I will have failed him. I already feel he shouldn't forgive me. And I miss my husband so much."

The television in the next room had gone silent. I pointed at the wall to remind Chloe that even now, when she was crying, we had to be quiet.

"You'll get up there," I whispered, like I knew all about it. But I sort of did. I mean, my God. She had to get there. "And your son'll forgive you. He'll just be happy you're there, whenever you get there."

"You don't know this." She sniffed. "You don't know any of this."

That was half true. I didn't know how we'd get across the

border. And I didn't know her son. But I knew that if either Caleb or I had a mom who'd just made one mistake and then actually felt bad about it, we'd take her back in a second.

"Well," I said, "the only way for you to get there is if I stay with you. So that's what I'm going to do. I mean, we've made it this far."

I got up to go to the bathroom, one, because I still had to go, and two, to show her that was the end of the conversation. She really should have understood at this point that she couldn't tell me what to do.

Before I closed the door, I thought of something. I took a few steps back toward her so I could keep my voice low. "Your real name's Sadaf?"

She nodded. She was still leaning against the wall.

"I'm saying it right?"

She nodded again.

"Okay," I said. "Thanks."

I'd still call her Chloe in my head, as I didn't want to mess up in front of other people. But I would know her real name later, when she was safe and gone, and just a memory in my head.

13

IN THE MORNING, I opened my eyes to see Chloe curled in a fetal position on top of her made-up bed. She had her hand pressed to her ear.

"It's worse?" I asked, sitting up. Both Tess's watch and the clock on the nightstand agreed it was after nine. But the room had the look of early dawn, with only a strip of daylight glowing gray between the heavy curtains.

She squinted at me like she didn't hear. She was already dressed, even wearing her coat. I pointed at my own ear, and she nodded.

I got up and went to the window to pull the curtains back. But there wasn't a lot of light to let in—the sky over Sherburn was a white fog, as far as I could see. In the parking lot, just beneath our window, a man blew on his hands before lifting a suitcase into the trunk of a car.

"You should let me look at it," I said, turning back to Chloe. She didn't move. I walked around my bed to hers and switched on the lamp above her pillow. I didn't know when she'd gotten dressed, or how long she'd been awake. She looked like she'd combed her hair. But the coffee maker by the television still had its cord unplugged and tied in a neat bundle.

"Hey," I said. "Let me see." Either she didn't want to, or she was having trouble hearing—I had to touch her coat sleeve to get her to move her hand and pull back her hair. When she did, I gasped, which probably wasn't the most tactful thing I could have done. But her whole ear was bright red, and so was the skin all around it, going down to her neck. I put the back of my hand to her forehead. Hot like a stove.

"It feels as if . . ." Her voice was quiet. "It feels as if there was a sharpened pencil placed just in my ear, and then someone kicked it, as hard as they could, farther in."

I sat on the edge of my bed. I'd thought today would be like yesterday, in that we'd just keep getting rides, getting closer and closer to the border. That was all the plan I had. But that wouldn't work now. She couldn't stand out in the cold to wait for a ride, not with a fever. And definitely not with a pencil kicked in her ear.

But it didn't seem like the kind of thing we could just wait out, either. If she had some kind of infection, nothing we could buy at a drugstore would help, and it probably wouldn't clear up on its own. It would just get worse. It seemed like Chloe probably knew all that. And she must know that there was no way for her to see a doctor, unless she turned herself in.

"What do you want to do?" I asked.

She sat up slowly, putting her feet on the carpet opposite mine. She was wearing her fluffy pink socks, and her big toe poked through one of them. She looked at the nightstand, where she'd left her book, her eyeglasses resting on top of it.

"I want to keep going," she said.

When we got to the gas station, she picked out medicine with a box that said it was extra-strength for relieving pain and also fever. She took two before we went outside, and they did seem to help a little. She stopped holding her ear, and she sometimes smiled at people as they went by. But from the side, I could see her jaw was clenched.

I was hopeful we wouldn't be waiting for long. We'd found a little spot between the store's front door and the propane tanks that was mostly out of the wind, and also hidden from the cashier's view by a poster in the window advertising lottery tickets. It said *YOUR LUCKY DAY?* in big white letters, which seemed like it might be good advertising for us, but maybe also some kind of mean joke.

We'd been outside for maybe an hour, cold and quiet, when it started to snow. Tiny flakes fell straight down, and they didn't melt when they hit the pavement, or the sleeves of my coat, or Chloe's hat, or my mittens on either side of our sign. And so after maybe twenty minutes, I knew we probably looked like those cows you see standing out in fields sometimes in winter, with whatever part of them facing the wind getting coated with snow, and still they just keep standing there, not even bothering to shake themselves off.

But I didn't know what else we could do. Most people didn't even look at us, and the ones who did kept moving. I couldn't blame the men, as the sign clearly stated we wanted a ride from a woman. But all the women kept walking by, too. Every time a woman walked by, I stared at her like I could use ESP to let her know that we were really having a hard time, and that the person beside me was in pain, and that neither of us was anyone to be afraid of. It didn't work. Most of them kept their faces pushed down into their scarves, so all I saw was the tops of their snow-dusted hair or hats.

Another hour went by. I say that like it was nothing, but it didn't feel that way when it was happening. My nose started to run, and I could hear Chloe sniffing too. It got hard to keep trying to smile at people who weren't even looking up, so after a while, I just watched the snow thicken on the oval roof over the pumps, and also along the cracks in the pavement. I kept thinking, okay, any minute now, somebody'll stop, because that was what had happened the day before. But I knew that really, just because we'd gotten lucky yesterday didn't mean there was any rule that said of course we'd be lucky again.

"Tell me when you need to go in," I said, my voice low, my lips barely moving. I was on the side of Chloe's good ear, but I didn't know if she'd heard me. I leaned in a little. "If you're hungry or you just need a break."

She nodded once, but that was all. I guessed she was thinking the same thing I was—that if we went inside for even ten minutes, that might be the exact time when the one person who would give us a ride walked by. We couldn't afford to be babies. I couldn't even let Chloe go sit inside while I stayed out with the sign, as somebody might come up and try to talk with her, or they might look at her more carefully if she was on her own. When we'd been inside buying the medicine, we'd both seen the front page of the local paper, with its picture of the dead man lying in the doorway of his house. There was also a picture of one of the Muslim women being led out in handcuffs with the two kids holding on to her coat. You could see the face of one of the kids, and how scared he looked, so maybe the photographer was trying to shame people. Then again, Chloe had said this was the woman someone had thrown something at, so at least one person wasn't shamed at all.

"I'm still doing okay," I said, as if Chloe, or anyone, had asked me. I dusted snow from my hood and locked eyes with an Asian woman hurrying into the store with her little boy. The boy had on a red snowsuit, but the woman just wore leggings and a sweatshirt that said *Gimme a slice! Big Al's Pizza.* She gave me a tight-lipped smile, but that was all.

I shook my head, watching the vapor of my breath float up into the gray air. It seemed to me a body could only take so much, whatever the mind was telling it. I mean, there was no guarantee we'd get a ride at all, not even if we stayed out here until dark. And that wasn't the worst of it. The police could come by for gas at any time. Or somebody might get weirded out by us and call them. I didn't even know if it was legal to hitchhike in Iowa.

We had to do something, and I didn't mean just hoping or praying. It seemed to me we had to start acting like this was the emergency that it was.

I looked down at our sign. It was holding up in the snow okay, as I'd gone over it with the clear tape again, and the ink hadn't run at all. I tugged off one of my mittens, so I could crease the poster straight across the middle. Then I held up the sign so the part about wanting a ride with a woman was upside down and facing me.

Chloe looked at me from the corner of her eye. I shrugged and turned away. We'd be okay. It seemed pretty clear to me, standing out there in the cold and sniffing my nose every five seconds, that you couldn't just rule out a whole group of people, even if they made up the overwhelming majority of killers and rapists. All I'd done just now was double our chances for a ride. I'd also at least quadrupled them for getting us chopped up in little pieces. I tried not to think about that.

And for a while, it seemed like I hadn't done anything. It turned out that men, at least the ones stopping for gas or snacks in Sherburn, Iowa, that day, weren't that excited about being included in our invitation or my hopeful smiles. In fact, most of them just seemed more likely not to look at either one of us after they'd read our sign. One man paused to cough something serious up from his throat so he could spit it on the curb, not that far from my feet. He didn't look at us either.

"I hate this town," I whispered. I didn't know if Chloe heard me or not.

But maybe ten minutes later, she nudged me and nodded over to one of the pumps. I followed her gaze to a tall, slender man leaning against an SUV, squinting at us, or maybe at our sign. He wore a dark peacoat with a red wool scarf knotted at the collar. Nothing about him seemed particularly worrisome. But he was a white man, and he looked like he got regular haircuts and shaved his face every morning. So as far as being a serial killer, he checked all the boxes.

I smiled at him. That felt weird, trying to give a smile that would win him over at the very time when I was trying to figure out if he looked like bad news himself.

He started to walk over. I turned to Chloe. "Nudge me if you get a bad feeling," I murmured. "If you don't like him, we won't get in."

"Hi," he said, his chin raised, though he was a good foot

taller than I was. He wasn't wearing a hat, and the snowflakes rested unmelted on top of his curly dark hair. "Let's hear your sales pitch." He glanced over my shoulder. "Make it snappy."

Kind of rude, I thought. But I launched into the story of how Chloe was my mother's cousin visiting from Portugal, and how we were headed up to see my mom in Minneapolis. I did my best to be as snappy as possible, all the while trying to be charming and just pathetic enough, too. I thought I did pretty well, especially considering my nose was running and I couldn't feel my toes anymore. He looked like he was listening close, and his eyes moved over both of us. But he didn't seem to be doing it in a creeper way. Whatever Chloe thought of him, she didn't give me a nudge.

He tilted his head at our sign. "What part of Minneapolis are you headed to?"

"Downtown," I said. It seemed likely Minneapolis would have one. "But any exit would be fine. We'll just call my mom to come get us when she gets off work."

I wasn't sure how that answer would go over, but he nodded like it made sense. "Listen," he said. "Do you know how to change a subject? Like in conversation?"

I blinked. "Yeah. I do it all the time."

"Then that'll be your job. My brother and I are headed to Saint Paul, and we can detour over to Minneapolis if you want a ride with us. But you've got to change the subject when he gets

270

going. Okay? That's the deal. That's how you pay for the ride."

I looked over his shoulder at his SUV. No one was in the passenger seat. His brother must still be in the store, or using the bathroom. And still no nudge from Chloe. It was up to me.

I took my old phone out of my pocket. "Okay if I take a picture of your license plate and text it to my dad? Just for safety reasons?"

"Whatever you want." He was already headed back to the pump. "But it would probably be better if you were both in the backseat before he comes out. It's my car, but he's often under the impression he has a vote on things when he doesn't."

I touched Chloe's arm and hurried behind him, holding out my palm to a little hybrid to remind its driver not to run us down. "Hey! How will I know when you need me to change the subject?"

He'd walked around to the driver's side, but he was tall enough that I could see his face over the roof. When he opened the door, he looked like he was taking a deep breath before going underwater, and the water didn't smell so good.

"Believe me," he said. "You'll know."

I felt more at ease once we got in the backseat, because it looked like the driver had at least one kid, which didn't seem like a serial-killer thing to have. The mesh net behind his seat had coloring books and a pack of crayons in it, and a half-sucked lollipop was stuck to my seat belt. Chloe and I were both wet and sniffing, and he turned up the heat while we waited for his brother, which was nice.

"You live in Saint Paul?" I asked, trying to be friendly. Chloe was hunched over behind the passenger seat, breathing a little heavy. I didn't want him to be freaked out.

"Yup," he said, and that was all. I got the message. He'd really only let us in the car so I could derail a conversation when necessary. And as there was no conversation going on just yet, he didn't want to talk.

The brother, when he finally came out, didn't notice us at first. He was maybe preoccupied, trying to hold both a coffee and a soda while he opened the passenger door with the edge of his hand. It was only after he'd sat down and set both his cups in the holder that he saw us. He said "Jesus!" and put his hand to his chest, looking at me and then at Chloe like we were a big spider and a snake.

He turned to his brother. "What the hell?"

You could tell they were brothers. The one who'd just gotten in had the same deep-set eyes as the driver, and they both talked in a quick way, their words clipped. But the one who'd just gotten in looked like he was only regular height, and he was wider across the shoulders, even just wearing a flannel shirt.

"Excuse me?" His eyebrows shot up. "David? Do you *know* there are two women in the back of your car? Who were not there before? Are you kidding me? You picked up hitchhikers?"

He was yelling. Chloe probably couldn't hear him as well, as she was sitting right behind him and had the protection of the seat, not to mention her clogged-up ear. She'd scooted right up against her door, her blue hat resting against her window.

"This is Amy and Chloe." The tall one, David, shifted the car into drive. "They need a ride to Minneapolis, and that's not so far out of our way. . . ." He shrugged, then checked his rearview like there was really nothing more to say.

"Unbelievable." The brother yanked off his hat and threw it at the windshield. He had the same curly hair as his brother. "Un-buh-leev-a-ble. Wow."

Nice manners, I thought. I mean, we weren't doing anything to him. If he faced forward, he wouldn't even know we were there, except for us both sniffing our runny noses. I sniffed again, and we rolled out of the lot, the windshield wipers beating away snow. The brother picked up his soda and sucked it through the straw, glaring at the road ahead.

By the time we were on the entrance ramp to the interstate, Chloe had closed her eyes. I was hoping she was just sleepy, and glad to be out of the cold. But just as I was looking at her, she pressed her hand to her ear again. And then a tear slid out of her eye and down her cheek, leaving a shiny trail.

I knew, right then, we were really in trouble. It didn't matter that we'd finally gotten a ride—not with her ear hurting her enough that she would cry like that. For now we were warm in the SUV, flying past farmhouses and empty fields, and even other cars. But once we got to Minneapolis, we had the whole rest of Minnesota to get through. It wasn't like her fever would just miraculously go back down, or the pain in her ear would stop. If anything, it would keep getting worse.

I listened to the beat of the wipers, trying to adjust my hopes. I could ask the police, very nicely, to make sure Chloe got to a doctor. Before we even called them, I could get Chloe's husband's name from her, and get a message to him in Canada, and their son, so they could know how hard she'd tried.

We'd been in the car for maybe twenty minutes when the shorter brother, the one in the passenger seat, slurped up the last of his coffee and started laughing. But it wasn't a real laugh. It was an unhappy laugh, and too high-pitched to be anything but for show.

"Pretty bold move, Big D. I've got to hand it to you." He looked over at his brother. "Picking up hitchhikers. Really smart."

David shrugged. "Just thought I'd help them out."

"That's nice. Interesting, really. As you won't help your own brother."

David didn't respond.

"It's just a loan I'm asking for. A loan."

David tilted the rearview mirror so I could see his eyes, and he could see mine. He bobbed his eyebrows at me like, *Okay, girl, you're on*, and it was only then I remembered we had a deal.

"How much farther to Minneapolis?" I asked. It was the best I could do. Chloe was still holding her ear, and now she was hunched forward again. It was hard to know if she was still crying.

"About two hours," David said, his voice as pleasant and sunny as a flight attendant in a movie. "Do you get up to visit your mother often?"

"Yeah," I said. "I just usually come a different way." I looked away so he wouldn't see me wince in the mirror. I should have said no. I should have said I hadn't ever visited her, not in Minneapolis, so it wouldn't seem strange that I knew nothing about the city, or even where to tell him to drop us off. I wasn't thinking. At least not as carefully as I should. It didn't matter. We weren't going to make it anyway. We were already done.

The shorter brother turned around. "So what's your story? You two just go around getting rides with strangers?"

"Yup." I held up my hands and waved them like they were little flags to keep his attention on me. But he turned a little more to try to look at Chloe over the edge of his seat.

"What's wrong with her?"

"Oh," I said. "She's just sad about my uncle dying. That's why she's here, visiting from Portugal. She's my mom's cousin, and she came over for the funeral. She doesn't speak English. She's okay though."

David tilted the mirror so I couldn't see him anymore. He

was looking at Chloe, too. "Is something wrong with her ear?"

"Yeah," I said. "It's giving her problems. My mom'll get her medicine. She'll be okay."

The brothers exchanged glances. I wiped my palms on my jeans.

"Okay," the shorter one said. "Well, which one are you? Chloe or Amy?"

"I'm Amy."

"Okay, Amy. Let me ask you a question." He put his left hand on the back of his brother's seat and looked at me over his shoulder. "Do you think family should help each other out?"

Up in front of me, the tall brother slapped his forehead. "Oh my God. You're ridiculous, Adam. You're a ridiculous person."

I cleared my throat. "Hey. Do you all know if you absolutely have to have ID to cross over to Canada?"

They glanced at each other again. Sweat sprouted out across my arms and my chest, and I got so itchy I had to unzip my coat and shimmy out of it, my neck straining against my seat belt. I knew I shouldn't have brought up Canada. I hoped David would just think I was doing my job and changing the subject. But part of me was still thinking maybe there was a chance for Chloe, even with the pencil in her ear. I was hoping these brothers might know some little trick for getting through the border, some secret that only Minnesotans were wise to. And maybe, if they understood what we were up against, they might even drive us all the way. I thought of football, the quarterback too far from the goal, the buzzer about to ring. A Hail Mary pass.

David shifted the mirror again. "I hear they're pretty strict about it. As much for getting out as for going in. Are you headed to Canada?"

"I was thinking about it," I said, like I hadn't really made up my mind.

They didn't say anything to that. After a while, the shorter brother, Adam, looked back over his shoulder and smiled at me. It was the kind of smile guys give you when they know they're pretty cute. I guess he was, for being over thirty.

"Okay, Amy," he said. "Back to what I was asking about helping family. I understand you're probably thinking about it now, because of your uncle dying. Your whole family is probably thinking about what really matters right now."

"Yeah," I said, looking over at Chloe, who was rocking back and forth a little, still holding her ear. David cleared his throat.

"Hey," I said. "It's really snowing out, isn't it?"

David nodded, giving me an appreciative look in the mirror. "It is! And you know it's only going to get worse, right? They're saying more snow, all day tomorrow. It's really going to hit."

I shook my head. As if things weren't bad enough for us. Even if somehow, by some miracle, Chloe's ear stopped hurting, we'd have to hitch the rest of the way up Minnesota in a genuine snowstorm. Chloe was still rocking back and forth.

"Like an actual blizzard?" I asked. It was all I could think of. I sounded like a ding-a-ling.

"Okay, enough about the weather." Adam turned around again, just looking at me. "So back to what I was saying about family, Amy. It's Amy, right?"

I nodded.

David raised his chin to the mirror. "They're saying two feet of snow, even more in the northern part of the state. Probably not the best time to visit Canada."

Adam waved him off again. "Okay, Amy. Let me give you a hypothetical situation." He turned back and touched the knee of my jeans, just for a second. "If you had disposable income, like say, enough that you just went to France with your spouse and two children for Christmas, and aside from that, every year you could afford to send both kids to private school as well, and you had a nice SUV that never broke down, and so did your spouse, everything was wonderful, et cetera, and then your brother, your brother who used to beat the crap out of anyone who picked on you when you were growing up, and let me tell you, that kept him busy . . ."

He paused to give me a look like, *You know what I mean.* Turned around the way he was, I couldn't believe he didn't notice Chloe rocking with her head down just behind him.

"Okay?" he continued. "And let's say this brother had fallen on hard times, and he didn't even have a car anymore, and he'd just been rebuked by his own parents, his own mother and father, for having the audacity to come to them for help." He held his hand out to me, palm up, like I had something to give him. "If this brother then came to you, asking for just a few thousand dollars, just what he needed to get back on his feet, let me ask you, Amy—would you let him borrow it?"

I wasn't sure what to say. I knew I was supposed to be hired for David. And maybe, being distracted by Chloe, I wasn't listening as close as I should have. But the proposition sounded reasonable to me.

David cleared his throat. "Um, Amy, he's leaving out a few details. Like that he plans to get on his feet at a poker game down in the Keys, which is always his plan." He held up one finger. "Unless it's a plan to invest in a company that doesn't actually exist, or a plan to flip a house with a bad foundation and problems with black mold in the vents." He glanced at his brother. "And he's leaving out the thirty grand I already lent him." He lifted his hands off the wheel to do quote marks around the word *lent*. "And also the fact that he thinks it's beneath him to get a regular damn job."

"You did lend it to me, David. It was a loan. Okay? We all get that it was a loan. Everyone understands that."

I slid my eyes over to Chloe. She was clutching at her ear like she wanted to pull it out of her head. I could think of nothing to do or say that would help her. I was trying to make something click into my brain, some plan, but it wouldn't come.

"And also," David said, looking at me in the mirror. "This is the first time our parents have actually said no to him, because they've finally figured out that he will bleed . . . them . . . dry. And he just spent our mother's seventy-third birthday making her feel bad about it."

"No," said Adam. "That is not what I did."

I didn't know if I was supposed to keep trying to change the subject. I was thinking I understood the problem, which was that the shorter brother, Adam, was a screw-up. But as soon as I heard myself think that, I felt ashamed. *Screw-up* was an Aunt Jenny term. She'd used it to describe my dad once, though as far as I knew, he didn't borrow money from people. He'd just been a drinker. That's how he'd died, though. He'd had a big screw-up at the end. But I always thought it was a point in his favor that he'd at least tried to walk home from the bar that night, when his car had been right in the bar's parking lot. He'd known he was drunk, and he didn't want to hurt anybody, maybe. So he'd walked. And that meant he wasn't completely bad. Not completely a screw-up. Aunt Jenny said he probably just walked because he was scared of getting a DUI. But I liked my way of looking at it, and she didn't know any more than I did what was in his head that night.

Adam was still talking. "If Mom was upset, it wasn't because of anything I said. It was because she wanted to help me, but Dad wouldn't let her. Because he's controlling"—he pointed at his brother—"like you."

Chloe started to moan, low at first, then rising up, like somebody pretending to be a ghost on Halloween. I stared at her, openmouthed. Both brothers turned around. David looked back at the road, and then turned back to Chloe again.

"Whoa," Adam said. "She's really not doing well." He gave me a hard look. "What does she have, exactly?"

"She's got water in her ear," I said.

"Like swimmer's ear? Just water?"

I nodded. "I guess it's infected."

He made quick eyes at his brother and turned back to the windshield again. The snow was coming down harder now. Already the fields and tops of tree branches on either side of the highway were blanketed white.

Chloe moaned again. I started to shake my head at her, but that wasn't fair, or even reasonable. If she could have stayed quiet, she would have.

David tilted the mirror at me. "She sounds like she needs a doctor."

I waited for Chloe to speak. If she wanted a doctor, if she wanted to give up, she should be the one to say it. She was silent, so I shook my head.

"She'll be okay when she gets the medicine. My mom has medicine for her."

"Antibiotics? Your mom has antibiotics?"

I nodded. My teeth were chattering, and I wasn't even cold.

David's deep-set eyes got even smaller. "Why does your mom have them? Why doesn't your cousin, or her cousin, have them herself?"

I tried to think. The brothers glanced at each other again. I had nothing to say. I was all out of lies. I had nothing.

"Listen," David said. "I don't know what's going on, but I'm getting off at the next town, and I'm taking her to an ER." He nodded at his brother. "Put in our location and find the closest one that comes up."

"No!" I slapped the back of his seat. "No! Don't do that!"

Adam nodded, his bottom lip sticking out. "This is a great idea you had, by the way, bro. Picking up these two. Seriously a smart move on your part."

"Shut up." David looked back at me in the mirror. "Why don't you want her to see a doctor? Are you worried about money?"

I didn't know what to say. I could say yes, but it seemed to me, just from the tone of his voice, that money wasn't a good enough reason not to go to the ER. He'd drive us there anyway.

"Amy," he said, not as friendly now. "What's going on?"

I shook my head. There was nothing to lose anymore. But I wouldn't give her up, not without her permission. I'd wait for her to do it herself. I could tell Caleb I'd done everything I could. I could tell myself that too. But I wanted, so much, for her to keep holding on, at least until she really couldn't.

"I'll tell you what's going on," Adam said. He laughed in

the high-pitched way again. "Think, David. She can't take her cousin, or whoever that is, to the ER. And she just asked about Canada. That's where they're headed. Without ID. Okay? Use your head. I don't think the cousin is Portuguese."

I could see David's eyes in the mirror, the new understanding lighting in. His hand moved fast through his curls. "Oh Jesus," he said. "Oh God."

Adam turned back to me.

"What's the deal?" He pointed at me. "You're a little liar, okay? And so help me, don't you lie anymore. I mean it. Tell us what's up, right now."

I couldn't speak. I mean really, physically. It was like my tongue wouldn't work. I was that scared.

Chloe held up her hand. "Leave her." She breathed heavily. "She's done nothing. I'm from Iran." She put her hand back to her ear. "I didn't register. I just want to leave. I want to be with my family. That is all."

We were all quiet again, the wipers beating. Adam shrugged.

"Yeah," he said, almost pleasantly. "This is way better than just giving me the loan, Big D. Way to go. You really showed me."

David took one arm off the wheel and made a fist, and for a second, I thought they were going to start fighting, like really fighting, while David was driving up the interstate. Chloe and I both put our hands in front of our faces, but then David put his hand back on the wheel.

"Shut up. Seriously. Shut up. Okay? This is serious." He turned back and glanced at Chloe. "What the hell are we going to do?"

"Uhh. Pull over and drop them off?"

He'd said it like it was obvious, like that was the only thing that made sense. But there was nothing on either side of the road except snow-flocked trees and grass. I held my breath and looked at Chloe. She had one hand on her ear, the other on her forehead, and she was rocking back and forth again. I knew people used to die from infections, before antibiotics.

"We can't leave them on the side of the road." David's voice was quiet enough I had to lean forward to hear. "She's in real pain. My God. And somebody'll find her." He lowered his voice even more. "Even if they aren't a nut, there's probably a rewar—"

He didn't finish the word. And I guessed why he'd stopped. Ten thousand dollars. Like a gift from above. His brother wouldn't need the poker game. Or if he wanted to go, now he could go in style.

But Adam turned to glare at David, and now he looked like he was the one who might deliver a punch.

"Thanks. That's really a nice thing for you to think about me."

David didn't say anything. Adam kept staring at him.

"I'm not going to turn her in for the reward, okay? That's disgusting. That's disgusting that you would think I would do that. I'm insulted. Offended." He thumped his hand against the front of his flannel shirt. "Deeply offended."

"Sorry," David said, like he meant it.

"Good. There's a big difference between asking for a loan from your own family and selling your damn soul. You know me better than that. Or you should. I didn't hear the same stories you did growing up? I didn't hear the same stories?"

"I'm sorry," David said again.

Adam looked out his window and shook his head. "But I also don't want to go to prison. And I don't think you do either. You want to wait until the next exit, fine. But then we're saying bye to your new friends."

"What about her ear?"

Adam held up both hands. "What would we do for her?" He turned around and looked at me. "Hey you, Little Miss Liar. Is there really a mom and medicine waiting for her in Minneapolis?"

I shook my head.

"Don't even start with the tears, okay? They won't do you any good with me." He pointed at me again. "I don't know what your deal is, or why you're helping her, but you just put me and my brother at risk for serious legal problems, okay? Without our permission. So I'm fresh out of sympathy for you right now. Forget the waterworks."

I nodded. I wasn't crying on purpose. I was seriously trying to stop. But I was thinking about the pencil jammed in Chloe's ear, and about her husband and her little boy in Canada. I knew he was right, that it had been wrong of me to lie to them. But I didn't want her to die in this car, and I didn't want her to get caught.

"You've got to help her." I wiped my tears away fast. I wanted him to understand. "She didn't do anything wrong. She just stayed too long because she liked it here. She liked being American. So she stayed, and now she's stuck."

He stared at me. He looked at me like he wanted to start laughing again, in the fake way, but he couldn't quite manage it.

"I don't have to do anything," he said. "And listen, no, I don't want the blood money. But I don't have to do anything for either of you."

"Adam." David's voice was low. "We at least have to get her to a doctor."

Adam's hands went to his head, then sprang up again like his head was too hot. "What doctor? What doctor are we going to take her to? What would we be risking? I'll tell you what. A federal offense. Treason. And let me ask you something, David. If the shoe was on the other foot, if we were down in her neck of the woods, do you think she'd risk it all for the likes of us? For the likes of you?"

David didn't say anything.

"You know what I'm saying?" Adam asked. "I mean, how come you and Stephen took the kids to France last month? Why didn't you go to Iran? Oh. That's right. That wouldn't have gone so well." He leaned around the edge of his seat to look at Chloe. "You people still executing gays over there? Apparently tolerance only goes one way."

"Stop it." David held up both hands. "We're not in Iran. We're about an hour outside Minneapolis. And we've got to figure out what to do. Right now."

"Yeah." Adam nodded, facing forward again. "That's right. We're not in Iran. It's different here, because they're not all coming over and bringing sharia law with them, you know? And wanting to push us out into the sea. I'm all for the containment. Believe me." He thumped his chest again. "I'm all for it."

Chloe was still holding her ear. "I did not bring sharia law with me." She said *sharia* in a different way than he did.

"Uh-huh. Well. When you get back to wherever you're going, you remember we helped you. Okay? My brother helped you." He leaned around the edge of the seat again. "A gay Jewish man. And his brother. Okay? We're Jews." He kept his gaze on Chloe. "These are Jews helping you. Remember that."

Chloe nodded. I crossed my fingers on both hands, wiping my cheek on the shoulder of my coat. He'd said it like they were going to help her. He'd maybe changed his mind, and I guessed why. He'd been trying to yell at her, to make himself hard, but he'd made the mistake of turning around to look at her, seeing her up close.

He turned back to the road again. He still looked mad, but I could see he was thinking, his dark eyebrows pushed low.

David looked at him. "I seriously don't know what to do. We can't take her to a doctor." He was whispering, maybe for Chloe's sake. "And I don't have any . . . amoxicillin or whatever lying around. Do you?"

Adam looked at him like he'd asked about the stupidest question ever.

David exhaled through puffed out cheeks. "Okay. Could one of us call our doctor and say we're out of town? I could say I came down with swimmer's ear, and I let it get infected? Then have them phone in the medicine and give it to her?"

"That won't work." Adam took his soda cup out of the holder. "They're going to want to see the ear. So unless we can remove her ear from her body, it's not happening." He tried to sip his soda, though it was empty now, the straw just sucking air. He shoved the cup back into the holder.

"What about Audrey Chang?"

I didn't know who Audrey Chang was, but Adam gave him a look that implied that David had now truly asked the dumbest question of all time. I had to sniff again, and I tried to do it quietly. I didn't want to interrupt them. I wanted them to keep talking, trying to work something out.

"She's a doctor, right?" David was still whispering. "She even works at an ER, right?"

"It's a walk-in clinic. And she's way over in Stillwater."

"Yeah. But she could call it in. We could pick it up any-where."

"Uh-huh. There's one tiny problem, besides, you know, her risking her license, and us risking arrest. Which is that she hates me." He lowered his voice. "I cheated on her. Remember? With her friend?"

David shook his head. "She doesn't hate you. She's always liking your posts. Even the dumb ones."

"No. That's just her pretending to be over it. Believe me. She hates me. She said I was disgusting." He pointed his thumb up toward his own chin. "She said that to my face."

"Okay. But would she help?" David nodded back at Chloe. "Would she be . . . sympathetic?"

"No idea."

"How can you not know? She was your girlfriend."

"That's not the kind of thing we discussed, okay? Believe it or not, it didn't come up."

We passed a green sign saying we were sixty-five miles from Minneapolis. I sucked my lips between my teeth, reminding myself to stay quiet. Best-case scenario, they would think of a way to get Chloe medicine. Worst case, they would drop us off at the edge of the road, or maybe even at a gas station. They weren't going to turn us in. But I could tell they were both pan-icked, talking even faster than they normally did. I looked over at Chloe, who was still hunched over, and shaking, too, though the car was warm. I put my hand on her shoulder and gave her a pat, as much for me as for her.

"Do you have her number?" David whispered.

"Audrey's? I have her cell."

"Then what are you waiting for? Make the call."

"And say what?" Adam's voice came out shrill. "What am I going to say? 'Oh, hey, Audrey. 'Sup? Yeah, it's Adam. Listen, I know things didn't go so well between us, but you know, I've got swimmer's ear that's turned into an infection, and I don't want to have to come in, and I think you're going to give me special treatment.' Are you kidding me? She'll think I just don't want to pay for a visit. She'll be nothing but annoyed." He looked up at the roof of the car. "I'd have to explain what's really going on and hope she's . . ." He made his hand into a blade and rotated it forward, like he didn't want to say the same word his brother had used, but he couldn't think of anything else.

Sympathetic. That was what we needed Audrey Chang to be.

14

AUDREY CHANG DIDN'T pick up. It didn't matter that while her phone was ringing, or while Adam said it was ringing, I had my fingers crossed again. It didn't matter that I was staring out at the snow flying into the windshield and thinking, *please, please, please*, begging I don't know who or what again.

"Voice mail," Adam said, hanging up. He put his phone back in the front pocket of his shirt, like that was the end of that.

"Call back and leave a message." David pushed his hand through his hair again. From what I could see of his face in the rearview, he looked pretty stressed out, probably because of Chloe. But maybe because the snow was really coming down now, and the road had gotten slick enough that he was tapping the brakes every now and then. Or maybe it was that traffic had gotten heavier after we'd crossed into Minnesota. Or maybe all of the above.

"Send a text," he said. "Tell her it's urgent."

"An emergency," I added, and Adam gave me a look like I was being irritating. I didn't care. I'd moved to the middle of the backseat, closer to Chloe. I had my hand steady on her arm now, just above her elbow. I didn't know if she wanted my hand there, or if I was just making her feel more caged in. She hadn't pushed me away.

"She's probably at work," Adam said. "She won't pick up on a personal call. And sometimes her shifts are twelve hours."

"Can you call the clinic and ask for her?" I'd tried not to sound like he was being dumb, but that was obviously the next step. My ninth-grade English teacher back in Joplin would have said, "I don't know. *Can* I?" I tried again. "Maybe you could look up the number?"

"I guess." He gave me a quick look over his shoulder, like he still thought I wasn't exactly trustworthy. Little Miss Liar, he'd called me. I had my own doubts about him. This time, after he tapped the screen and put the phone to his ear, I leaned in toward him, my ears straining to hear a voice on the other end. For all I knew, he wasn't really calling anybody. He might just be pretending to try.

I didn't hear anyone answer. But before Adam spoke, he took a breath like he was getting ready to sing, and his voice came out deeper than usual.

"Hello," he said. "I need to speak with Dr. Chang as soon as possible."

If he was, in fact, talking to someone, then he was being smart about it, making his voice so low and serious. He sounded like he owned the place, or like he was the hero in a movie, and a time bomb was ticking, so everybody better listen up. If I'd been the receptionist hearing that voice, I would have paid attention.

"Please tell her it's an emergency." He rubbed his lips together, waiting, and then he said "Thank you," his voice still deep, but also sincere, like he was trying to stay on the receptionist's good side.

But the next thing he said was his name and number, and then he said "Thank you" again in the deep voice, and that was the end of the call. After he put his phone away, he looked at his brother, and then at me, like, *Oh, well.*

I narrowed my eyes. He'd been scared from the beginning. He'd wanted to put us out on the side of the road as soon as he'd known about Chloe. I guess it was nice that he didn't want the reward money, that he wasn't going to turn us in. I'd give him that. But I had a feeling he hadn't called anyone either time he'd dialed, and that the deep voice he'd used had been just for us. And it wasn't even like he was being patriotic. He just didn't want to risk his neck.

I hated him for that. I really did. Because he'd heard Chloe cry out. He had to understand how much she was hurting. And there he was, sitting up front and looking out at the snow like he was waiting for a call he knew he didn't have to worry about, because it would never come. I wanted to reach up and grab hold of his handsome face, digging in with my nails. I thought of the pepper spray in my pocket. Not that. I didn't want to hurt him that bad. I just wanted to help him think about what it meant to be in pain.

Screw-up, I would say. *You selfish screw-up.*

His phone rang.

"Hello?" he said, his voice not as deep as before. "Audrey. Thank you. Yeah. I'll explain. But I just want to say right now—oh my God. Thank you so much for calling back."

I tried to picture her in my head. She was probably Chinese, or at least half, and she'd be wearing a lab coat and maybe a name tag, with a stethoscope hanging from her neck. She might have her own office, or she might be calling from a common area, leaning on a wall next to a scale and a poster of what a body looked like under the skin. She probably had an annoyed look on her face, listening, on what was likely a busy day in the middle of flu season, as the ex-boyfriend who'd cheated on her tried to explain what the emergency was without really spelling it out.

"Yeah," Adam said, switching his cell to his other ear. "I get what you're saying. But I'm pretty sure it's bacterial . . . No. Okay . . . Right. I know I'm not a doctor. You're absolutely right. But she said she got water in it. That's how it started. Like swimmer's ear . . . Okay. I understand. But the thing is, Audrey, she really can't come in. I'm not saying it's inconvenient or too expensive. I'm saying that she *can't*."

He was talking all around it, saying anything he could to avoid having to say the words *Muslim* or *illegal*. Maybe he didn't want to scare her. I stared out at the fast-falling snow, my hand resting on Chloe's arm. She was taking deep breaths, every inhale and exhale loud enough for me to hear.

"It's all right," I whispered, squeezing her arm. "Everything's gonna be all right." I wasn't at all sure this was true.

"Okay," Adam said. "Please don't hang up. I know you're busy. But please just listen. She can't go to any doctor, is what I'm saying. You see what I'm saying? Okay. How about this?" He slowed his words. "One of the reasons she can't go to any doctor is that she doesn't have any ID." He paused. "That she can use. My brother picked her up just a little while ago. She's trying to hitchhike to Canada."

He'd said *Canada* even more slowly than he'd said everything else, giving emphasis to each syllable, and that must have been what did it. After that, he didn't have to give any more hints. But it wasn't a done deal at all.

"I know," he said, nodding at the dashboard. He picked up his empty coffee cup and set it down again. "And I wouldn't have called you. I wouldn't have. The thing is . . ." He turned and looked around the edge of his seat at Chloe. "She's really in pain. I would say agony, if I'm being honest. David said we at least have to get her something for the pain, you know? And he's right. He's right."

I stared at the back of his head, at his pale little earlobe, feeling so sorry for what I'd been thinking about him before. I'd called him a liar and a coward and a screw-up. I'd done it in my head, but still.

He switched the phone back to his other ear. "Do you want to talk to her? You want me to put her on?"

Apparently the answer was yes, because he turned around and put the phone under Chloe's head, where she could see it, though I wasn't sure her eyes were open. "Say something," he said. "Listen. I know it hurts. But I've got a doctor on the other end of the line. If you want her to help, you've got to tell her yourself. You've got to let her hear what I mean."

Chloe nodded. I took the phone and held it to her good ear.

"Yes," she gasped. "Yes, I am in so much pain." It was good she had her accent now, and also that she was crying, so Audrey Chang would understand this wasn't a joke. She must have been hard to understand, but she managed to confirm that she'd gotten water in her ear the week before, and that at first her ear had just felt numb, and then it had started to hurt, and then she'd woken up this morning with the pencil jammed in. When she didn't seem like she could say any more, I handed the phone back to Adam.

"Okay? Audrey? Will you help her? Please?"

I wanted to reach up and put my arms around him. Not in

a romantic way. I mean that all at once I felt this tenderness for him, this person I barely knew. And it was strong, almost what I felt for Caleb all the time. I was sorry for thinking that he was a coward and a liar, and I was sorry that he had money problems and that he didn't have a car, and that things didn't seem to be working out for him in general, and that he was always borrowing money. Maybe he was a screw-up, but he was being brave right now. I wanted to take off my seat belt and lean forward enough to take his hand and hold it. Sounds weird, I know. But that's what I felt just then.

He put the phone against his chest and looked at David. "Where are we?"

"Uh. Next exit is Lakeville."

He put the phone back to his ear. "We're coming up on Lakeville. Yeah. Okay. Right. Yeah, I can wait. Of course." He stared up at the roof of the car. "Yeah. Hi. Okay. . . . Yes. Oh, great. That's fantastic. The CVS on Dodd. In Lakeville. Under my name. Thank you. Oh my God, Audrey. You're the best. I—" He paused. "Audrey?"

He touched a button, then put his phone back in his shirt pocket.

"Thank you," I said, even nicer than I'd planned, as it was pretty clear she'd hung up.

Adam's phone said the CVS on Dodd was only fifteen minutes away.

"Fifteen minutes," I told Chloe, because I wasn't sure she'd heard. "We'll have your medicine in just fifteen minutes. You got that? You're going to be okay."

I believed it. Or I wanted to. I at least knew we'd get to the CVS, even with the snow coming down and the taillights in front of us blinking red every time a driver tapped the brakes. We'd passed two cars that had slid off to the side of the road, but the SUV was doing great, and David was a steady driver. I tried not to think about how Audrey Chang might have only prescribed antibiotics, and nothing for the pain. What mattered was that now there was something for Chloe to hold on to, a possibility that she wasn't going to die without her family in the back of somebody's car.

But just as we came up on the exit, Adam started shaking his head.

"I've got a bad feeling." He looked at David, not at me. He put his hands on the back of his neck. "I mean it. I just got a real bad feeling about this."

"Stop it," David said. "You already called. It'll be fine. And I've got to concentrate."

Adam shook his head. "Listen to me. Okay? Just listen. Remember that time I got busted? And I knew? Remember? I called you up that morning and told you I had a bad feeling? And what was it, four hours later, there was a knock on the door?"

David didn't say anything. Good, I thought. Because it was crazy, what his brother was saying. We'd already worked out a plan. All we had to do was pick up the medicine. Was he really thinking we were going to let Chloe keep getting worse because he had a bad feeling? Something his brain just made up?

"I'm telling you, I got that same feeling now, David. I've got it bad. What if they're waiting for us at the pharmacy? They know we're coming, and they know she's with us. This is crazy, what we're doing. We've got to stop and think."

I glared at him, my hand steady on Chloe's arm. He was the one being crazy. He'd gone from saying "what if" to just assuming it was true.

"What are you saying?" David glanced at him again. "You think Audrey called the police?"

"She might have."

"Do you think she would do that? Is she that kind of person?"

"I don't know! I don't know what she thinks about this kind of thing. And even if she didn't call them, somebody might have been listening in. You know? She didn't call me back from her cell. She was calling from the clinic's line. That receptionist was probably curious what the emergency was. Seriously. Would you just pull over for a second? We need to think about this. We're talking about prison, David. We've got to stop and think."

"You're being paranoid." David made his hand flat, like a wall between them. "We're just going to a pharmacy. We're picking up a prescription. There won't be any police."

"And what if there is? I'll tell you what—we're not talking about a slap on the wrist. We're getting arrested for treason. Both of us." His voice was getting louder. "I'm not just thinking about me here. What about Ethan? What about Riley? Huh? What about Stephen? Do they get a say in any of this?"

The fact that he wasn't saying anything made me think he was getting scared too. I looked down at the coloring book in the seat pocket. There was a ballerina on the cover. *Color the Great Paintings of Degas!*

"You'd lose everything. And they would too. And my God, what about Mom? I'm just saying we have to think about this. Before we do something we can't undo."

The SUV made a sharp right, the back of the car skidding out on the ice. I grabbed David's headrest to keep my balance.

"Sorry," he said. He'd pulled into the nearly empty parking lot of a Hardee's. A man in a Hardee's jacket was shoveling the front walk. Beyond the roof, I could see the overpass of the interstate that we'd just gotten off, cars flying by in the snow.

"Sorry," David said again. The snow had covered the lines in the lot, but he eased the car into what seemed like a space and took the keys out of the ignition.

I held my breath, hoping he just meant sorry for turning fast and making the car slide. I knew he might have meant more than that.

Chloe moaned again. I don't think she did it on purpose, but David put his face in his hands.

"Oh my God." Adam stared up at the roof of the car. "This is a nightmare."

"I don't know what to do," David mumbled. He was hard to hear through his hands.

Go get her the medicine! I wanted to say. They had to go get it. What would happen to her if they didn't? I was thinking I'd go myself, no problem, but the prescription was under Adam's name. Then again, if there really was a chance that the police would be waiting there, then I didn't want to be the one to convince Adam he had to go give his name to the pharmacist and then see if he'd be arrested. Plus we'd be out in the parking lot. They would get us too.

"Leave us here," Chloe said. She was wincing, but she'd sat up a little. "We can wait in the restaurant, the Hardee's. You can get the medicine by yourselves, please, and if there is no problem, you can bring it back to us here. If the police are there, you can say you lied to the doctor. Say there was never any hitchhiking woman, that you pretended to have my voice." She paused, blinking slowly. "Say it was a test, to see that she still loved you."

Whoa, I thought. That was good. I was a little jealous that she was the one who thought of it. Of course that was what we should do.

"Is that illegal?" Adam asked. "Lying to a doctor like that?" He looked at his brother, and then at me. "I'm just curious. I don't care. It's not like treason. That's fine with me. Okay. That's a deal. That's workable. But that's where it ends. We'll drop them off, get the medicine, bring the medicine back here, and then we'll be on our way. Alone. Okay? I'm good with this new plan.

But we can't do any more."

"Okay," David said, his voice so quiet I could barely hear. He put the keys back in the ignition and drove up to an entrance of the Hardee's, which was considerate, making it so Chloe and I wouldn't have to walk across the lot in the snow. But now I was the one with the bad feeling. I wanted to see his face.

"Hold on a second," I said, picking up my backpack. "I'll get out on my side and then come around to help her out."

But after I got out and shut my door, I moved up to David's door and gave his window a tap. The glass rolled down slowly, and I could feel the heat coming out, mixing with the cold around me. His face was more narrow than his brother's, and his eyes looked kind, though that didn't necessarily mean anything. That was just the way some eyes looked.

"Um," I said, because I still didn't know how to say it.

He lifted his eyebrows like he meant to listen. But he didn't look at me, and I knew then I was right to be worried. He'd wanted to help. He'd wanted to help from the start. But his brother had gotten him nervous, talking about prison, and his family, and what they would do if he got arrested.

"Do you know how long you'll be?" I asked.

"No idea." He still had his hands on the steering wheel, and he seemed to be staring at my flag pin. I was thinking he didn't want to meet my eye.

"You'll come right back, though? With the medicine?"

He nodded. Snow was falling in through his window, land-ing on the front of his peacoat and catching in his hair.

"Okay," I said. "We'll be inside. Waiting."

I suppose I could have asked him to promise to come back. But if he'd already made a decision, a promise wouldn't make any difference. For some people, that's just a word.

When we got up to the front of the line, the boy behind the reg-ister took a deep breath.

"Smiles-are-free-get-yours-today-may-I-take-your-order?" He smiled with his mouth, but his eyes gave Chloe a worried look. I didn't think he recognized her face, or even thought she was suspicious. It seemed more like he could tell something was wrong. She wasn't holding her ear, but her cheeks were still tearstained, and she kept her gaze on the stainless steel counter.

"She okay?" he asked.

I nodded. "She just went to the dentist." I tapped the side of my cheek. "Still numb. Could I get two sodas? Mediums are fine."

I figured she wouldn't be able to eat, and even though I'd only had another pack of mini-doughnuts at the convenience store in Sherburn that morning, I knew I wouldn't be able to get anything down either. I didn't even want caffeine—I was wide-awake, jittery, and my eyes felt dry. I'd only bought the sodas so we wouldn't be loitering.

"Sorry," I whispered once we were over by the soda fountain. "Did you want coffee?" I was on the side of her good ear. "Or food? I can go back and get whatever."

She grabbed my arm. I mean, she really grabbed it—I almost spilled my soda. She was still breathing hard, her mouth open, but her grip on my arm stayed tight. For a second, I thought she was getting ready to faint, and I was about to tell her she couldn't do that. She just couldn't. Somebody would call an ambulance, like they'd done for me at the Arch. I looked behind each of my shoulders. The lobby of the restaurant was almost empty, as it was the middle of the afternoon, and also maybe because of the snow. If I could just keep her upright, I could get her to a chair without anybody seeing.

"It's okay," I said. "Let me help you."

She shook her head. "I want you to go," she whispered. "To the hotel across the street." She paused to swallow, and I could see by the look on her face that the pencil was still jamming in. She let go of my arm and closed her eyes. "It's just across. Wait for me in the lobby."

"What?" I waited for her to open her eyes, and I shook my head. I didn't like this idea at all.

She reached into her bag. "Go." She swallowed again, looking around to make sure no one was watching. "Check in." She slipped me a wad of bills. "I'll come as soon as they bring the medicine."

"I can't leave you here," I said, maybe too loud. Nobody was around, but I turned on the ice machine and leaned in close to her good ear. "What if somebody tries to talk to you?"

She pushed my shoulder. Kind of hard.

"I said go! Go, Sarah-Mary. They could be followed back. I don't know. And even if they're not, there is no reason for you to sit with me. It does me no good, and it is dangerous for you."

I shook my head. She pushed my shoulder again, and I almost lost my balance, my backpack heavy behind me. I stepped back and looked around. Nobody had seen, but if she kept this up, somebody would probably get concerned.

"Please," she said. I could tell by the way she said it how much it hurt for her to talk. "Please. Just go."

An old man walked up with an empty soda cup. He stood behind us, waiting. Chloe stayed where she was, staring at me.

She was all business. That was clear. There was nothing to do but go.

I stood just outside the door we'd come in, watching snow fall in front of the drive-thru. The hotel across the street was a Sleep-n-Eat, with a sign promising a free breakfast buffet with *WAFFLES*. I passed my soda from hand to hand so it wouldn't feel so cold.

I supposed Chloe was right, or a little right. I'd be safer if I waited for her at the hotel. But then again, did she really think that if the police showed up, I'd just watch it all go down from across the street like I was watching television? Was I going to stay in a room she'd paid for, and wake up and get myself some *WAFFLES* in the morning? I knew she didn't feel well, but it was a little insulting. I'd already said, very clearly, that I would see her through.

I walked around the back of the restaurant. One of the drivers waiting in the drive-thru clicked her locks down as I went by, like she was anxious I was a criminal, just trying to look like a high-school girl with her backpack. Which I guess was what I was. When I got around to the other side, I peeked in through one of the windows. The lobby was empty enough that Chloe was easy to spot, sitting by the windows that faced the street. She would have seen me probably, but she was hunched over, her hand on her ear again. Her soda sat on the table in front of her, and her straw lay beside it, still wrapped in its paper sleeve.

I slipped inside and found a seat behind her, with a little divider between us. If I leaned out and stretched my neck a little, I could see the edge of one of her boots.

My gym teacher in Joplin once spent about half an hour telling us we should be careful trying to save a drowning person, and that it wasn't like in the movies, where you can swim up and grab them and bring them back to shore, both of you coughing a little but otherwise fine. He said that when a body is really getting ready to drown, it gets so frantic that it tries to use anything coming near it as a raft, including you if you swim out to help.

So maybe you die and they live, or both of you die together. It doesn't matter if the person you're trying to save is a nice person or not. The body takes over, he said. It's a survival thing.

I believed him. And his main point—that we should try to grab some kind of flotation device before setting out to save someone—seemed like good advice. At the same time, I was thinking that if I were ever drowning, and someone was swimming out to help, I would try hard not to let my body take over and kill them. My gym teacher made it sound like it wasn't even a choice you could make, but probably a few people had it in them to keep their heads, and turn away from help so as not to take anybody else down with them.

Apparently, Chloe was one of those people. She wasn't actually drowning, not yet, but she still had that pencil pushed in her ear, and she must have known that the chances of her seeing her family again weren't looking so good. And here she was, pushing me away, thinking about my safety.

I didn't know if it was an Allah thing or just a Chloe thing. Whatever it was, all it did was make me know I couldn't leave her there alone.

Most of the other tables stayed empty. The drive-thru was busy, but not too many people seemed to want to get out of their cars in the snow, though the same guy had to keep going out to shovel the walks. For at least a half hour, if anyone did notice Chloe sitting by herself, hunched over and holding her ear, they didn't say anything.

But then a man pushing a dust mop through the lobby stopped near her table. I could tell he was a manager, or at least he was dressed like my manager at Dairy Queen, wearing a tie over a button-down shirt. Only this manager looked old enough to be my manager's dad. He didn't have any hair except for a couple inches of gray curving around the back of his head.

"Ma'am? Are you okay?"

He sounded nice, like he was really worried about her.

"Are you sure?" he asked. She must have nodded.

"Is there someone I can call for you? Are you not feeling well?"

I held my breath. I should have given her the marker. She could have used a napkin for paper. She would have been smart, writing out that she'd just gotten back from the dentist, and that she was waiting for a ride. But even that might not have helped for long. I'd never seen anybody sitting by themselves in the lobby of Dairy Queen hunched over and holding their ear, and maybe crying, too. It seemed like the kind of thing a manager wasn't supposed to ignore.

Even when I leaned forward, I couldn't see anything of her but her one boot. But I could see the manager as he turned around and waved somebody over from the counter. I hoped it would be the boy who'd taken our order, so he could tell the manager what I'd said about Chloe's cheek being numb. Then again, the boy might recognize me, sitting over by myself, and that would seem pretty strange to him if he remembered we'd come in together.

Anyway, what I was hoping for didn't matter, as it was an older blond woman who walked into the lobby, her gaze moving over the manager's face like they were using ESP to talk.

Even with my backpack, I got there before she did.

"Hey there," I said, sliding into the seat across from Chloe. "Sorry that took so long." I held up my soda cup to both the manager and the blond woman like it was proof of admission. "Everything okay?"

"That's what I was wondering," the manager said. "She seems to be not feeling so well?" His voice was friendly, but the blond woman kept her gaze on Chloe. She wore dark red earrings that matched the shirt of her uniform, and she had small, smart-looking eyes.

"She had a rough day at the dentist." I looked at Chloe and clicked my tongue. "My dad was supposed to pick us up, but he got stuck in the snow. He'll be here soon, though."

"That's too bad." The manager gave Chloe a sympathetic look. "I hate going to the dentist."

"What dentist was it?" the blond woman asked. Now her gaze was on me. She'd asked it in a pleasant way, but I was thinking wow, how lucky for us that a person who maybe should have been working as a gotcha district attorney happened to come out from behind the Hardee's counter. For a second, she had me stumped.

"Oh no," I said, waving my straw at her. "Can't say. I don't want to give him a bad name." I laughed, I hoped just enough, wrinkling my nose at the manager. He laughed too, but only like he wanted to be polite. "Seriously," I said. "My dad should be here soon, and she's already doing better. Thanks though."

Chloe nodded, even smiling a little. I actually thought she really might be feeling better, but after the woman went back to the counter, and the manager got far enough away with his mop, she put her palm to her forehead and turned away, and she made a little crying sound. Clearly, the pencil was still digging in.

I leaned across the table. "Can you take any more of the medicine you bought?"

She shook her head, just barely. "I've already taken the limit. And it's not touching it. I have never felt pain like this in my life." Her voice wavered. "Even giving birth. That was nothing to this."

She turned her face to the window, looking out at the snow. She was deciding. I knew she was.

I leaned my head back as far as I could, trying to see around the partition to the counter. I was thinking about getting up to see if the blond woman was there, scooping up fries or taking an order, or doing anything besides calling the police because she recognized Chloe, or thought she did, and hadn't believed me for a second.

"Just hang on a little longer," I whispered. I turned back to look out the window. People were driving slowly because of the snow, and though it was just a little after four o'clock, most everybody had their lights on. So it made sense that the brothers were taking so long. It didn't mean they weren't coming back. They could come back any minute.

A woman carrying a child on her hip shuffled through the snow in the parking lot. The child looked maybe five years old, too big to be carried, but she was wearing tights and ballet slippers, and she cuddled in close to the woman's neck like she was afraid of the snow. The woman held out her tongue to catch a snowflake, and after she chomped down on one, or pretended to, she smiled and said something. The girl tilted back her head and laughed.

Chloe's hand was still pressed against her ear, but her eyes were on the girl, and all at once, she looked miserable in a whole new way.

"You thinking about your son?"

She closed her eyes and nodded.

My own mom was probably in Virginia, maybe spending time with that guy she'd met online, working on her own plan. Maybe she sometimes worried that she was a bad mother, or missed us, like Chloe missed her son now. But probably not for long.

If you asked Aunt Jenny what was wrong with my mother, she would say it was that she didn't have God. If Aunt Jenny ever talked to Chloe enough to not be scared of her, she might even say that's exactly what was right with her—that believing in Allah was enough like believing in God to make her a decent person, and the kind of mom that would feel guilty about leaving her kids, or letting them leave you. But that's not right. I mean, obviously I don't have kids. But clearly, I don't leave people in fast-food restaurants, either. I think the thing that's missing in my mom, and maybe a lot of people who do things that are way worse, is that they don't care so much when other people hurt. Or if they do care, they work around it in their head so they don't have to feel bad about it. Given some things I've seen in the news, I knew there were plenty of religious people, from here and all over, who could pull that trick at least as well as my mom.

But Chloe wasn't one of them.

"How'd you get water in your ear?" I asked. I wasn't sure if she would answer or not. She was rocking back and forth again, her eyes closed. I was mostly trying to distract her.

"The bathtub." She kept rocking, but she opened her eyes. "The friends who hid me, they had a tub in the basement. I couldn't take showers upstairs because someone might come by. I was in the tub when someone did come by, the neighbor we were worried about. She stayed, and she stayed. The water was getting cold, and I wanted to rinse my hair and get out, but I was afraid to turn on the faucet, in case the neighbor could hear." She shrugged. "So I dipped my hair back into the water, and some got in my ear."

That was so unfair. Even with how hard she'd tried, and even with all the good luck we'd had, just a few drops of bathtub water was what was going to do her in. Maybe not. But now it had been almost an hour since the brothers left us. They could be back on I-35 North, headed up to Saint Paul. The medicine, and maybe the police, would be still waiting at the pharmacy, if Audrey Chang had even called the prescription in. Both brothers would probably feel bad about not coming back. They'd wanted to help, at least before they'd gotten scared.

"Still waiting for your dad, huh?" It was the blond woman again. She'd sneaked up to our table. She had a squirt bottle in one hand and a rag in the other, but she wasn't using them yet. And the empty tables around us all looked pretty clean.

I nodded.

She turned to Chloe, her small eyes steady. "Seems like you should call a cab or something, since you're hurting so much. Do you live around here? Are you from here?"

Chloe nodded. She looked like the saddest person I'd ever seen.

"Whereabout?"

I leaned forward. "Why do you ask?" I smiled. But we both understood the conversation had just gotten less friendly.

The woman shrugged, keeping her gaze on Chloe. "You look familiar to me."

I held my breath. She knew. Or she was close to knowing. She knew she was on to something.

"Everybody says that to her." I forced a laugh. "Aunt Chloe, you must look like a lot of people."

Chloe didn't look at me. She probably couldn't. She was either too scared, or she was hurting too much.

"She doesn't look like you," the blond woman said. She smiled, and I thought, my God, how much longer can we keep this up? And why should we even bother? Chloe needed a doctor. The brothers weren't coming back. If this woman wanted to make ten thousand dollars out of it, well then okay. I guess at least somebody could come out a winner.

And then I saw someone moving toward us: Adam, still just wearing his flannel shirt, and out of breath, his boots tracking in snow. He was holding a white paper bag, the kind you get from a pharmacy.

The blond woman was still looking at me. "I mean being your aunt," she was saying. "Must be by marriage?"

"Yeah," I said, looking around her to give him a wave. "Well, hey. What do you know—here's my dad now."

We were lucky in that almost as soon as Adam slid into the booth next to Chloe, the manager came out and told the blond woman that a charter bus was coming in fifteen minutes, and that he needed all hands on deck. Adam waited until she was out of earshot before he said anything.

"Sorry for the wait." He put the pharmacy bag on the table. "There was a line."

"It's okay," I said. Chloe stared at the bag. She had her hand over her ear again.

"I can't stay long. David's in the car." He nodded out the window to where the SUV was parked. The wipers had cleared enough snow off the windshield that I could see David in the driver's seat. He lifted his hand off the steering wheel to give a quick salute.

Adam opened the bag and took out a small bottle. "These drops, they're for the pain, okay? The pharmacist said it would numb it instantly, way different than what's over the counter." He turned to Chloe. "So let's get this one in before I explain the rest. If you lay your head down, I'll put some in right now."

I looked around. I was surprised he wanted to put the drops in himself, and that he wanted to do it right there in the Hardee's. But I figured he might as well. Maybe a charter bus was on its way, but for now, the lobby was dead. I wasn't sure how Chloe would feel about letting him put drops in her ear, since her ear was so close to the hair she wasn't even supposed to show. That was no problem, though. By the time I'd turned back to Chloe, she already had her head on the table, bad ear up. She left her hat on and closed her eyes.

The drops took about five seconds to work. I'm serious. You

could see it in her face, the relief, almost as soon as they went in. I was thinking, thank you, thank you, all the people in the world who spent their lives coming up with medicine. They never even got to meet all the people they helped.

Chloe sat up and looked at Adam, blinking fast. "Thank you," she whispered. "Oh. Thank you so much."

"Okay." He turned to me. "This one's the antibiotic. It says that you're supposed to just take one every twelve hours, but the pharmacist said I could double up tonight and tomorrow morning, and that would help it get better faster. But she can keep using the drops until then. Got it?"

I nodded. It occurred to me that Adam must have had to act like his ear was hurting in the pharmacy. He'd had to hold it and wince, just like Chloe had been doing, so the pharmacist would believe he was in pain.

"How much was it?" I asked. I was just asking for Chloe. I knew she'd want to pay him. But he made a face like I'd said something crazy.

"Thank you so much," Chloe said again. She was sitting up straight, blinking at the ceiling like someone had just turned on bright lights.

"Thank Audrey," Adam said.

"Yes," Chloe said. "But I thank you, too." She smiled at him, pulling her hat back down. "You've saved me. One person. You know what that means."

"Yeah, yeah." He was already standing up. "I've saved the

world. You've read the Talmud, I guess." He shrugged. "Weird. But impressive."

"It is the same for us." She looked over his shoulder, and then hers. "It is in our book too."

"Huh." He tilted his head. They smiled at each other, their eyes talking like they had an inside joke. "That's good to know."

"It is," she said, still friendly, but serious now, like whatever it was they both knew wasn't a joke at all.

We waited until the bus came and things got busy enough in the lobby that we felt safe to slip out the doors. Adam walked out with us. No one was paying attention, but we still acted like a little family, though none of us looked alike.

15

THE NEXT MORNING, she was still asleep when I woke up. I was starving, so I left a note on our room's coffee maker.

> *Gone down to breakfast.*
> *I'll bring you back some bacon.*
> *Ha ha just kidding! I'll get you*
> *a bagel or something. C U SOON.*

I tried to be quiet on my way out. Her bag was in a different spot than it had been in the night before, and I guessed she'd gotten up early to pray and take her medicine before going back to bed. But now she was sleeping hard with her mouth open, like she'd lost consciousness and gone peaceful in the middle of saying something.

I'd slept well too. After we walked over from the Hardee's,

we were so tired that we were both in bed, lights out, by seven. We hadn't had any dinner. Now I felt almost dizzy as I walked down the hallway to the elevator, my boots quiet on the maroon carpet. But I also felt optimistic. We'd gotten Chloe's ear fixed, or at least on its way to being fixed. And we were already in Minnesota. Two states down, one to go. A dad and two little kids got in the elevator with me, and when the dad said "good morning" in a cheerful way, I said it right back, and meant it.

But as soon as the elevator's doors hummed open and I looked out the lobby's front windows, my high hopes fell considerably. It was hard to believe that so much snow could have fallen in little flakes—cars in the parking lot were buried up to their door handles. A plow rumbled down the road between the hotel and the Hardee's, spitting out a wall of white. And more snow was still coming down, though it was hard to tell what was falling and what was getting blown around by the wind.

"Oh, come on," I said, like I could argue with it.

A man walking through the lobby nudged my arm. "It's January in Minnesota, dear. What'd you expect? A heat wave?" He got into the elevator laughing like he'd just said the funniest thing in the world.

Over in the breakfast room, some of the people sitting at tables had their coats on and their bags next to them, like as soon as they finished their instant oatmeal and coffee, they were going to rush out and drive, blizzard or not. But other people looked like they had no immediate plans aside from getting their money's worth from the buffet. A woman in line for the waffle maker was telling somebody "Well, we already missed the rehearsal dinner, so we're just going to give it another couple hours to settle down before we even try to head out."

That sounded smart to me. The breakfast room was warm and bright, and the buffet would have been Caleb's dream, with little boxes of different kinds of sugary cereal set out, and bagels with cream cheese packets, as many as you wanted, free for the taking—not to mention the waffle maker and the tub of batter at the ready. Most people were talking to each other or looking down at their phones, but there was a television, which, at the moment, showed a weatherman pointing to different-size snowflakes on a map of Minnesota.

I frowned, taking it in. Minnesota was a tall state, and if we hadn't even made it to Minneapolis yet, we were at the very bottom of it. We still had a long way to go.

I started thinking about how nice it would be to just take a little break, instead of going out in the cold with Chloe and trying to find some shoveled-out space to stand with our sign. I wanted to sit at a table all morning, warm and dry and eating bagels and drinking all the free coffee I wanted, and not even doing anything visibly illegal, with Chloe safe up in the room. I knew we couldn't waste the time, but still, it was a nice fantasy.

That's when I had the idea. I couldn't believe I hadn't thought of it before. Live and learn, as they say.

I got a napkin, an orange, a toasted bagel, and a packet of cream cheese for Chloe, as I had to run back up to the room for supplies anyway. She was still asleep, so I set it all on the nightstand. Ten minutes later, I was back downstairs in the breakfast room. I made myself a waffle, perfectly crisp at the edges, and I also got a coffee with extra cream, a glass of orange juice, and a bowl of Cheerios with milk. I even got a newspaper from the stack at the front desk. Just before I sat down, I taped the sign I'd just made to the edge of my table:

HEADED NORTH?
MY AUNT AND I WOULD
LOVE A RIDE!
WE HAVE $$$ FOR GAS

I knew the breakfast attendant saw the sign when she came out. But she looked too busy to bother with me, or maybe she didn't care.

The paper's front page was almost all about the bus in Detroit. They'd caught the men who'd done it: two men from Egypt who'd skipped out on the registry. In their photos, they both looked as cold and mean as you would expect a person would have to be to blow up people, including a kid, that they didn't even know. The inside of the paper had two pages dedicated to pictures of fugitives—ten rows of ten on each page. It took me a while to spot Chloe on the second page, fourth row down. Her real name, Sadaf Behzadi, was printed underneath.

Some of the other fugitives had Mexican names—there was a Maria Rosario Villalobos, and right next to her, an Ana Villalobos. Neither of them looked anything like Tess. But most of the fugitives had Arabic-sounding names, or names that just sounded generally foreign, though there was one bulgy-eyed blond guy name Brian T. Goodrich who looked like someone had snapped his picture right after sneaking up and saying "Boo!"

"How far north are you headed?"

I looked up. The speaker looked about twenty-five, and he wore a black hoodie that said *WISCONSIN* across the front. His hair was slicked back, still wet from the shower, and he looked like he'd nicked his chin shaving that morning. The cut was still bleeding a little.

I wiped my mouth with my napkin. "How far north are you going?"

"Winnipeg."

I nodded like that was just regular good news. But I knew Winnipeg was in Canada. And nothing about him seemed worrisome. His eyes were large and sort of amber looking, and though his skin looked especially pale against the black of his hoodie, he had an open, friendly face.

"Wow," I said. "That's exactly where we're headed. Me and my aunt."

He could be a killer, I thought. He could be a killer dressed like a college student from Wisconsin. Or he could be a killer who really was a college student from Wisconsin. Either way, he wouldn't necessarily be put off by the fact I'd have my aunt with me. He could just kill us both.

"Well"—he shrugged—"you can ride up with me if you like."

"Thank you!" I said. I was being polite. I hadn't made up my mind. I could say no, and try to hold out for a woman, or at least a family. But this was a bird in the hand, and he was going right up past the border. We'd done the right thing the day before, getting a ride with the brothers.

"When are you leaving?"

He took out his phone. His nails were clean and trimmed. "In the next half hour. Would that work for you?"

Like I was a paying customer. Maybe he wanted the gas money. "You're not worried about the weather?" I asked. I thought, Or that one of us is actually a fugitive trying to get out of the country?

He shook his head. "The plows have been out all night, and I've got studded tires. My girlfriend lives in Winnipeg, so I make the drive in weather all the time. I usually head up to Fargo, and then make a straight shot up I-29. I plan to get there in time for dinner."

I nodded, my hands squeezing my knees under the table. It

was too good to be true. Really. But maybe not.

"Is it okay if I text a picture of your license plate to my dad?" I smiled like I was embarrassed. "He worries. He's a cop."

I watched his eyes. They didn't change.

"That's no problem." He glanced at his phone again. "I'm Tyler, by the way. So you want to meet me down here at a quarter till nine? You and your aunt will be ready?"

When I got back upstairs, Chloe was sitting at the little desk by the window, reading her book and finishing the last of her bagel.

"How's the ear?" I asked.

She used a napkin to wipe cream cheese from her lip. "So much better, thank you. I put in a few drops just now, but already I don't need them as much."

I nodded. "Well. I may have more good news."

She was quiet as I described Tyler. I could tell she was anxious, or at least not sure. Her gaze moved across the ceiling.

"We can wait if you want," I said. "Or you can meet him yourself when we go downstairs. If you don't like him, we'll wait."

I meant it. I didn't want this to be all on me. But it seemed to me anyone, man or woman, would be a risk. It was a matter of which one we wanted to take. And if we said yes to Wisconsin Tyler, it would be the last ride we'd need.

She waited a while before she said anything.

"In time for dinner?" she asked. Her voice cracked on the last word. She wouldn't be having dinner with her family tonight, as they were way over in Toronto. But I knew she was thinking about them.

I nodded. She nodded too, and that was that.

By the time we got downstairs, Tyler already had his truck shoveled out, though snow was still falling on the roof and the hood, and also on the flat cover over the truck bed. He was still scraping the windshield when I went around the back with Chloe to get a picture of his license plate. His tailgate had some serious rust damage around the hinges, but his registration sticker was up-to-date, and he didn't have any bumper stickers, worrisome or otherwise. I thought about getting in the backseat with Chloe, as it looked big and comfortable, like the backseat of a car. But Tyler's duffel bag sat behind the driver's seat, and also I didn't want to be rude and make him feel like our chauffeur.

He slid the scraper under his seat before he climbed in. "Everybody ready?" he asked, looking at me, then back at Chloe. He had on dark sunglasses now. "Buckled up?"

Chloe didn't answer, and he seemed fine with that. I'd already explained she was visiting from Portugal, and that she didn't speak English. He hadn't had any follow-up questions, on that subject or on any other. In fact, even after we got on the interstate, it seemed like I could have sat in the back without him even noticing. He didn't say one word to me, and the only time he looked away from the road was to check the rearview.

I supposed he was just focused, which made sense, given the weather. We passed the flashing lights of highway patrol pulled over next to a car crunched into the rumpled back end of another, and a blinking sign hanging from an overpass told us to *WATCH FOR ICE*. Still, after we got past the exits for Saint Paul and Minneapolis, and the traffic thinned again, it seemed like it'd be okay to talk.

"We'll be glad to give you gas money," I said. I didn't want him to feel like he had to ask for it.

"That's okay." He glanced over his shoulder and turned on his blinker. "I'm making the drive anyway."

That was nice, I thought. Still, it seemed like everyone who'd given us a ride so far had a reason. Either Jesus had told them to pick us up, or they'd wanted to talk, or they wanted gas money, or they wanted somebody around to change the subject. The Amish people had just been quiet, but they still probably fell into the Jesus category.

"Do you go to school in Wisconsin?" I asked. I knew I was tempting fate. I mean, if Wisconsin Tyler didn't want to save my soul, or bring up Detroit, or talk to me about quilts for four hours, I could have just stayed quiet and thankful. But eventually, I was going to have to tell him that Chloe didn't have any ID, and that I didn't have a passport. I was thinking that it would be nice if we could have some kind of warm-up conversation first.

He nodded. "UW." He glanced at me. "Sorry. I like to concentrate when I drive. Nothing personal."

"No problem," I said. I only felt dumb for a second. He'd said it wasn't personal, and it wasn't like he had on the stereo.

But after a while, sitting there in the quiet, it occurred to me what might be really going on with him. A lot of his behavior would make sense if he had something illegal in the back of the truck, or even in his duffel bags.

I know that might sound paranoid to a lot of people. But back when Tom lived with us, he'd sometimes beg my mom and us to come with him on these drives that for a while seemed pointless. We'd drive and drive, and then he'd run into somebody's house real fast, leaving us in the car, and then we'd drive a little more, and he'd run into somebody else's apartment, and we'd go on like that for a few hours. He called it visiting friends, but I knew something was up, as they were pretty quick visits, and even my mom stayed in the car. Or sometimes on a Saturday he'd get a phone call, and then as soon as he hung up he'd say, "Let's all go down to Springfield. I'll take y'all to the mall." When we got there, he'd go off on his own for a while. One time after he came back, he gave me and Caleb two hundred dollars each to buy new school clothes, and then we all went to Applebee's, and then bowling.

So it wasn't hard for me to put things together and get that Tom was making deliveries on these drives. What I couldn't figure out was why he always wanted us to come along. So one day I just asked him. First he denied it, but when I didn't let up, he said, "Okay, Sarah-Mary. Okay. Just don't say anything to your brother." He said he really did like our company, but he also said that if he had us with him, he didn't fit the profile so much, and it was less likely he'd get pulled over. Or if he did get pulled over, the car might not be searched.

I suppose that would sound pretty awful to most people, that Tom used us, his girlfriend and her two kids, as a cover for driving around with bags of weed. But Caleb never even knew what was happening, and as I said earlier, Tom was nice to us. So even if I should have been put out about the using thing, I wasn't.

And now I was remembering that whenever we went on one of those drives, Tom had been an especially careful driver. After a while, that was how I knew if he had something in the car. If he didn't, he'd sometimes speed a little, or make a quick call from the highway, or turn up the radio loud and sing along with us when he liked the song. But other times, he was Mr. Follow-Every-Rule. We could talk, but he wouldn't. Even if other cars were flying by us, he wouldn't go over the speed limit, and no way would he get out his phone.

I glanced over at Tyler. He was still wearing the sunglasses, but I could see his eyes from the side, steady and focused on the road. Obviously, if a person needed to sneak a bunch of marijuana somewhere, it probably wouldn't be Canada. But he might be bringing in something else, something that was illegal there, too. And if he had two women in the car with him, one older than he was, and one younger, so much the better.

I knew I might have it all wrong. There was a chance he was just a nice person who liked it quiet when he drove. In any case, I wasn't about to start asking twenty questions, or let on at all about my theory. People were always forgetting to play dumb in movies—they'd tell the killer, *I know you're the killer!*, usually while they were alone with the killer on the edge of a cliff, or in an abandoned barn with a scythe on the wall. Whenever I see a scene like that, I always think that if it were me, I'd tell the killer, *Hmm, I have no idea what's going on. I'm just kind of hungry. Want to go into town and get something to eat?*

I turned around to see that Chloe was asleep, or pretending to sleep, her head against her window, her hat pulled over her eyes. Tyler appeared content to just keep driving, which was exactly what we needed him to do. It seemed like for once I could just relax. I popped the earbuds out of Tess's watch, slipped one in each ear, and settled in for an easy ride.

North Dakota was a whole other new state for me—I took a picture of the *Thank You for Visiting Minnesota* sign, and also the *Welcome to North Dakota—LEGENDARY* sign so I could show

Caleb later. But really, North Dakota didn't look any different from what I'd seen of Minnesota. There weren't any mountains, and the fields and trees and even the guardrails were covered in the same blinding white.

When we stopped at a gas station just outside of Fargo, a line of cars was waiting for a mini-plow to clear snow from around the pumps.

Tyler glanced at me. "Why don't you two go on ahead and order your lunch here while I'm filling up. I'd like to be on the road again in about fifteen minutes. You can get something to go and eat in the truck."

"Sounds good," I said. I got that he wasn't really asking—he was telling us to get our lunch to go. I hustled out, waving to Chloe like I had to tell her she needed to hustle too. I was thinking she'd be happy that he was in such a hurry, as she probably didn't want to spend an extra half hour hanging around a busy gas station that probably sold newspapers with her picture inside. But as soon as we were in the women's bathroom, she grabbed my arm. Before she said anything, she pushed the button on the hand dryer so no one in the stalls could hear.

"You have to tell him I don't have the ID," she whispered, getting out her ear drops. "We're close to the border. If he doesn't want to take me through, or he doesn't know how, it is better if he leaves us here, by a city."

I nodded, looking down at the muddy slush on the

bathroom's floor. She was right. I couldn't keep putting it off. But I still didn't know what he would say. I'd been riding alongside him all these hours, and I didn't have a take on him at all, other than my theory of why he might be going to Canada, and why he'd picked us up. I'd already decided I wasn't going to mention my theory to Chloe. She'd be uncomfortable with it, maybe, even the possibility. And what she didn't guess wouldn't hurt her.

When we came out into the store, Tyler was standing just outside the front windows, talking on his phone. Chloe and I picked out our sandwiches and drinks and got in line to pay. A road map was taped to the counter in front of the register, and right on our route, where I-29 touched the Canadian border, someone had written in ball-point pen, *SAY GOODBYE TO YOUR FREEDOM*.

Chloe stared at it so long I wanted to nudge her. She'd lived in the US long enough to know that whoever wrote that just meant they didn't want to turn in their guns. It didn't have anything to do with her, or what would happen to her at the border. Still, I wished I could tell her, *Don't worry about that. That's where you'll be saying hello to your freedom!*

There were people all around us, though, so I couldn't say anything. And anyway, she must have known, as I did, that a lot could happen between here and there.

* * *

331

As soon as Tyler put his phone away, I went outside, with Chloe following behind.

"Lot of snow, huh?"

He nodded and took a step back from me.

I pushed my hair out of my face. "And wind, too." I pretended to kick snow off my boots, waiting for a couple coming out of the store to pass by us. On the other side of the interstate, a man shoveled snow off the flat roof of a truck stop.

"So listen," I said, speaking more quietly now. "It turns out my aunt lost her ID. She doesn't have anything with her name on it."

He cocked his head. I could see my two reflections, side by side, in the lenses of his sunglasses. I didn't look as scared as I felt.

"And this is really crazy," I continued, "but I myself don't actually have a passport. I just have my driver's license."

"You need a passport for the border," he said. "You can't get out, and you can't get in. They don't mess around."

He'd said it like that was the end of it. Nothing else to add.

"Hmm." I nodded, waiting as another man walked by. "There aren't any, like, back roads or anything?" I took a breath. No backing out now. "If it's out of your way, we could pay. Like three hundred dollars?"

An old woman with a plastic kerchief over her hair was making her way from the handicap space up to the sidewalk. Tyler moved past me to hold open the door for her, staying quiet until she was inside. After the door closed behind her, he rubbed his lips together. It was hard to tell, because of the sunglasses, but it seemed like he was looking at Chloe.

"Your aunt's from Portugal?"

He asked like he believed it, or like he would if I said yes. But I imagined he knew when to play dumb, too.

"Yep," I said. "Just visiting."

He took off his sunglasses. "I do know a way." His amber eyes were steady on mine. "We'd have to go back into Minnesota. It'll take a little longer, but not that much. For three hundred dollars, I don't mind."

"Really?" I was almost 100 percent happy. I was only a little scared. "That'd be really nice. Thank you!"

"Sure." He checked his phone again and slid his glasses back on. "Just let me run in and get a few things for the road. And I've got to text my girlfriend and tell her I'll be late." He used his clicker to unlock his truck. "You and your aunt can wait inside. I'll be right out."

He was already moving around Chloe toward the door. As soon as he passed her, she looked at me, and I could see in her eyes, how scared they seemed, that she was thinking what I was—there was a chance, a good one, that he was going inside to call the police. If that was what he was doing, it made sense that he'd want us waiting in his truck, secure and ready for pickup.

Forget the three hundred dollars. He could make ten thousand with far less trouble.

She stepped close to me, touching the sleeve of my coat.

"Sarah-Mary. We'll say good-bye here. Now. You have to go."

"What? Go where? Where am I gonna go?"

She nodded toward the interstate. I knew she meant the truck stop on the other side, where the man was still shoveling the roof.

"You want me to run across? Like a deer?"

"Yes. Watch for cars, but please go now. In case he's calling the police. If he isn't, I don't need you anymore. He knows, Sarah-Mary. You could see it on his face. He will either take me or he won't." Vapor streamed out from her mouth. "There's nothing for you to do for me. Here." She tugged off her glove, reached into her bag, and pulled out her red wallet. "Here's two hundred." Her hand was shaking. "Fargo will have a bus station. Call a taxi to get into the town. Don't hitchhike by yourself. Take the bus home. Please know I will always be so grateful to you. But please go. Please."

I opened my mouth to argue with her, but just as a fat snowflake landed on my bottom lip, it occurred to me that I didn't have to argue anything. I turned around and started walking toward Tyler's truck. If he was turning us in, we were already done. We might as well get out of the cold.

I got up in the front seat of the truck, closed the door, and stared straight ahead. I knew she'd get in behind me. She had to. I didn't want to rub it in that she didn't have any choice, and that she didn't have any say in whether I stayed or went. I would have hated it, too, thinking someone else was going to get in trouble trying to help me, especially if I'd done nothing wrong in the first place.

After a minute or so, she climbed into the back. She didn't say anything, and I didn't turn around. I was already listening for sirens, for any kind of warning, and I imagined she was too. But there was just the snow falling softly around the truck. Cars drove up to the pumps, and drove away from them. A tall woman on her way up to the door started to slip, but she held out her arms and kept her balance.

"I'm sorry," I said. I didn't turn around. "I know me staying is just making you feel worse. I know you've already got enough on your mind. But I can't go until I know you made it. Get mad at my brother if you want." I shook my head. That wasn't right. That wasn't all of it. "Or consider it me trying to make up for everything. I'm trying to be a good American to you." I closed my eyes. That had come out wrong, too. I couldn't make it all up to her, even if she got out.

She didn't say anything. I turned around and saw she had her face in her hands. All I could see was a little bit of her hair and the top of her blue hat. I didn't know if I'd made it even worse, saying what I'd just said. She'd come over here in the first place because she thought this was the one place she'd be free, and safe. Now her sister was in Nevada, and all her friends. She'd lost her house and her job. And maybe her husband and son.

I couldn't make up for that. But I was at least going to stay with her until the end, good or bad. I couldn't promise her that, because she'd never let me. But too bad, I'd already promised myself.

I looked back out my window and saw Tyler coming out of the store, the hood of his sweatshirt pulled up. He walked in front of the truck, a plastic bag with something in it swinging from his hand. He opened his door, slid in behind the wheel, and reached between the seats to put the plastic bag in back. After he closed his door, he just sat there, looking at me, his sunglasses still on. I couldn't say anything, partly because I was so relieved, but also because I didn't know what he was waiting for.

Chloe reached up with three hundred-dollar bills, folded in half. He took them and pushed them into his back pocket.

"All right." He stretched his seat belt over his chest. "Everybody buckled in?" I nodded, and he glanced at Chloe in the rearview. "Okay then. Let's go to Canada."

The engine growled awake, the truck rolled forward, and just like that, we were on our way.

I hadn't even unwrapped my sandwich before we were back in Minnesota, heading north on Highway 75. It was plowed as well as the interstate, but there wasn't nearly as much traffic, and it seemed like enough of a back road to me. But after a while, we turned onto a two-lane that was even quieter, and then we turned left, and after another long while, right again. We kept stair-stepping like that, with nothing to see out the window but snow-covered fields, and every so often, a house or a barn or a hand-painted sign advertising firewood. Finally, we passed a sign that said *Fertile, Minnesota, Pop. 842.*

"Guess it's not that fertile," I said. Tyler didn't so much as smile, and I was polite enough to turn away before I rolled my eyes. I appreciated that he was still being careful, but even with a fugitive and whatever else he had going on in the truck, it seemed like he could lighten up a little, now that there weren't any other cars around.

He cleared his throat. "I'm going to listen to an audiobook for a while." He was already fiddling with the stereo.

"That sounds good," I said, meaning it. "Whatcha got?"

"Uh, I forget the title. It's a guide to smart investing."

I'll admit that from the get-go, I wasn't super excited about the subject matter. But the book was even worse than I thought, with no storytelling at all, just a guy reading in a flat voice about shares and Wall Street indicators and commodities, and using the phrase "increase wealth rapidly" like twenty-five times. It would've put me to sleep in just a few minutes if I'd kept listening, and as it didn't seem likely Tyler would take offense, I slipped my earbuds back in, looking back over my right shoulder at Chloe. She was awake, staring out the back window. Maybe she was listening and picking up investment tips, but it looked like she was just thinking, and the expression on her face seemed so sad, or maybe just tired. I was thinking she'd be excited, now that we were getting so close to the border. But she might have been thinking these fields and farms were the last she'd ever see of the United States.

It was weird to think I myself would actually be in another country soon, at least for a few hours. As soon as Chloe was safe and gone, I could call Tess. She'd been back from Puerto Rico for a whole day now, and I knew if I called her, she'd drive up to get me. I could tell her the truth, once it was safe to. But she would be the only person I'd tell about Chloe, ever, except for Caleb. I'd tell everybody else I'd run away, then after a few days, changed my mind. I'd be in trouble with Aunt Jenny, and maybe the law. But at least I'd get to see Caleb, and let him know Chloe was fine. He was probably so worried about both of us. I'd left on Wednesday, and it was Saturday now. All these days in between, he'd had to lie to Aunt Jenny, and anyone who asked, and say I'd left him, just like our mom had left him, at the McDonald's. He had to listen to whatever bad things people had to say about me while he was probably getting more worried about me every day.

Tess might be worried too, after listening to that crazy voice mail. She might have gone to the Dairy Queen to try to catch me working, and heard I'd missed two shifts while she was gone.

But there wouldn't be anything she could do about it. I'd told her not to tell.

I was still thinking all this out, looking out the window and braiding my hair in little strands by my ear, when I felt the truck start to slow. For a second, I thought we were running out of gas. That happened on the highway with my mom once, and I remembered how the car had slowed, then stopped, and how we'd all looked at each other so surprised like, *You're kidding. A car really needs gas to work?* But Tyler seemed calm as he eased the truck in front of a plowed drive, iced-over snow crunching under the tires.

I sat up, looking around. There was no reason to stop here. There was nothing. Maybe he needed to pee. That was possible. Still, by the time he put the gear in park, my hand was in my coat pocket, and I'd flicked the safety off the pepper spray.

"What's going on?" I asked, trying not to sound scared.

The engine was still running, and the windshield wipers whacked back and forth, pushing away falling snow.

"The road's getting really bad." He moved his palm along the edge of his cheek. "And I know from experience they don't plow as often, the farther north you go. We'll be better off stopping for the night if we can."

I didn't believe him. It wasn't snowing any harder than it had been when we'd stopped in Fargo, or even when we'd first set out from the hotel in Lakeville that morning. But whatever I believed or didn't believe, there wasn't anything I could do. We were way out in the country. The only building I could see, way off in the distance, was somebody's green-roofed house, and I didn't know how long it had been since we'd passed a gas station. I wanted to turn around and look at Chloe, and see what she was thinking. But I didn't want to take my eyes off him. The wipers kept their steady beat.

"We've got to get to Winnipeg tonight," I said.

He laughed a little, not in a mean way. Just like I didn't understand.

"Well"—his eyebrows moved up, then down—"I was in a hurry myself. And then I took this back road, because of your . . . lack of documents. And I'm sorry, but the snow's really piling up. I don't want to be out in the middle of nowhere when it gets dark."

I nodded. Maybe he was telling the truth. If he just wanted to go to a hotel, we could do that. I steadied my breath before I spoke.

"Where are you thinking of going?"

He got out his phone. "Well, I pulled over here because my buddy has a hunting lodge just a mile or so up this drive. It's closed for the season, but he stays through. I'm sure he'll give us a couple of rooms if he's around. And then we can start out in the morning." He held up one finger. "Hold on. I'll call and make sure he's there."

He was acting like he was being reasonable, like he was just making the best out of a bad situation. But all at once my coat felt tight and hot. Even if I didn't have Chloe with me, even if I was just with Caleb or anybody not wanted by the law, I would never agree to spend the night in some winter-closed hunting lodge in Who Knows Where, Minnesota. This was a start of a horror movie if I'd ever heard one.

"Hey, Dale. It's Tyler. Yup. Hey, listen. Are you around now? In the lodge?" He lifted his chin, his gaze moving around the windshield. Maybe he was really talking to someone. I considered that I could try to grab the phone from him and see for myself, but that didn't seem smart. If he was lying, that would just set things off in a direction I wasn't ready for them to go in. Really, there was nothing for me to do but sit there and watch him with my finger on the pepper-spray trigger.

Out of the corner of my eye, I saw something move along the floor of the truck, a strip of bright blue. The ice scraper. Chloe was sliding it toward her. I held my breath. At least there were two of us. We'd do okay, maybe, with pepper spray and an ice scraper. Unless he had a knife. Or a gun.

"Aw, that'd be great," Tyler said. "Yeah. I'm actually right at the start of River Road. Yeah. But here's the deal. I've got a couple of hitchhikers with me, a girl and her aunt. What? Yeah, I know. But they're fine. Nice people. Quiet. Anyway, they'll need a room too. I'm sure they can pay the rate. Will that work?"

I told myself it was possible he wasn't lying. It was possible that we'd really go to some closed-down lodge, get our own room with a lock, and start out for Winnipeg in the morning. And if that was really his plan and we flipped out now, if I pepper-sprayed him or Chloe tried to club him with his own ice scraper, we'd definitely regret it, not just for his sake, but for ours.

He put his phone away and looked at me. "Okay. He said he'll get two rooms ready for us." He smiled like I'd won a prize, like this was something I'd told him I wanted. "He's a good guy. We go way back, so he's not even going to charge us. And he's getting out clean sheets and everything."

He put the truck in gear and checked the rearview, like there were any other cars to worry about.

"Hey," I said. "Wait a minute." I tried to make my voice go deep, like I was serious and someone to listen to, but I was so scared I just sounded strange. "I appreciate you asking your friend for us, and all the trouble you've already gone to. But we'd rather stay in a regular hotel. I'm sure you understand." I tried my best to smile. "Is there a gas station or something around here? Somewhere you could drop us?"

He did the laughing thing again. "Uh . . . not unless you want to try your luck at somebody's farm. You could go around knocking on doors." He kept both hands on the wheel. "Listen. I told you I was taking a back road. The closest hotel would be in Thief River Falls, and that's some twenty-five miles back. I'm sorry, but I just don't feel comfortable doing that in this weather."

I tried to think. There had to be a way out. "What about dinner?"

He shrugged. "Dale'll probably offer us something. The last time I was there, his wife made spaghetti, and it was amazing. But she wasn't planning on us, so I don't know. They're hospitable people, though."

I gave him a long look. He hadn't said anything about a wife when he was on the phone.

"Oh." He blinked, his lips parted. "Are you . . . scared? Are you thinking I'm going to do something to you?"

I didn't say anything. My hand was still in my pocket. It was hard to imagine Chloe hitting anybody with an ice scraper, much less stabbing them with it. But she would. If he made a grab for me, I knew she would.

"Look," he said. "I'm just trying to make sure we get to Canada alive. It's not like that. Dale's got a wife, Ellie, and she's really nice. And anyway, you're gonna have your own room. Like a regular hotel room. Maybe not as nice." He laughed again, but it was a frustrated laugh, like he was trying to communicate with a crazy person. "A free room. And then a ride to Canada. It's a pretty good deal."

There wasn't really a decision to make. If he'd planned to get us way out here, where we couldn't say no, he'd already done it. And maybe it would all be okay.

It seemed like Chloe agreed, as she hadn't tried to club him yet. I waited a few seconds, just to see, but she stayed quiet.

"Thanks," I said. "That'd be great."

The road he turned onto was plowed, though only enough for one lane. It snaked its way around clusters of trees, the narrow trunks grown close together, the bare branches cradling snow. I stretched my neck to peer around every turn, but all I saw was more trees, and snow falling on snow. It would have been peaceful to look at, maybe, if I knew there really was a hunting lodge up ahead. But I could only take in short, quick breaths, because it was starting to seem a lot more likely that Tyler, if that was even his name, was going to stop at a clearing and kill us. He would bury us here. He'd have a shovel in the back of the truck. And wouldn't that be a way for me to go, after all my years of watching movies and thinking I was smarter than the people who got killed in them, and that it could never happen to me.

But then we came around another turn, and there it was—a long log cabin–looking building, one story, with eight windows and eight numbered doors, all evenly spaced and facing a plowed parking lot. The office was off on one side, its pitched roof rising a little taller than the rooms, like the head of a dark caterpillar. A sign just to the right of the glass door read *Welcome to the River Road Lodge!* The walkway to the office was shoveled except for what might have fallen in the last hour, but the rest of the building, including the doors to the rooms, were half-covered with snow. Tyler parked next to a smaller truck with a plow attached to the front.

"Well." He didn't look at me. "It's not a Hilton. But it'll have to do."

He got out of the truck. I looked over my shoulder at Chloe, who held my gaze and shook her head just once. I didn't know what that meant, exactly—what it was she was saying no to. But I agreed we shouldn't move just yet.

"You getting out?" Tyler asked. He'd left his door open, and snowflakes drifted onto his seat. I didn't say anything. I wanted to see the wife. I wanted her to come out here and ask us if we liked spaghetti.

He ducked, looking through the back window at Chloe. He shook his head and did the laughing thing again, like we were both just acting so strange. "Okay," he said. "I'll be right back."

I checked the ignition. He'd taken his keys. I turned around.

"I don't know what to do," I said.

She shook her head, her gloved hand over her mouth. I turned back to my window again, watching him make his way up the shoveled walk to the office door. He still just had on his Wisconsin sweatshirt, with no coat over it, and snowflakes settled on his shoulders and the back of his hair. He tried opening the glass door. When it didn't open, he knocked on the glass and cupped his hands around his eyes.

"You got the ice scraper?" I turned around again.

She nodded, glancing down. She had it tucked between her boots.

"But he might not plan to harm us," she said. "He might just want to stop for the night. Look." She nodded toward the cabin, where a bearded man in a flannel shirt had opened the office door. Tyler turned around and pointed at us, looking like he was explaining something. The man nodded. Tyler smiled at us, and gave us a thumbs-up, then followed the bearded man inside.

I turned around again, nodding down at the plastic grocery bag. "What's in there?"

"Crackers. Beef Jerky."

"What about the duffel bag?"

She hesitated. "You want me to look through his things?"

"Yeah." I turned back to the office door. "I'll keep watch. I just want to know what's in there." I didn't know what I thought she'd find. Drugs. A gun. Heavy rope. If he'd wanted to hurt us, he'd already had plenty of opportunity. I still wanted to know what was in the bag.

"There is only clothes," she said. "And a toothbrush. Toothpaste." She zipped the bag closed, smoothing the top like she wanted to undo what she'd done. "But we can't go in. We can't."

I tried to think. We couldn't lock him out. He had the clicker. We could get out and run, but to where?

"I am so sorry," she said, and I could hear she was trying not to cry. "I am so sorry that you are here. This is my fault. All of this has been my fault."

"You told me to leave," I said. "You told me twice." I was thinking I was the one who should feel bad. I could have told her back in Fargo that I thought Tyler might have something illegal in his truck. I'd told myself that it was just a theory, and that I didn't want to scare her. But it was a pretty good theory. And she might have been right to be scared.

She touched my shoulder. "Here he is."

Tyler moved carefully over the walk, a pale yellow bundle in his arms. The bearded man waved from the doorway, then went back in.

Tyler opened the door to the truck. It seemed like a good sign that he'd opened the driver's door. He was keeping his distance.

"Okay," he said, ducking enough to see my face. "Here's the deal. His wife's in Florida right now, visiting her sister."

We stared at each other. He glanced back at Chloe.

"But here are the clean sheets. And here's the room key." He put the folded yellow sheets on his seat. A key attached to a green plastic diamond sat in the middle. "You're in number two. I'm in number one. He said he left the bathroom sink running a little so the pipes wouldn't freeze, and you shouldn't turn it off. Okay?"

He was speaking to me slowly, like I wasn't very smart, or like I was famous for my crazy temper. I nodded.

"I'm not going to so much as knock on your door. But I'm going to be out here at nine a.m. tomorrow, ready to go. Dale said it's going to stop snowing tonight, and that'll give the plows time to get up north."

I nodded again. All of this sounded reasonable. I was starting to feel dumb.

"I'm going to have mac and cheese with Dale in his place, and he said you're both welcome to join us, but if you're . . . uncomfortable with that, I can give you my crackers and beef jerky I bought back in Fargo. Okay? It's in the plastic bag there in the backseat." He held up his palms. "So all I need right now is my bag, and I'm going to go inside, and you can do what you want. But it's probably too cold to sleep out here. I wouldn't recommend it."

Chloe passed his bag up through the seats. I felt bad that he was having to act like the truck was ours. And that he had to give us his beef jerky and crackers. There was a chance he was a good person, and we were treating him like he wasn't.

"Okay," he said, nodding to Chloe, and then to me. "See you tomorrow."

He closed his door, jingling his keys with a wave. We watched him go up the walk and disappear through the door. And then it was just us, sitting in the truck, the cold already settling in.

16

AS SOON AS we got in the room, Chloe pulled the ice scraper out from under her coat and raised it like a baseball bat. I checked the lock, fixed the chain, and pressed my back against the door.

She took a step forward. "You stay here."

I grabbed the sleeve of her coat. When she looked back, I shook my head. No way was I going to stand there by myself while she walked around a cold and musty hunting-lodge room that even in daylight looked like a prime location for a murder. The walls were covered in wood paneling, and the only decoration was a framed poster of a mallard duck taking flight from a lake. Beneath the poster was a stripped double bed with a folded green cover at the foot, and next to that was a little desk lamp sitting on a nightstand that wasn't as tall as the bed. A couple of dressers stood against the opposite wall. One had a television on it, the old box-shaped kind, secured to the wall by what looked like a bicycle lock.

Chloe yanked back one of the plaid curtains, letting in the silvery light of the clouded sky. We moved toward the bathroom together, my hand still tight on her sleeve. She pushed open the door and jumped in with both feet, keeping the ice scraper raised. Water dripped from the faucet of the sink. I flung back the shower curtain, ready with my pepper spray, but there was nothing in the tub but an orange stain by the drain. Still, when we came out of the bathroom, we went through the same procedure with the sliding door of the closet, only finding some wire hangers and a couple of wool blankets folded on the shelf. I got down on my hands and knees to look under the bed, but the frame was too low to the ground for anyone to be hiding under.

"Okay." Chloe looked up at the low ceiling. "It is okay. It is fine."

She went back to the door and held her hand against it while she slid off her boots. We'd already tracked snow onto the gray carpet, but I pulled off my boots too, taking giant steps on my way back to the bathroom so I wouldn't get my socks wet.

When I came out of the bathroom, Chloe was fiddling with the thermostat. Something in the heater under the window started to hum.

"That's encouraging," I said, my voice a little too chipper, like we were just a couple of ladies on a weekend trip and our biggest problem was that the heat wouldn't work. I didn't want to think about our actual situation, or how far away we were from anyone who could help us, even if they would.

She went over to the dresser that didn't have the television on it and tried to lift one side. "It is heavy," she said. "You will help me move it to the door? We can put our things inside to make it more heavy?"

I got on one side of the dresser, and we half-slid, half-carried it to the door. We pushed our bags in the drawers, hers on top of mine. I put the plastic bag with Tyler's crackers and beef jerky in the third drawer.

"That's all we can do," she said, turning on the overhead light. She moved around me to close both curtains before she pulled off her hat. Her hair was smashed flat where her hat had been, but still wavy on the bottom.

"Maybe it will be fine," she said, giving me a little nod like we were agreeing it was true. "Maybe there is no problem."

I looked at Tess's watch. It was almost five. We'd have about sixteen hours, at the most, before we knew if there was a problem or not.

I didn't even check to see if we had hot water. It seemed to me that if I was stupid enough to take a shower in that place, I might as well find some ominous music to play and then go ahead and get a knife to stab myself with forty-five times so I could just get it over with. Chloe was apparently of the same mind: she took her bag with her into the bathroom, and I heard the sink running, but not the shower. She came out wearing her wide-legged pants, the white sweatshirt, and a yellow pair of socks.

"You like *Jeopardy!*?" I asked, nodding at the television. There weren't any chairs, so I was on the bed we'd made up, sitting under the mallard duck. "That big guy on the left is killing it, and they haven't even hit the Daily Double."

She pushed her bag back into her drawer. "I do like it," she said. "I play against my husband, and I often win." She turned around, holding a rolled-up mat and a brown velvet bag that looked like something you'd keep jewelry in. "But now I need to pray."

"Oh." I sat up, glancing back into the bathroom. It was the only place I could go to give her privacy.

"Just do as you were. It will not take so long." She tucked the mat under her arm, pulled a long white scarf out of her bag, and used one hand to drape the scarf over her hair, pushing the long end over her shoulder. It looked right the first time she did it, and she didn't even have a mirror. She reached into the bag again and brought out something silver, small enough to fit in the palm of her hand. She squinted down at it, then turned, a little at a time, until she was nearly facing the wall opposite the window. She walked to the other side of the bed, still facing that same direction, and spread out a green-and-gold mat about the size of a bath towel.

"You need me to turn off the television at least?"

She shrugged, setting something small and circular on the mat. "No. I am fine."

That was nice of her. In my experience with religious people, when they tell you they're getting ready to pray, that means they usually want you to be quiet, or they even say "let us pray," like they just assume you're in on it. Or they're pretty much telling you you're going to be in on it, so you might as well bow your head. That was certainly true at Berean Baptist, which I understand, as it was a religious school. But it was even true when I was in public school in Joplin. Right before our spring choir concert, our teacher was really nervous, and she had us all pray together that we would sing our best and bring glory to God through our voices. And of course, Aunt Jenny always said grace at the table. In all of those cases, it never killed me to just close my eyes and bow my head to be polite. But I didn't know what to do around a praying Muslim.

Whatever she said, it seemed kind of rude for me to leave the television on, with people calling out their question-answers and Alex Trebek saying "no" while someone was trying to pray. I picked up the remote, hit the power button, and lay on my side, facing away from Chloe. Her back was to me, but if she turned around, I didn't want her to feel like she was being watched. And anyway, even with the locks, and the dresser we'd moved, it seemed like one of us should keep an eye on the door.

* * *

Before we went to bed, she prayed again, even though she hadn't done anything since the last time she prayed except eat beef jerky and crackers and watch television with me. She had to go through the whole deal of getting her mat out again and setting it up in the right spot—it seemed to me she could have just left it out from last time, but I guess not.

I watched her put her prayer things away before I took out my earbuds. I was ready for bed, the blankets pulled up to my armpits, though I was still wearing my sweater and jeans. I'd already decided to sleep in my clothes. If somebody tried to bust through the door chain in the middle of the night, I wanted to be ready. My boots were next to the bed.

"Hey," I said. "Can I ask you a question?"

"You just did." She looked at me over her shoulder and smiled.

Ho ho ho, I thought. Chloe made a joke. It was sort of a lame one. But still. Good effort.

"I'm sorry." She turned around, still smiling. "What is the question?"

"You ever get tired of having to pray so much?"

She frowned. I frowned back. I hadn't meant it the way it came out, like I was pretending to just ask a question but really trying to convince her of something. I sounded as bad as Patty Charlson from seventh grade, who once asked me, with a really nice and caring look on her face, why I wasn't more worried about spending eternity in hell, as I had not accepted Jesus as my personal savior and could not be convinced by Patty to do so, or even come with her to church. That always got on my nerves, when people acted like I was a sad story because I didn't believe what they did.

But I wasn't trying to talk Chloe into or out of anything. I really just wanted to know.

"Sorry." I waited to let the word settle in. "What I mean is, is it like something bad will happen to you if you don't pray? Like you'll go to hell if you don't do it enough?"

She leaned on the dresser, tilting her head back and forth like she had a marble rolling around inside. "No. It is not that. I want to do it."

I nodded. It didn't seem like there was much more I could ask without feeling like I was cross-examining her, like I was the atheist version of Patty Charlson. Also, with religious people, you have to be careful because sometimes if you ask too many questions they start to think it's the green light to start trying to convert you when really you're just curious.

She walked around to the other side of the bed, setting her ear drops on the night stand. "It's a time for me to remember God, and to remind myself to be and do good." She got in bed slowly, careful not to tug on the cover or the sheets. I could smell her lotion, or her soap, whatever she put on that was minty. "I do it because it is pleasing to God, but it's pleasing to God because it is good for my soul, just as the movement is good for my body." She put her head on the pillow, looking up at the ceiling. "And to answer your first question, no, I do not get tired of it. Some days I think I am too tired, or too busy. But it is when I am tired that I need prayer the most. It restores me."

"Okay," I said. I wasn't going to argue with her about it. But she'd just prayed, and she still looked pretty tired.

She smiled like she guessed what I was thinking. "It is not exactly what I mean. It would be better to say that when I pray, I'm reminded that God does not want me to be sad or afraid." She shrugged. "And that I don't need to be."

"You're not afraid now?" I tried not to say it like I didn't believe her. But I myself wasn't looking forward to her turning off the lamp. We hadn't heard Tyler's door, or anything from his room, for a while, and I told myself that was a good sign. For all we knew, he was already asleep, getting rested up for tomorrow's drive.

"I'm less afraid than I would be." She pulled her hair back and lay her head back on the pillow. "I might even be able to sleep."

Maybe it was the God thing that was the difference. Or maybe I was just more jittery by nature. But long after I heard Chloe snoring—nothing loud, just a whistle between her teeth when she exhaled—I was still lying there in the dark with my eyes open and my head buzzing like I'd just slammed an energy drink. I could hear the trickle of water from the bathroom sink. My feet were cold, but I already had on both pairs of my socks. So there was nothing to do but lie there with cold toes and try to keep reminding myself that Chloe was right—there might not be any problem with Tyler. It was entirely possible, maybe, that he had really just been worried about the weather.

I turned on my side, facing the dark outline of the closed curtain. Chloe's breath kept whistling, and the water kept trickling from the sink. I thought I heard something outside, some kind of cracking sound, but then I didn't hear it again. When I closed my eyes, I saw the old man who'd gotten shot in Sherburn, and I heard the thuds of the body, hitting the door and then the ground. The people he'd been hiding were probably in Nevada now. I hoped the one who needed medicine could get it.

It was a hard thing to consider that a lot of the people put in the safety zones might not have done anything wrong, except share a religion, at least in name, with people who were crazy. If I put myself in their shoes, I could understand the bad spot a lot of Muslims were in. I mean, if some atheists started going around killing people, which I knew some of them already did, but I mean if they started saying, *We're killing all these innocent people in the name of atheism!*, I'd be horrified just like everybody else, but it's not like I'd change my mind and not be an atheist anymore, or start going to church of my own free will so no one would think I was a killer. I'd think, *That's messed up. But that's not me.* I wouldn't just stop thinking what I think. I wouldn't want to pretend, either. But I'd hate to be lumped in with killers when I myself hadn't done anything wrong and had no intention of killing anybody, just cause of what I did or didn't believe about God.

I turned over again, trying to find a softer spot on my pillow. The edge of the blanket we'd gotten down from the closet felt scratchy against my chin, and it seemed like it might be the main source of the room's musty smell. I was hungry, but not for beef jerky, which was all that was left in the plastic bag. I was wondering when and where we might stop for breakfast in the morning when I heard the muffled slam of a car door.

I sat up in the darkness. Silence. Chloe breathing. And then, so quiet I almost didn't hear it, the outer edges of someone's voice in the parking lot.

I slid out of bed and felt my way across the room. I told myself it would be okay. Someone was just out in the lot. Maybe Tyler had left something in his truck. Everything was probably fine.

I pulled the curtain back slowly, just a few inches. The sky had cleared, just as Tyler had said it would, and the moon was so bright against the snow on the ground I had to squint. Even without any lights in the parking lot, it was easy to see a two-door car idling at an angle next to Tyler's truck. A man with a blond ponytail was lifting the trunk door of the car and talking to Tyler, who used one arm to push snow off the plastic cover over the bed of his truck. The man helped him move the cover to the side, and Tyler reached in the truck bed and lifted what looked like a twenty-pound bag of dog food—I could see a picture of a dog on the side of the bag. He handed the bag to the other man, who put it in the trunk of his car.

"Sarah-Mary? What is it?"

I jumped back from the curtain, my hand on my throat. I couldn't see anything but dark.

"Why are you by the window?" Chloe's whisper was low and gravelly. "What do you see?"

"Hold on. Don't turn on the light." I turned back to the window and moved the edge of the curtain again. The trunk of the car was closed now, and both the ponytail man and Tyler were putting the plastic cover back over the bed of Tyler's truck. When they finished, the man got in his car.

"It's okay," I whispered. I didn't want Chloe to think there was an emergency. There wasn't. The truck that I'd assumed was Dale's, the one with the plow on the front that had been here when we'd pulled up, was still parked in the lot, the windshield covered in snow. So Dale was still here. And Tyler was still here. All that had happened was that Tyler had moved some things out of his truck to a third party. That didn't have to be any business of ours.

"Please tell me what it is you see."

"Just wait." Even with two pairs of socks, the floor felt cold on my toes.

When I looked back out, the car was rolling away. Tyler hurried up the shoveled path to the office, blowing into his hands. When I couldn't see him anymore, I stepped away from the window and told Chloe she could turn on the lamp.

She stayed quiet, sitting up in bed, her head just under the mallard duck, as I told her what I'd seen. I was trying to convey to her that everything was fine, but I couldn't get my knees to stop wobbling, which made no sense, because really, nothing I'd witnessed was particularly worrisome. But I had to sit on the edge of the bed and press down on my knees to still them.

"I don't think it was dog food," I said. I wasn't sure she understood. The lamp by the bed gave off a dim yellow glow that cast half of her face in shadow. At first, she didn't say anything, and I thought I'd have to spell it out.

But then she said, "I see."

"I wondered if he was moving something. I should have told you."

She nodded like she wasn't mad. Or she was thinking about something else.

"It's probably got nothing to do with us," I added. I couldn't figure out how it would. And he hadn't bothered us yet. He'd just given us crackers and beef jerky and gone back to his room. Still, I had a bad feeling there was something I wasn't putting together, a riddle I hadn't figured out.

Chloe reached over to the nightstand for her glasses. She kept looking all around the room, and she seemed distracted, or like she was thinking something but not saying it.

"Well," she said finally, glancing at her watch. "It is only a little after ten. And I won't be able to go back to sleep for a while." She tucked her hair behind her ears and gave me a smile that didn't look happy. "We can watch television?"

I was fine with that, but I thought it was weird how she asked in such a nice way, her voice gentle, like I was a little kid who'd had a nightmare and needed to be consoled. She used the remote to click through channels until she got to the news out of Grand Forks, which didn't seem like the most exciting choice to me. But I got back on my side of the bed, folding my pillow under my head.

"Maybe there's a movie or something," I said. "You could cruise the channels."

She nodded, still looking at the screen. "This first," she said. "Just to see."

I didn't want to be rude, but I was thinking, see what? I mean, local news shows always looked pretty low-rent compared to Aunt Jenny's cable shows, and Grand Forks's news was no different. The anchor had a flag pin just like ours, and she had a nice speaking voice, but she was just a regular-looking woman who never would have made it on the cable shows, and anyway, there wasn't a lot anyone could have done to jazz up the long opening piece about a meeting on municipal waste. After staying on that topic way too long, she moved on to a story about a fire at an Indian restaurant that was still being investigated, meaning nobody knew anything yet. I sighed to show I was bored, but Chloe either didn't notice or she ignored me.

She didn't even change channels during the commercials, which were local as well, so we both just sat there and watched as a Grand Forks car dealer wearing a spandex suit and eye goggles ran between two lines of parked cars with a chainsaw, saying he was going crazy cutting down prices. The next commercial was for a pizza place that delivered, the number flashing at the bottom of the screen, and they were mean enough to show a slice of thick-crusted pizza being raised up out of a pie, strands of melted cheese hanging down.

"Oh my God," I moaned, cradling my belly. "I could very much go for some of that right now. You think they deliver out here?"

It was just a joke. I mean, obviously. We didn't even have a phone that would make the call, and we were probably twenty miles outside of any delivery range, even in regular weather. But Chloe didn't smile or even acknowledge that I'd said anything, and it occurred to me that maybe she was mad at me after all. I supposed she had a right to be. If I'd told her my theory about Tyler when we were back in Fargo, she could have decided we were done with him, and we could have hitched with someone else. She would probably have been in Canada by now. Or at least a normal hotel room.

"Hey." I nudged her elbow. "I feel bad about not telling you I thought Tyler might—"

She held up her hand. The news had come back on, but instead of the anchor, *SPECIAL SECURITY REPORT* was written in black against white, and there was a picture of the flag underneath. There was different music, too, something exciting, with more drums. But when the anchor came back on, she didn't seem any more pumped than she'd been when talking about the municipal waste.

"We're breaking in to our scheduled reports to tell our viewers that during the last commercial break, our Channel 5 Nightwatch Team passed on an unconfirmed report that police in Northwestern Minnesota are currently en route to apprehend a Muslim fugitive in a remote location about fifty-five miles northeast of Grand Forks."

I turned to Chloe. She looked back at me, and the expression on her face made me feel like maybe I'd heard wrong, and everything was still okay. She didn't seem scared, or even surprised. She had the face of someone hearing a sad story about something bad that had happened a long time ago, something already done and over. She put her hand on the sleeve of my sweater.

"Sarah-Mary," she said, using the same gentle voice she'd used earlier. "You understand? That is us. They are coming for us already." She didn't even seem surprised. And it was only then that I got it—this was why she'd wanted to watch television in the first place. She'd known. Or she'd suspected. She'd just been checking to make sure.

"Do you see?" She put her palms to her cheeks and slid them down to her throat. "He knew what I was back in Fargo. But he couldn't call, because he had something in his truck. He got rid of it so he could call and get the money."

"WNDR does not encourage anyone to interfere with police business, but any of our viewers interested in learning the specific location of the suspects can check our website, as WNDR is always committed to keeping our viewers informed on matters of public safety."

I shook my head. We were so close, so close to the border, so close to her husband and her little boy. This couldn't be right, that everything could end like this because of one mistake I'd made. I got up and hurried around the bed to the window.

"Turn off the lamp," I whispered.

The room went dark, and I used just one finger to move the curtain back. Outside, all was silent and still. The almost half-moon glowed above the trees and the two trucks in the lot. But of course she was right. We were in a remote location, and probably about fifty-five miles northeast of Grand Forks. The police were on their way, and worse than that, maybe other people. If they got here before the police, they'd throw rocks through the window. They'd throw rocks at us.

I let the curtain fall. "Then we've got to go!" I whispered. "Let's go! You can turn the light on. He's not out there. But we've got to move."

She turned the lamp back on, but she didn't get up. She tapped her finger against the diamond on her wedding ring.

"Move where?" She said it more like an answer than a question, watching me as I hurried back around the bed to grab my boots. I got what she meant. It was freezing outside, and dark, and we were way out in the country. But we couldn't just wait there with the wood paneling and the mallard duck and the yellow light for the first car to roll up into the lot outside. Not when I was the one who'd gotten her out here.

"Sarah-Mary," she said. "You know he is watching for us. He won't just let us run away."

"He wasn't out there when I looked." I pulled up the zipper on my boot so fast it bit my finger. "Listen up, Chloe. I'm walking out of here in one minute." I went over to the closet and grabbed my coat. "Get up and come with me. Okay? Please?" I let my voice break. I'd cry if I had to. I'd pull out all the stops. "Okay? I'm scared to go out by myself."

She didn't ask me where I planned to go, which was good, because I didn't know. Less than a minute later, we were both ready, coats and boots zipped, hats and gloves on, our bags on the floor beside us as we scooted the dresser away from the door. She was still wearing her pajamas, her wide-legged pants stuffed into her boots. I'd left my toothbrush and comb in the bathroom, and my pulse was a drumbeat in my head, *go now, go now, go now, go now, go now.*

But once we pulled the dresser away and Chloe undid the chain lock, she paused to look at me, her hand on the doorknob.

"You are ready?" she whispered. She had the ice scraper tucked under her arm. "We'll go right to the trees. A straight line."

I held my breath. She turned the knob, opening the door just a crack at first, and then wider, and wider still, until I could see out as well. All was quiet outside, the snow by our door undisturbed except for our own tracks from the afternoon. The stars were out too, twinkling high, but the air coming in was cold enough to sting my cheeks. She held her hand out to me and I took it. Then we ran out into the night.

I think part of me knew, even as we ran, even as I kept my gaze on the trees beyond the lot like they were a finish line, that Chloe was right about Tyler watching for us. After all the trouble he'd gone to, and all he stood to gain, it wouldn't have made sense for him to just stay inside, warm and cozy, and assume we'd stay put as long as needed. But the night kept quiet as we kicked through the snow, and I could only hear the crunch of its iced-over surface under my boots and Chloe's, and I let myself hope as I sucked in cold air, holding tight to Chloe's gloved hand. But then I heard more crunching behind us, moving fast, and I didn't even have time to cry out before the sleeve of a down jacket moved fast and tight around my neck. I fell back into a body, padded and wide, as another arm clamped around my waist.

"Hold on now!" he yelled, but not in a mean way. He might have been talking to himself. "Just hold on!"

It wasn't Tyler. It was the other one, Dale, the lodge owner, smelling of cigarettes, his bristly beard pressed against my cheek. The more I thrashed, the tighter he held me, and out of the corner of my eye, I could see that Tyler had come up behind Chloe in the same way. Or he'd tried to. He had his right arm around her neck, and her left arm pushed down, but her right arm was still free, stabbing at his leg with the ice scraper.

I pulled up both legs and brought down my heels against Dale's shins.

"Hey!" he said, like he was surprised I was fighting, like he'd just expected me to go limp in his arms. "Just settle down, okay? It's her they want. They don't even know about you. You stop fighting us and you'll be okay. We'll get you back into town. Come on now. It's over for her. Be smart."

Tyler cried out, but he and Chloe had moved behind me, or we'd moved forward, and I couldn't see them anymore. My hat was gone, the air cold on the tips of my ears. I pulled my head away from Dale's cheek and brought it back hard.

"Hey!" he said, louder now, though he only tightened his arms. "Come on now. Jesus! I got a heart condition, okay?"

I didn't care about his heart condition. But I got that he was pleading with me when he didn't have to, and I could feel in the way he held me, with enough space between his arm and my throat that I could breathe, that he didn't want to hurt me. Chloe cried out behind me, and when I tried to turn my head, my nose pressed up into Dale's tobacco beard.

"Be smart," he whispered. "You're the reason I didn't get my gun, and I wouldn't let him borrow one. There's no reason for you to get hurt. But he'll hurt you, okay? I'm your friend. I'm your friend here."

"You better let go," I hissed. I didn't want to hurt him either. But he wasn't my friend, not if he wasn't Chloe's. I didn't care if he was going easy on me or not. And maybe some people will think worse of me for what happened next, or think I'm some kind of animal, which maybe I am because here's the truth: next thing I knew, I'd pushed my nose down a little more so my mouth was right up against his bristly beard, and I clamped my teeth into his jaw like an attack dog, and I kept clamping. Even after he cried out and gripped at my head, and yelled "Oh! Oh, please!" I didn't let go. He grabbed my shoulders from behind and tried to push me away, and I felt skin give way between my teeth, then warm blood on my tongue, but I was a pit bull, locked on. What happened next was up to him.

We fell into the snow together, with me still biting down

and tasting blood and him clawing at the back of my head. He grabbed hold of my hair with both hands and tried to pull my head away from him. I didn't let go, and he didn't let go, and just as I got my hand in my pocket, I felt a giving way above my ears as two fistfuls of hair tore from my scalp, the roots coming out like jagged hooks. His breath caught with the surprise of it, and his hands flew up, newly freed, and in that second I had the safety cap off the pepper spray and the can in his eyes. I unlocked my teeth and turned my own head away before I pushed hard on the trigger.

His scream, when it came, rattled my heart like someone had reached into my chest and shaken it. My own eyes burned, but I could see his hands were over his eyes, clumps of my torn-away hair still threaded between his fingers.

I had to step on his chest to get to my feet. Once I was up, I turned in a circle, gasping and coughing until my stinging eyes found Tyler. He was hunched over Chloe, who was down in the snow, writhing and punching and kicking as he tried to grab hold of her. I ran toward them, and his bulging eyes looked up at me just before I pressed the trigger again, harder and longer than I had before. At first, I thought it didn't work. He grabbed the back of my neck, and I was the one sucking in the stinging heat. But then his chest fell away from my pounding fists, and before I even opened my eyes, I screamed for Chloe to hold her breath and get up, get up, and run.

17

THE TREES WOULD have been safer, but the snow was too high to run through. So we kept to the tire tracks in the road, and there was the bad feeling of being in a chute of some kind, like nowhere to go but forward. But once the screams faded behind us, I heard nothing except for our own breathing and the steady beat of our boots. Every time we rounded a turn, I peered back through the trees. I didn't know how long we had until Tyler or Dale would be able to drive, or until the police, or the people who'd seen the news and were already racing out here to beat them, reached us.

When we reached the main road, Chloe held up her hand to show she couldn't go any farther. She bent forward, her elbows on her knees, her bag swung behind her for balance. I walked in circles, my throat burning, my watery eyes blurring my vision. The cold seeped in and stayed where my hair had been torn out. I pulled up my hood.

"Which way?" I panted, as if that were a reasonable question, as if Chloe was supposed to pull out her compass and figure out which way was north so we could just walk to Canada from however far away we were before anyone found us. I knew it didn't matter which way we went. There was no plan that could save us.

Chloe straightened and pulled her hat low. She had a cut on her lip, still bleeding, and she'd lost her glasses too. She peered down the road in one direction, and then back in the other. I did the same. In the moonlight, the road looked lavender, fading to gray and then darkness in either direction.

"I don't know," she said, breathing out through chattering teeth. She looked up, so I looked up too. And I have to say, even in that moment when I was so freezing cold and winded and kicked in the heart because I understood now that she wasn't going to make it to Canada, and that all of this trying and scheming we'd done had just been for nothing, I couldn't help but notice the stars. I guess the lights of Joplin and even little Hannibal were bright enough to shut most of them out, because I swear I'd never seen so many. It was like someone had shaken diamonds out across the sky.

One of my teachers in Joplin told me that a long time ago, people used to think that the sky was a dome and the stars were just little pinpricks that let in the light of heaven, and as crazy as that sounds, I could see how they would think that. But in my opinion, it was even more amazing to think what stars really were: big balls of gas so far away that the light took years to get here, sometimes thousands of years. If thinking about that didn't make a person shake her head and have nothing to say, I didn't know what would.

"My family once rented a house by the sea," Chloe said, still looking up. "Just for a few days. I was six. Maybe seven." She smiled, her cheeks flushed from the cold. "My father loved the beach. It was too cold to swim, but we'd stay out late, and the stars looked just like this. There were this many."

I nodded, the frozen snot under my nose going tight. You don't think about Iran and the outback of Minnesota having anything in common, but I guess we were looking up at it.

"They're here," she whispered. I followed her gaze to our left, where a pair of headlights, still maybe a mile away, moved steadily down the road. I shook my head, but that was all I could do. Whoever it was was driving fast, like they couldn't get to us soon enough.

Chloe grabbed my arm and pulled me back to the edge of the drive. We jumped high over the ridge of snow and staggered into the trees, my boots sinking deep until we reached a thicket that let down what felt like five pounds of snow when my shoulder brushed against it. We fell behind its cover, still as stones until the headlights swept over the thicket.

The engine roared, then faded. I peeked out to see the back

of a white Suburban just before it disappeared around a turn.

"Was that the police?" Chloe whispered.

I shrugged to show I didn't know. I could see how the police would want to drive out in an unmarked car, with no flashing lights or sirens. They wouldn't want to give us any warning. But it was just as likely somebody who only wanted to watch, who had a GPS and the address from the news station's blog, and maybe, even on a night like this, lawn chairs in the back. And just thinking about that made me feel so lonely, even with Chloe beside me. Because we were alone. I was the only one helping her, and I wasn't enough. Too many people were against us, who didn't care anything about how we were feeling now. I'd thought I was so smart, and so good at scheming, that I'd be able to get her through. But that was just dumb. I was one person. One person wasn't enough.

Chloe peered through the thicket. "When it is the police, when we know it is them, we have to go to them, Sarah-Mary. You understand? We will freeze to death if we stay out here. Even if we don't, they'll find us in the morning. And if the police aren't the ones to find us, it will be worse. We are better off with the police."

She looked at me, waiting, until I nodded. I knew she was right.

"I'm so sorry," I said, and my heart clenched in, because it was such a small thing to say, and not enough in the face of everything she was about to lose. But I was sorry. Sorry that I'd said we should go with Tyler. Sorry that she'd had to run in the first place. Sorry that she wouldn't be with her husband and son tomorrow, or the day after that, or the day after that.

She started to say something when another pair of headlights glinted through the trees, this time coming from the right. She touched my arm and we ducked low again, listening as the engine hummed louder. Melted snow seeped in through the knees of my jeans, but I stayed still. She kept her hand on my arm, whispering words I didn't understand. I held my breath, glad that if she was praying, at least she wouldn't feel as alone or as afraid as I did. Because soon enough she wouldn't even have me. I wouldn't have her either.

The headlights moved over us. Chloe kept whispering prayers I didn't understand, *Allah* the only word I understood. It was a green van, and now I could see the taillights. They were almost at the turn when the brake lights flashed. The van idled, the hum of the engine steady. There was no reason for them to stop out here. Chloe's grip tightened on my arm.

"They could not have seen us," she whispered. "It's impossible."

But the van didn't move, and I started thinking maybe they had some kind of night-vision goggles, like soldiers used in wars. I sucked in cold air and held it. Maybe they were looking at us now, laughing at us because we thought we were hidden, like

Caleb when he was little, hiding in plain sight with his hands over his eyes. Exhaust floated up and fanned out over the van's back doors. Whoever it was had Nebraska plates.

Chloe started to pray again, whispering fast and barely moving her lips. I pressed my wet mitten over my nose. My eyes still burned, but I watched without blinking as the front passenger door opened, and a tall, wide-shouldered man got out. The side door slid open, and another person, harder to see, jumped out and took a few steps toward the trees.

"You stay here," Chloe whispered. She wiped her mouth, smearing blood. "You understand? Only I will go out now. You stay for now, and go to the police when they come."

I tried to yank her back down beside me. They hadn't seen her yet.

"Please," she hissed. "If I can have just one thing. Just one thing left. At least you will not be hurt. Give me that." She choked on the words. "Let me at least have that."

She started to step out from behind the thicket. I lowered my head and stayed still, an ache blooming in my chest. They'd hurt her. But she was right. They'd hurt her whether I was with her or not.

"Sarah-Mary!" the big man yelled.

Chloe froze, still in shadow. She glanced down at me, but I could only shake my head. I didn't understand. I'd never told Tyler my name. He couldn't have told anyone.

"Sarah-Mary! Are you out here? Sarah-Mary!"

A girl was yelling too, harder to hear.

"Sarah-Mary? Are you out here?"

I was dead, maybe. Or we were freezing to death, falling asleep, and I was just thinking nice thoughts as I died. But I knew the girl's voice. I knew who that was, calling me.

"Sarah-Mary?"

I squinted through the thicket. I still couldn't see anything but their dark outlines, but now I saw the second person was tall and thin, wearing a hat with pointy ears. And I knew it might be a trick of the mind, a dream of what I wanted more than anything. But if we were already dead, then it didn't matter. And if this was real, and if by some miracle we were still alive, I would be so grateful, because oh my God, oh my Allah, oh my anything-you-wanted-to-call-it, this meant everything.

So you're probably thinking it's just a little too crazy that Tess Villalobos, seventeen years old and just back from a trip to Puerto Rico, was somehow able to find me hiding behind a snowed-over thicket in Northwest Minnesota in the middle of the night. I can tell you I thought the same thing, and I was still thinking it after the big man hustled us through the van's sliding door and told us to get in the very back seat and Tess piled blankets over our heads and somebody else slammed the doors shut and whoever was driving did what felt like a nine-point turn and screeched back out onto the main road so fast that my head knocked hard into Chloe's shoulder and I had to apologize.

I stayed mystified as we bumped along in the dark like that, me whispering that it was okay, that it was for sure going to be okay now, and that no, I didn't know who the man was, or who was driving, but I knew Tess and that was enough, and I was sure everything would be fine. I was talking to myself as much as Chloe. The van was warm, even too warm under the blanket, and I had to keep sniffing as all the snot in my nose came unfrozen, and if you've never had to keep a blanket over your head as you're riding along fast on a curving road, try it sometime. You'll hate it.

But finally a man's voice from up front said we were far enough away that we could sit up and take off the blankets, as long as we kept them in our laps and stayed ready to duck.

When I sat up, taking deep breaths of fresh air, Tess was in the middle seat but turned all the way around, her eyes way more popped out than usual. She looked at Chloe, then at me.

"Oh my God," she said. "Are you okay?"

I nodded. I was having trouble believing it, but yes, it seemed I really was okay, though the back of my skull still hurt where Dale had pounded on it, and my scalp burned where my hair had come out. My teeth had stopped clicking together, and I could feel my fingers again. Chloe seemed okay too, though she looked strange to me without her glasses, and her lower lip looked swollen around the cut. She squinted past Tess up to the front of the van, where the big man sat in the passenger seat, his bald head visible over the headrest. A black man wearing a beanie cap was driving. I didn't know him, either.

Tess looked at Chloe. "Are you okay?"

Chloe nodded. She seemed scared to talk, or maybe she was thinking she still had to pretend she couldn't speak English.

"Good. I'm Tess." Her voice was soft. "Nice to meet you."

"This is the friend I called from Sherburn," I explained. I wanted Chloe to know she didn't have to be afraid.

Tess reached over the back of the seat and slapped my shoulder hard.

"Sarah-Mary! Do you know how worried I've been? You leave a message like that and then don't pick up when I call you back? I tried calling that number all night, and in the morning when we were going to the airport, and then on the layover in Miami, and as soon as we landed in St. Louis." She tugged off her cat hat. Her hair was blonder than it had been. "But you never answered, and I didn't know if you were dead or if you'd just run away or what, and I couldn't even tell my mom what was going on because you said not to. I was going out of my mind."

"I'm sorry," I said, meaning it. But right away, I understood I should just stop there. The only excuse I had for stomping that disposable phone to death was that I hadn't wanted to get Tess in trouble, or to bring her into my problems, and I could see by the way she was looking at me now, mad but mostly like she was about to cry she was so happy to see me, that if I told her I hadn't wanted to give her my problems, she'd probably slap me again.

"Poor Caleb was the one who had to tell me."

I blinked.

"Yeah. He sneaked out of your aunt's house last night and ran all the way to my window. You want to talk about somebody who's worried. I don't think he's slept since you left. He thinks you're dead, Sarah-Mary, and that it's his fault."

Chloe and I looked at each other. At least he'd known he could go to Tess, and he'd remembered when she'd get back in town. He was smart. But he was only eleven. All this time, he'd been all alone.

"He was a mess." Tess shook her head. "He was crying. He made me promise I'd go find you. I told him of course I would do everything I could, that he didn't need to make me promise. But he made me promise."

Chloe caught my eye again, and this time, we both smiled a little. "Yeah," I said. "I know how that goes."

"So I promised him, and gave him a ride home, and this morning I got up early and left a note for my parents saying I was going up to Omaha for the weekend, because, you know, better to ask forgiveness than permission." She nodded in the direction of the bald man. "That's my Uncle Tim. My aunt stayed home with my cousins."

The bald man turned around and waved with one of his big arms. His eyes were bulgy like Tess's, and also like her mother's. Now I was following, at least a little. This was the uncle who lived in Omaha, the one who'd had Muslim friends.

Tess nodded at the driver. "And that's Ray. He knows people who know how to get someone across." She looked at Chloe. "He says you'll be in Canada in just a few hours."

Chloe bowed her head. I heard the breath rush out of her as she whispered something into her hands.

Ray turned around and said "Nice to meet you" to me, and then *"As-salam alaykum"* to Chloe. She smiled and said something back to him I didn't understand. That was strange, going from being the only person Chloe could talk to, and the only person who could talk for her, to sitting and watching as she had a foreign-language conversation with someone we didn't even know. Also, we were going against her rule of riding with a black driver who was more likely to be pulled over. But I guess it was dark out, and if he was willing to take the risk, she was in the homestretch now.

Tess stayed turned around, resting her chin on the back of her seat. "Aren't you curious how I found you?"

I nodded.

"Guess!"

"I can't," I said. I wasn't in the mood to guess. My scalp hurt where my hair had come out.

"All right." She clicked her tongue like I was ruining her fun. "Don't think I'm a stalker, okay? I seriously forgot." She reached over the seat and pointed at my wrist. "It's the watch. I was almost in Omaha before I remembered I had a tracker for it on my phone. My mom had it on auto-pay, and I was hoping she forgot to cancel. I guess she did, cause we've had a global position on you for about the last ten hours."

I looked down at the watch, its small and silent screen. I never would have guessed. But that was really something. When Chloe and I were out in the woods, thinking we were so alone, Tess and these two men I didn't even know had been racing toward us, knowing just where we were. All because of something strapped to my wrist, so light I barely felt its weight.

I guess my jaw must have gone slack, because Chloe nudged me.

"That's engineering," she whispered, and gave me a smug little smile.

Tess's uncle turned around. "We've got water up here." He had a big voice to go with his big body. "Anybody thirsty?"

Chloe and I nodded, and he passed two bottles to Tess to pass to us.

"I'm guessing you're Sarah-Mary?" he asked, looking at me.

I nodded. "Thanks for picking us up."

Everybody laughed, even Chloe. I got the joke. Understatement of the year. My nose was running full-on now. Chloe handed me the tissue packet from her bag.

Ray glanced over his shoulder. "And your name, sister?"

Even with him saying "sister" like that, I almost jumped in and answered for her. I was that used to our routine. Before I could get a word out, she put a light hand on my knee.

"Sadaf," she said. "My name is Sadaf."

I closed my eyes, working to make my brain change over. There was no reason for me to keep calling her Chloe anymore, even in my head. I could call her Sadaf all I wanted now. And I would. I was used to Chloe, in the habit of it, but I wouldn't want somebody to call me something that didn't have anything to do with me. She knew my real name, and I knew hers.

"And thank you for your help," Sadaf added. "Thank you so very much."

Nobody laughed this time, probably because you could hear in her voice that she was about to cry.

Ray and Tess's uncle both said they were honored, and Tess turned around and nodded to show she was honored too.

"But how?" she asked. "How will I get across?"

Tess shook her head like she didn't know, and her uncle did the same. Only Ray glanced back over his shoulder and gave her another quick smile.

"You ever seen *The Sound of Music*?" he asked.

Sadaf tilted her head. "Yes," she said, sounding nervous, like she maybe had the same image that I did of the von Trapp family climbing up over those mountains at the end of the movie.

If she was in for that kind of hike, in this weather, he probably shouldn't smile about it.

"It'll be a little like that." He looked back at the road. "We're going to go see some nuns."

Ray cut the lights just before we turned onto a private drive, but the moon was bright enough that I could read *St. Vincent's Home for Aged Sisters* on a sign sticking up out of the snow. Behind the sign was a two-story farmhouse with a green porch light and a wooden cross by the door. An extension with the look of a long mobile home was attached to the right side of the house, with a wheelchair ramp running along the front.

"The nuns are aged?" Tess's uncle asked. He sounded as unimpressed as I was. Maybe I was still thinking of *The Sound of Music*, but I'd been expecting a stately abbey with gates, or at least a church with a steeple. This little farmhouse with its flat-roofed extension looked as low-rent as Berean Baptist.

"Some of them are aged," Ray said. We continued to roll forward, though slowly, by only the light of the moon. "The young ones do the caretaking." He paused. "Relatively young."

Sadaf ducked to get a better view, her lips rolled in so they didn't show. She tapped her gloved hands against the knees of her pajamas like she was providing her own drum roll.

"How come all the windows are dark?" I asked, loud enough

for Ray to hear me. "I thought the nuns knew we were coming."

Tess turned around and gave me a look like I was being rude, or paranoid. I understood Ray was doing us a favor, and that he probably knew what he was doing. And I didn't want to make Sadaf more anxious than she already was. But a half hour earlier, I'd heard Ray call somebody and say we'd arrive a little after one. It was ten past one now, so we weren't late. It seemed like somebody should have waited up.

"They know we're coming." Ray's voice was pleasant, but he didn't say anything else as we rolled right past the farmhouse. We approached a barn with peeling white paint, and it was only after we turned in behind the barn that I saw a crack of light between the big wooden doors.

Tess turned around to give me an I-told-you-so smile as Ray cut the engine.

"We can all go in." He stretched his hands out over the wheel, pulling on one wrist, and then the other. "Sadaf. You'll want to bring your things."

Tess's uncle opened the van's side door and helped each of us out, telling us to be careful and to watch for ice. I was only thinking of hurrying, and of getting out of the cold and up to the doors, but Sadaf, walking just ahead of me, slowed her pace by a scattering of rocks and gravel the plow must have scraped up. Just as I moved beside her, she bent down, snatched up one of the rocks, and pushed it in her coat pocket.

"Why'd you do that?" I whispered.

She either didn't hear me, or she didn't want to say. My guess, which made me sad, was that she was so scared and tired that she didn't trust anybody anymore.

"It's okay now," I said, and I hoped she at least believed it after we'd followed Tess through the doors and into the barn, where two older women stood smiling at us like they either didn't mind the odor of cow manure or they'd just gotten so used to it that they couldn't smell it. Bright lamps hung from one of the rafters, and though the barn wasn't exactly toasty, it was warmer than outside. There were three stalls on our left, and their doors were closed, but I could see scattered hay and the black haunches of a cow through the lower opening of one. Next to the stalls, rectangular bales of hay were stacked high on a pallet next to a black tarp. Along the far wall was a rider mower, a Ping-Pong table with a shoebox on it, another pallet with bags of feed piled on it, and next to that, a salt spreader.

"Welcome," one of the women said, rolling the door shut behind Ray. She was white, as tall as Tess's uncle, and almost as wide across the shoulders, and though she had a wooden cross hanging from a black cord around her neck, she wasn't dressed like a nun. She wore a brown turtleneck under overalls, and duck boots that squeaked when she walked. "We're so glad you're here!" she boomed. "I'm Sister Janice, and this is Sister Eva."

Sister Eva smiled and gave us each a nod. She was Asian,

about my height, her dark hair gone gray at her temples. She wore a baggy sweater, a long skirt, and red galoshes that said *Property of Brandon* on the outside of each.

"You all are nuns?" I asked.

Sadaf gave me a nudge. But Sister Janice seemed pleased. "Oh yes!" she said, her blue eyes bright. "We've just gotten out of the habit!" She kept a straight face for a second, then she started laughing while Sister Eva made a face like maybe it was a joke she'd heard too often.

Sister Janice looked at Sadaf and went serious. "I see you're injured, dear, there on your lip. If it's recent, we've got some Tylenol back at the house. Or would you prefer an ice pack?"

Sadaf's hand went to her lip, her gloved fingertips grazing the cut. "I'm fine," she said. She touched the rim of the blue knit hat like she wanted to make sure it was straight. She still had her flag pinned to the side.

"Are you the only one leaving?" Sister Eva asked. She had a low voice, and an accent I didn't recognize, so *leaving* sounded like *leabing*.

Sadaf nodded.

"You can walk fine?" Sister Eva glanced at Sadaf's boots.

Sadaf nodded again. She didn't ask how far, or what we were all doing out there away in a manger, which was what I wanted to know. Ray had walked over to where the hay was and stepped up on the edge of the pallet, and without even asking anybody, he reached up with both hands and tugged one of the bales from the top. He turned around and lowered the bale to the tarp. When he stepped back up on the pallet to reach for another, Tess's uncle took a few steps toward him.

"Is this something we need to do?" he asked. "Can I help?" He was already taking off his jacket like he assumed the answer was yes.

"Only if you have a good back." Sister Janice followed him to the pallet. "They're about forty pounds each. Don't strain yourself."

I guess Tess's uncle wasn't worried about it, because he reached up and brought down a bale without even stepping on the pallet. And then Sister Janice reached up and pulled down a bale, giving it a little toss onto the tarp—maybe just to show she could.

Sister Eva turned back to the rest of us. "I can't reach the high ones," she said. "I always have to wait until the stack is lower before I can pitch in, and even then I have to take care."

Tess and Sadaf both looked at me like I might know what was happening. I didn't. We all looked back over to the hay bales. Neither Ray nor Sister Janice was restacking the bales with any particular care. It was like they were just trying to get the weight off the pallet as quickly as possible. I squinted down at the pallet, realizing.

"Are you kidding me?" I still had my mittens on, and I

pressed one to each side of my head like I was trying to hold in my brain. "You all have a tunnel in here? There's a tunnel coming out of this barn?"

Sister Eva nodded like it wasn't so surprising. "The border's not even half a mile away." She touched the sleeve of Sadaf's coat. "Don't worry. The passage is narrow, but tall enough for even a grown man to walk upright. And it's safe. Your guide is walking over now. Or I should say under." She checked her watch, which was digital, with a neon pink strap that fastened with a silver strip of duct tape. "She should be here in ten minutes. Do you need to use the bathroom before you go? I can take you into the house."

Sadaf shook her head.

"You're sure? It's no trouble."

"We just went," I said, because I didn't want her to keep hassling Sadaf about it, and also because it was true. Only a half hour earlier, Tess had announced to everyone in the van that she'd needed to pee since Fargo, and after Ray pulled over, Tess, Sadaf, and I got out and walked far behind the taillights for privacy, and then relieved ourselves in the middle of the dark road, as none of us wanted to wade into the high snow on either side. Mid-stream, I'd called out that I was sure I was getting frostbite where I definitely did not want to get frostbite, and both Tess and Sadaf laughed, though I hadn't been joking.

Sadaf set her messenger bag on the barn's dirt floor. "I should help," she said, moving past Sister Eva. By the time she got over

388

to the pallet, the top three rows of hay had already been moved to the tarp. She staggered under the weight of the first bale, so we all went over to help, though Sister Eva told us there was no real hurry, and the four of us smaller people should be smart and lift in pairs.

I'll admit that the only reason I helped was that I would have felt bad just standing around when everyone else was working. I hadn't gotten any sleep since we'd left Lakeville the previous morning, and it wasn't as if the earlier part of our night had been easy. But it turned out helping move the hay was a good feeling. I partnered with Sadaf, and after we lifted and set down just a few bales, I was warm enough to want to take off my coat, and that was the first time I'd felt warm in a while.

I was also grateful to have something to distract me from the fact that if everything went as planned, Sadaf and I were about to say good-bye. It was what I wanted. But it seemed like it was coming up too fast. In just a few minutes, maybe, she'd be gone from me. Probably forever. Already I felt an ache in my chest, as real as if I'd swallowed something sharp.

After the last bale was moved, Sister Janice lifted the pallet, and Sister Eva pulled back the small blue tarp that had been underneath it. And there was the hole, the size of a Monopoly board, and not so deep that I couldn't see dirt at the bottom. A rope ladder lined one side, held in place by two wooden stakes dug into the barn's floor.

Sadaf was quiet, peering down.

"That's just the way up," Sister Janice said. "The actual tunnel is much larger."

"Will I have light?"

"You'll have a headlamp. Like a miner."

"How in the world?" Tess's uncle was on his hands and knees, peering down. He looked up at the nuns. "You're telling me you dug a tunnel over half a mile long?"

"Oh, *we* didn't." Sister Janice waved her hand. "Someone brought in a boring machine. A smaller one, but still." She sighed. "What an amazing piece of machinery. They rolled it right in through those doors." She waved her hand toward the doors we'd come in.

He stared at her with astonishment, then turned his bulgy eyes to Ray, who held up his hands as if to say he hadn't been there to see it happen. I studied Ray for a moment, taking in his narrow face and the red scarf that looked home-knit tucked into the collar of his coat. He was the second Muslim I'd ever met. That I knew of, at least. I wouldn't have known Ray was Muslim if I'd passed him on the street.

Tess's uncle shook his head at Sister Janice. He was still freaked out. "You know someone with their own boring machine?"

"Ah. We're in touch with many people who want to help." Sister Eva smiled. "Some have resources, and some only have time. The latter is how we got all the dirt out. Some of our own neighbors carried it off, sack by sack, in the backs of their trucks.

We had three college students out here last summer, staying with us to help care for the older sisters. They did just that during the day, but they were out here every night, carrying out dirt." She shrugged. "In the end, we had to turn away offers to help."

"People are so angry about what's happened," Sister Janice added, looking at Sadaf. "They're desperate to do what they can."

We all waited. It was the first time anyone had mentioned the reason Sadaf had to leave, or why she might have a cut on her bottom lip, or why there even had to be a tunnel in the first place.

"It's very kind," Sadaf said.

I frowned. Of course that was what she would say, being as nice as she was, and I supposed that was true. The tunnel must have taken a lot of work, not to mention risk. I'd put in work and risk myself these last few days. But it wasn't like any of us was going to leave tonight with warm, fuzzy feelings inside. All we'd done was make a way for her to leave. For sure, Canada with her husband and son was better than Nevada without them. But she'd wanted to live here in America, and stay an American, and everyone would have been better off if that's what she could have done. Even with her being born someplace else, she was as American as I was, maybe even more, because she'd had to work so hard to get here, and she had Thomas Jefferson quotes memorized in her head. I knew part of her was Iranian, and would always be. But she had an American heart.

And now she had to take it somewhere else.

"You'll like Canada," Sister Janice said. "We hear good reports from the people who've gone over, and from our friends there. It's so welcoming. Everyone says it's the new America."

It hurt me, hearing that. Ray, and Tess, and her uncle all seemed pained as well. Sister Eva gave Sister Janice a hard stare like *maybe you should stop talking*. But if that's what Sister Janice thought, she had the right to say it. It was just hard to hear that someplace else was the new America. If that was true, then where did we live? What was it? Where America used to be.

All seven of us stared down into the hole, and for a while, no one had anything to say. I was thinking about *The Sound of Music* and how Captain von Trapp was super patriotic about Austria and didn't like it when somebody tried to change the flag over his house. And then near the end, he's up on stage with all the kids and Maria, and he's so broken up about having to leave he can't even finish the "Edelweiss" song, and Maria has to jump in and start singing with him, and then they get the whole audience, everybody but the bad guy who liked to say "Heil Hitler" to sing along too, and the singing gets loud and powerful. That was a nice moment, like they were all using that pretty song to stick together and tell the Heil Hitler guy where he could go.

Still, the von Trapps were the ones who left, and I don't think they ever went back.

"Here she is," Sister Janice said, nodding down at the hole. A beam of light swept along the bottom of the hole, and then shone up at us so bright my eyes shut tight against it. Even when I opened them, I was bright-blinded, with purple worms obscuring my vision. By the time I could see clearly, Ray and Tess were helping the guide up out of the hole, the back of her backpack scraping along the other edge. She was a small person, at least a head shorter than I was. She had on a bicycle helmet with a penlight attached to each side. After she reached up to switch off the lights, I could see her face, which was round, with a deep dimple in her right cheek. She had large, dark eyes, and she looked enough like Sadaf that I thought she might be Iranian too. She didn't look much older than I was.

"Sorry I took so long. The snow slowed the drive for us." She didn't sound like Sadaf. I couldn't hear any accent at all. She unfastened the chin strap of her helmet, and when she lifted it, I saw she wore a white headscarf, the ends double-wrapped around her neck.

"Let me take your helmet, Amina dear." Sister Janice towered over her. "Would you like some water? Would you like to sit for a few minutes?"

"I'm okay." Amina, I guess her name was, took all of us in with a friendly smile. "So who's coming back with me? Just one, right?"

Sadaf raised her hand. The girl nodded and said, *"As-salam alaykum."* Sadaf smiled and said what sounded like the same thing in reverse. And here's the truth—while they stood there grinning at each other and saying their special Muslim words, looking so much alike that they could be mother and daughter, my heart hurt. I know. It's embarrassing to admit. You'd think I'd just be happy for Sadaf going to where she'd be safe, and with at least some of her family. And this Amina girl she'd probably have a lot more in common with.

Amina tugged off her backpack, unzipped it, and pulled out another bicycle helmet, rigged up with two penlights like the one she'd been wearing. "Do you want to try this on?" she asked. "It's adjustable, so you can probably fit it over your hat." She lowered her voice. "And if you want to take your hat off when we get down in there, you can take the helmet off for a second."

Sadaf smiled as her new best friend helped fix the helmet over her blue hat, adjusting the strap under her chin so it wouldn't pinch. Of course they were going to go as soon as possible. No point in waiting around. Sadaf probably couldn't wait to get away from here. But I could feel the pressure behind my eyes, and my lower lip started to tremble. My hands felt hot, and I pulled off my mittens.

Sister Eva carried the shoebox over from the Ping-Pong table. "Sister Mirasol baked oatmeal cookies," she said. "She wanted to come out herself, but she's on duty tonight." She took the lid off and held out the box. "If you're not hungry now, you could take some with you. She put just a few in each bag, so please take as many bags as you like."

Sadaf and Amina both thanked her, and they each took a bag of cookies out of the box. In all the time Sadaf and I'd traveled together, I'd never seen her eat a cookie or anything with sugar in it. I guessed she was either being polite, or taking them as a treat for her son, Jahan.

"Well"—Amina gestured toward the hole—"are you ready? I should go in first."

Sadaf looked down at the hole, blinking.

"I go back and forth all the time," Amina said softly. "Don't be afraid."

"I'm not afraid." Sadaf looked up as if she'd been startled. "I need to say something." Her gaze moved from the men to the nuns and then to me and Tess. "I don't know that I can say thank you enough." She put her palm against the zipper of her coat. "I can say that I am glad this is the last I will see of America." She shook her head, realizing how it sounded, or how it might sound, like she was just glad to be leaving. But I got what she meant—if she had to go, she was glad that nice people would be the ones seeing her off.

"We're just sorry it's this way," Tess's uncle said, and he sounded like he really was sorry, almost like he was going to cry, which surprised me, because he'd just met Sadaf, and also because he was a big, bald man who looked like he could be scary. But he was like Captain von Trapp maybe, and just as mad about his country, only he was deciding to stay.

I had my own lips rolled in and my teeth clenched tight, because I didn't want to start crying and having Sadaf feeling bad for me when she must be so excited to see her husband and her little boy. I raised my eyes to the rafters, working to keep them dry. I was fine. I was good, actually. I'd done what I'd set out to do. I'd done exactly what I'd promised Caleb.

"I could have a few minutes with Sarah-Mary?" Sadaf's voice wavered when she said my name, and that was all it took to make my vision go blurry. I heard Amina say, "Of course," and then Sister Janice saying that they could all sit for a while, and Sister Eva said the bales made good enough chairs and maybe they could all have some of Sister Mirasol's cookies. Someone, maybe one of the nuns, or maybe Tess, or one of the men, patted my shoulder, and then Sadaf took my arm and steered me across the barn to where the rider mower sat.

When I could see again, my tears wiped from my eyes, I gestured to the mower's seat. "You can sit if you want." I meant it as a joke, but I started crying again, so the joke didn't really work. Sadaf shook her head and stayed standing. We were only thirty or so feet away from everyone. I knew they could hear me blubbering. There wasn't anything I could do.

"Your son's lucky," I said. "Don't ever think you're a bad mom."

I don't even know why that was what came out of my mouth, out of all the things I could've said to her then. But she acted like I'd hurt her, like I'd hauled off and slapped her across the face. She made a little whimpering sound and reached out and grabbed my hands, her leather gloves cool against my fingers.

"Your brother is lucky to have you, Sarah-Mary. But I'll

worry about you." She glanced over to where everyone else sat on bales of hay. "I am glad you have your friend."

"Yeah, I'm fine," I said. I pulled one of my hands away and wiped my cheeks. Let my pity party commence. I guess I was the one who'd invited her to it. "I'm fine," I said again.

"All right." She didn't let go of my other hand. "I only mean to say I care about you very much. And I wish you had someone to look after you more. I wish I could have met you under different circumstances. I would have liked you to be one of my students."

I had to laugh at that. Me in an engineering class, doing math and looking at wires, or whatever it was they did.

"Don't laugh. You are smart. I hope you will do something with your mind. And more than that, with your good heart." Now her green eyes brimmed. "Because it is a very good heart you have. Do you hear me? Sarah-Mary, you are one of my favorite Americans. And if that sounds like low praise under the circumstance, I can tell you, it isn't." She pulled her hand away and reached into her pocket. "You see this rock?" She held up the rock she'd picked up outside, which actually just looked like a piece of gravel, gray and smaller than her thumb. "I took it so I could take some of America with me, a souvenir, because there is so much I will miss about this country. I wish I could take something of you."

I tried to think. I'd left my backpack in the van, and what was in there anyway? At this point, nothing but dirty clothes. I had my flag pin, but she had one herself. I reached up and felt for my earrings, but I'd left them, along with my toothbrush, back at the hunting lodge. My mittens were probably covered with snot.

Once it came to me, I was sure. I didn't have to ask Tess. She'd given it to me. It was mine to give.

"No." Sadaf shook her head. "Please. This is not what I meant."

But I'd already undone the buckle and slid it off over my hand. "It's perfect," I said. "Don't you see? I'll know for sure that you made it, as soon as you're out of the tunnel. I'll be able to see on Tess's phone. And if I pay for the subscription, I'll know if you stay in Canada, and what city. And you know, maybe someday . . ."

She let me place the watch in her palm, but she was still shaking her head.

"It's got good music on it," I said. "You should try it out. Seriously. I want you to at least listen to a few songs. Listen to Sketchy first."

"All right. Yes. Sketchy. But you take mine. You should have a watch."

She slid her own watch off her wrist. It was heavier than Tess's, and sort of old-person looking, with tiny Roman numerals on the face and what may or may not have been a real diamond in the center. The band was pretty, thin and silver. After I fixed the latch, it felt snug against my wrist.

"Thank you." She showed me Tess's watch, now buckled around her wrist. "I'll wear it every day, so you will be able to see me. Or the light that is me." She waited until I looked up at her. "Thank you, Sarah-Mary. Thank you for helping me."

"They're the ones actually helping you." I sniffed and nodded over to everyone else. "They've got a plan that'll work. They know what they're doing. I'm the one who about got you caught."

She touched my arm. "You did help me, as much as you could. And I am saying thank you."

I wiped my cheeks again. I didn't know what to say. It wasn't the kind of thank you that you could just say "oh sure no problem" to. You had to take it in and hold it. I could tell by the way she was looking at me she wanted me to. So I did. But then I said, "My pleasure," and we both laughed, because obviously not all of it had been a pleasure, especially the parts where we almost died. I meant it, though, in the larger sense. She knew I did.

"Okay, then," I said, meaning I was ready if she was. She couldn't just keep hanging around to make me feel better, as she'd only be safe after she got through the tunnel. And the sooner she said good-bye to me, the sooner she'd get through the tunnel, and then make her way to Toronto. Still, she held out her arms to me, and I stepped in close, my chin resting on the shoulder of her white coat. I put my arms around her and squeezed, breathing in the smell of her minty soap. Her hat was soft on my cheek, and the flag pin pressed against my ear.

It's a weird thing, hugging. Like I don't know who made it

up, or if they do it in every country. When I was little my mom would complain that I hugged back too tight. I probably did. I remember in my mind I was trying to have her pressed into me, like if I hugged her hard enough and long enough, some part of her would stay with me, and I'd have her even when she was away. It sounds like something a little kid would imagine, but really, that might be what people in general are going for when they hug. They want the other person to leave an impression on them, not one you can see, but something like it. They want to leave their impression, too.

I must have walked with Sadaf back over to where the others waited by the opening, but I don't remember doing it. I have a flash of standing beside Tess and watching as first Amina, and then Sadaf, climbed down the ladder into the hole. Sadaf's messenger bag was on her back, and the penlights were bright on her helmet. When she got to the bottom, she said, "Oh, yes. It opens up," and then, I guess talking to us, "Good-bye, friends! Thank you!"

I remember being surprised at how fast their lights disappeared.

Tess nudged my arm. "You okay?"

When I looked up, everybody seemed like they were waiting on something. It took me a second to realize it was for me to move. I guess I'd been looking down the hole for a while.

"Sorry," I said, stepping aside. Sister Janice pulled the tarp back over the hole. I took my mittens out of my pockets, thinking

I would help move the hay back. But I couldn't make my hands go in. One mitten fell to the floor.

"Hey," Tess's uncle said, his big voice gone soft. "Tess, why don't you and your friend go sit down over there and let us do this?"

"I'm okay," I said, or tried to say. It came out all warbly.

But Tess already had her arm around me. She steered me back across the barn, whispering that I was going to be okay. When we got by the rider mower, she pointed at it and told me to take a seat. Maybe she was just joking, too, but all at once I felt so tired, my legs aching beneath me. So I climbed up to the seat of the mower.

"Well, look at you in the driver's seat. That's a sign of what's coming, is what that is." Tess gave me a long look. "Sarah-Mary. You know you're missing some hair?"

I reached up and felt for where my hair had come out. The wounds stung at my touch. When I brought down my hands, some of my fingertips had blood on them.

"It'll grow back," she said. "If not, we'll call you Patches." She stopped smiling. "What happened?"

I rested my head on the steering wheel. I felt like I could still taste blood in my mouth. I'd maybe swallowed a tiny piece of Dale's jawline. I'd wait to tell her that. I was still so hungry, but I didn't want a cookie. I wanted dinner, a regular meal, and then a good night's sleep, though the sun would be up soon.

"Well," Tess said, "whatever it was, I can tell you now I'm

impressed." She shook her head, her big eyes steady on mine. "I knew from the start you had something in you. But I had no idea. Let me tell you something. I know that when we get back, you're going to be in the doghouse for a while. That's fine. We'll wait it out. Because eventually, you and I are going on some serious adventures."

That got me to smile. She was right that when I got back, I'd be in trouble, and not with just Aunt Jenny, but with Mrs. Harrison and Pastor Rasmussen. They wouldn't ever know about Sadaf, but they'd know I'd lied to all of them. There'd be consequences for that, on top of all the regular miseries that had been there before I left. But whatever they did wouldn't kill me. I'd seen someone killed for real. I could handle a little persecution, and even getting spanked with that damn paddle.

In fact, I was almost excited to light out for home. I couldn't wait to see Caleb and let him know I was just fine, and that I really had done as much as I could, and that Sadaf was free with her family. I'd show him the GPS light on Tess's phone. I'd make sure he understood that as scared as he must have been these last few days, he should feel proud of himself, because he was the one who made me promise to do the right thing, even when I thought I shouldn't. It felt good to know he'd be proud of me too, for keeping that promise, and in the future, for whatever I might try next.

ACKNOWLEDGMENTS

I am forever indebted to Kelly Cannon, who talked through the arc of the story with me and read drafts of every chapter. Her insights and suggestions were invaluable; I feel fortunate to know someone so smart and observant who is also hilarious and generous with her time. Kelly, you are completely worth the drive to a certain bakery franchise at any Kansas City location.

I am also grateful to Shabnam Hashemy, Sharareh Hashemy, Neena Haider, Giselle Anatol, Janet Yates, and Mary O'Connell for sharing their experiences and perspectives with me, and for reading drafts. I am so appreciative of their time, their feedback, their encouragement, and their kindness.

I am lucky to be married to Ben Eggleston for a number of reasons; his being a thoughtful listener when I am writing a book is one of them.

The always smart Jennifer Rudolph Walsh was an early and helpful reader. After working with Margaret Riley King for almost a year on this book, I have so much respect for her integrity and her wisdom. And of course, I want to thank Tara Weikum and everyone at Harper for their belief in this book and the care they have taken with it.